# Praise for Peter Murphy's
## *Born & Bred:*

"The author did a splendid job in portraying many diverse relationships, city life, church life, family life, corruption and crime, which makes it an engaging read."
– Hotchpotch

"As the first book in a series, Murphy has created a lasting story with great potential in future installments."
– Savvy Verse and Wit

"*Born & Bred* is part historical fiction, part political thriller and part social commentary. With a bit of magical realism thrown into the mix it makes for a commanding read and a compulsive page-turner."
– Brendan Landers

## And for *Wandering in Exile:*

"Engrossing and significant.... A moral book and a worthy read!"
– Brendan Landers

"The author stirred a multitude of emotions with his tale."
– Beth Art from the Heart

T0168134

# All Roads

# All Roads

## Peter Murphy

The Story Plant
Studio Digital CT, LLC
P.O. Box 4331
Stamford, CT 06907

Story Plant paperback ISBN-13: 978-1-61188-212-4
Fiction Studio Books E-book ISBN: 978-1-936558-63-6

Visit our website at www.TheStoryPlant.com

First Story Plant Printing: June 2015

Printed in the United States of America

0 9 8 7 6 5 4 3 2 1

Hurt people hurt people. That's how pain patterns get passed on, generation after generation after generation. Break the chain today. Meet anger with sympathy, contempt with compassion, cruelty with kindness. Greet grimaces with smiles. Forgive and forget about finding fault. Love is the weapon of the future.

– *Yehuda Berg*

*For: Sean, Barry, Richard, Paul & Ciaran*

# Chapter 1 – 1997

"HI, MY NAME IS DANNY B. AND I'M AN ALCOHOLIC."

"Hi, Danny," everyone answered and settled in to hear him speak.

"As some of you might have guessed from my accent, I was born in Ireland, where we like to have a drink now and then." The whole meeting laughed so he waited for a moment. He was still shy when it came to talking honestly about himself, but it was getting easier.

"Anyway, right after I was born, my mother was put in an asylum, my father went to England, and I was left with my granny. She was, I suppose, a good woman who tried to bring me up to believe all the stuff that she believed in. Only I never felt right about God and all, because I couldn't understand why he wouldn't let me have my mother with me."

He paused for a drink of water and to get a better grip on his composure. He was trying to speak from his heart and it was causing a lump in his throat. "My granny was always telling me what a great man my grandfather was—how he was a hero and all—and that my father wasn't. She used to say that how I behaved would decide which one I'd end up being like.

"Then, when she got sick, my mother and father moved back in with us and we tried being one big happy family—except family isn't always a very pleasant experience. It is for some people, but not as many as we'd like to think." Some people laughed at that.

"My granny died when I was a teenager and I found out that she was the one who had sent my parents away. I was so pissed at her and all the stuff she had tried to teach me. That's when my life started to go really wrong and I ended up getting involved with things I shouldn't have."

He paused to see if Anto had anything to add. He usually did, but lately he seemed happy to let things go. It seemed as though the longer Danny was sober the less Anto had to say.

"But I managed to get away from all that and came to Canada where I was going to have a fresh start. Only problem was that I brought myself with me, and before long I was drinking heavily. You hear people say that they never intended to become alcoholic and I totally get what they mean. When I was younger, I hated my father for his drinking. Back then I thought he had given up on life and I wasn't going to let that happen to me. But I had all this stuff going on inside me and drinking was the only way I could feel good about myself. That, and smoking drugs. I was in a band back then and I was able to tell myself that it was all just part of the scene.

"At first, I was just doing what everyone else was doing; only when they went off and started to make lives for themselves, I was still drinking and acting the fool. Even after I got married and had kids."

He thought about mentioning his uncle but he wasn't ready to talk about all that yet. Martin's death was still like an ulcer. And he was a bit pissed that it was Anto's ghost that got to haunt him. At least Martin once cared about him.

"I now know"—he smiled wistfully at the crowd—"that normal people just smarten up and get on with things. Not me, and after a while I began to resent my wife and kids for intruding on my drinking, and that didn't make for a very happy family life. I used to try to tell myself that drinking wasn't the problem, that it was my job, or the way I was brought up, or that Mike Harris was in power. Anything rather than face the truth."

Nobody laughed at that, but a few nodded sympathetically.

"Anyway, after a few years they all got fed up with me and made me go to meetings. My wife had been sneaking over to the dark side on me—to Al-Anon meetings." Everyone laughed at that.

"So I came, but I didn't want any part of what you people tried to tell me. I just came to get the heat off for a while. I managed to dry out a bit but I didn't find much contented sobriety. I did learn all the slogans, though, so I could use them at home when anybody bugged me; but deep down I knew I was just bullshitting everyone again, and after a while I picked up another drink.

"I'd managed to convince myself that I wasn't really an alcoholic and, because I'd learnt about my other problems, I'd be able to drink like a normal person."

He paused for another drink of water as everyone smiled back at him. "But all those meetings I'd gone to had screwed up my drinking. I couldn't pretend anymore because, deep down, I knew what I really was and I knew what my real problem was. And no matter how much I drank I could never get back to the happy places drinking used to take me. I felt like a piece of crap and I had to drink because I couldn't stand myself. I despised myself when I was drunk, and I was full of guilt and remorse when I wasn't. I was trapped and hopeless."

He paused again and briefly looked around. Frank was sitting near the back, and Billie was sitting in the second row, smiling and encouraging him. It was a struggle but they were all making it, one day at a time.

"My wife had tried to kick me out when I started again but she had to take me back for the kids' sake. I knew that and took full advantage and behaved like a total arsehole.

"That was another thing I hated about myself. But now that I have come to accept this program, I understand what was happening. In the first step, where it talks about being alcoholic and not being able to manage our lives—I was living proof of that. I didn't care that my wife and kids were scared of me, never knowing when I was going to go nuclear again. I didn't care because the only thing I ever thought about was where my next drink was coming from, even when I had one in my hand.

"After a while I couldn't stand being around my own wife and kids so I moved into our basement. I had a bar down there and a couch, and as long as I had a good supply in, I didn't care about anything else. My family all tried to get on with their lives while I lived like a troll in a cave, only coming out to go to work—and the liquor store." His voice wavered and his eyes welled up, but he was determined to be honest. "I was living in my family's house like a wild animal."

He checked around the room for disapproval but there was none.

"Only my daughter would come down to see me, and that just made things worse. At least with my son it was obvious— he hated me. My daughter still wanted to believe in me, and I couldn't stand the look in her eyes. I suppose it reminded me too much of how I must've looked when I was a kid.

"Anyway, I blew that too. I got drunk and lost it on my son one day and my wife kicked me out again. To try and make up for it, I stopped drinking and went on anti-booze. But, to be honest, I only went on them so everybody would think I was trying.

"Then I got drunk while I was taking them and ended up in the hospital. When I got out, I'd nowhere else to go and went to see a friend from the band. I didn't know that he was in the program. If I did, I'd have gone somewhere else—only I didn't have too many other places to go.

"Anyway, he said I could stay with him if I started going to meetings again. I wanted to tell him what to do with his meetings—and his steps—but by this time I was totally beaten. I'd reached the bottom and kept thinking about what the steps said about insanity. At first, I didn't think of myself as mad, but someone once said that it was doing the same thing over and over and expecting different results. I could totally relate to that. I knew when I picked up a drink that I was playing Russian roulette, but each time I told myself that it would be different. It was. Each time things got worse.

"You see, I didn't want to believe in all the stuff you people go on about, but I'd nowhere else to turn. I had a lot of issues with gods and higher-powers and all that, but people just kept telling me to keep coming back. My sponsor used to say that I never let what people say drive me out of a bar so . . .

"He was right, and bit by bit one thing started to make more sense to me. I was an alcoholic and I couldn't manage my own life—even when I wasn't drinking. And then, after another few months I started to think about what you people told me, that a power greater than myself could restore me to sanity.

"As I said, I used to object to the word sanity, but my sponsor and I drank together, and he was more than happy to remind me how insane I was. He also said that my higher power could be whatever I was able to believe in and, if I didn't have anything else, I could believe in the power of the program. I went along with that and after a few more months, when the fog began to clear, I began to start every day by making a conscious decision to turn my will and my life over to the idea of trying to be a better person.

"Keep an open mind on what I say, because I'm still not sure what my higher power might be, and the great thing is that I don't have to worry about it. They told me that if I keep bringing the body to meetings, and if I try to live by the steps, the rest will fall into place.

"I still struggle with the urge to drink but I'm learning to deal with that. I call somebody, usually my sponsor, or I go to a meeting, and it works. I come in gasping for a drink and I leave thinking about something else. It works, and one day at a time I've managed to avoid picking up that first drink. And if I can keep it together for another few weeks, I'll be celebrating one year."

Everyone clapped at that and a few called out, "Keep coming back."

"If you're new, then take it from me that it does work. If someone like me can do it then so can you. And I'm not going to lie and say everything is rosy or anything like that. My wife filed for a divorce and we're just dealing with all that right now.

It bothers me a lot, but with meetings and all the support I get from you people, I can avoid picking up that first drink.

"I've been told that we have to clear away all the debris of the past and that's what I'm trying to do. My wife has started to let me see my little girl again and I'm learning to be grateful for that. My son still doesn't want anything to do with me and there's nothing I can do about that right now.

"All I can do is go to meetings and stay sober one day at a time and let the future look after itself. So if you're new, or you're like me and coming back, keep at it. It does get better. Every day you don't pick up that first drink is a better day.

"Looking back, I've always let the things other people do get to me. For years I resented them all: my mother and father, my granny, even my own wife and kids. But since I started practicing the steps, I'm starting to see things differently.

"I once heard a guy at a meeting talk about how hurt people hurt people. He said it was like a sickness that kept getting passed on and that instead of giving in to it we should try to break the cycle. That's what I'm trying to do now. I'm trying to change the way I react to things that used to bother me. I'm trying to learn about the principles of Love and Tolerance. And I'm not doing it to become a saint or anything like that. I'm doing it because it is the only way I can survive. Sometimes, I think it's the only way any of us will survive."

As he returned to his seat everyone clapped, and some reached out to shake his hand. Danny Boyle, who had come through all that life had thrown at him so far, was as happy and hopeful as he had ever been in his life because, deep down inside where it really mattered, he felt he was no longer alone.

\*

At the back of the hall, where the smokers crowded near the door, ready to step out and light up right after the Lord's Prayer, Anto hovered unseen, until Martin squeezed in beside him.

"Ah, Martin. Are you well?"

"I'm fine, Anto, thanks for asking. How's he doing?"

"I don't want to jinx him or anything, but I think he might finally be getting it."

"Well I hope you're right—he never was the brightest—but all credit to you, Anto. He never would've made it this far on his own."

Anto shuffled. He still wasn't used to compliments. *Poor bastard,* Martin thought, *he never had much of a chance either.* Guys like Anto and Danny who had strayed from the path never really got a fair chance again, despite all that people went on about kindness and forgiveness. The world was just waiting for them to screw up again. *But everything always works out in the end,* he reminded himself and smiled.

"It had feck all to do with me." Anto shrugged. "I was just doing my penance."

"You know you won't have to hang around much longer. It must be getting to you."

Anto paused. He wasn't used to making decisions anymore. "Martin, do you remember what it was like waiting for a bus on a fine morning? You wanted it to come but you didn't mind waiting either. Everything was so nice around you." For a moment Anto almost looked like the young lad he had once been, before life had turned and twisted him.

"You know your mother is still praying for you?" Martin mentioned as casually as he could.

"Isn't there a way to let her know I'm all right?"

"There is, but wouldn't you rather tell her yourself?"

"I don't think I could face her. You know what Irish mammies can be like."

"I do. I think she'd be thrilled to bits."

"Maybe, but only after she clouted me around the ears a few times. Besides, who's going to keep an eye on him?" He nodded towards Danny, who was surrounded by people shaking his hand and thanking him for sharing. He almost looked a little guilty and a bit embarrassed. "Guys like him and me have to look out for each other."

Martin tried to hide his smile. Anto was finally beginning to realize so much that had escaped him in life. "There are others."

"Like?"

\*

"Patrick Reilly?"

Patrick looked up into the face of a tall man who stooped as though the cares of the world were too much for him. But his eyes had a strange little twinkle and were still a bright shade of blue. Miriam had written a number of times to remind them to get together and Patrick had been putting it off. He kept all memories of her in a little chamber in his heart and wasn't sure if he could trust himself to revisit them—something that would happen when her name came up.

"Father Melchor?" Patrick couldn't help himself and deferred to the older Jesuit.

"Call me John, please."

"Well, John, I'm very happy to finally meet you." He rose while the older man sat and waved to catch the waiter's eye. "Can I get you something?"

"Yes." John smiled as he checked his watch and nodded. "I would like a limoncello if it's not too early."

"Not a bit of it," Patrick agreed with enthusiasm and ordered two. It was a hot afternoon and the crowds of tourists milled around the old rotunda, snapping photos and gaping at everything. Patrick still loved dropping by and watching it all, even though Giovanni didn't work as much as he once did. "And are you glad to be back in Rome?"

The Jesuit looked at him for a moment as he chose his words. "To be honest, I am very conflicted. There is so much to be done in the world and I am to see out the rest of my days here. I'm in disgrace and now must end my days as a minor bureaucratic functionary." He smiled wistfully and raised his glass. "Still, there are far worse places to be."

Patrick sipped his drink and agreed. Rome had become his island. He'd been so happy for the last few years. He practically lived in libraries now, with his nose in a book, as his mother used to say. His uncle had been right about that: he was happier that way.

He placed his glass back on the table and looked at John Melchor. He was gray and careworn but still looked like a film star. He had a strong jaw and piercing eyes. Patrick's face was becoming rounder as the years went by and his eyes were soft.

"This is one of my favorite places."

"Rome?"

"Well, yes, but I meant right here in the rotunda. An uncle of mine used to spend his time here too. I guess that's why I'm drawn to it."

"And not because it celebrates Pantheism?"

John Melchor may have been joking, but Patrick wasn't sure. "Well, I'm just a simple scholar. I wouldn't understand such things."

"As you wish." The Jesuit laughed and raised his glass again. "To your uncle's memory. I'm sure he was a great man."

There was something in the way he spoke that made Patrick pause. John Melchor was looking at him as if he were waiting for him to put the pieces of a puzzle together.

"He was, only I didn't understand that when he was alive. He was my bishop, too, and it was very hard to see past that. I didn't really get to know the man he was until after he was gone."

"That's an odd way to get know someone."

"Oh, don't mind me. I'm so used to being alone that sometimes I think out loud. I suppose I just wish I'd more time with him, man to man."

"Well, Patrick, this is the Eternal City. Who knows what might happen?"

John Melchor looked at him again as if he could see what was going on inside him, and Patrick swallowed the rest of his drink. There was something about the old Jesuit that invited him to speak of the night in Campo De' Fiori—the night he thought he heard his uncle's voice. "Who knows indeed? The man who owns this café often tells me stories about the talking statues. Do you know about them?"

Even as he said it, Patrick was sorry he'd brought it up. Miriam had warned him that John hadn't been the same since he'd been shot. She wrote that he seemed to believe that he had some type of transcendental experience. "Though it might have had something to do with all the morphine they had to pump into him," she added.

"The whisperers of dissent? Patrick, I have spent my whole life listening to them."

\*

"Have you had a chance to go through the papers I sent over?" Deirdre asked after the waitress brought their coffees. She had chosen the diner because it was busy and far enough away from her office. She didn't want anybody from work witnessing any aspect of her personal life, especially if things became messy. She didn't think they would. Danny was never that type of guy—unless he was drunk—but she wasn't taking any chances. She hadn't talked with him face-to-face since before they separated, preferring instead to communicate through Frank, but this was different; this was the end, and they would negotiate it in person, and in relative privacy.

"I did, yeah."

"And?"

"I'm fine with everything."

"Danny, you're giving up your half of the house."

"I know. I just think it's fair after all that happened. I'm trying to make amends, Deirdre. I want you and the kids to be able to go on without having to move and all that. I just think it's fairer this way."

"Have you talked to a lawyer?"

"No. I don't like lawyers."

"Nobody does, Danny, but this is important."

"Look, Deirdre, everything was my fault and I want to try to make things right. I want you and the kids to be able to go on without any more of my bullshit. I don't need anything. I've got my own place and I can manage fine."

"I still think you should get legal advice." She almost felt guilty—as if she were taking advantage of his reformation—but a part of her was angry at him too. He was why they had to go through all of this.

"I don't need it. I'm trying to do what's right and there's feck-all lawyers know about that."

He meant it as a joke, so she smiled. "Danny, you know that things are over between us?" She almost felt bad saying it but she had to put it out there.

"I know, but I still want to have a relationship with my kids. I know Martin isn't ready and I don't blame him, but I want to be able to make things right between them and me someday."

He seemed to be expecting her to say something about that, but the time wasn't right. He had put them through this before, pretending to get his act together and letting them get their hopes up. She wasn't going through any more of that. This time they were well and truly over. Still, she was a little sad for him, even after everything. "Well, I still think you should have someone take a look at them."

"I don't need to." He reached inside his jacket and pulled out the pen she had picked out for the kids to give to him one Christmas. He signed and initialed where she had marked and handed the papers back. They didn't make eye contact but she could tell he was almost crying. She collected the papers and placed them in her briefcase. It felt so unreal. Twenty years of their lives ended by a few signatures, calmly and quietly after all they had been through. Deirdre raised her cup and finished her coffee to give him a chance to compose himself.

"Well then?"

"Yeah, I guess that's it."

"By the way, Grainne has a sleepover planned for Saturday night. Did she tell you?"

"Yeah, but she said she'd be free the next weekend."

There was something else happening that weekend but Deirdre didn't mention it. She would shuffle a few things and let him see her. If he really was trying this time, then she wouldn't do anything to deflect him, and issues like custody could derail anybody. No, she wouldn't do anything petty or spiteful. He deserved that much.

"Goodbye, Danny."

"Goodbye, Deirdre."

She walked back to the office. She would be late, but she needed the time to make the transition. Seeing Danny again awoke so many feelings she had lulled to sleep. She was still angry at him—and not just for discarding what they had together. She could handle that as long as she remembered what she had learned in Al-Anon. Danny was suffering from a disease.

At first, she had found that hard to accept—it just seemed far too convenient—but over time it had made sense. He wasn't just the monster he had become. There was still some of the sweet and shy young man she had once fallen in love with. But his drinking had distorted all that.

There had been so many times she couldn't understand why he didn't just stop. Days and nights when she functioned robotically while questioning everything they had become together. If he really loved her . . .

Now, she knew it was not that simple. Danny was fighting for his life, and it was a battle he was going to have to fight on his own. There was nothing more she could do for him, and she certainly wasn't going to let it spill over into the lives of her kids. At least no more than it already had.

Sometimes she felt she was abandoning him, but they had talked to her about that at the meetings. She had to do what was right for her and the children and, even though she was separating him from his family, it was what he needed. The people at the meetings had been very clear about that: Danny Boyle would have to choose how he was going to spend the rest of his life, and he would have to make that choice alone. It hardly seemed fair after the way things had been when he was younger, but there was nothing more she could do.

That was what was really bothering her. All her time and energy and love counted for so little in the end. Nothing she had done, or said, had been of much value. Danny was destined to go and meet whatever life had in store for him, and the power of love was nothing more than wishful thinking. It might even have been better if they'd never met.

*Detach, detach,* she reminded herself with every step, even as her emotions churned. She would still get angry from time to time but that would pass. She would feel sad for him, too, and all they might have been together. And she would feel a little sorry for herself. But she had more than enough to do looking after herself and her children. Danny Boyle couldn't be her problem anymore. Hopefully somebody else was looking out for him.

\*

"Oh, Mrs. Boyle. I can't get over the size of it."

They were sitting in the middle of St. Peter's Square enjoying ice cream, after having seen the basilica. It was enormous, and Jacinta couldn't help but wonder if it was all really necessary. They had to put on a big show back in the old days but things had changed. She thought they should sell off some of the stuff they had lying around. It would probably feed half of Africa for a few years.

It had almost made her smile, standing in the middle of it all, thinking like that. Nora wouldn't have approved, and if Jerry had been with her he would have said she was being a bit racist or something. As time went by she missed him more and more. It would have been so much better if he were with her.

"And did it make you feel closer?"

Mrs. Flanagan was still in awe and didn't seem to hear a word Jacinta was saying.

"To God, like? Did you feel closer to him?"

When Mrs. Flanagan finally focused on her she was smiling. "Oh no, not to God directly, but I did get the impression that there was somebody there to take messages. It was probably a saint. The place must be full of them."

It was full of something, Jacinta agreed, but kept her thoughts to herself. Half the people there looked gobsmacked. Jerry used to say that was why they had made it so big—he was always going on about stuff like that. He used to say it was to make you feel small and insignificant. That was why he was never going to be caught dead there. She never really listened and now she regretted it. She hadn't paid enough attention to all the little things about him when she could.

He would have enjoyed the tourists though—the ones that weren't gobsmacked and walked around like a bunch of heathens. There were a few pilgrims, too, scuffing around on their knees, and Mrs. Flanagan in the middle of it all, looking as though she might burst into tears at any moment. Jacinta had to look away so she didn't laugh out loud. She didn't of course. "From your lips to God's ear. Isn't that what they say?"

"Who?" Mrs. Flanagan still looked as if she were somewhere else.

"When you were inside—you must have felt like your prayers were finally being heard."

"Do you really think so, Mrs. Boyle? That's so nice of you to say."

She had that look again. She'd often said that if it weren't for Jacinta she'd have gone sheer mad from all the grief. That always made Jacinta uneasy. Mrs. Flanagan seemed to take her words as gospel, even though she knew Jacinta had been in the hospital and all.

"Well if they can't hear your prayers from here, they mustn't be really there."

Jacinta hadn't meant to say that out loud, but seeing Rome with Mrs. Flanagan was far more than she had bargained for. She had to keep reminding herself that she was doing it for her Danny—in a roundabout way. If she could help Mrs. Flanagan find a bit of peace—well, some good had to come out of it. All she wanted now was for Danny to be cured. Only Mrs. Flanagan was far crazier than anybody she'd met in the hospital, but she was religious about it, and everyone was more accepting of that.

"Oh don't say that, Mrs. Boyle." Mrs. Flanagan really looked shocked and blessed herself with her ice cream, a few drips falling on her pants. She daubed them with her fingers and licked them clean. Jacinta had never seen her look so happy, even if she was gobsmacked.

"I was only joking, Mrs. Flanagan."

"Oh, but you shouldn't. They might hear."

Jacinta was about to say something when she realized Mrs. Flanagan hadn't mentioned Anthony since they came out, and she had managed to work him into every other conversation they'd had since they left home. Starting in the taxi, and then in the airport, and then on the plane, even though Jacinta put on headphones and tried to watch *Jerry Maguire*.

"He's the spitting image of my Anthony." Mrs. Flanagan had nudged her every time Tom Cruise came on the screen.

"So, do you want to go back to the hotel before we meet with Fr. Reilly?"

"I hope I'm not putting you out but I'd like to sit here a little while longer. It's very strange, Mrs. Boyle, but I know you'll understand. You see, when I was inside I got the feeling that Anthony would know I was here." She turned and waited for Jacinta to answer.

"Good enough, Mrs. Flanagan, and if Anthony hasn't shown up by the time we have to leave, we can come back tomorrow."

Jacinta wanted to sound as patient as she could, but she didn't really believe in pilgrimages anymore—or any of that stuff. But she had to try everything if she was going to save Danny. Still, she couldn't wait to dump her on Fr. Reilly for a while so she could have a few drinks in peace. He wouldn't mind.

So Jacinta and Mrs. Flanagan sat for over an hour in the shade of the saints, enjoying their ice cream while it lasted and watching people file in and out of the basilica. Up and down the steps where kings once had to sit in sackcloth and ashes. The nuns had told Jacinta all about that when she complained about her penance one day. She had told them she could never be sure if she had said enough. She used to get confused having to say everything ten times.

\*

"I hope you don't mind." Fr. Reilly blushed a little as he sat down with them. He was about to tell another lie. "But a friend of mine called as I was coming out so I had to invite him along too."

He hadn't. Patrick had phoned John and asked him to come. He needed a foil between him and what he used to be. He'd been surprised when Mrs. Boyle called and explained what she was up to, as though Patrick would understand and approve. He'd managed to put off seeing them for a few nights but he'd run out of excuses. Besides, Mrs. Boyle made a point of reminding him of the time he'd brought the two of them together to talk about their sons and all that happened that night in the mountains. She almost made him feel that she'd been the one doing him a favor.

"The more the merrier." Mrs. Boyle laughed and seemed genuinely relieved.

"He's a Jesuit." He'd been seeing a lot of the older priest and was learning to enjoy his company, even if the things they talked about were often disquieting. Sometimes John could get a bit strange.

"Lord bless us and save us." Mrs. Flanagan looked concerned.

"But he's a fine man, only he can seem a little different at first. At least until you get used to him." He wanted them to be ready in case John Melchor got into one of his moods. "So, did you have a nice day?"

"Oh we did, Father. We even got to say a few prayers in St. Peter's. It was such a blessing."

Patrick glanced at Jacinta before he answered and caught her making a face.

"It's a grand place to pray all right." He usually avoided it. It was a bit too ostentatious for his tastes. "And did you enjoy it, Mrs. Boyle?"

"I did indeed, only I'm glad I'm not the one who has to keep it clean."

Mrs. Flanagan looked a bit perturbed by that but Patrick laughed a little. He'd never thought about that before. He and John had often discussed the more obvious point: It was hard to champion the plight of the poor while clinging to all the trappings of wealth and power. Patrick was certain that Jesus wouldn't have liked it. He probably would have gotten angry as he did in the temple long ago. "And have you seen much of Rome?"

"Not yet." Jacinta rolled her eyes. "Mrs. Flanagan is very fond of praying. We've spent the last three days in the Irish churches: St. Agata's, St. Clemente's, St. Isidoro's and, of course, St. Patrick's. Mrs. Flanagan had wanted to work her way up to St. Peter's, like a pilgrimage, you see." Jacinta nodded to him so he would understand.

"For the sake of my Anthony's soul, Father," Mrs. Flanagan added. "We felt that God would hear us better here."

Patrick had almost forgotten all the crazy stuff people revealed to their priests. It was no wonder that poor old Fr. Brennan had ended up the way he did. Patrick had promised to go back and see him, only he'd left it too late.

"Ah." Patrick rose, delighted by the diversion as John Melchor approached. "Here's my friend. Father Melchor. And these two ladies are Mrs. Boyle and Mrs. Flanagan."

As John joined them Patrick took a moment to gather all he'd have to be again. He'd nearly forgotten how to be around them and almost felt impatient with all the superstition he'd once been part of.

"Ladies." John raised his hat and smiled. "I'm delighted to meet you." He offered his hand but Jacinta was sipping her wine and Mrs. Flanagan looked nervous.

\*

"I see." John Melchor nodded when Mrs. Flanagan had finished sharing the story of Anthony, murdered in the mountains with no one to tell her why.

"I have been praying every day since . . ." Mrs. Flanagan started to shudder a little. They were on the second bottle of wine and it seemed to be taking a toll on her.

"Of course you have." Patrick tried to soothe her from across the table.

"But, God forgive me,"—Mrs. Flanagan made the sign of the cross—"I never felt that my prayers were properly heard before. But God couldn't be that cruel, could he, Fathers?"

The two men hesitated, so Jacinta jumped in. She'd had more wine than the rest of them. "Maybe it's because he's a man. Men always say they love you and then put you through the fires of hell."

The two priests smiled at that, but Mrs. Flanagan didn't.

"But don't worry," Jacinta continued. "If this doesn't work we can go to Lourdes and talk to his mother. She'll put the skids under him. Mothers always stick together." It might be better for Danny, too, she considered. Lourdes was where everybody went to get cured.

"Ah now, Mrs. Boyle. You shouldn't be talking like that in front of the Fathers."

"Don't worry about us," John Melchor assured her as he poured more wine. "It's something I have often thought myself."

"I don't mean any disrespect," Jacinta explained, "it's just that sometimes praying feels like lining up at the butcher's counter and waiting for your number to be called."

"Don't be talking like that in front of the holy Jesuit. He'll think we're all still pagans."

"Don't concern yourself on my account." John Melchor laughed. "All the best Catholics are really good pagans at heart. I learned that in Central America. They have their own saints down there and they pray to them to intercede on their behalf. I guess we all still live in fear of the god of the Bible. It's understandable. He was very temperamental."

Mrs. Flanagan looked pleadingly at Patrick, expecting him to stand up for God, but John continued. "Trust me, Mrs. Flanagan, your prayers have been heard and God will surely act in his own mysterious way."

"Are you sure, Father?"

"I'm certain of it."

"Well there you have it."

Jacinta was clearly enjoying herself and looked for a waiter to bring more wine, but Mrs. Flanagan was tired and wanted to get back to their hotel. Patrick settled the bill and he and John walked them there like gentlemen.

*

"Are you sure you should have said that to Mrs. Flanagan?" Patrick chided gently when they were alone again, mindful that John was more used to talking with academics than ordinary people. "She might take the wrong meaning from it."

"I doubt it. That poor woman is so worn down by grief that she'll find solace in anything. They both are."

"Well, I hope everything works out for them."

"I'm sure it will, Patrick, but it'll probably take a few miracles along the way."

Patrick might have asked John why he looked so assured but they were crossing the Campo De' Fiori, right under Bruno's statue.

"Tell me more about Anthony and Danny Boyle," John asked nonchalantly.

# Chapter 2 – 1998

"WHERE'S MOM?" Grainne called from the hallway. It was almost nine and she was supposed to have been home by seven. And she had someone with her.

"Out," Martin answered from his room. He didn't want to have to deal with her. His mother would ask what time she had got in and he was going to have to fudge it again. He was tired of getting caught between them.

"Where?"

"I don't know. I think she had a meeting or something." He did know. She had gone for dinner with Eduardo. But they both thought it was better that Grainne didn't know. His mother felt that Grainne wasn't ready for her to move on from their father but, sometimes, Martin felt that Grainne was just using the whole thing to get her way.

He had been preparing for a test. He had to do well if he was going to go for scholarships. His coach said he was good enough to make it into the Ontario Hockey League and could even make it in the draft in a few years. It was flattering, but Martin had been around hockey long enough to see the price that had to be paid. Guys who had devoted everything were getting cut all around him. He was still going for it, but he would have a plan B. He already knew that life made its own cuts.

"This is my troll of a brother," Grainne explained and pushed his bedroom door open in case further evidence was required. Her friend looked in and smiled.

"Hi, Martin."

She flushed a little when he looked over. Her name was Rachael and she lived in Moore Park. She was older than Grainne and Martin was surprised they were friends. Rachael was one of the hottest girls in grade nine.

"Close my door. I'm busy." It sounded worse than he had intended. He always talked to Grainne like that, but she knew he didn't really mean it, even when he did. He was just a bit flustered. He'd never talked to Rachael before, but since the beginning of term he saw her everywhere and, lately, she always smiled when he walked past. He never reacted when he was with his friends, swaggering around in their hockey jackets, but sometimes when his friends weren't looking he'd look back at her. The last time she'd caught him.

"Rachael and I are going into my room and no one is to bother us."

"Mom's going to ask about your homework."

"God! You're such a . . ." Grainne stormed off but Rachael lingered for a moment.

"Bye, Martin."

"Yeah, bye." He could have kicked himself. He'd wanted to be much cooler.

They were listening to *Faith*. Grainne was obsessed with George Michael and had posters of him all over her room. She'd even gone around singing "I Want Your Sex" until their mother insisted she stopped. Martin had complained, too, but his mother had just laughed and told him he was just as obsessed by hockey. "At least hockey," he had blurted out without thinking, "doesn't turn people into sluts."

His mother hadn't jumped all over that. She just raised her eyebrow to let him know she expected better of him. They had talked about it. Grainne was being a total pain, but it was what she had to do to get through. They were all still a little damaged.

Grainne and Rachael were laughing at something. He hadn't heard Grainne laugh like that in so long that it almost made him smile. "That's so, like, cool," he heard her through the wall. She was doing that thing she always did, acting and sounding like whomever she was with. It was as if she had a different personality for every person she met. Most of the crowd she hung around with were dorks. Everyone was dorky in grade seven, but when Martin was in it they didn't go around like they were proud of it.

They had only been in the same high school for a few months, but she was already embarrassing him. She was acting flirty all the time, and the other guys were starting to notice her. She was still going over to her father's too. He only went at Christmas and met him somewhere for his birthday. He never wanted to, but his mother insisted. His father was still a dork. He'd stopped drinking again but that didn't change anything. And he was always trying too hard. Grainne milked it for all she could, but it just made Martin angry. Especially when his father bought him a Wayne Gretzky autographed stick and his mother made him hang it on his wall. He hated looking at it. It brought up all kinds of feelings that he couldn't sort out. It was easier when he just pretended that his father didn't exist anymore.

His mother was due home by eleven so he banged on the wall at ten-thirty and banged again when Grainne didn't respond. It was how he kept her out of trouble.

"Okay, okay. God! You're like a prison guard."

He waited by his door until they came out. Rachael had made a phone call and they were giggling about something.

"Martin, Rachael's parents didn't answer. Would you walk her home? Pretty please," Grainne asked when they saw him, her voice softer and sweeter. Rachael stood behind her and watched his face. They were both smiling like cats but he didn't hesitate.

"Yeah, okay."

*

When he returned his mother was waiting for him. She was sitting on the couch with her legs tucked under her and her high heels kicked off under the coffee table. She had turned the lights down and poured herself a glass of wine.

"Everything okay, sweetie? Grainne tells me she had a friend over and that you were a gentleman and walked her home."

"Yeah."

"Want a sip?" She let him have one every so often. She didn't want him to be afraid of alcohol.

"No thanks."

"So, is she nice?"

"Yeah."

"You don't normally like Grainne's friends."

"She's different."

"Oh?"

"Yeah. Did you have a nice . . . evening?"

His mother shook out her hair and took off her earrings. She had makeup on too. All the guys in school noticed her and they all had the "hots" for her. Doug was the worst. When they went drinking on the hill behind the school, he let it slip out. They were all drunk, so he probably thought no one would remember. Martin did. He only had one beer and didn't finish it. He didn't like drinking like that. Normally he wouldn't, but it was the hockey guys.

"Martin, what would you think if we all went out with Eduardo some evening?"

He just shrugged. He wanted to but he didn't want to show it.

"Is that a yes?"

"Yeah."

"Oh, Martin, stop grunting and talk with me. The reason is, your father called me today. He wants to take you and your sister shopping on Saturday. He wants to bring his girlfriend along. Would you be okay with that?"

"Yeah, I guess so." He knew what his mother was up to. If Martin accepted his father's girlfriend, Grainne would have to accept Eduardo. It seemed fair, only his mother would insist she was doing it for Grainne's sake—so Grainne could see that everyone could get along even though everything was different. It would help with her trust issues. Martin didn't care. He liked Eduardo. He was cool.

"What's she like?"

"I'm sure she's a very nice person."

"Then why is she going out with him?"

"Maybe she likes him."

"Or feels sorry for him."

"Martin, that's very cynical of you. People meet and fall in love, even damaged people. So, tell me about Rachael. Is she nice?"

"Yeah."

*

Deirdre finished her wine and got ready for bed. It was all going to work out fine.

"Each new beginning is the start of the next failure." Danny's voice echoed as she removed her makeup and applied her night creams. For the most part she had exorcised him from her life, but whenever they had contact he'd linger for a while. She dismissed him again and checked herself in the mirror. Since they had separated she had taken good care of herself and was fighting the war against aging. And while not so much winning, she was going down with a fight. She was forty-one but could easily pass for mid thirties. Wise enough to know what she was getting herself into.

Eduardo had been cut off from his kids, as well as his parents and everyone they knew. When he left his wife, he had left his tribe. If he had hooked up with an Italian or, at worst, a Hispanic it might have been okay, after enough time had passed. But he had left his wife for a British woman.

"Irish," Deirdre had corrected him when he tried to explain it all to her. He needed to feel part of a family again. And Grainne needed to know that life went on and often led to new and greater times. Deirdre knew she had to let it play out slowly. She'd see how the shopping trip went first.

*

Traffic was bad so her mother agreed to drop them off at Simcoe St. She had wanted to leave them right at the door where their father would be waiting. Queen Street West could be a little too much for a girl Grainne's age, she had said. But Grainne pointed out that Martin would be with her, and it was the middle of the day.

Only Grainne wasn't happy that Martin was wearing his dorky hockey jacket. She wasn't even sure why he had come along. He didn't even like their daddy. He was so . . . God! And he wouldn't even let her stop and look in any of the small boutiques along the way. They had the kind of stuff that the older girls in school were wearing, punky and retro.

"I just want to look. God!"

"You wouldn't like it. You only like stuff with big logos."

"Yeah, right. Like you'd know what I like." She was about to get all . . . when she saw her father standing by the doorway of Club Monaco with some woman beside him.

"Daddy." She ran to him as she had when she was younger. He tried to pick her up and twirl her a little but she was too big for that now. So he just hugged her as if he hadn't seen her in so long. They had just been to the movies two weeks ago. He could be so . . .

"Grainne, this is Billie."

The woman leaned forward and smiled all stiffly. "Hi, Grainne. It's so nice to meet you. Your daddy has told me so much about you. And you"—she turned to her brother—"must be Martin."

Martin just grunted and didn't look up—like he was acting all bored.

"C'mon on then. Let's do some shopping." Grainne tugged her father's arm and, when he turned back to her, linked arms with him and dragged him inside. Billie followed with Martin who was all . . . He could be such a scrub sometimes.

Grainne knew her father was acting all nervous and was trying to involve his girlfriend every time they looked at something. At first Grainne just pretended like she wasn't even there but when Billie started agreeing that the stuff wasn't too old for her, Grainne smiled and even let her pick out some shirts and dresses.

She even let Billie hold them against her while she tilted her head and squinted a little. "Maybe something brighter," she would say as she put it away and rummaged for something else. "Or something looser," when she looked at Grainne's tiny breasts and tried again.

A few times her father objected. He thought she was too young to go around looking like that, but his girlfriend just laughed. Grainne didn't even have to work on him. Billie did it all for her. She came into the change room, too, with all that they had picked out. She said that Grainne should try them all on and they could decide from there.

She even made her father and Martin sit outside while Grainne strutted back and forth in each different outfit. She loved being the center of attention, even if Martin was glaring at her. And when it was time to decide, and Grainne was preparing to squeeze out a few tears if she had to, Billie said she should take the lot and that she wanted to pay for them. Her father tried to argue, but Billie wouldn't hear it. She linked arms with Grainne and marched to the checkout.

Two dresses, three skirts, a few shirts, two sweaters and two cargo pants. It was quite a haul. And her father seemed happy. "So, do you like your new clothes?"

"Yeah, and the best part is that Mom is going to hate them."

"Well I'm just happy to see you getting on so well with Billie," he whispered when she rose on her toes to kiss his cheek. "It's so great to see everybody happy and enjoying themselves."

*

Billie wasn't. Not really. But she kept smiling for Danny's sake. His daughter was a spoiled little princess and she had just gone and spent a fortune on her. She had to; she really wanted the little brat to like her and had promised to take her shopping again—just the two of them. And now she had to work on Martin, who looked like he just wanted to be anywhere else. Billie knew exactly how he felt.

"And what kind of stuff do you like?" she asked as she walked out beside him, while Danny followed with all Grainne's bags under one arm and his daughter under the other—just as he and Billie did when they walked home from gigs together.

They had only been living together for a few months, having waited the "AA year." Everything was different from before, but in recovery, everything else was too. He had changed and so had she, but they still loved each other. It was different this time, though. He wasn't just him anymore. It was him and his children, particularly his daughter. She was a part of everything they talked about.

The only time Billie ever really felt as though they were a couple again was when they were in bed. Even then it was different and a bit strange at first. Sober sex was difficult, but they had the past to remind them.

For everything else they had the program. They talked about it and how it impacted every facet of their lives. Danny was almost evangelical, but she understood. When life got difficult, Danny became more programmed. It was almost like a religion with him, but they did talk openly and freely; and after all the years she had spent hiding from reality, she was happy about that. Except they never spent enough time talking about themselves. He was always going on about how much he missed his kids. Maybe if they got that straightened out they would have time. It was going to be hard, but she was determined to get the little brats to like her.

"Nothing around here," Martin answered gruffly.

"So where do you hang out?"

"I don't."

"Sure you do." She wanted to put her arm around his shoulder like a friend, but he didn't seem like that type of kid. "You hang around with your hockey team. That's hanging out, no matter what you call it."

"Whatever."

"Oh, you're the strong silent type?"

"Whatever."

"So what would you like to do?"

"Go home."

"Why? Are you not enjoying yourself?"

"No. And I don't see why I have to do this. Next time, just invite Grainne."

"But your father wanted to see you too."

His eyes grew harder and narrower. "Why? He doesn't even like me."

"Sure he does."

"You don't know what he's really like."

"And are you so sure people can't change?"

"Whatever."

"Listen, Martin, this is just as hard on him as it is on you."

"How would you know?"

"Because it is not any easier on me."

"Then why did you come?"

"Because I'm with your father now."

He didn't say anything but he did look up at her. His eyes were hard. The kid had eyes like a hawk.

"What do say that you cut me a break so that I don't have to spend any more time with your little sister? We could cut out on shopping and go for something to eat. You look like the type of guy who could manage a steak."

"Sure," he agreed and smiled the way Danny did.

"Thanks, kid." She paused to light a cigarette but thought better of it.

"Billie?"

"Yeah?"

"I'm going to be okay with you being with my dad."

"Good, kid, because I'm going to be okay with you."

*

The morning of his seventy-fifth birthday was cool but sunny. John Melchor had decided to take the day off and celebrate. It wasn't as though he'd be missed. They had him translating footnotes, and someone else proofed everything he wrote anyway. He called Patrick but he was busy. John envied him a little. Patrick still had a purpose in the world, but at least he had found the time to wish him a great day and agreed to meet for dinner later.

So John had the day to himself and was going to enjoy it as if it were his last—a determination that grew a little more with each birthday. He left his lodgings and walked along the Via Giulia, past the Santa Maria dell'Orazione e Morte, built by Confraternita del Suffragio, the Church of the Dead, and one of his favorite places in the whole city. He had visited the crypt and stood face to face with the skulls of the past. It was a pilgrimage he had to make. When he was shot, the dead had hovered around his bedside for days.

Being back in Rome suited him, even though he still grumbled. For all that his soul yearned to go out and fight the good fight, his body was past it. He stayed involved and did his part through letters to newspapers and politicians, drawing attention to the things that were often forgotten. He had tried to pester Patrick to be more active, too, but had gotten nowhere.

"Render unto Caesar?"

"It's not my place to say, John."

"That's all very well, Patrick, but sometimes the shepherd has to chase the wolves away." He knew Patrick saw the world as one big wheel that just kept trundling around and around. He had often said that everything made far more sense when this was understood.

"And sometimes he just has to move them to safer pastures." Patrick smiled. "Things are not getting better or worse—not where it really matters. Civility, like civilizations, comes and goes and the poor still trundle on. All we can do is spread a bit of comfort and hope where they are needed."

"A bringer of comfort . . . like Simon of Cyrene?"

"Well, I wouldn't go that far, John, but sometimes just having a helping hand or a shoulder to cry on is the best medicine. I think it's one of the things the example of Jesus asks of us. I know the world is run by rich and cruel people who hire men to go around and do their killing for them. It's always been like that. And I know when the Church tried to set up a new and fairer order, it just made a total mess of it. But with all due respect, John, I don't think priests are cut out for getting involved in the temporal world."

John had bristled at that and reminded Patrick that, as a Jesuit, he was committed to the fight against social injustice.

Patrick had just smiled again. "I appreciate that and I do admit that I'm becoming a bit of a Trappist. I wasn't a very good priest when it came to dealing with other people's problems. I'm much better suited to the cloisters."

Still, John liked his company and appreciated his friendship. Most of the men he worked with gave him a wide berth. He was tainted by his past, and no one wanted to get too close in case they might be tarred by the same brush.

He turned onto the Via Paola and walked toward the Ponte Sant' Angelo. He wanted to watch the river for a while. As he walked he could hear the whisperings of the dead, harder to hear when the city was awake. At times like this he wondered what his life would have been like if he had been a normal person, with normal problems.

*

Billie walked past the liquor store twice and looked inside each time. The windows had been decorated for the Christmas season and everyone inside looked so happy. She wasn't, and turned away again. She should just get on the subway and go home. And, if she still felt like taking a drink, she should go to a meeting.

She should, but life should have been a lot better by now. It wasn't. Danny was in a funk over Grainne. She was supposed to spend Christmas with them while her mother and brother went skiing for the holidays. They were probably going with Deirdre's boyfriend but Billie didn't think she should mention that. It didn't matter anyway. It was canceled, and Danny would have to make do with just seeing her on Christmas Eve. Billie didn't see why it was such a big deal. People made too big a fuss over Christmas, and Danny made far too much of his relationship with his daughter.

Billie had known it was going to be difficult, but she'd had no idea how much she'd have to give up for a kid she really couldn't get to like. They had begun to disagree over that. He felt she was being insensitive, and she thought his daughter was soaking him for all she could get. It wasn't just money. It was everything else. Every time she had a problem with her brother she called, and Danny would spend an hour on the phone listening to her. She would also get him involved when she had problems with her mother. Billie thought Danny should stay out of it, but had kept her thoughts to herself until the other night. They were just sitting down to dinner when the call came.

"Just leave it ring through," she had suggested as she placed his plate before him. He didn't, and she ate alone while his food got cold. They had planned to go out and catch a movie but she knew that wasn't going to happen now.

"Sorry, I had to deal with that. The kid is having a fight with her mother."

"What about?"

"Her mother won't let her to go to a sleep over."

"Maybe she's not ready, Danny."

"I think she is. Besides, I don't think her mother handled it very well."

"Do you really think you should be getting between them?"

"I'm still her father."

"I know, but sometimes kids try to take advantage when their parents are divorced."

"She's not like that."

"Okay, then."

"I mean it. She's a good kid."

"I'm not saying she isn't. It's just that . . ."

"It's just that you don't like her. That's the real problem here."

She should have let it go but she didn't. "Danny, that's not fair. I'm not good with kids but you can't accuse me of not trying."

"Well, I think we all have to try harder."

"I am trying, Danny. I want things to be good for all three of us, but sometimes I think Grainne is . . ."

"Is what?"

"Well, she's just a kid, Danny. They're all a bit self-obsessed at that age."

"And how would you know?"

"Because I was just like that." She wasn't. She had lied to make him feel better and it almost worked.

"Maybe you're right, but you got to see it from where I'm sitting. It's like I'm stuck between two relationships."

*And that worked out so well for me the last time,* Billie thought but didn't say. She was just about to reach forward and touch him. They could even go to bed. Everything was better after they did it. She'd almost reached him when the phone rang again. It was Deirdre wondering what gave Danny the right to undermine her. It was never going to end.

"Screw it," she decided aloud and turned back and went inside the liquor store. She bought a bottle of white rum. It didn't leave too much of a smell and she could mix it with Coke. Danny would be gone all evening and she would be sleeping by the time he got home. She didn't intend to get hammered; she just needed to take the edge off. She shouldn't, but she couldn't see any other way. The program might be working for Danny but it wasn't for her. She had tried. She had gone to meetings and done all the things they told her to do, but it didn't make any difference.

She had hoped that if she got her act together they could go back to what they had once been, back when he lived on Jarvis Street. She had hoped she could rekindle the side of him that sang about the world with such poignancy. He was never cut out for the life he chose with Deirdre.

That was another thing that had always bothered her—he hadn't chosen Deirdre over her. He had just gone along with her because of the past, and because he felt obliged. Billie should never have reacted the way she did but she had been hurt. She was, despite all her bravado, insecure when it came to love. That was why she drank too much.

Besides, cocaine was her real problem. Admittedly, she always gave into it after she had been drinking, even when she knew she shouldn't. But she had kicked it, and from now on she would just stick to booze. She just wouldn't let Danny know for a while.

\*

After the kids sidled off to their rooms—Martin to study and Grainne to talk on the phone— Deirdre tidied the kitchen and poured herself a large glass of red wine. She kicked off her shoes and settled on the couch. She flicked around a few channels but there was nothing that interested her. *As Good As It Gets* was still in the VCR so she started it from the beginning. The last time she watched it she felt a bit like Carol, but this time she was feeling more like Melvin.

It had been one of those days when she wished she worked without any human contact. Most of it had been taken up by a young woman from Corporate Services who was threatening to file a complaint, citing sexual harassment. She claimed she was overlooked for a promotion because she had declined her manager's advances.

That type of thing always made the whole bank tremble and a flurry of emails fluttered down to Deirdre's desk. She had to interview both parties separately and report back to senior management. She was always called to clean up little messes before they got bigger, just like at home.

The young woman claimed her manager forced himself on her near the washroom of the restaurant that hosted the last Christmas party. Deirdre wasn't sure about that. She had been at that party and remembered the young woman drinking far too much and being far too flirty, but she couldn't say any of that. She just made notes and nodded along, even when the young woman broke down and cried. She did offer her the box of tissues she always kept on her desk and calmly asked why the complaint wasn't made earlier. She could understand, but she had to ask. If she didn't, someone else would.

The manager had a very different story. He said that she followed him and forced herself on him. It was probably closer to the truth, but he was the kind that always hovered far too close to the line between what was appropriate and what was not.

Regardless, Deirdre remained placid as she took notes, but she had to ask how the young woman managed to force herself on someone who was bigger than she. He admitted he'd been drinking a bit and didn't realize she was going to take it so far. Deirdre just nodded along and then asked if the young woman had ever been considered for the promotion. He told her she was and that she'd made the long list. She even offered him a tissue when he cried about what would happen if his wife and children ever found out—not that anything happened. He hadn't let it.

Deirdre would make her recommendations in the morning. The young woman should be given a settlement in lieu of the promotion and shuffled away. She could feel vindicated and the bank could avoid any type of stain. Deirdre didn't want to judge her, but she had seen too many like that—women who used their tits instead of their brains. If the young woman had been thinking she would have gone for someone better than a department manager. There were far hornier old goats on the higher floors. And the manager should be formally reprimanded and sent for sensitivity training. He'd be red-circled then and given every encouragement to seek employment elsewhere—with a clean record. He could take it and leave. It was cold but what did he think would happen?

She went for more wine, checking on the kids on her way back. Martin grunted when she looked in on him. He had his books open and was furiously typing away. He had an essay due and would stay up until it was done. Grainne was lying on her bed, busy yakking away with a friend. Deirdre didn't react in case she had brought any part of her day home with her. Things were messed up enough, and she'd been thinking about Grainne when she was interviewing the young woman. She just shook her head and went back downstairs.

She sat back on the couch and sipped. Life was so much easier to deal with when she wasn't personally invested. Melvin Udall would totally agree. Eduardo had canceled the trip because of his mother.

"She went ahead and made all the arrangements without telling me."

He had phoned full of indignation. Deirdre wasn't too surprised, just disappointed. Not so much in him, just in the way things were turning out these days. It was what her mother used to call "one of those trying times, but often they turn out to be blessings. In disguise," she'd add if Deirdre's father was around.

And she wasn't surprised when he made it obvious that he was going to have to go alone. "I know what they're planning for me," he had explained, growing more indignant as he did. "And I'm mad about it, too, but I have no choice. I have to go to my mother's."

It was the essential difference between them. Everything was a big deal with him. He admitted it openly and claimed it was very Portuguese. At first she had liked all of that—all the bright energy that sparkled when they were together. But the other days—when all his guilt and sadness engulfed him—were just far too much.

She didn't make a big deal out of it and quickly reassured him. "It's okay, Eduardo, I understand. Besides, we can try again at March break."

"I'm not going back to them, you know that?"

"I know, Eduardo. I know."

"Dee-dree, I love you now and I promise you that nothing will change between us."

But it already had.

As the movie closed so satisfyingly, Deirdre felt miserable. She had been so upset about the trip being canceled that she had decided that Grainne would be staying with her for Christmas. It was a little mean-spirited of her and not at all like the principles they had talked about at the meetings.

She hadn't been in a while. She told herself it was because she was too busy, but there were other reasons. Too much of her life was still taken up by Danny. He was still a factor in every decision she made and she was getting very tired of that. Sure, he'd always be the father of her children and she would always have to take that into account, but she couldn't go on tip-toe-ing around him, always afraid that anything she did might send him spiraling down again.

His recovery was his business now and had very little to do with her. She hoped he would make it, but past experience made her skeptical. Danny always had difficulty adapting to the world around him. He always became caught up on what they had been taught as children. She had learned that it was better to go along with things as long as they got her where she was going. She worked hard and wanted to enjoy the comfort and security that afforded. She supported her charities and volunteered when time allowed. She did her part and she was content with that.

Danny had never been able to find a way of doing that. For him it was still a matter of the world being full of lies and deceit and, instead of doing something to change that, he'd sit brooding and feeling sorry for himself. She had indulged him before and that just made things worse. No, Danny Boyle would have to face the world head-on and learn to deal with it by whatever means he could.

Her mother would have thought she was becoming heartless, but Deirdre had never told her how bad things had gotten. Part of it was she wanted to be understanding—Danny was suffering from a disease—and part of it was shame. She was working on ridding herself of that, but sometimes just remembering what it had been like . . .

Besides, Danny had Grainne for her birthday and every second weekend, and sleepovers, so she should really spend this Christmas at home. Grainne was showing all the signs of being troubled, and Deirdre needed to spend some time with her.

She had called to let him know and Billie had answered. She quickly agreed that Deirdre was absolutely right and Grainne's stability was more important. She would let Danny know and he could call back. She sounded disinterested and a little out of it, but Deirdre didn't care. At least she had let them know.

She wished she hadn't now. Grainne was making her pay. She was so tempted to book the three of them into a hotel in Montreal for the holidays. Only not in the one that she and Eduardo had . . .

"Mom."

"Martin. All finished?"

"Oh, yeah. Can I ask you a big favor?"

Deirdre sat up because she knew it was going to be important.

"Can Rachael come over on Christmas Day? She's never had a Christmas and asked if she could see ours."

Deirdre could see how much it meant to him. "Sure, only it mightn't be our best."

# Chapter 3 – 1999

"THAT'S ANOTHER SOBER ST. PATRICK'S DAY, done and dusted." Danny smirked as he carefully shaved the last of the cream from under his chin. A part of recovery was looking as though he cared; the old-timers had been adamant about that. They said that if he ever wanted to become a living example of the power of the program then he'd better start looking like a winner.

Danny liked the sound of that and started to send his shirts to the dry cleaner, too, and enjoyed their crisp, white cleanness. He always wore the best ones to meetings. He liked the effect it had when he talked with one of the new guys afterwards. He could tell they were looking at him as if he had it made. Except the old-timers. They still looked at him like they could see right through him.

"Nothing to say?" he asked the mirror as he daubed aftershave on his face. Part of his new morning ritual, after making coffee from freshly ground beans, was to talk with Anto while he shaved. He needed to talk with someone. Things with Billie were strained and had been since Christmas.

She wouldn't admit it but he could tell she was having a tough time. He'd tried to help but that didn't go too well. He understood. It was one of the things the old-timers warned him about. Two recovering alcoholics, together—it was hard enough to try to get along with a normal person. And it was probably hard on her that he was doing so well.

*Yeah, you're a real power of example to us all.*

"I'm doing my best, you know?" He shrugged to change the subject. It was probably a little insensitive of him to be going on like that—given that Anto was where he was. He'd started to include him in the list of those he thought about when they said the Lord's Prayer—even though he was still praying to an ambiguous higher power. "What's bugging you?"

*Nothing.*

"Nothing? I've never known you to have nothing to say."

*It's nothing, Boyle. I just think you might be getting a bit carried away with the image of recovery—and not actually doing it.*

Danny stopped to consider that. It was the feeling he'd been getting from the old-timers too. It bothered him—a lot. He'd been doing everything they'd told him—well, almost everything—and they still wouldn't cut him a break. Sure there was all that stuff about moral inventory and defects and short-comings. He'd get around to them. Right now he was just trying to help others. "You know what they say, Anto. Fake it 'til you make it."

*That sounds like when we were kids and we all had to pretend to be good Catholics.*

"Don't remind me. I'm still trying to get over all that bull-shit. Do you remember all the crap they tried to teach us? Especially that fecker, Muldoon. I'd love to go back and give that gobshite a right earful."

*Yeah.* Anto sounded a little tired and frustrated.

"Guys like him are why I'm the way I am, filling our heads with bullshit and saying everything is our fault when the whole world is in the state it's in. Except Fr. Reilly. At least he tried to help."

*He did, yeah,* Anto agreed, almost sounding contrite. *And do you remember the bishop?*

"Him? He and my granny were friends. He used to scare the shit out of me."

*Me too, until just after my parents kicked me out. He stopped me on the street one day to ask how I was doing. I told him I was fine but he could see I wasn't. He gave me a few quid and then he said something I have never forgotten. He said that no matter how bad things got there would always be someone who'd be willing to help.*

"What do you think he meant?"

*If I knew that, I wouldn't be here with you.*

\*

"Where better to eulogize the dead on a Good Friday?"

Patrick didn't like the Church of the Dead. He appreciated what it was about but it was just far too morbid. However, he did like when John Melchor did stuff like this. Whenever they had to mark an observance he'd make it into a full ritual, complete with mystical symbolism—just like the way things used to be before Vatican II. Patrick missed some of those days, only John's rituals were getting very dark. His doctor assumed it was because of what happened in El Salvador and increased his medications. John took them and continued to shuffle calmly through his days, but whenever he was with Patrick he'd let his inner demons out to play. Miriam said it was cute and that it was a sign of how much he trusted Patrick. "He isn't like that with just anyone," she had assured him. They still called each other a few times a year just to keep in touch. They were older and wiser now and had left all the awkwardness behind.

"Okay, John, Santa De' Morte it is then. The usual time?"

John liked to get there after the "Celebration of the Passion of the Lord" had cleared out and the whispers of the dead eddied back into all the nooks and crannies. John would always dress perfectly for the occasion in his long black coat and his broad brimmed hat. And his gleaming white collar.

"Oh, don't worry, I will." Patrick had bought black slacks and a black turtle neck, and his raincoat was a very dark blue. It would pass for black in the dark.

John believed in showing great respect where it was deserved. "They died secure in the false hope we gave them," he'd mutter as if to himself. "The least we can do is honor them for that."

Patrick never knew what to say to things like that. John could become morose and it took forever to get him out of it. Sometimes—Patrick laughed to himself—John was almost as bad as Dan Brennan, and he wasn't far behind. He felt bad about indulging him but, as he'd learned with Dan, what else could he do but go along with it all and hope that nobody else noticed?

"Very good, John. I'll see you then." It was his own fault. He was always saying that being a priest meant giving comfort and solace to the poor and the sick and the insane. That's what the example of Jesus was for him.

"Very well, John, but you'd better let me get off the phone so I can get ready."

"Anthony Flanagan?" Patrick could hardly believe it. John had just told him that the whisperers were saying he needed their help.

"Yes, Anthony Flanagan," John repeated impatiently. "The one who was killed over twenty years ago. And bring your umbrella. It's starting to rain."

\*

As soon as they knelt in the shadows John went a bit trance-like, but Patrick didn't mind. It gave him the chance to sort things out. John was on one of his missions for the dead and it was best to play along and make sure no harm came to him. Besides, it gave Patrick time for his own reflections.

For most of his life he'd spent Good Fridays dwelling on all he'd been taught: that the only Son of God had allowed Himself to be stripped and beaten. He'd let them crown Him with thorns and nail Him to the cross.

When he was younger Patrick struggled to understand what was going through the minds of the Jews and the Romans, but now he understood. Jesus had the power of God in Him but

He let them do what their wicked hearts desired. Truth and Love frightened dark minds and cold, black souls; and Patrick wasn't just thinking about the people of the time. Things were the same today.

He didn't like to discuss it with John but it was obvious that Christ wouldn't have wanted anybody fighting for Him or His ideas. The whole point of His sacrifice was that those who suffered and died at the hands of the world would be rewarded with everlasting life. It was that simple, and that was probably why everyone overlooked it, preferring instead to focus on what they thought others shouldn't do. Sometimes, when he thought about what they'd done with the Savior's message, he almost despaired, but he preferred to focus on hope. It was a year since they had signed the *Good Friday Agreement* in Belfast and it was beginning to look as if it was going to hold this time. It wasn't so much the beginning of peace but the end of the strife—or the beginning of the end. They'd be haggling for years, but that was far better than shooting and bombing each other. After a thousand years, even the Irish grew tired of the fighting.

"He's here," John whispered in the darkness of the church, silent and draped until Sunday morning. Soundless but for the chanting of the dead, chanting the *Improperia* antiphonally.

"Who?"

"Anthony Flanagan."

"Anthony Flanagan?"

"Yes, Patrick, Anthony Flanagan. Who were you expecting? Anyway, he says hello and apologizes for making that false confession to you."

"Oh, tell him not to give it a second thought."

"I already did."

"Is there something else he wants?" Patrick didn't know what else to say. It was so absurd that it was probably really happening. He'd never told a living soul about Anthony's confession.

"He wants to talk with his mother."

\*

"Not at all, Father. Sure isn't it lovely to hear your voice again." Jacinta had been having a bit of a lie-in before she and Gina went to lay flowers on their parents' graves. They did it at Easter because they had both died in April.

"Mrs. Boyle." Fr. Reilly cleared his throat and Jacinta could picture him, twisting himself into knots, as Nora used to say.

"Yes, Father?"

"I was wondering if you were thinking of visiting Rome again anytime soon."

"It's funny you should say that, Father. I was just talking to Mrs. Flanagan the other day and she was saying the very same thing."

She and Mrs. Flanagan still met up in the Yellow House to break the monotony, and sometimes Jacinta even looked forward to it. Since they returned from their first trip she'd noticed Mrs. Flanagan wasn't so morose anymore. She seemed to be waiting on the good news Fr. Melchor had alluded to. "Would you come back with me?" she'd asked.

"I will if you want. Only I thought we might try Lourdes this time. You know, for the change."

"Maybe another time. It's just that I've been having this strange feeling lately. It's like my Anthony is calling out to me. It's only when I'm sleeping, mind you, but it's been almost every night." She paused to sip her sherry and to gauge Jacinta's reaction. "I hope that doesn't sound too strange."

"Not a bit of it, and I'd be more than happy to go again. Didn't we have great gas the last time?"

It was a lie but what else could she say? Mrs. Flanagan had found so much hope the first time that Jacinta was afraid another visit might just take it all away again.

"She was?" Fr. Reilly interjected hesitantly.

"Yes. She's convinced she's going to get more good news this time." Jacinta decided to help him along. "And even if she doesn't—it will be nice to see yourself again. Will your friend be there?"

"Yes he will. In fact, he's the one who asked me to call you."

"Well then, it is settled. Mrs. Flanagan put great stock in what he had to say."

"Yes," Fr. Reilly agreed, but sounded a little put-out.

"But then, he is a Jesuit," Jacinta reminded him so he wouldn't feel so bad.

After she hung up, she thought about it. It was all very well and they'd have a great time, but what if Mrs. Flanagan didn't find any peace? It might break her heart. That was the thing about being a woman. For all that they suffered, their hearts were still very brittle.

*

Things had been rough since Christmas and, as far as Billie was concerned, it had all been Danny's fault. He'd become a real prick about everything—chiding her about not getting out to meetings and how she was practicing the steps. She was hurt by that, but she knew what was really bugging him. He'd gone on a dry drunk over Grainne. He hadn't actually taken a drink; he just did all the other stuff—acting like a spoiled brat and throwing little temper tantrums. And he'd kept it up for weeks, even though he was still going to his meetings.

Still, she loved him and felt bad that she'd been sneaking drinks behind his back. She wished she didn't have to, but there was no way she could explain it. She'd tried the program and it really wasn't for her. She wasn't an alcoholic—she was just a bit messed up. Everything she believed life was about— art, music, expressions from the soul—were being drowned out by the jingle-jangle of commercialism. Everyone she knew was selling out and just going along with it all.

Besides, Danny was becoming one of those guys who stayed sober by telling others how to do it. She tried to be understanding, but he was making it so hard, and now they were barely on speaking terms. They hadn't slept together in a while either. She'd used the excuse of working later hours and they both seemed to accept that. Really, she was afraid he might smell alcohol on her breath, especially if they started doing anything.

That was another thing about recovery that really got to her—it was all about making life so dispassionate. She hadn't said anything, but since Danny had gotten sober he had no time for his music or any of the things that really made life interesting. Part of it was that when he had been with his family, that side of him had been discouraged. Billie didn't think much of Deirdre and it wasn't just rancor. Deirdre was one of those people who were all about the straight and narrow—the type of life that Billie wanted no part of, and the type of life that had strangled Danny's soul.

She couldn't say any of that to him, but she wanted to try to help him find that side of himself again. It was buried somewhere beneath the mounds of shame he'd piled on himself. He took all the blame for the way things had gone with Deirdre—and everything else in his life.

That wasn't how Billie saw it. Danny was one of those life had selected for special treatment—artists, poets, musicians—people who saw life as it really was and didn't let themselves get distracted. Maybe, after he'd learned to get a handle on his drinking, Danny could be one of those that left some record of their existence.

She decided, as she finished dressing and touching up her makeup, that she'd try again. The weekend was coming up and she had some time off. They could go down to Kensington and just walk around. With any luck they might bump into the people they used to be. She left a note on the kitchen table as she called a cab. She signed it "Billie" with a little heart over the second "i". She hadn't done that in years.

\*

Danny really needed a meeting and when they got to the slogans, the "live and let live" one hit him hard. He wasn't doing so great at that. He understood where Billie was coming from—theirs wasn't the life she wanted. But he was too scared to even let her talk about it. He was so afraid of going back out that he was doing what he always did—masking it by becoming a self-righteous arsehole. The old-timers had terrified him when they talked about the poor devils who had gone back out. They said the last thing those people needed was some reformed drunk getting all evangelical on them. Danny hadn't meant to. Staying sober was so hard.

But they'd managed this far. It was time he started having a little faith again—in the program and the great ambiguity that was still his higher power. And in himself. He felt better as he thought about it and settled in to listen to the speaker. He was one of those "god-guys." He kept referring to the "Big Book" with a touch of southern drawl. He was one of those guys who was about a year sober and had found Jesus, and he was now determined to tell everyone how to find him too. Danny never liked guys like that, but the old-timers told him to listen anyway—he just might learn something.

Instead, he went back to thinking about Billie and how he was going to make it up to her. He'd start promptly admitting when he was wrong and he'd make amends—only not in those words.

By the time he got home he was reformed again but Billie wasn't there. She'd said she'd be late and he wished she wasn't. He wished she was there waiting for him so they could just sit together and talk—as they used to. It would be like in the apartment on Jarvis—only they were older and, in his case, more foolish. They needed to get back there and just be the two of them again. That's when life was good.

When he found her note, he actually cried. Then he got down on his knees and gave thanks. Danny Boyle, who had screwed up everything he'd ever touched, was getting another chance to be happy. He'd been a real prick to her but he was going to make up for it now. In the morning he'd make her breakfast in bed. And that would just be the beginning. He was going to change everything. He'd been a total shit about Grainne. She was his daughter, but even he could see that she was a bit much sometimes. And Billie wasn't really the maternal type.

He got up as quietly as he could and cut grapefruit into slices like oranges because Billie liked it that way. They had no bread so he put little pieces of cheese on crackers and made a pot of coffee. They both drank far too much and only used freshly ground beans from Timothy's—a new indulgence in place of the old. The sugar bowl was empty, but they had a box of brown cubes somewhere in the back of the cupboard. He had to climb on a chair and when he reached in, he saw it. A bottle of rum—or half a bottle, to be more precise. He took it down as he stepped off the chair, never taking his eyes off it. He shook his head and put it in the middle of the table.

*

It was the first thing Billie saw when she came out, and for a moment considered bluffing her way through. She could say that she knew nothing about it—that it must be there from before, even though none of that made sense. She was busted, and even though all that she hoped for the weekend began to flutter away, she was relieved.

"Do we need to talk?" he asked in his sponsor voice. He always spoke like that when she got a bit edgy. It didn't help. In fact, it usually made things worse.

"Yes, I have had a drink." There was no point trying to deal with it any other way. She was an adult for Christ's sake, and he could take or leave her as such.

"When did this happen?" He looked shocked and dismayed—as if it was a surprise.

"When you were being a total prick to me."

"Are you going to stop?"

"Are you?"

"Billie, we got to separate things here."

"That's why I moved into the other room."

"You know I didn't mean that."

"I know, but I did." She didn't mean to get so angry, but just having to explain herself was really getting to her. And she had just sat through three months of him being a total asshole. Screw him if he had a problem with that.

"So what do we do now?"

"You tell me, Danny." But she couldn't look him in the face. He was standing there, with his big surprise on the table in front of him, looking like a broken-hearted kid. "I'm sorry." She shrugged and stepped a little closer to him. "It's just that I want us to be together, Danny, just like we used to be."

\*

"Are you warm enough?"

Rachael nodded but she was shivering a little. "Come here." Deirdre extended the blanket that was draped over her shoulders and pulled her a little closer. "If you're going to come to his games, you're going to have to learn to dress much warmer." Rachael nodded as she snuggled a little closer. She tried to say yes but her teeth were chattering. "You poor dear." Deirdre began to rub her back and coaxed her even closer.

"I've never been to a rink before," Rachael finally managed as Deirdre's warmth began to spread through her.

"Never? Didn't you go skating when you were little?"

"No. My parents were very protective." She smiled shyly and Deirdre gave her another little squeeze. She really liked the kid. When she came over for Christmas she made the whole thing seem magical again, asking about every little decoration that Deirdre had put out without thinking. For the first time in years she saw Christmas for what it really was—a time for family, whatever family meant.

Deirdre and Martin had gone all out decorating inside and out and had made a point of making sure there were a few things for Rachael under the tree. The poor girl broke down and cried when she found them. It was just a bawneen scarf and mittens, but Rachael clutched them against her for the whole evening, with Martin in attendance like a perfect gentleman. Rachael was having quite an effect on him.

She had a very positive impact on Grainne too. She'd been in a funk since they had to cancel their plans but lit up the moment Rachael arrived. It was that thing she did, being someone else with someone else. Later she told Deirdre that Rachael's parent were weird. Her father was all nervous and twitchy and her mother was worse, "like she was already having a breakdown waiting for him to have his." They had moved from Montreal and had no family in Toronto.

"So, how's school?" It was trite but it was all Deirdre could think of. She approved of Rachael and didn't want to scare her away too. She and Eduardo were taking a time-out. After seeing his family he was conflicted. He admitted it when they were in bed one evening. They stole time when the kids were out but he never stayed over—she wasn't ready for that. They'd just finished and she was lying on his chest listening to his heart.

She sat up a little drawing the sheets with her as she rose, slowly exposing more and more of him. "Excuse me?"

"What's the matter?"

"You wait until after to tell me?"

"Yes, because we're like one now and I want to share everything. That's what love really means."

She grabbed her robe and slowly walked into her bathroom, taking the sheet as she went. When she came back out she was clutching her robe against her as if she didn't want to brush up against anything he might have touched. "And I always thought that love implied being in love with just one person at a time."

He was still smiling, lying totally naked on her bed like an opened gift. "You love your children and you still love me. I love my kids but I still love you. I'm not choosing between you and her. I just cannot risk losing them."

She wasn't angry; she was just pissed off. She tried to hide it but he sensed it. He sensed all her moods, even the ones she wished he didn't. Sometimes she missed that part of Danny that gave her so much space. Eduardo could become very needy and had to have constant reassurance. She just couldn't do that this time, and a few days later she phoned him and told him to stay away until he had sorted it out.

"Dee-dree. No. Don't say things like that."

"Eduardo, you need time to think about this. If you decide on me, I will take you back. And, if you decide not to . . . well then this is still the right decision." He argued but she didn't change her mind. She felt very cold but it was the right thing to do. Relationships were still difficult. She wished she'd dated more before she got married. She wouldn't want either of her kids to . . .

"It's good, thank you, Mrs. Boyle."

"It's 'Fallon' actually. Ms. Fallon. I don't think women should take their husband's name. It gets far too awkward when you change husbands." She meant it as an ice-breaker, but Rachael just looked a little shocked. "I'm sorry," Deirdre added. "I'm just a little cynical right now."

Rachael smiled again but now she looked a little confused.

"So, you're actually enjoying school. I think Martin does, too, but Grainne—she's an entirely different story." It was out of her mouth before she could stop it. She hadn't wanted to sound like a typical mother. "Do you understand hockey?"

"Well, not really."

"Then let me explain." She moved her arm to point at the ice but Rachael stayed close to her. "The three good looking guys are the forwards." She pointed to Martin and his wingers. "They're the guys that shower regularly. And the more jock looking guys"—she pointed to the two guys near the blue line—"are the defenders. They're the type that sits at the back of the class making strange noises." Rachael was laughing but still holding on tight. "And the guy in the net, he's one of those kids that fall in love with Goth poets."

Rachael was still laughing and tried to smother it by putting her hand to her face. She was going to become a very beautiful woman, dark haired and with eyes that could smolder. "And those guys . . ." Deirdre pointed to the other team. "They make our guys look good."

As the game went on Deirdre was learning everything she needed to know about Rachael. She was taking school seriously because she had plans to go on to university. "And what do you think you'd like to become?" She felt as if she were interviewing an intern.

"My father wants me to become a lawyer."

"Do you like the law?"

"I guess so."

Deirdre couldn't help herself—her maternal side took over. "Would your parents mind if you came to our house for dinner? We're going to have a Mexican night."

Rachael smiled and nodded. "My parents won't mind but I will have to phone them."

"There's a phone outside beside the snack bar, and we can get hot chocolate while we wait for Martin."

His team had won the game but the coach would still keep them for a while. Martin said that he loved the sound of his own voice. So Deirdre rose and rolled her blanket and cushion, one under each arm, and ushered Rachael along.

*

"I really like your mom."

Martin was walking Rachael home and they always cut through the cemetery. She said she wasn't frightened, but she let him put his arm around her waist and hold her close. She had said that she really enjoyed Mexican night. His mom had even made them teeny-margaritas. She put in a little tequila but added more to her own. Grainne had two and started talking like she was in *Sex and the City*.

"Yeah, my mom's pretty cool. I just wish my sister wasn't such a pain."

"She's not so bad. I like her. I don't have any sisters."

"What are your parents like?"

"Well . . ." Rachael responded as if she had rehearsed it. "We're secular, anti-Zionist Jews, but you probably don't know what any of that means."

"Not really. We never went to church either."

"Never?"

"No, my parents were against all that. My father had a tough time growing up."

"Well my father is against everything. His family was from Hungary and Joel Brand was his uncle. Do you know who he was?"

"Sure, he played in goal for the Leafs back in the Stone Age."

"Not according to my father. He says he was the greatest man that ever lived. He tried to save Jews from the Holocaust."

"Wow. What happened to him?"

"He's dead now, but my father says that Zionists wouldn't let him, and the Hungarian Jews were sent to the concentration camps. Most of my father's relatives never survived."

"Wow. I didn't know that."

"About the Holocaust?"

"No, everybody has heard of that."

"Yeah, well, since then my father doesn't like anything Jewish. My mother says he's like a troll in a cave."

"Maybe I shouldn't meet him then."

"Oh, he'll like you. He hates the English too. He says they went along with the Zionists; but he was happy when I told him you were Irish."

"Did you tell him that my parents were secular, anti-Catholic Irish?"

"Really?"

"No. My father is just an asshole."

"Don't talk like that, Martin. It's disrespectful."

"You don't know my father."

"No, but there must have been something good about him. Your mother married him."

Before Martin answered they heard a groan from behind one of the head stones. He stepped in front of her and waited."Martin," a voice called, "I've come for your soul." Doug jumped out but Martin and Rachael didn't react.

"Martin, it's me."

"Go away, Doug. You've been drinking again."

"C'mon, old buddy." He joined them and put his arm around Martin's free shoulder. "Where're we going?"

"Go away, Doug."

"I can't. I'm scared of being here alone. Just let me come with you guys."

"Go away, Doug."

They couldn't get rid of him until they reached the fence. He was too drunk to climb it and went back to his friends, who were finishing a case of beer.

"Sorry about that. Doug can be a bit of an asshole."

"Yeah, what a defenseman."

"Yeah. I see my mother's been talking with you."

"She was just explaining hockey to me."

"Wow, she must really like you."

"She just wants what's best for her son. What mother wouldn't?"

*

Jacinta and Mrs. Flanagan waited for the lights to change and for the other pedestrians to go first. They kept forgetting which side the cars were on, and twice Jacinta had nearly walked into a passing moped. "I just don't want you getting your hopes up."

She was a little concerned. Mrs. Flanagan had been as giddy as a goat since they arrived. They were on their way to meet the two priests at the Piazza Navona and they'd all walk over from there. Fr. Melchor was going to take them to a church where Mrs. Flanagan might finally find some peace. Fr. Reilly seemed reticent about it, but Mrs. Flanagan and the old Jesuit were adamant. Jacinta wasn't too sure, but they were almost there now.

"I can't help it, Mrs. Boyle. It's just a feeling I have."

"Are you sure it's not jet lag? When Jerry and I used to fly to Canada, we used to get it really bad. He always got it worse, though, but that might have been because he always drank too much on the plane. He was a very nervous flyer. Not like me. As long as I have a cup of tea and a good book, I'd be happy on the *Titanic*."

"Ah, no, Mrs. Boyle. It's nothing like that. I think it's because of the holy Jesuit. They're all great friends with God you know."

*Sweet Jesus*, Jacinta prayed silently. *Please let Mrs. Flanagan find her son this time before she drives me straight back to the hospital.* "You have great faith, Mrs. Flanagan."

"Sure you have to. Anything else would be an insult to God. I never gave up on Him, you know. I knew my Anthony would have to spend his time in purgatory, but I always knew that things would be grand in the end. Do you not worry about things like that?" Mrs. Flanagan looked unsure of what she was about to say. "You know, about your Jerry?"

"I don't," Jacinta decided after she thought about it. "I'm sure that wherever he is, he is content. He was always a great one for making friends and there was never much badness in him. Not really, you know."

She did wonder about him sometimes. He'd never come back to her the way Nora had, but then again there was never any reason to. She hoped he was happy and that he'd made up with his father by now. There were times, though, when she wanted him to come back and scare a bit of sense into Danny. He'd stopped drinking but there was still a lot of badness in him. And she didn't think too much of the one he was with now. She called herself Billie and dressed like a hussy, and never looked Jacinta in the eye. That was always a sign.

"Well, here we are now." The evening was still warm and the crowds came and went. The restaurants were full and the whole piazza was buzzing. "I hope they'll be able to see us in this crowd. You know," Jacinta added to lighten the mood, "this is like waiting for fellas."

As they walked to the church with all the skulls, the holy Jesuit looked more like the priest in *The Exorcist*, only he didn't have a bag. It was just as well. Jacinta didn't think she'd be able to handle it if Mrs. Flanagan's head started spinning around. She stayed close to Fr. Reilly as they made their way through the dark, narrow streets. Jacinta was more comfortable with Rome during the day, but at night she always felt as if things were moving and muttering in the shadows. It made perfect sense to her—after all that had gone on there.

The church was dark but for a few fluttering candles and a few of those lights that looked like candles. "In Rome, too!" Jacinta muttered. "You'd think with all the money they have they'd be able to keep real candles going and not have the place looking so cheap. And it could do with a good cleaning—and an airing out. It's awful musty. You'd think with all the nuns in Rome that they might be able to . . ."

"Shush," Fr. Melchor interrupted her sharply and turned toward Mrs. Flanagan. "He's almost here," he whispered and smiled encouragingly.

"Oh, sweet Mary and Joseph, thank the Sacred Heart." Mrs. Flanagan clasped her hands and looked up toward the dark ceiling.

"Amen," Jacinta quietly added, with as much deference as she could manage, not wanting to disturb them anymore as they knelt in the silence and waited for Fr. Melchor to speak again. His head was in his hands as if he'd forgotten about them, and was deep in prayer.

"He wants you to know your prayers saved him," he said so suddenly that it startled them all.

"Ah, God bless him," Mrs. Flanagan whispered when she recovered. "And I want him to know that he's still my little boy."

Jacinta peered around but couldn't see anything. She wasn't surprised. When Nora came to talk to her it was just her voice; only now she couldn't hear anything either. "Did he get to hear her?" she finally whispered to Fr. Reilly, after the old Jesuit had sat for a while staring off into the dark. She was beginning to wonder if he hadn't nodded off.

"Maybe." Fr. Reilly tapped her elbow as he rose. "You and I should go over and light a few candles by the side altar. We could light a candle for Nora? I'm sure she'd be very happy with that."

He seemed to be trying to mollify her and she might have reacted, but before she could, Mrs. Flanagan stood up and started hugging the shadow around her. She began to cry, letting out all the tears she'd been storing since that night in Cruagh Wood. It almost got Jacinta going, too, but she didn't want to draw any more attention to herself. Fr. Reilly was ready to catch Mrs. Flanagan if she fainted. The old Jesuit was still kneeling but looked up at Mrs. Flanagan.

*

"And now, Patrick, she is happy."

The two priests were walking back from the ladies' hotel and Patrick was having doubts. He'd been indulging John—not wanting to upset him—but the whole thing was spiraling out of control and was probably going to end badly. Mrs. Flanagan didn't seem to care. She'd practically floated home, she was so happy. Patrick wasn't ready to talk about it, but John ignored his reticence.

"I haven't done anything that our Church hasn't done before."

"Well now, I'm just not sure that we should be giving her false hope. She thinks she was actually talking to her dead son. I'm not sure about things like that. It could confuse her."

"Patrick, she needs to believe that her son is finally safe. This is the comfort and solace you talk about. You wouldn't deny her that?"

"No." Patrick could never win against John; he was far too much of a Jesuit. "Only I prefer giving it on the basis of something more . . . tangible."

"Like blind faith?"

"I suppose you're right."

"I hope so, Patrick." John turned and faced him. "By the way, your uncle wants to talk with you."

"My uncle?"

"Yes, your uncle. Who were you expecting?"

# Chapter 4 – 2000

THE WORLD DIDN'T GO SPINNING OUT OF CONTROL. Computers didn't crash and planes didn't tumble from the skies. The lights still worked and there was water in the taps, and for the most part people didn't die in their sleep and just woke up to another day.

"Just the beginning of another new year and a new decade." John had almost made it sound prophetic. "And the beginning of the third millennium since Christ walked the Earth, for those who still believe in such things."

Patrick had let that one go. After the night with Mrs. Flanagan he decided to let sleeping dogs lie. John seemed to understand that and hadn't mentioned Patrick's uncle again either. He could probably sense that Patrick wasn't ready. He wasn't. He'd been reading his uncle's writings again and they were still so unsettling. It was heresy against all that Patrick had been taught to hold sacred. And coming from his uncle and his bishop, it was impossible to dismiss.

Still, Patrick reminded himself after looking for something to cheer himself up, it was the International Year for the Culture of Peace and that had to mean something, even if it was just holding fancy dinners to raise money for the cause.

God help him, but he was getting a bit cynical, too, and quickly corrected himself. It was, he decided with all the hope he could muster, another chance for the whole world to step toward the bright shining future that was still well within its grasp. They were heading into a new world order that promised jobs and prosperity for all. He opened his curtains to take it all in. Rome, that had seen and done it all so many times before, was peaceful. Most of its citizens were sleeping off the revelries of the night before. In the Eternal City, Giovanni had often assured him, millennia came and went like the seasons.

Patrick had woken late too. Almost an hour after his usual time, even though he had spent his evening alone. Giovanni had invited him to spend it with his family, but he was getting old and went to bed early, leaving Patrick to referee any sibling squabbles that might arise.

*And it is the World Mathematical Year*, his academic side chimed in to banish any wistfulness. This year would mark his thirty-fifth as a priest. He looked over at the Holy See and wondered if anybody else would remember that. It wouldn't matter; a life of service was its own reward.

*

Frank kept reminding himself of that as he listened stoically. Danny was reciting his litany of all that was wrong with the world. Frank had been like that himself a few times.

All things considered, Danny was doing okay. He was just sick and tired of his job and feeling a bit sorry for himself. "You can't even just go ahead and say the obvious anymore because someone might get offended. You can't even say hello to some of them without being all politically correct and all. It's getting as bad as Quebec."

"How many meetings have you been getting out to?"

"I just told you, I spend my whole day in meetings, listening while total morons have their say—and taking forever to say nothing in the end. They don't even know which meeting they're in but they still have to add their two-cents, usually about stuff they know nothing about."

"That many?" There was a time when Frank might have become exasperated, but listening to Danny whine reminded him to be grateful.

"And most of them only come so everybody thinks they're busy. It'd be better for everybody if we paid them to stay at home instead, so those of us who actually do a bit of work can get on with it."

"God, grant me the serenity . . ." Frank muttered, but Danny ignored him. He was too pumped up on indignation. He'd better be careful on that stuff; it was one of the things alcoholics couldn't afford. Frank had seen too many guys go back out because of that.

"I mean it. I've been working there for twenty years and now I have to take orders from someone who was in diapers when I started."

"The courage to change the things I can? You could always quit and do something else." Frank smirked but he really wanted to laugh. They were all the same. A few months off the drink and they began to think their shite smelled like roses. It was understandable, though. For far too long they had felt like their hearts and souls were drowning in it.

"Yeah, they'd love for me to leave and I will when it suits me. A couple more years and I'm gonna take one of those early retirement deals they're always offering. Then they can all kiss my arse."

"Ah, the wisdom."

"Ah, Jaze, Frank, do you never give it a rest?"

"No. And I won't until you start trying to be grateful, you bollocks. You're sober now. Isn't that enough?"

"I know, but it's been almost three years. I would've thought things would be better by now."

"They are. You're just not seeing it because you're still whining about all that's wrong."

"Glass half full?"

"The glass is all full and just make sure it stays that way." Frank tried to look stern but he couldn't. They all went through rough patches from time to time. Getting sober wasn't something that just happened to you. It was more like climbing out of the grave. And you had to do most of the digging yourself. And it didn't help when you went to a meeting looking for someone to feel sorry for you and you bumped into the old-timers. "You dug yourself in to it. What did you expect?" they'd say. "Just keep digging and don't pick up a drink. And keep coming back."

And then they'd wander off and leave him alone as if he had a cold or something. That used to really piss him off but over time Frank learned to love those guys. They said it like it was—like Buddha or one of those guys that sit up on mountains. They cut through all the shite that everybody else was just inhaling and exhaling.

He wanted to be one of those guys with Danny, only Danny was still thinking like a Catholic—that if he just kept his head down, pretending to be doing the things he was supposed to, everything would be all right.

It was a bit like that, only instead of just doing the right thing you had to *become* the right thing too. Frank was still having trouble with that, but talking to Danny helped. It helped him see how impatient he could still become—not as bad as Danny, but then he'd been sober longer.

He also knew what was really going on. He hadn't seen Billie at a meeting in a while. Danny had said they were just giving each other space to practice their own programs and not trying to do it together. The old-timers were always going on about that, too, but Frank didn't believe him. There was more going on, but it wasn't his business until Danny told him.

Getting sober in a world that was going mad wasn't easy for any of them. Everyone around them could get away with being assholes—being all righteous and all, without having to worry. Recovering alcoholics couldn't. It wasn't as if they had to become saints or anything, but they had to learn to live by principles distilled down to the basics, so even the most damaged and frightened could grasp them. "And that hope," the old-timers assured them when they faltered, "will grow like an acorn if you don't choke it off."

"I'm not worried about picking up a drink, you know." Danny insisted, and waited for Frank's response.

"Maybe not, but you will if you keep going around bitching about everything. The world is still all messed up—only you've changed. You know what the old-timers say about getting hungry, angry, lonely or tired. Other people might be able to handle it but we can't."

Love was a dangerous thing, too, only he couldn't say anything about that. Not until Danny brought it up. Two recovering alcoholics in one relationship was at least one too many— probably two. "It's very simple, Danny. We can stay sober or we can go back out. I've made my choice. I'm going to stay sober because if I get my shit together there'll be one less asshole making problems in the world."

*

Frank was right and Danny always felt better after they had one of their little chats, even if it did remind him of when he was a kid and had just been to Confession. Sometimes he missed those days, but he could never get back there again. Too much had happened for him to ever be that naïve again.

That was something else that was really bothering him, but he couldn't talk about it with Frank—he would have gotten all bent out of shape about Danny not being grateful and all. Sometimes it felt like that was what the program was trying to do to him.

Maybe Billie was right. Maybe he was just a restless soul that was becoming stagnant. Maybe the real problem was that he was trying to live the wrong life. He'd tried being a normal person when he was with Deirdre and look how that turned out. He wasn't cut out to be one of those guys who just kept their heads down and put up with all the shit for a paycheck. He'd seen what happened to the old guys from work who had done that. Most of them died within a few years of retiring.

Billie kept telling him that he could be so much more than that. She kept telling him that he had a voice and something to say. He liked hearing that but he found it very hard to believe.

She'd said that was because he was still carrying around all the guilt and shame that the priests and the nuns had heaped on him. That was the real problem; he'd been raised to feel unworthy, and when shit went wrong—he always blamed himself, deep down inside. She said that was why he used to get angry and lash out at everyone around him. He'd been hurt and, instead of coming to terms with that, tried to pretend he wasn't bothered. Until it became too much for him and all his repressed anger would erupt over everything.

That was beginning to make more and more sense to him. He had to find a way to vent before too much pressure built up. The problem was that you weren't supposed to do stuff like that in case it offended or upset someone.

Billie said that music was the perfect outlet—that he could take all that was bothering him and write about it. But even just thinking about what he'd write made everything boil up inside him and, at the meetings, they warned him against that.

But all they had to offer was some vague idea of a higher power, and he had seen enough god-pushers to know what they were really like. They made Anto and the other heads back in the scene look like angels.

Besides, if he did get back into music he'd be around alcohol again and he wasn't willing to risk it—even if he was trapped in a miserable existence. That was it: he was trapped in limbo and there was nothing else he could do. He'd still go to meetings and all of that stuff, but he wasn't really getting that much from it anymore. The program was being taken over by the Jesus crowd—even the old-timers were remarking on it. It wasn't what he'd signed up for, but he wasn't ready to risk it on his own just yet. Not until he had proved everybody was wrong about him.

*

"Of course I was in the right," Deirdre continued as she ducked her head into the fridge. She'd been updating Miriam on her recent run-in with Grainne. She had asked to go to Doug's basement party but she was only fourteen—still far too young. It wasn't because Deirdre disliked Doug—he was practically family—but he and his friends were getting far too fond of beer.

"And?" Miriam was visiting on her own. She'd told Deirdre that Karl was busy with something and had been traveling so much she was beginning to feel like a nun again. Deirdre insisted that Miriam come and spend Easter with her. She was still on her own since Eduardo had gone back to his family.

"And she has made my life a misery since." Deirdre returned with her arms full and placed everything on the counter. Grainne hadn't really. In fact Deirdre had been glad of the distraction. "I'll peel and you can chop." They were having Mexican again. It was everyone's favorite.

"And you let her?" Miriam selected a knife from the block and began chopping; onions, peppers and avocados, all sliced or diced into separate bowls. She often volunteered at local missions—to help feed the hungry—and had developed expertise.

"Yeah, I suppose I do. It's just that things with her father have been a bit rough lately. He still sees her but he never has her stay over anymore. I think there might be trouble in paradise."

"Oh?" Miriam invited her to say more, but Deirdre shrugged and refreshed their margaritas.

"Does Grainne get along with his girlfriend?"

"When it suits her."

"Well I think you should crack down on her once and for all."

"You would, once a nun . . ."

"Didn't you hear? The pope recently apologized for the wrongdoings of the Roman Catholic Church throughout the ages. Mind you, he was on his way to Israel and probably wanted to get a head start on guilt."

"Oh, Miriam, that's a little anti-Semitic of you."

"Don't get me started. I'm so tired of the Holocaust being used as a rationale for what's going on in Lebanon and Palestine. You'd think they'd know better by now."

"Well, please don't say things like that when Martin's girl-friend is here. She's Jewish."

"Too bad. I'm sick and tired of being muzzled by Jewish sensibilities. What they should be offended by is what is being done in their name."

"Well, please don't bring it up later. Rachael is a very sweet girl but her home life is not great. Apparently her father wants nothing to do with anything Jewish—even family. It's all over something that happened during the war."

"Okay, I'll behave myself. Is Martin serious about her?"

"Very."

"And how do you feel about it?"

"I really like her, only . . ."

"Only what?"

"Only I wish they had met when they were older—after they had been in a few other relationships."

"And not make the mistakes you made?"

"Precisely."

"What's the ketchup for?"

"You'll see."

"Your princess? You know you're not doing her any favors?"

"You're beginning to sound like Martin."

"Well he's right. She needs you to show her some proper direction. All this tit and ass wiggling has them confused. It's not girl power unless you want to empower bimboism."

"Oh, Miriam, you're still such a nun. What about Madonna? Don't you think she's smart?"

"She might be, but that's not what she's selling, and we're all selling some part of ourselves."

\*

Miriam was totally different when they sat down to eat. For all that she had to say beforehand, she was charming with the kids. Even with Grainne, asking about every detail of her life and listening patiently as Grainne answered in her best *Valley Girl* impressions.

The kids always called her "Auntie Miriam" and Deirdre could see how much that meant to her. She sat with her elbows on the counter, between Grainne and Rachael. Her face was bright and warm as she giggled and laughed as much as they did. She'd had a few margaritas but the girls hadn't. They were just heady from being around her. Even Martin was affected and stood on the other side of Rachael, leaning across her so they were touching.

Deirdre was content. They were warm and happy together, and she could sit back and enjoy it while it lasted. Eduardo had phoned to wish her a happy Easter. It was a bit unfair of him but he wouldn't have considered that. He was being needy but she could hear the sad loneliness in his voice, almost sounding like one of the *Fado* singers he used to make her listen to when they lay together and he'd open up and pour his heart out. He could be such a little boy, and she had more than enough mothering still to do.

He said he regretted it now. He told her he'd made the biggest mistake of his life, but he said that about a lot of things. Still, it caused a flutter deep down. Little bubbles of hope tangoing with a little selfish delight. She should let him cool his jets for a while but she missed him too. Only she couldn't tell him that. Instead, she told him she couldn't talk—that she had company and was far too busy. He pleaded a little but she was resolute, even if she wasn't being totally honest. She wasn't ready to let him back into her life. Not until she was sure he was going to stay. And she wanted to punish him a little for discarding her so easily.

"Well," Miriam said, loud enough to get her to look over. "When I met your mother, Ms. Fallon," she added to make sure Rachael felt included, "she used to like to spend her nights in churches . . ."

"Don't you dare." Deirdre rushed forward.

"Tell us," the girls almost squealed.

"Yeah, Mom. Let's hear what you were like."

"Martin Jeremiah Boyle, you're supposed to be on my side."
And before Miriam could continue, Deirdre brushed past them
and put on Ricky Nelson. *Sometimes*—she smiled to herself and
began to sway and gyrate—*the past belongs in the past.* And before
long they all danced the rest of the evening away.

*

On the anniversary of the day he was ordained, Patrick stepped
out of his apartment into one of the hottest days of the summer. Tourists sweltered and scurried from shade to shade. The
smell of their sweat, and all the things they used to mask it,
mingled in the manky musk that drifted up from the debris of
the dark years. He was going to spend the day reflecting on his
life before meeting John for dinner. He had called to congratu-
late him, and Patrick was surprised that he remembered.

It had all been so different that day thirty-five years ago
in Maynooth, when a gentle rain freshened everything around
them. His mother had tried to contain herself but couldn't and
cried warm, happy tears along with the rain. His father, who
always kept one eye on the weather, was prepared and raised
his big black umbrella over the three of them as they shared
a rare moment of public affection. His uncle was there, too,
prouder than punch but careful not to encroach.

They'd all gone now but they were still warm in his memory, and he'd celebrate the day in their honor. He decided to drop
by Pontecorvo's book store first. They'd left a message: Signore Davide had found the book Patrick was looking for and he
could drop by and pick it up. It was like getting a present.

The book store was an old, musty place in the heart of the
Ghetto di Roma, a place Patrick often walked through when his
heart was heavy. It was just across the river, near the Theatrum
Marcelli, but the words of Pope Paul IV still hung over the
place like a pall and had since 1555.

> Since it is completely senseless and inappro-
> priate to be in a situation where Christian

piety allows the Jews (whose guilt—all of their own doing—has condemned them to eternal slavery) access to our society and even to live among us; indeed, they are without gratitude to Christians, as, instead of thanks for gracious treatment, they return invective, and among themselves, instead of the slavery, which they deserve, they manage to claim superiority: we, who recently learned that these very Jews have insolently invaded Rome from a number of the Papal States, territories and domains, to the extent that not only have they mingled with Christians (even when close to their churches) and wearing no identifying garments, but to dwell in homes, indeed, even in the more noble dwellings of the states, territories and domains in which they lingered, conducting business from their houses and in the streets and dealing in real estate; they even have nurses and housemaids and other Christians as hired servants. And they would dare to perpetrate a wide variety of other dishonorable things, contemptuous of the very name Christian. Considering that the Church of Rome tolerates these very Jews (evidence of the true Christian faith) and to this end we declare: that they, won over by the piety and kindness of the See, should at long last recognize their erroneous ways, and should lose no time in seeing the true light of the catholic faith, and thus to agree that while they persist in their errors, realizing that they are slaves because of their deeds, whereas Christians have been freed through our Lord God Jesus Christ, and that it is unwarranted for it to appear that the sons of free women serve the sons of maids.

*Cum Nimis Absurdum* had, with all the weight of papal infallibility, condemned Rome's Jews to yet more centuries of segregation and, as he walked the narrow streets, Patrick was always mindful of his share of inherited guilt. Davide Pontecorvo's forefathers had come to Rome as slaves before the spread of Christianity and had lived at the edge of all that came and went since.

Davide was a friend of Giovanni's and often came to the café where they talked and laughed about all that they remembered, sometimes slipping in and out of the old *Giudeo-Romanesco*. They'd known each other since that day in October 1943. Davide's family had hidden in the Vatican and Giovanni's father sent him over with food. They'd remained friends since. "We are Romans and we stick together, no matter who sets themselves up to rule over us." Giovanni was proud of that and of the seven thousand who had been saved in monasteries and churches around the city.

The old man was busy with another customer so Patrick rummaged for a while, browsing the shelves of books stacked to the ceiling. Signore Pontecorvo's family had been saving books from pilferers and pillagers for centuries, and even now most of the clientele were referred. Patrick felt at home there even though the old man always seemed to be overshadowed by the wings of death—not unlike John.

Giovanni had told him that most of the things the old man had loved had been taken from him, some forcefully and some by the slow gnawing of time, and now he could only find true solace amidst dusty old tomes that most people never knew about. And when it was time for Patrick to pay for his book and leave, the old man looked over his glasses and shook his head.

"Today, you do not pay."

"Well that's very kind of you, Signore, but I must."

"Not today. Today is a happy day for you and I give you this as a gift."

"That is very kind of you."

"Kindness?" He smiled and wrapped R. H. Charles' *The Book of Enoch* in brown paper, tied it with string and handed it to Patrick with a strange little smile on his face. "It is the only way for us all to live together."

*

Dinner with John was far less pleasant. The news of the wider world had swirled in again and unsettled the old man. "They have finally withdrawn from Lebanon," he remarked, with more than a touch of rancor. He wasn't anti-Semitic; he was anti-war in all its shapes and forms.

"Do you not think, John, that it could be a goodwill gesture? You know, before Camp David? Maybe this time peace will be given a real chance."

Patrick so wanted to believe that, even if it was too late for the dead and disfigured women and children in the refugee camps. They were the ones Jesus would have been most concerned about—the poor innocent pawns in a deadly game of tit for tat.

He didn't want to dwell on that tonight and he wanted to change to subject. "It is an odd thing to think that Judaism was already here when word of Christ was spread. I can only assume that piqued a few popes along the way."

"Yes," John agreed. "And we must always feel a degree of shame about how the Church behaved back then."

It was something Patrick's uncle had written about. He too had shared in the guilt of Europe having once endorsed those who stood against the communists only to let the greater evil rise unchecked. "We sowed the seeds," he had written, "and yet in a way, if one is to believe in what it says in the Bible, we were all just playing our parts in God's grand plan." Patrick was hesitant about accepting that but he had always been bothered by the god of the Old Testament. "A vicious, vengeful thing of man's creation. And you can learn all you need to know about people by the gods they create," his uncle had also remarked.

"We are, despite all that we know about ourselves, just prisoners of the past," John continued. "But we can choose our guards far more carefully."

Patrick didn't respond. He knew the old Jesuit was worried. Bush and Cheney had won the Republican ticket, endorsed by the righteous and the rich. John had been less concerned under Clinton. "The kinder face of Imperialism," he used to call it.

"If they win we will have a rising clamor for confronting those who do not share our Judeo-Christian view of the world.

"Soon," he spoke again, thinking aloud, "our masters will once again convince us that we have a need to go to war with the Muslim world."

They finished their meal in silence as John sat as though he was pondering the whisperings of the dead, and Patrick looked back along the road he had come.

He couldn't hear the dead but he had read all they had left as warnings, crying out to the living, beseeching them to rid themselves of the devils they'd raised as gods. The culture of hate, they told him in a thousand different ways, made no sense. And the dead never spoke of vengeance. Never.

Perhaps it was because they were finally content.

*

Toward the end of September it was obvious; Mrs. Flanagan was giving up the ghost.

The doctors weren't sure what was causing it, but she was failing right before their eyes. She told Jacinta what was going on. "I want to go and try to catch up on some of the time I missed out on with my Anthony. You understand, don't you, Mrs. Boyle?"

Jacinta did but still felt she had to make some kind of argument for living. It was reflex. "But what about the rest of your family? Don't you think they'll be lost without you?"

"They've had me for all of their lives, but Anthony—he's been alone all this time with no one to turn to."

"Are you sure that's how it works? Are you sure that you and Anthony will get to meet?"

"I am. When he got out of purgatory he came to see me instead of going on, don't you see?"

"And he's still waiting?"

"He is, indeed. He comes and talks to me every night as I'm falling asleep."

If it had been anyone else she would have thought the dying woman was delusional, but Jacinta knew better. She raised her old friend's hand to her lips and kissed it softly. "Well then, as long as you're sure."

"I am indeed, Mrs. Boyle, and let me thank you once again for all that you've done. I'd have had no peace if it wasn't for you—and the holy Jesuit. But I have peace now and there's nothing else I want from this life."

She was good to her word and died a few days later. Jacinta went to the funeral and almost smiled. She wanted to tell Mrs. Flanagan's family but she couldn't. They would think she was going mad again. And after Mrs. Flanagan was laid to rest, Jacinta walked around the old graveyard to pay her respects to all that she knew there.

The whole world was different now and she wondered what they'd make of it. Nora would be happy that they finally closed Long Kesh. "It never did a bit of good," she'd sniff, "except to make the people harder." Jerry would agree with her. He always said it did wonders for IRA recruitment—something that always happened when governments treated people like terrorists.

Jacinta still missed them all, and that feeling lingered through the evening as she pottered around the large empty house where they all had lived. Things hadn't always been rosy between them, but now she felt left behind—left alone to deal with whatever was going to happen with Danny.

"If you're not too busy," she said to her bedroom ceiling as she finally lay down to sleep, "maybe one of you could drop by and let me know what it is I'm supposed to do about him."

She wasn't surprised that it was Martin who came to see her. He'd always been so good to her but she couldn't let on. "Well it took you long enough. And I don't suppose you've heard anything from that Jerry of mine?"

*Jerry? He's fine. He's with his parents—they have a lot to catch up on.*

"I'm sure they do."

*C'mon, Jass. The past is over. People move on. Besides, they'll all be waiting for you when you get here.*

"Are you so sure I'll be going there?"

*Yes, I'm sure. You've already done all your suffering.*

She was so happy to hear him say that. She'd always wanted to believe it but she could never be sure. The nuns had filled her head with guilt and all kinds of nonsense that never totally went away.

"Martin . . ." She hesitated. It wasn't the type of thing she was used to asking people, even dead ones. "Why are you still here?" She assumed he would have been in the better place but, then again, he had gone and gotten himself cremated. "Are you not at peace?"

*I'm fine, Jass. I'm just fulfilling an old promise.*

"The one you made to Nora?"

Danny still phoned every other week and tried to sound as he did when he first got sober, but his mother could tell. "Is he going to be all right?"

*Yes,* Martin answered, the way he always did when she became concerned. *Only he has a few more trials and tribulations to go.*

*

Billie was sitting at the table when Danny got home, long and lean with her black dress clinging to her hips and waist. Her hair was still up but a few strands had escaped down the back of her neck. She had her pearl necklace on and played with it as she watched him come in. She had kicked her shoes off and poured herself a glass of wine.

They had an uneasy truce about that. He was trying to live and let live, and she was trying to let him. She'd explained her position: she was no longer an alcoholic. She may never have been. She did have a problem with cocaine but she'd left that behind. She understood how, in his reformed zeal, he could misunderstand but she really wanted him to be able to accept it.

She also told him that she still loved him and wanted to stay with him. She would understand if he couldn't, but she really hoped he could.

"How was your meeting?"

"Fine. How was the show?"

"The art was beautiful, the crowd was happy, and my boss made a shit load of money. All in all, it was better than getting slapped by a frozen fish."

She waited until he smiled and rose and put her arms around him. She didn't kiss him in case she had wine on her lips. "Oh, Danny boy, you look like you have all the cares of the world on your shoulders."

"I'm okay."

"No, you're not. Why don't you go and relax. The hockey is still on. I could bring you a cup of tea."

The Leafs were losing so he switched to the news and listened to the media's veiled displeasure with the recent protests in Prague. Fifteen thousand had come out to decry the workings of the IMF and the World Bank, and the consensus of the panel of political experts was that they were malcontents, trouble makers, and probably communists, even in the city of the Velvet Revolution.

It was the same when they covered Temple Mount, except they used words like "terrorist" and "Islamist Extremists."

It was the one thing that had really begun bothering him. People whose idea of a foreign vacation was a trip to Disney were forming opinions about the world through the narrow little window of their TVs, getting narrower and narrower. "It makes you realize that we're so lucky to live in the best country in the world," the panel would agree smugly, after serving up more and more doom and gloom. Danny had to change the channel again.

"Danny?" Billie returned with two cups of tea and settled at the opposite end of the couch. "I was talking about you with some people at the show. They're musicians. Would you ever think of doing it again?"

"I'm too old for all that."

"I don't think so. I think you should sit down and write a few songs again and then, when you're ready, you could meet these guys."

"What would I write songs about?"

"You could sing about all the stuff that's bothering you."

"They'd just be dirges."

"With the right sound they could be good, and I think it would be great for you."

He looked directly at her for the first time in months. Age had been pecking at the corners of her eyes and around her lips but she still looked beautiful. She was still that woman who'd turned his head all those years ago in the Windsor. Only now she had far more depth. She'd learned all she needed to know about sorrow and failure and she had come through it all.

Not unlike himself. He reached for her hand and trembled as their fingers entwined.

\*

As Christians everywhere rose to celebrate Christmas Eve, word came of the bombings. Churches all over Indonesia had been targeted.

"It's only the beginning," Karl warned them. He had been brooding for months over things he wouldn't share with Miriam. That was why she insisted they go to Rome—to be with friends, her only family now.

"Perhaps," John answered cautiously.

"The warning shots were fired when they attacked the *Cole*, Padre."

"Or, perhaps that was just retaliation for our attacks on them. We did fire our missiles at them two years ago."

"But this is a direct challenge. They killed seventeen of ours. We cannot allow that to go unanswered."

"We have before. We let our only friend in the region attack the USS *Liberty* and kill twice as many. How do you differentiate between the two? Is it because the Islamists do not have influential lobbyists? Our elected representatives have always been available to the highest bidder and we did get our pieces of silver for each of the *Liberty* dead."

"The world is full of dangerous men."

"Yes, and we have elected those who will go hand in glove with the worst of them."

"And what would you have us do, Padre?"

"I would have us select our enemies and our friends far more carefully."

"Now boys," Miriam had to interject. She was getting so tired of it all. "Can we not call a Christmas truce?"

Karl nodded, but John just turned and stared at her.

She knew that look. He was disappointed in her. He would think she had become what he once called "a selective liberal." One of those who chose their outrage by gender, color and whatever was topical. "American Liberalism," he had often said, "is nothing more than the yapping of domesticated dogs at the end of short leashes."

It almost made her cry, something Patrick noticed.

Sometimes Patrick thought that Americans could be very trying, and Miriam was practically one of them now. He presumed it was because they'd all grown up watching westerns and liked to see themselves as the good guys. He heard them all around the city: "We liberated this place and look at how they treat us. We're just walking wallets to them."

There was some truth to it. The people of the Eternal City had learned how to survive no matter who was liberating them, and there was always somebody trying.

"Well." He raised his glass. "A merry Christmas to us all."

They raised their glasses but weren't enthusiastic. The Year for the Culture of Peace had been far too hard on them all. He'd been a fool for ever getting his hopes up; he knew better by now. This life was never supposed to be anything but chaos and disorder. That was the challenge of it all. They weren't supposed to just go along with it all—they were supposed to shun it and all its trappings and seek the solace of God.

He tried to focus on that as he walked home alone, but from every side street and from the old places, he could almost hear the whispers of dissent—still echoing through the Eternal City. Still decrying the way things were.

# Chapter 5 – 2001

"I T ALL BEGAN WITH THE BARBER, PASQUINO," Davide Ponte-corvo began and settled back into his chair. Like all old men, he and Giovanni hashed and re-hashed the things they loved talking about.

"He was a tailor," Giovanni interrupted, but Davide just shrugged and sighed. They'd been competing since they were kids. They both considered themselves experts on their city. Giovanni even took Patrick aside one day to tell him, "Signore Pontecorvo, he knows what books tell him and that is a good thing, but Giovanni"—he paused to swell out a little—"he knows the people."

They were sitting at the back of the café as it was far too cold to sit outside. It was a quiet day. There were very few tourists about and Romans could get on with their day-to-day in relative peace. Signore Pontecorvo visited on Mondays and Patrick was always welcome to join them.

"He was a barber."

"Everyone knows that Pasquino make the robes for the bishops and the cardinals."

"Then everyone is wrong."

"Of course, everybody is wrong but you." Giovanni looked over at Patrick to see which side he was on, but Davide held up his hand.

"He was a barber and every day he went to the Vatican to shave and cut the hair of the bishops and the cardinals. And because he was just a barber, they talked like he couldn't understand them. Now Pasquino was a wise man and, for a while, he kept all that he heard to himself." He paused to sip his *Macchiato* and to gauge Patrick's face.

Giovanni had also told him that Signore Pontecorvo's sister had been one of those who were taken that day in October. And her husband and her four-year-old boy. They were never seen again—not even after the war. "Gone," Giovanni had explained as his face grew troubled. "Like smoke," he'd added as he sat back and looked out at the piazza where people from all over the world walked in and out of the Pantheon.

"But the people," Davide continued, "they know that a good barber always has news and came and asked him to tell them what was really going on. At first, he no want to say anything, but the people asked until he did." He paused to see if Giovanni had any other corrections but he just nodded along in collusion.

"Then, Pasquino became the most famous barber in all of Rome because everyone wanted him to cut their hair so they could hear what he had to say. And then, after he died, the people named an old statue after him."

"Some say," Giovanni jumped in when Signore Pontecorvo paused to sip his coffee, "that it was the people who started to put the messages on the statue, telling the rest of the people what was really happening: 'Da quando è Niccolò papa e assassino, abbonda a Roma il sangue e scarso è il vino.' Since Nicholas became pope and murderer, there is more blood than wine in Rome."

Now it was Davide's turn to sit back and smile as Giovanni leaned forward with one elbow resting on his thigh. He turned his hand downwards as if to settle things. "But other people say that it was the ghost of Pasquino. He didn't like when the bishops and the cardinals acted like the big shots and wanted the people to see. The statue told the people the truth, and the popes—they no like it.

"Pope Adrian, he want to throw Pasquino's statue in the river, but the people of Rome, they no let him. Then he send his soldiers to try to keep Pasquino's statue from talking, but the spirit of the people could not be silenced and the statue of Marforio began to talk too. 'Dimmi: che fai Pasquino?' Tell me, what are you doing, Pasquino? it asked; and Pasquino's statue say, 'Eh, guardo Roma, chè non vada a Urbino.' I watch over Rome, to make sure it's not moved to Urbino."

"And then," Giovanni added, when they finished laughing, "Madama Lucrezia joined *il Congresso degli Arguti*, the Shrewd Congress. And *l'Abate Luigi.*"

"And don't forget *il Babuino.*" The two old men were laughing at his expense, but Patrick didn't mind. He envied them for all that they could share.

"They called it the conversation of wits and it goes on to this day. In Rome"—Giovanni leaned forward again for emphasis—"even the dead get to have their say: 'Quod non fecerunt Barbari fecerunt Barberini.' What the Barbarians did not, the Barberini did."

As Patrick walked back to Trastevere he thought about it all. The old men had been having fun with him and he didn't mind. He was just happy to be included. It made him feel that Rome was finally coming to accept him—that they no longer saw him as one of those who just passed through for a few days or a few years. Patrick Reilly, once from a small biteen of a place a few miles from Windgap, was becoming a citizen of the Eternal City.

He'd known about the pasquinades but didn't say. The old men knew that, too, but their retelling was far more Roman, and he wanted to immerse himself in that. He was tired of the world outside, still in constant strife despite everything the rise and fall of Rome had taught them—that the gold and glory of empires and nations went to those at the top and the rest of them snapped and snarled at each other for the little that trickled down. Beaten back into submissions until their master's enemies were at the gate. Then it was for them to go out and pay for the sins of their leaders.

He couldn't go along with it all anymore and was beginning to cut himself off from all that was current. He spent his free time thumbing through the dusty pages of the old books that Signore Pontecorvo had found for him, one every other week or so. He'd been avoiding John, too, since Christmas. The old Jesuit was filled with broodings, seeing the portents of doom at every twist and turn.

Miriam was also quiet and hadn't written. Patrick was no expert on relationships but even he could see that she and Karl were having difficulties. He thought about offering some help and support but what could he do? Relationships were just not his forte.

\*

Deirdre felt the same way. For the first few years after her marriage ended, she had privately laid most of the blame on Danny. Even though she'd admitted her own faults, he was the one who trampled over everything they were together. Yet as time passed, it always nagged her that there was more to it than that. She didn't dwell on it. She didn't have time for pondering the depths of her own psyche anymore. She was far too busy raising kids and holding on to her career. Women like her had everything and the burden was far more than they had ever considered. "Be careful what you wish for," her mother's voice often reminded her.

She had supported and encouraged Deirdre through all that happened, but always with a faint hint of condescension, as if somehow more could have been done to help Danny. It still haunted Deirdre on those nights when she lay awake, too tired to sleep. The accusation stung but when she argued, she sounded like all those other women who blamed all their failures on men.

They were everywhere. Many of the women at work were convinced it was the only reason they were overlooked.

Particularly those who spent most of their days socializing and gabbing on the phone, criticizing anyone who managed to get ahead, intimating that they had slept their way up. "Give head to get ahead," they whispered to each other with disdain and knowing nods.

That infuriated Deirdre. She knew better than to shit where she ate and was meticulous about keeping her lives separate. She attended work functions but always left early after one drink and after she had done the circuit, chatting with colleagues' wives, sharing what they had in common as mothers. Superficially, of course. They all had perfect children and stable homes and made a point of saying that she was marvelous for being able to do it all alone.

It always felt like a slap with a long silk glove, but she'd learned to keep smiling and how to politely excuse herself. Single women, especially accomplished ones, were not very welcome in the good wives' club.

Besides, they really had so little in common. Most of them were trophy wives to older executives doing it all for the second time. Most of them had nannies and cleaners and therapists for when the husband's other children intruded. And when their husbands drifted off to talk about golf or the market, they would drink too much and share far too many details of their married lives—always casting themselves as empowered, except when their husbands did something without permission, like spending money on themselves or their other children. Then they portrayed themselves as victims.

Deirdre hardly listened. She knew they were really frightened of her. She got to spend the day with their husbands who had left other wives. She was tempted to flaunt that sometimes but she knew the men she worked with. They were, despite their suits and spacious offices, just little boys who should never be encouraged and sometimes had to be discouraged.

"I really feel sorry for them," she had told Miriam the last time she visited.

"And well you should. Poor little trophy girls with nothing but rich husbands and pampered lives. They never get to go out and play in the real world like the rest of us. But don't worry too much; they're specially bred for it."

"Listen to us—we've become a right pair of misogynists."

"Not at all," Miriam corrected her, so nun-like. "You just have to keep up with the times. Feminism today is all about self-justification. Today's woman must be empowered and have no room for doubts."

"Easy for you to say."

"And for you. You will always be able to tell yourself that you did the best with what you had."

"Are you referring to my failed marriage?"

"Not in particular, but now that you mention it . . ."

"Yes, Miriam. I picked Danny Boyle knowing everything I did and I was an active participant in all that happened between us. Happy now?"

"I would have been much happier if you had listened to me and never got mixed up with him."

"That die had been cast long before you came along."

"Predestination, you're such a bitch."

It was. That was why she had been so indulgent with Grainne, compensating and trying to make things right. She knew she had to move past all of that. "It is," they had told her at Al-Anon, "all very well to be in touch with your feelings, but you can't give them control over your life."

She was guilty of that. Every time her feelings were hurt she set about reordering the world around her, convinced she was doing it to make things better for all of them. Sometimes she was, but other times she was simply trying to impose what suited her through the passive-aggressive way that mothers had—the iron fist in the velvet glove.

"They have always had it," Miriam had assured her when she confessed to it. "Women always had the power to change things. Women raise families and hold the future in their hands."

"Even when they were chattel?"

"The men who imposed that were some mothers' sons."

"Oh, Miriam, you have no idea how it works."

"Really? Where do women learn to be such little bitches to each to other? It's not something that's taught in schools. It's there by the time they get there. Mind you, nothing is done to discourage it."

"Should we go back to teaching the example of Mary?"

"No, but surely we can teach them not to be so self-absorbed. And to have the confidence to be themselves and not a clone of someone they see on TV."

"Oh, the changing times," Deirdre mocked a little. Sometimes she was miffed, being lectured on parenting by a childless ex-nun.

"Seriously, Dee. They can't even think for themselves. Or about anybody else. And they're only happy when they're shopping."

"Not like when we were young?"

"No, Dee, not at all like when we were young."

Raising children was such a crap shoot, particularly alone. Deirdre had been lucky with Martin, and while she wanted to assume all the credit for how he turned out, Grainne exposed her for all that she could have done better. And she wasn't the worst of them. The neighborhood kids were even worse. Deirdre had done well with what she had.

Still, while relationships could be broken by the actions of one, far more often they were nothing more than lopsided arrangements people found themselves trapped in after attraction had faded. And she and Danny were no different. All the warnings signs had been there from the beginning but she ignored them. Then, after the children came, she bound herself in the sanctity of family and prolonged everyone's misery, including Danny's. And even though it was all in the past now, it still mattered. It mattered in how she was with her kids and it mattered in how she was going to deal with Eduardo.

He had left his wife again, just after Christmas, and called her as if he expected Deirdre to invite him straight back into her life. She didn't. She listened to him complain about all the terrible things he had been put through. He said his wife was still a peasant at heart and didn't understand him. Deirdre did. He was just a little boy who liked to fall in and out of love. Deirdre listened but didn't take sides. And when he was finished and waited for her to agree, she told him that he had to sort his life out before he called her again.

He did. He found an apartment and called again at the beginning of February. It had been a long, cold day and he always knew how to make her feel warm inside, so she gave in and agreed to meet him again. She had to check the family schedule, but she would. She was too young to be alone.

Friday the sixteenth was best. Grainne would be staying over with a friend and Martin and his friends were going to Buffalo for a hockey game. They would all pile into Doug's mom's minivan and spend the night in a motel. Deirdre didn't want to think about what the rest of them might get up to, but she could trust Martin to stay out of trouble.

"That will be perfect." Eduardo almost purred. "We can make it our special Valentine's."

She had to laugh at that. He could do romance so effortlessly and she was so much wiser now.

However, she was a little foolish after a few bottles of wine and agreed that he could come back for a nightcap. "One drink," she warned him as they got out of the cab and hurried inside before the neighbors noticed.

"Dee-Dree?" He stood with his arms by his side and his palms turned forward, as if to show he had nothing up his sleeves.

"Don't look at me like that." She laughed as she ushered him inside.

"Like what?" he murmured as his lips fluttered against hers. She didn't even get to take her coat off. He just opened it and wrapped his arms around her, touching her through her clothes; and when she responded, hungrily searching for his lips, he backed her against the wall and reached between her legs.

She let him because she wanted him. It had been far too long. She curled her leg around his hip and pulled him closer as he tugged at the buckle of his expensive Italian belt. And when he was free, she draped her arms around his neck so he could raise her a little. He didn't even stop to remove her panties. He just pulled them aside and plunged into her. She gasped loudly and threw her head back against the wall, but that only urged him on. His face straining as he pushed harder and harder, pushing her up against the wall, and letting her slide down as he pulled back. He moved slowly and deliberately, sensing her and responding as her intensity grew. She moaned and clasped the sides of his head so she could see his eyes. "Yes," she encouraged, "oh, yes."

She started to pound down upon him and he had to brace his knees and press against the wall with one hand, the other tight around the small of her back, holding her against him.

"Oh Christ," he announced, and let it all out.

"Jesus," she agreed as they both came in a flurry of twitches and groans until they were spent.

They did it twice more in her big bed and were tired and sore by morning, when she rose and showered without waking him. She made coffee, too. Small dark espressos. But he came down before she could surprise him. He was wearing her long white robe, tied at the waist but still showing his broad, dark chest.

"Morning," he tested, boyishly.

"Morning." She smiled back and let him take her in his arms, his scent evoking little spasms deep inside her. He kissed her gently and his breath was fresh. So was he, and she had to fight him off and send him upstairs to get dressed before Grainne came home.

"Last night?" he asked when he came back down.

"Yes," she mewled. "Last night?"

"Does it change things?"

"Yes."

"Does it mean we can be together again?"

"It means we can be lovers, for now."

"Just lovers?"

"For now. Let's just take things slowly until we are both sure that this is what we want."

"I don't need to take things slowly. I know what I want. I want to be with you."

"And I think I want to be with you, Eduardo, but I have my children and I will not change things until I am sure."

"Love is not something to think about. It does not happen here." He patted his head. "It happens here." He took her hand in his and placed it over his heart. "This is where I carry you."

She would think about it and probably still do it, but not yet. And after he had gone she had more coffee and smiled to herself. It would be so much fun to introduce him to the good wives club.

*

They were still cold when they came out. Martin took off his jacket and wrapped it around Rachael's shivering shoulders. The sun was bright but it was March and they had just been chilled to the soul. They had been to the Holocaust Museum on a school outing so that they, and future generations, would never forget. How could they? They had been face to face with the grainy images of men, women and children who had been vilified from birth and finally sorted and marked for extermination like vermin—a sad legacy of the world their parents brought them into. Most of the kids had walked around in stunned silence, but Martin had kept one eye on Rachael all the time.

Usually, when they went to the art gallery or other museums, some of the kids would horse around until their teachers reined them back, but not here. Overwhelmed by the horror, they knew they were there to bear solemn witness and to make sure it could never be allowed to happen again.

It must have been even harder on Rachael who touched the names on the wall like she was touching all that was left of friends and family. She cried openly and Martin didn't try to stop her. He just stood close to her, touching her arm when it was time to move on.

It got to him too. Pictures of broken people with haunted eyes, behind barbed wire, waiting for the horrible end plotted by minds that had been seduced by pure, unadulterated evil. It made him angry and it wasn't just for Rachael's sake. He was angry that he belonged to a species that could do something like that. He could understand blind rage—he had seen it often enough on the ice—but this was something different. This was what happened when men sat behind their desks, coolly and calmly designing and planning the most efficient way to exterminate an entire race. That frightened him.

They kept meticulous records, too, as if they were proud of it all. And pictures; undeniable proof that would live forever even after the smoke from the crematoriums had blown away. Martin had read about it and thought he understood but here, face to face with the ghosts of the six million, and listening to the faltering voice of an old survivor, it became so real that he too had to fight back his tears.

"It might be better," Rachael said to him as they got closer to her house, "if we don't mention where we've been." She had recovered for the most part but her dark eyes were still soft from all her tears.

"Okay, but why?"

"Because of my father. The Holocaust brings up all kinds of bad memories for him."

"I can understand why."

"It's not what you're thinking, Martin."

He looked at her and saw the veil of mystery close behind her eyes. He had yet to meet her parents and she said as little as possible about them.

"Okay." He took her in her arms and held her against him. She seemed to melt against him and raised her head and smiled. "You know," he added as he tried to keep his heart from bursting, "that I will never let anything happen to you." It was clumsy but it was how he felt.

"I know, Martin."

He held her close as they walked to the door and she kissed him before she went inside.

*

The summer was passing and the trees along the Tiber had begun to yellow. The days were still hot and thronged with tourists but the evenings were beginning to cool. Those who could afford to leave the heat of the city were returning, and life would go on as it had for thousands of years. But the world outside was about to be changed forever, and in the middle of *Ludi Romani*, when the ancients had honored the king of the gods, death came swooping from the skies.

Even though the voices in his dreams had been warning him for a few nights, John was horrified and couldn't turn away. No one could as the tower blazed and burnt. And then, as CNN showed the second plane glide in, almost serenely, and strike the second tower, it all came flooding back.

**

They were coming home from church, almost gliding along in the big old Buick with the gleaming white-wall tires. They had prayed for peace, and while his mother was content with that, his father had the radio on low. He had been following Hitler's panzers as they rolled across the steppes of Russia, inching closer and closer to Moscow. "It will all be over by Christmas," he assured them, regardless of the irony. He was no fan of the Nazis; he just didn't want his country involved again.

"I hope so. You don't think we'll get dragged into it?"

"Why would we? We have oceans between us."

His mother seemed assured and went back to checking things off her list. Every Christmas she gathered the hats, mitts, and scarves the congregation gave to the poor and needy and brought them home to wrap in bright, shiny paper. His father contributed too, and made sure every package had a little toy because the children's smile would help to warm their parents' hearts. He smiled at her and turned the radio up a touch. Just in time to hear that Japanese planes had attacked American ships in Hawaii. It all seemed so unreal at first, but as they spent the rest of the day wrapping gifts, the news grew worse and worse.

"It will mean war, won't it?" His mother was frightened and looked to his father.

It almost broke her heart when John signed up. "It is not for a Christian to go out and seek revenge," she reminded him with a tone of resignation. His father was against it, too, but understood and drove him to the recruitment office in the grand old Buick with the spotless white-walls. They sat for a moment as they watched the lines of indignant men shuffle forward, impatient but jovial—as if they were going on a grand adventure.

"I will give you my blessing for what it's worth, but I cannot claim to be happy about this."

His father had always been cautious about anger, believing it was a sin against the love of God. He had wanted John to finish his education and join the family business. "You are going to join a war that might cost you your life—or worse, your soul."

\*\*\*

When he'd had enough of the hours and hours of repetition, of expert rumors and panelist's conjecture, and the constant rerunning of the images of dust-covered New Yorkers wandering through a moonscape, and the towers exploding, over and over, John turned it off and went outside. He hesitated at the door but he had to go out. He had to walk by the Tiber and gather his thoughts. Life would never be the same, so he may as well get used to it. Everyone would have to. They would have to find their way through the shock of it all. War hadn't visited the American homeland in so long. They had been exporting it for years and now it had come back to them.

There would be a period of mourning. Flags would fly at half-mast and politicians would line up for their chance to step into the spotlight of history. But in time that would give way to anger and from there revenge was just a stone's throw away. He had seen it all before. He had been part of it then and he was part of it now, even from his exile. He was still at heart an American but he was also a Christian, and Jesus had been explicit: love your enemies.

The river ran deep and dark, but ripples flared where the lights of the city reflected, red and yellow like little fires. Even Rome, that had seen so much more, was nervous as night fell, and John walked back toward the only place he was sure of finding peace, in Santa Maria dell'Orazione e Morte, in the company of the dead. They were whispering as he entered: *The city to which the whole world fell has fallen. If Rome can perish, what can be safe?*

John Melchor knelt as he had not knelt in years, as a true and humble penitent, and let the cloak of arrogance slip from his shoulders and shatter on the stone floor. He freed his heart from dogma and cried without restraint. He, who should have known better, and still professed a certainty about what Christ had said, had once let loose the fires of death from the skies. Yes they had been at war—a war they hadn't started. And yes, terrible things had to be done in wars; but that night, above the wooden houses of Tokyo, he saw the face of Satan in the billowing fireball below.

He saw him many times in the darkness that followed that night in San Salvador, and he had seen him again in the billowing black smoke of the twin towers.

"Blessed be the Lord, for he showed his wonderful love to me when I was in a besieged city," he remembered from the pages of Psalms that fluttered through his mind. He said it more in hope than conviction. He had become a Jesuit to silence the demonic guilt that met him at the gates when he was discharged back into a world where murder was still a crime. While much of the class of '45 simply got on with life, there were many like him. The war had taken away everything they used to be.

He tried to go back but he couldn't. His parents did all they could to recreate the innocence that had been shattered but that just made things worse. He spent his days on the veranda staring off into the depths of his soul, black and tarnished now. And at night he dreamed he was back in the plane, hunched over his bomb sights. And each night, when his target was aligned, he dropped his bombs on his father's house. He'd squirm and thrash about but he couldn't wake until he had watched his father and his mother turn to ash and blow away.

For a while he found some solace in the local bars where he was treated as the returned hero and plied with whiskey. Night after night he would drink until he was oblivious. Only then could he go home and collapse upon his bed. By the summer of '46, his father had had enough and took him aside.

"I can't claim to understand what you're going through but I can't sit back and watch anymore. Your mother and I have talked and we both feel it would be best if you took some time to travel. You could go in search of whatever it is you've lost."

"Do you think it can be found again?"

"Perhaps, or maybe you'll find something better."

"What do you think it is that I've lost?"

"Your soul. I warned you this might happen and now that it has I take no pleasure in being right. But have courage, son. You are not the first person to be lost in war only to find a better purpose."

"I wish I could believe that. How can you be so sure?"

"Because your mother and I still believe in you."

**

So John Melchor wandered in the wilderness for a while, drifting down the west coast seeking reaffirmation in anything that opposed what he had once believed. In time he crossed the border while the rumblings of the next war began, but the burning women and children of Tokyo followed and waited by his bedside, or wherever he had passed out after another day of mescaline and tequila.

It took time but he made his way through it. The discipline of the air force proved useful as he rebuilt himself in the manner of Ignatius of Loyola, who had also suffered in battle. Retreating when he lost his way and practicing the *Spiritual Exercises* the Spanish prince had left them, John re-emerged into the world full of reformed zeal. And when the tremors of the world threatened to shake him off his new pedestal, he found strength and balance in the pages of *De Civitate Dei contra Paganos, The City of God against the Pagans*, Saint Augustine's words of calm to the bewildered survivors after Alaric sacked the Eternal City. And they guided John through all that followed when once again he became a mercenary in the never-ending war between the cities of God and Man. He used his collar in Chicago and San Salvador, fingering it as he made the rounds of the rich and liberally minded. Shaming them into supporting the poor and downtrodden, preaching like a Manichean as he went:

> These are the considerations which one must
> keep in view, that he may answer the question
> whether any evil happens to the faithful and
> godly which cannot be turned to profit.

He needed the words of the bishop of Hippo again as all that he had been in the City of Man ached for his fellow Americans.

> And that you are yet alive is due to God, who
> spares you that you may be admonished to
> repent and reform your lives. It is He who has
> permitted you, ungrateful as you are, to escape
> the sword of the enemy, by calling yourselves
> His servants, or by finding asylum in the sacred

places of the martyrs.

Despite the eyes of the dead, John Melchor cried again and searched the shadows for peace.

> But the peace which we enjoy in this life,
> whether common to all or peculiar to ourselves,
> is rather the solace of our misery than the pos-
> itive enjoyment of felicity. Our very righteous-
> ness, too, though true in so far as it has respect
> to the true good, is yet in this life of such a kind
> that it consists rather in the remission of sins
> than in the perfecting of virtues. Witness the
> prayer of the whole city of God in its pilgrim
> state, for it cries to God by the mouth of all its
> members, "Forgive us our debts as we forgive
> our debtors."

As the shadows flickered, the dead of Tokyo slowly gathered around the altar. They did not speak; they didn't have to. They stood in silence behind their Noh masks and condemned him. He had made so many promises to them. He had sworn to spend his life ensuring that what had happened to them would never happen to anyone again.

One by one they stepped forward and removed their masks so he could see their faces, twisted in pain as they slowly turned to ash and settled to the floor.

"'The sins of men and angels," John prayed in earnest,

> do nothing to impede the great works of the
> Lord which accomplish His will. For He who by
> His providence and omnipotence distributes to
> everyone his own portion, is able to make good
> use not only of the good, but also of the wicked.

The last shadow removed his mask and smiled.

> But not even the saints and faithful worship-
> pers of the one true and most high God are safe

from the manifold temptations and deceits of
the demons. For in this abode of weakness, and
in these wicked days, this state of anxiety has
also its use, stimulating us to seek with keener
longing for that security where peace is complete and unassailable.

John knew him well. He was the devil he had seen so many
times before. Not the devil of imagination, horned and hid-
eous. This devil wore a suit and a shy smile. He spoke so reasonably, quoting Augustine as if he had inspired him.

For even they who make war desire nothing
but victory—desire, that is to say, to attain to
peace with glory. For what else is victory than
the conquest of those who resist us? And when
this is done there is peace. It is therefore with
the desire for peace that wars are waged, even
by those who take pleasure in exercising their
warlike nature in command and battle. And
hence it is obvious that peace is the end sought
for by war.

"I can never accept that," John said as determinedly as he
could. But his voice wavered. "I will never accept you."

"But you already have. You know in your heart that the
gods of man are the true devils. You know what will happen
next. We will have another bloody crusade to honor your gods.

How much more powerfully do the laws of
man's nature move him to hold fellowship and
maintain peace with all men so far as in him
lies, since even wicked men wage war to maintain the peace of their own circle, and wish
that, if possible, all men belonged to them, that
all men and things might serve but one head,
and might, either through love or fear, yield
themselves to peace with him!

"Come with me, John, and renounce the great lie of peace. You know it is beyond your kind."

*

"We should fight them over there so we don't have to fight them here," everyone agreed as they sat around the office waiting until it was time to go home. "We have to protect our way of life."

Danny just shook his head and walked away. The war drums were pounding and everyone around him was falling into step. The armies of the West were getting ready to avenge the dead, killed by those who hated freedom and democracy. He had heard it all before. It was the same language he'd heard growing up when the people of Derry were set upon. He knew better then and he knew better now. The world he had to find peace and serenity in was a mad house—and it was getting worse with each passing year.

Even guys at the meetings went along with it, except a few of the old-timers who had been to war before—but most people didn't listen to them. Instead they listened to voices of outrage that dominated the airwaves. They made it all sound so obvious and understandable. They were fighting the good fight against the forces of evil—just as they did in the Bible. Some even went as far as calling it a crusade.

"Onward Christian soldiers," Danny hummed to himself as he rose to get his coat and leave. He just wanted to get home and be with Billie. She understood how he felt. She would let him talk and not argue with him.

That was the big difference between her and Deirdre. Deirdre would have tried to get him to change his way of thinking. She would have said it was for his own good—that going against the flow was one of the things that caused him so much angst. She would have reminded him that he had always been like that.

She had a point, but her solution was to just try and go along with things. He had tried that, but the longer he was

sober the harder that became. How was he supposed to practice rigorous honesty when the whole world was reveling in lies
and deceit? How was he supposed to find peace in a world that
was spoiling for war?

"You're different from them," Billie had told him. "You're
not able to put your head down and follow along. For better
or worse, you've seen through the veil." She was always saying
stuff like that and telling him that he had the soul of an artist.

"Piss artist," Anto would have said if he were still around.
Danny missed him. His mother had phoned and told him what
happened in the church in Rome, but Danny didn't believe it.
He didn't say anything because his mother, and Mrs. Flanagan,
needed something to believe in. Everybody did, and lies were
far more comforting than the truth.

Still, he hadn't heard from Anto since then and that made
him stop and wonder.

Billie said it made sense—that Anto had unfinished business and had now moved on. She was into all that New Age
stuff and Danny just smiled and nodded along with her. It
made as much sense as all the stuff he had grown up with.

The only issue he had with it all was that if he was Anto's
unfinished business, what was supposed to happen next?

Frank was always saying he had to become a light in the
darkness, and Billie was always saying that he could become a
voice crying in the wilderness, but Danny wasn't sure. He still
wasn't ready to trust himself but he had to do something. He
couldn't just go along with things. That wasn't what he had
sobered up for. Life was just too dark if you couldn't have a bit
of fun now and then.

## Chapter 6 – 2002

IT WAS TIME FOR ANOTHER FIESTA. They all needed something to change the mood. It had been another cold, dark winter and it was still only February. And it was Martin's last year of high school. Things were going to change and they mightn't get as much time together anymore.

Deirdre was so proud of him. She was proud of both her children but Martin was turning into such a fine young man. It was his idea that she invite Eduardo. He said she didn't have to hide him. He even got Rachael involved. "Yes, Ms. Fallon. We're all dying to meet him."

Rachael practically lived with them now and Deirdre didn't mind. Grainne was so much easier to deal with when she was around. Rachael had become like a big sister and kept the peace, alternating her loyalties as evenly as she could. And she was an only child.

"Yes, Mom." Grainne had joined in and put her arm around Rachael as they both smiled synchronously, almost like cats. "We're dying to meet him. Is he like . . . all dreamy?"

"No he's gross and greasy and he has a moustache like Saddam Hussein," Martin teased them.

"Who?"

"The guy on TV with the chemical weapons."

"Oh him. He gives me the creeps."

"I'm impressed, Grainne. I hadn't noticed how much you paid attention to world affairs."

"I'm not a moron, Mom. Jeez."

And before Martin jumped in, Rachael ironed out the wrinkles. "That's not what your mother meant. She was complimenting you."

"Yes, Grainne, I was. And I'm very proud of you." Her daughter smiled as she hadn't since . . . Deirdre couldn't remember when and wanted to make this one last. "And what do you think of him?"

"Well, he gassed people . . . and he attacked Kuwait. And everyone says he has links with terrorists . . . and he's all like . . . old and gross."

"Wow, air-brain, I'm impressed too."

"Martin, be nice," Rachael scolded before Deirdre could.

"Yes, Martin," she added anyway. "Girls are not encouraged to pay attention to things like that."

"Mom. Hello-a, I'm still in the room."

"I know, sweetie. I just don't think we should let your brother ruin things with his misogyny."

"Yes, Auntie Miriam," they all chimed in, in unison. They always did that when she was about to rant. She didn't mind. Except she didn't want to sound like Miriam, even if she was her best friend in the whole world. Things weren't going very well for her. It looked like it was over with Karl. They both probably knew it, but neither of them knew how to get out. And Deirdre couldn't tell them—not until Miriam brought it up. "Well I hope you're all going to behave yourselves when Eduardo is here."

Everything was chopped and diced and carefully arranged on platters. The bowls of dips were in the fridge and she would take them out when he arrived, along with the corn chips— if Martin hadn't devoured them already. She had time for a shower, but just a quick one. She wanted to be fresh and clean and relaxed when he got there. The kids were going to catch a late show afterwards and made a point of telling her that they'd be home late and would probably sleep in in the morning. "It's no big deal, Mom," Martin had assured her after she gave him some money to treat Rachael and his sister. "It's your house too." He was just returning the compliment; she had respected his privacy when he started taking Rachael to his room and closing his door.

Well, she did after Grainne caught her standing by his bedroom door with a basket of his laundry. She'd been watching her for a while and reminded her of that the next time Deirdre intruded on one of her phones calls. They were all trying to learn how to give each other more space.

Grainne and Rachael insisted on helping her get ready and did a wonderful job on her makeup, even if she looked a lot like Sophia Loren. But she couldn't go along with them on the clothes. Rachael wanted something long and black and flowing, something alluring that would appeal to Eduardo's "Romanesqueness." And Grainne tried to dress her like one of the girls on Isabella Street long ago, the ones that all knew Danny by name. She overruled them and wore jeans. They were a little tight around her ass but she covered it with a light, lamb's wool sweater, the powder blue one with the V-neck.

"Misdirection." She winked at herself in the mirror and adjusted her breasts. The girls had insisted that she wear her smallest bra—everybody was doing it now. It gave her enough cleavage to keep his eyes above her waist and maybe, if he could find them in the gauze of shadow the girls had applied, look into her eyes. She was reconsidering her lipstick when he arrived. Martin had been posted to let him in and help break the ice, but she heard Grainne get there first.

Deirdre rose and checked herself one last time. The girls had assured her that her lipstick was a muted red, but in her reflection it looked more like something you might wear if you were dating a vampire. But it would have to do. Besides, she decided as she walked toward the stairs, she would leave a lot of it on her margarita glass.

He was standing in the hall, still in his expensive black coat, with his black leather gloves in one hand as he struggled with his overshoes with the other. When he finally peeled them off, he placed them on the rubber mat. He rose when he saw her coming down the stairs like a bride. "For the ladies." He retrieved the three roses from the hall table. "And for the gentlemen." He handed Martin an expensive bottle of wine.

*

Danny had gone into a right funk when he heard about it—Grainne had shared every detail until Billie deflected her.

And it wasn't just that. The whole world was getting to him. It was getting to her, too, but she could have a drink. Danny had no outlet—nothing to blow off some steam when the pressure got to him. He hadn't been going to meetings, but she didn't think it was her place to say anything—not unless he brought it up. And he didn't. He just sat in front of the TV every night watching as the world got ready to tear itself apart again. He said it reminded him of when he was a kid, right after Bloody Sunday.

She had to do something to snap him out of it. She tried sex, seducing him in black bustiers and long stockings, but it was becoming too much effort. She worked evenings and got home far too late. It was time to get his soul back on the road.

"Some friends are doing a gig on the seventeenth and wanted to do something Irish."

"Tell them to do 'The Black Velvet Band' and 'The Unicorn.'"

"They're not that type of band. They're more jazzy."

"Tell them to do some Mary Coughlin then."

"I told them you might consider doing a few songs with them."

"Me? I don't do that anymore. I'm too old for all that shite."

"You're only forty-five, much younger than Dylan and he's still going strong—and Mick Jagger."

"I couldn't, Billie. I haven't picked up the guitar in years."

"Well, you'll have a few weeks to get ready. The guys are even willing to do some rehearsals."

"I don't know, Billie. I'd probably be shite."

"No you won't and we can bring Grainne if you like."

She knew that would get to him. Even he must be getting tired of his daughter going on and on. Everything was "Eduardo this ... and Eduardo said that." It was time the little brat saw what Billie had always seen in her father—an artist that never should have been burdened with the petty details of life.

*

They didn't bring her but it was probably just as well. The Dominion on Queen was old, like a beer parlor, but reclaimed with eclectic touches that made it perfect for *après*-show parties. It was one of Billie's regular haunts.

The band was good, too; a stand-up bassist with a pork-pie hat and a dour-looking drummer who kept time with practiced nonchalance. The sax player, Bobby, had wandered north from Alabama following the old freedom train. Marvin (The Moose) played piano or accordion depending on his mood. They were tight and played off each other, handing melodies and harmonies around like ear candy. They did their usual set before wandering into a dirgy, haunting version of "Molly Malone" in honor of the day.

"We're gonna take a break," the Moose advised as the song finished, "but don't go anywhere. When we come back we'll have a treat for all of you who are celebrating St Patrick's Day."

"Yeah, man," Bobby agreed, "our brother Danny Boyle is gonna come by and lay something really Irish on your asses."

Billie could tell Danny was nervous as he strapped on his old battered Guild and checked levels. "Happy St. Patrick's Day," he greeted the room when he was ready. "I hope you're all getting shit-faced." The crowd roared back in approval and raised their glasses.

It was almost the way it used to be—only everything had changed. He looked more like a real musician now and not the young man flirting with it all. He tentatively strummed a G chord for a while as the band settled in around him. Then a couple times through G, D, E-minor as they found a funky groove. Then through G, D and B-flat, with Bobby beginning to add some flourish as they repeated it and finished on an A-minor—the chord that always set the mood.

"This is a song written about a fella that went out to America and didn't do so well," Danny said without looking out at the crowd. But Billie could tell; it was all starting to come back to him.

"He should've come here, instead," a drunken voice heckled.

"Yeah," Danny laughed. "Yeah, he should have." And after a few runs through A-minor, F and E, he began to sing:

> Here's you boys, do take my advice
> To America I'd have you not be coming.
> For there's nothing here but war
> Where the murdering cannons roar
> And I wish I was at home in dear old Erin.

His voice was a little rusty and shaky, but Bobby wrapped sweet sounds around it and The Moose smoothed over any cracks.

> And it's by the hush my boys, and that's to hold your noise
> And listen to poor Paddy's narration.
> I was by hunger pressed and in poverty distressed
> So I took a thought I'd leave the Irish nation.

Pork-Pie was bowing his bass and the drummer added chimes, blocks and cow-bells.

> Well I sold my horse and plough, I sold my pig and cow
> And from that farm of land I parted.
> And my sweetheart Biddy Magee oh I'm sure I'll never see
> For I left her on that morning broken-hearted.

> Then myself and a hundred more to America sailed o'er

Our fortunes to be making we were thinking.
When we landed in Yankeeland they shoved a
gun into our hands
Saying, Paddy you must go and fight for
Lincoln.

General Meagher to us said, If you get shot and
lose your head
Every mother's son of you will get a pension.
In the war I lost my leg, all I've now is a wooden
peg
By my soul it is the truth to you I mention.

Now I think myself in luck to be fed on Indian
buck
In old Ireland the country I delight in.
And with the devil I do say, Oh Christ curse
America
For I'm sure I've had enough of your hard
fighting.

Bobby soloed for a while and Danny seemed lost, but the band carried on, ducking and diving and exploring all that the melody could yield. But they brought it all back together for one more chorus.

Here's you boys, do take my advice
To America I'd have you not be coming.
For there's nothing here but war
Where the murdering cannons roar
And I wish I was at home in dear old Erin.

"My brother, Danny," Bobby announced when the crowd settled back down. "Let's get him to do another 'cos the Irish, man, they got soul."

They followed with "The Fairytale of New York" even though it was out of season, and everyone loved it and joined in where they could. The Moose pounded the piano and the whole place shook like an old music hall. And when it was done, when the drunks at the back finally let the chorus end, Danny smiled and tried to leave the stage but they wouldn't let him. "One more?" The Moose asked the crowd and they roared back.

After a hurried confab the drummer started a brisk tattoo on his snare.

"With all this talk of war, and all," Danny spoke in time to the rhythm, "I was thinking of an old song that sums it all up."

Danny and Pork-Pie joined in, adding chords and a bass line and raising the intensity as if they were ready to march into battle. Bobby twirled bugle notes in the background as The Moose squeezed away on the accordion. And when it all melded together, Danny began to sing:

> While goin' the road to sweet Athy, hurroo,
> hurroo
> While goin' the road to sweet Athy, hurroo,
> hurroo
> While goin' the road to sweet Athy
> A stick in me hand and a tear in me eye
> A doleful damsel I heard cry,
> Johnny I hardly knew ye.

> With your drums and guns and guns and
> drums, hurroo, hurroo
> With your drums and guns and guns and
> drums, hurroo, hurroo
> With your drums and guns and guns and
> drums
> The enemy nearly slew ye
> Oh my darling dear, ye look so queer
> Johnny I hardly knew ye.

> Where are the eyes that looked so mild, hurroo,
> hurroo
> Where are the eyes that looked so mild, hurroo,
> hurroo
> Where are the eyes that looked so mild
> When my poor heart you first beguiled
> Why did ye skedaddle from me and the child

Oh Johnny, I hardly knew ye.

Where are your legs that used to run, hurroo,
hurroo
Where are your legs that used to run, hurroo,
hurroo
Where are your legs that used to run
When you went to carry a gun
Indeed your dancing days are done
Oh Johnny, I hardly knew ye.

I'm happy for to see ye home, hurroo, hurroo
I'm happy for to see ye home, hurroo, hurroo
I'm happy for to see ye home
All from the island of Ceylon
So low in the flesh, so high in the bone
Oh Johnny I hardly knew ye.

Ye haven't an arm, ye haven't a leg, hurroo,
hurroo
Ye haven't an arm, ye haven't a leg, hurroo,
hurroo
Ye haven't an arm, ye haven't a leg
Ye're an armless, boneless, chickenless egg
Ye'll have to be put with a bowl out to beg
Oh Johnny I hardly knew ye.

"Sad verse," Danny called back over his shoulder and they
all toned it down.

They're rolling out the guns again, hurroo,
hurroo
They're rolling out the guns again, hurroo,
hurroo
They're rolling out the guns again
But they never will take my sons again.

They all stopped abruptly except the drummer who began
to build to a crescendo. And when he was there, Danny raised
his head to the ceiling and sang from the depths of his battered

heart: "No, they'll never take my sons again, Johnny I'm swearing it to ye."

Billie kissed him when he sat back down, even though her lips were wet with wine. "Danny boy, that was beautiful." He became shy and flustered but Billie could tell—he was happier than he'd been since . . . before.

"Do you think," he asked with a smirk, "the world would get any worse if I had a beer?"

*

*Dim Sum* in The Bright Pearl on St. Andrew Street was always busy. Bustling with carts of steamed tidbits, forcing their way through the babble of Babel, but a few words pierced the din: *Har gow, Guotie* and *Char siu baau.* After Mexican, it was their second favorite way to eat together, sitting at round tables covered with sheets of brilliant white plastic, easy to peel off when stained by chopstick mishaps. Deirdre, Grainne and Martin were all experts, but Eduardo struggled and ended up using his like spears. Rachael didn't even try and asked for a fork. And, as the dishes were placed on their table, they all ate furiously to try to make space for whatever was coming next. Deirdre didn't mind. They were all together and they were all happy.

"Oh, my god, I need a *Coke.* I have all this like . . . grease in my mouth."

"Then eat some of the vegetables." Deirdre had ordered them though they rarely touched them. She'd eat a few but they were so bitter. Martin would eat some, too, coated in soya and any other hot pastes the servers had left.

"Oh, Mom. I'm not a kid anymore."

"Sorry, but I'm still your mom. Rachael, would you like some vegetables before Martin devours them all?"

Poor Rachael. She had tried everything, even the pork before Deirdre could tell her what was what. She smiled like she was really enjoying herself but sometimes, after popping something strange into her mouth, she looked a little frightened. Eduardo was doing much better and was taking chopstick lessons from Martin. "So this is why you are so good at stick handling. Show me again."

Martin looked chuffed and plucked at the rings of slippery squid. He caught one and effortlessly dipped it in the dark, tangy sauce before raising it to his mouth, winking at Rachael as he did.

"Okay." Eduardo shook out his shoulders and stretched his arms with his fingers locked until they cracked. "Now I have it." He went for the squid, too, and chased one around the plate. He stuck with it and raised it near his mouth before it began to wobble. He panicked, rushed and lost it, right into his tea cup, causing it to spill. The watery green tea pooled for a moment before joining the watery yellow mess Deirdre had made when she tipped over the little bowl of curried tripe.

"And this," Eduardo announced after he had fished the flying squid from his tea and popped it into his mouth, "is why the Portuguese invented the fork."

"Some people"—Deirdre smiled around her tea cup so the kids couldn't see—"would have realized what the little bowl is for. You place the food in it and raise it to your mouth. Or you can go on using your tea cup."

He smiled back and didn't care who saw. "And this, this is just one of the reasons why I love you."

"Ew."

"Grainne, are you embarrassed when people say they love each other?"

"Yeah, especially when one of them is my mother. And it's all like . . . emo."

"Martin?" Eduardo turned to him, pleading his case. "You agree with me?"

"She's just jealous no one will ever say it to her."

He had probably meant it as a joke but it lingered like a fart. Before Deirdre could dispel it, Eduardo did. "Martin. You're her brother and she's not supposed to look like a woman to you, but to other men she will be very beautiful. After she turns sixteen, you'll see. The boys will be lined up around the block."

It was a bit creepy to think about but it worked. Grainne's growing breasts heaved and she was smiling as she put her head down to her straw.

When they had eaten as much as they could, and had segregated what they wanted to take home, the dessert cart passed. Deirdre tried to shake it off but Eduardo insisted and ordered more.

"This"—he held up a *po taat*—"is what we in Portugal call a *Pasteis de Nata*"

"Do you get them delivered?"

Martin could be very dry, and if Eduardo noticed he didn't let on. "These were invented in Belem for our sailors to take around the world.

"You're welcome," he added when no one responded. The proud Portuguese in him could get a little tiring, but he did try to balance it with saying great things about being Irish too. Only the kids didn't like being reminded.

"Well, I think they're delicious." Rachael smiled at them all and finally looked as if she could eat something without fear.

*

Deirdre and the girls went back into Courage My Love for the second time. They had seen a few items but had wanted to check the other stores first. Rachael had her heart set on a bright pink angora with little yellowed pearls. Grainne thought it was too girly, but Deirdre thought Rachael could pull it off. "It's probably from the fifties, or early sixties."

Eduardo motioned Martin to hang back. "Let the ladies shop and you and I can talk. Your mother tells me you haven't decided yet."

Martin had applied to four different universities. "I haven't been accepted yet."

"You will. You'll have your pick."

He probably would. He had maintained an A average and was particularly strong in math and science. Western or Waterloo were obvious choices, but Rachael was hoping to go to McGill, in Montreal.

"And what about hockey?"

"I'll keep playing, but I think it's time I grew up and got a real life."

He looked like his mother when he said that and it made Eduardo smile. "Yeah, you and me both." Eduardo had started a new job with an investment company: "Vulture Capital Inc.," he often joked when he complained about having to prove himself all over again. "And what do you want to be afterwards?"

Martin wanted to be more like Eduardo than his father. He wanted to make enough to marry Rachael and buy a nice house around Lawrence Ave. and raise kids. She would be the perfect mother and he would be nothing like his father. They would have two kids and two cars, a cottage in Halliburton and a spotted dog. And a white picket fence. He had no idea how he was going to do it all but he wasn't concerned about that. He could deal with each step as it happened. What was bothering him was that in a few months he and Rachael would be separated. "Maybe I'll start the next Dot-Com bubble."

"Well, let me know. I'm sure my firm will want to get in on the ground floor. But what about Rachael? A man has to do what is required to make it in the world, but it means nothing if he's not with the woman he loves."

Martin liked that about Eduardo. He could never remember his father talking about stuff like that. He was still thinking about it when the girls emerged. Deirdre had bought them each something. The pink angora for Rachael and a spangly top and striped pants for Grainne; something that she could relive *Boogie Nights* in.

*

"School's out . . . forever," Grainne sang as she passed in her disco outfit, a beer clutched in her hand. It was just the summer break, but everyone was ready to party like there was no tomor-row. Doug's parents had gone away for the weekend, leaving strict instructions: he could have a few friends over but there were to be no wild parties. Doug had agreed and only invited his friends; but they invited their friends and the house was already full.

"Who invited the guys from Northern?" she asked as she stopped by the kitchen again. She had put on makeup too.

"I dunno. I just asked a couple of girls from N.T." Doug put his arm around her but Martin didn't mind. Doug was like family.

"You should tell them to leave. They're all like . . ." Grainne grabbed her crotch and sucked on her beer again.

"They're okay. They're the football team. After a few beers they'll pass out anyway."

"You hope." She sashayed away, looking much older than sixteen.

"Take it easy on the beer," Martin called after her.

"Give her a break."

"I haven't killed her yet. What more do you want from me?"

"Martin!" Rachael laughed and took another swig of his beer. "Don't be such a big brother."

"Yeah, bro'," Doug joined in. "Take the night off. It's the last summer of high school."

"Not for her it isn't."

"Chill, bro', chill."

"Leave him alone, Doug, he's just being protective." Rachael leaned against Martin and nudged him with her hip.

After everybody got wasted, or high from toking in the back garden, or popping their parents' pills, and the gang from East York Collegiate left, they all settled down. The hockey crowd had taken over the basement and were playing beer pong. The Emos were on the stairs discussing elaborate suicides, while the Goths were on the upstairs landing looking bored. Some-body was vomiting in the washroom and somebody had pissed on the rose bushes. Martin and Rachael decided it was time to leave and Doug tried to dissuade them, half-heartedly. He had gotten wasted too.

\*

"It's the end of the world as we know it," Martin sang as he climbed on the back of one of Mel's moose at the corner of Bayview and Moore, one of many that had sprouted up all over the city. Rachael had gone quiet and he knew what was on her mind. The world was about to change on them. "And I feel fine."

"Come down," Rachael said, but at least she was smiling again. "Someone might see."

"Let them." He slid down and took her in his arms. "What's bothering you? You've been very quiet since the party."

"I'm just thinking about what will happen when we go away in the fall."

"And the children go to summer camp," Martin sang whimsically. It was one of the songs his father used to sing to him when he was little.

> And then to the university
> Where they are put in boxes
> And they come out all the same.

"Seriously, Martin, aren't you concerned?"

"No, why would I be? It's just another four or five years of school."

"I meant about us. I'll be in Montreal and you'll be in London."

"I trust you."

"And I trust you, but I don't trust all the other girls that will be fawning all over you."

"Have I told you lately that I love you," he sang in his best Van Morrison voice; something else his father sometimes sang to cheer his mother up. Rachael cheered up, too, but he could see she was worried. He hated when she was like that. "Here." He reached into his pocket and pulled out his high-school ring and knelt before her. "Rachael Brand, will you do me the honor of accepting this pre-engagement ring?"

She looked as though he had given her the whole world and, as he kissed her, he made a promise to himself: one day, he would.

On his way home, he heard them before he saw them, swaying and staggering along.

"Oh. Hi Martin."

Doug was embarrassed but Grainne didn't care. She just stuck her tongue out as she hung on to him. "I was just seeing Grainne home."

"And he told me that he loves me," Grainne laughed and hiccupped. "Dougie loves me, only don't tell Mom."

"C'mon." Martin laughed as he took his sister by the arm. "Let's get you to bed."

"Ew, I'm not going to bed with you. I want to go to bed with Dougie."

"C'mon." Martin laughed again and gave Doug a playful punch on the shoulder.

"See you around?" Doug asked as if he was unsure.

"Always, bro, always."

*

"Was Grainne drinking last night?" Deirdre asked from behind the business section of *The Toronto Star*.

"She might have had a few beers." Martin tried to make it seem like it wasn't a big deal.

"Don't you think she's a bit young for that?"

"Mom, she's sixteen. Besides, when has she ever listened to me?"

"Well I don't think it's right. She's foolish enough."

"She was okay—Doug was looking out for her."

"Doug? That's a bit like the wolf minding the sheep."

"Doug's okay."

"I meant the other way around. There are enough problems in the world as it is."

*

John Melchor was getting worse. He was seventy-nine years old and his doctor was worried about possible delusional disorders, but John wouldn't hear of it and insisted it was the world around him that was really mad. It was hard to argue with him, especially when he quoted Bernard of Clairvaux verbatim:

> O ye who listen to me! Hasten to appease the anger of heaven, but no longer implore its goodness by vain complaints. Clothe yourselves in sackcloth, but also cover yourselves with your impenetrable bucklers. The din of arms, the danger, the labors, the fatigues of war, are the penances that God now imposes upon you. Hasten then to expiate your sins by victories over the Infidels, and let the deliverance of the holy places be the reward of your repentance. Cursed be he who does not stain his sword with blood.

A friend had phoned Giovanni who had phoned Patrick to tell him that John was having another one of his episodes in the Campo De' Fiori. He was standing in front of Bruno's statue in the middle of the piazza, quoting the dead to the passing crowds.

"Hence," John passed on the words of Pope Urban II when he roused the swordsmen of Europe to his Crusade,

> it is that you murder one another, that you wage war, and that frequently you perish by mutual wounds. Let therefore hatred depart from among you, let your quarrels end, let wars cease, and let all dissensions and controversies slumber. Enter upon the road to the Holy Sepulchre; wrest that land from the wicked race, and subject it to yourselves ... God has conferred upon you above all nations great glory in arms. Accordingly undertake this journey for the remission of your sins, with

the assurance of the imperishable glory of the
Kingdom of Heaven.

"Is not so bad," Giovanni explained after Patrick got
there. "Is Rome. Nobody listen to anybody here." He could tell
Giovanni was embarrassed for him; he became so much more
Italian when he was.

"Should we not try to take him home?"

"I try, but he say no."

"Well we have to do something."

"We will. We'll listen to him and when he's finished—we
take him home."

"But what if the police come by?"

"We'll tell them that he is a talking statue."

"All who die by the way," John continued as they approached
him casually,

> whether by land or by sea, or in battle against
> the pagans, shall have immediate remission
> of sins. This I grant them through the power
> of God with which I am invested. O what a
> disgrace if such a despised and base race, which
> worships demons, should conquer a people
> which has the faith of omnipotent God and is
> made glorious with the name of Christ! With
> what reproaches will the Lord overwhelm us
> if you do not aid those who, with us, profess
> the Christian religion. Let those who for a long
> time, have been robbers, now become knights.

And as Giovanni and Patrick stood and waited for him to
finish, and the words of the long dead pope drifted off toward
the Vatican, a small crowd gathered around them.

"Patrick." John nodded as they stepped forward to lead
him away. "Your uncle wants to talk with you. It's about Danny
Boyle."

\*

Danny ordered a second beer but he wouldn't have any more. He was learning to enjoy them without getting shit-faced. Now that he had sorted out so many of the things that were wrong with him, he could manage that. Provided he didn't overdo it.

He'd even started having a few glasses of wine with dinner, too, but he was careful. He knew Billie was keeping an eye on how much he drank. He could tell she was a bit conflicted—relieved that he wasn't on edge all the time, but a little guilty too, as if somehow she was responsible.

She wasn't. Danny had been sober long enough to learn that he was just a heavy drinker with other problems; and while many of these problems came to the surface when he was drinking, he could avoid them if he could teach himself to drink normally.

He was cautious about it, though, and only drank in bars where he wouldn't run into anybody he knew. He was still just getting the hang of it.

Sometimes, he felt guilty, but as Billie had convinced him, he was full of guilt and shame and that was something else he had to learn to outgrow. He was just having a few beers, for Christ's sake, like any normal man. No one could begrudge him that.

This time, he assured his reflection in the mirror behind the bar, was going to be different from all the other times he had started again. Danny Boyle, by the grace of his nebulous higher power had recovered. He smiled at himself and couldn't help noticing that he was beginning to look a bit like his uncle Martin.

## Chapter 7 – 2003

"WHERE'S MY DAD?"

Billie sat up immediately, almost dropping the phone. Grainne was coming by to spend the day with her father. They'd forgotten and had sat up late, drinking, and were still in bed. She nudged Danny hard but he just muttered and rolled over.

"Oh, Grainne, we weren't expecting you 'til . . ." She had to lean over to see the radio clock. Shit! It was almost midday. "I'll be right there."

"Ew." Grainne wrinkled her nose as she walked through the living room. Billie had managed to hide the empty bottles and her underwear but she had left the wine glasses and ashtray on the coffee table.

"Mornin', sweetie," Danny said shyly when he emerged from the bedroom and propped himself up by the coffee machine. He was hung over, and it was better that he stay there until they got some coffee into him.

"Afternoon. It's afternoon. I can't believe you forgot I was coming. That's like . . . so . . ."

"Oh, Grainne, take a pill." Billie shouldn't have said it but the kid was too much sometimes.

"Excuse me?"

"Grainne, just cool it until we get some coffee. Please?"

"Daddy?"

"C'mon, Gra, we had a bit of a late night. Let me just get a coffee into me and then we'll be all set. Okay, sweetie?"

"Oh, I see."

"You see what exactly?"

"Billie, don't start."

"No, Danny, I'm not starting anything." She pulled two cups from the shelf and almost slammed them down. Her hands were shaking and she dribbled some as she poured. "Here." She handed Danny his and moved past him.

"Hello-a?"

"You're too young."

"Daddy, can I have one?"

Danny handed over his and poured himself another.

"Ew." Grainne put her cup down. "This is gross. Can I get a mocha latte instead?"

"I can't make those. What if I put in sugar and lots of milk?"

Grainne looked around the messy kitchen with disdain and smiled. "Never mind. Eduardo is always making us different types of coffees."

"Then you should've had one before you came over." Billie should have let it go. She just wanted to get in the shower—and stay there until the little bitch left.

Grainne didn't say "Ew." She didn't have to; her face said it all. But before Billie could react, Danny turned to plead with her. "You know how to make that, don't ya? You could show me."

"Sure, just let me jump in the shower first."

"I don't suppose you'd show me before?"

"Oh, Danny, let me shower. I won't be long. You don't mind waiting, do you Grainne? I won't be more than five minutes."

"Whatever." Grainne shrugged and turned so her father couldn't see her face. "Bitch," she added under her breath.

Billie should have let it go.

"Excuse me?"

"Nothing."

"It's not nothing. Danny, you heard?"

He didn't even look up at her and Grainne smirked and mouthed "bitch," again.

"I saw that."

"Dad?"

"Billie?"

"She called me a bitch, twice."

"C'mon." Danny took her in his arms and steered her toward the shower. "Go and have a nice shower and everything will be grand when you come out."

She almost did, but Grainne did it again and Billie didn't even stop to think. She marched over and slapped her smirking young face.

"Daddy?" Grainne shrieked and lowered her face into her hands to squeeze out her tears. And when she raised it, the mark of Billie's hand was becoming clear.

She stayed in the shower until she heard them leave, and when she came out she saw the note he had left on the counter. "It might be better if you weren't here when I get back."

She decided to stay with a friend until it all blew over, but Danny refused to take her calls for a week.

"I can't have you around my daughter anymore," he explained coldly when he finally did.

"I am so, so sorry, Danny. I just snapped."

"I know and I can't let it happen again. You can come by and take your stuff—and anything else you want. Only not when I'm here. I don't want to see you again. Ever."

\*

"Well now, between you and me, Father, things are not great for Danny right now. He's gone back on it."

Jacinta was having lunch with Patrick in a little place on the Via Sistina. The man who owned it was the spitting image of Pavarotti. Jacinta had heard about him and just had to eat there. She was staying up the street, in the Hotel King, and the restaurant was just a few doors down. It wasn't bad and Patrick was happy to see her. He was beginning to enjoy her odd visits and the snippets of news of her family.

"Only I'm keeping my fingers crossed. He broke up with that Canadian one so there's still hope."

"And is Deirdre still seeing someone?"

Miriam had kept him up to date on all that had happened between Danny and Deirdre. He was very sad about it but what could he do? He had thought about Danny often since the day John had mentioned him—only none of it made any sense to him. Besides, he had proven himself to be totally incompetent when it came to dealing with other people's problems.

"Isn't he living with her and my grandchildren? I hope he isn't making them all foreign on me. It's bad enough that they're Canadian."

"Oh, you don't mean that, Mrs. Boyle. I'm sure you'd love them if they were purple and had six heads each on the pair of them."

"You don't have children, do you, Father?"

"No, Mrs. Boyle, the good Lord saw fit to spare me that."

"Well let me tell you, you're probably better off. There's no end to it. Even when they're half a world away. And I wouldn't mind so much only things are so good at home these days. It's a pity they ever left. They'd probably still be together and the children wouldn't have to be getting used to a new father. Or at least if they did, he'd be one of us."

"So things have never been better back home?" Patrick decided to steer them back to common ground. He still read *The Irish Times* and *The Independent*. The college had them delivered every day and he had lots of time for reading. As he approached retirement, he was teaching less and less.

"You'd hardly know the place anymore. And now, with the euro, there'll be no stopping us. Our Donal has been selling apartments in Spain and the whole country is going mad for them. Gina was just telling me that they're going to buy a part of a little island for themselves too."

"And would you think that all the changes are for the better, Mrs. Boyle?"

"They are and they're not, Father, but we all have to get used to bit of change now and then. Only . . ." She paused to take a drink from her wine. "Some days I can't help but feel that it's all happening too fast. It's enough to make your head spin." She looked a little pained for a moment but smiled at him. "It must be so nice for you here where nothing ever changes."

"Oh, we've change here, too, only Romans are slow to adapt. I suppose they've seen it all before."

"Well, back home nobody even bothers about the British anymore. Nowadays, it's all the Germans this and the Germans that. It's like they're running Europe again."

"You might be right, Mrs. Boyle."

"I suppose they still dislike them over here because of the war and all."

"I suppose they do, but probably not the war you're thinking of."

Mrs. Boyle sipped her wine again as if she was getting ready to ask him a favor. "Do you still see the holy Jesuit, Father?"

"I do," Patrick lied—another little white one. He had been avoiding John since his breakdown. "Only he hasn't been too well lately. His old mind is beginning to slip."

"That's too bad, Father, because I was hoping to ask him a favor."

"Is it something I could help you with, Mrs. Boyle." He knew what she was going to ask and dreaded it, but he was still a priest and he had to try to offer what comfort he could.

"I doubt it, Father. Not unless you've seen my Jerry around."

"No." He laughed. "I haven't; but then again Jerry was never a great one for spending time in churches." Mrs. Boyle laughed too, but he could tell she still wanted something. "Was there something else you wanted to ask Fr. Melchor?"

"There was. I wanted to ask him if there's anything that could be done for Danny. I know it's a lot to ask, but he worked miracles for Mrs. Flanagan. Do you think he might be able to do something like that for me?"

Patrick was flustered, but Mrs. Boyle was looking straight at him. God forgive him, but he was going to have to go along with it all for now. "Well, the next time I see him I'll be sure to ask. But he mightn't be well enough for it anymore."

"Will you be seeing him before I leave?"

**

Giovanni and Signore Pontecorvo had broken the news to him. They sat him down between them and sipped on little glasses of grappa—a private stock Giovanni reserved for his closest friends. John had been preaching again to the crowds in the Foro Romano, warning them about the trap of revenge, even as his country was pushing the world toward war in Iraq.

> And now, brethren, I appeal to you by God's
> mercies to offer up your bodies as a living
> sacrifice, consecrated to God and worthy of his
> acceptance; this is the worship due from you as
> rational creatures.

Apparently, he'd been putting on quite the show, too. Standing on a rock and pointing all around him with a book in his hand, reading the letter of St. Paul to the Romans. One of Giovanni's nephews had been leading a tour and had called immediately and stayed on the phone until his uncle could get somebody there.

"I told Marcus to distract him," Giovanni explained while Signore Pontecorvo nodded sympathetically, as though it was something that could have happened to any of them.

Marcus had tried. He had smiled up at John and waved, but John had a faraway look in his eye and continued regardless.

> And you must not fall in with the manners of
> this world; there must be an inward change, a
> remaking of your minds, so that you can satisfy

yourselves what is God's will, the good thing,
the desirable thing, the perfect thing.

Romans had seen worse and passed with a smile. And the
tourists thought it was part of the tour and began videoing.

Thus, in virtue of the grace that is given me, I
warn every man who is of your company not to
think highly of himself, beyond his just esti-
mation, but to have a sober esteem of himself,
according to the measure of faith which God
has apportioned to each.

John had even begun to direct his sermon to them, looking
from camera to camera.

"Americans." Giovanni shrugged as he retold it all. "They
really know how to put on a good show."

Each of us has one body, with many different
parts, and not all these parts have the same
function; just so we, though many in number,
form one body in Christ, and each acts as the
counterpart of another.

The Asian tourists were confused and their interpreter
couldn't explain. "A talking statue," Marcus suggested, and
everyone seemed happy with that and gazed at John with
amazement.

The spiritual gifts we have differ, according to
the special grace which has been assigned to
each. If a man is a prophet, let him prophesy as
far as the measure of his faith will let him.

John had paused, as if to see if they understood. He had
raised his arms to encompass all of them.

Your love must be a sincere love; you must hold
what is evil in abomination, fix all your desire

upon what is good. Be affectionate toward each
other, as the love of brothers demands, eager to
give one another precedence ... bestow a blessing on those who persecute you; a blessing, not
a curse. Rejoice with those who rejoice, mourn
with the mourner.

Another tour had joined them and soon Marcus's words
were passed around. "Talking statue, talking statue," rippled
off to the edges of the growing crowd.

Do not repay injury with injury; study your
behavior in the world's sight as well as in God's.
Keep peace with all men, where it is possible, for your part. Do not avenge yourselves,
beloved; allow retribution to run its course; so
we read in scripture, Vengeance is for me, I will
repay, says the Lord. Rather, feed thy enemy if
he is hungry, give him drink if he is thirsty; by
doing this, thou wilt heap coals of fire upon his
head. Do not be disarmed by malice; disarm
malice with kindness.

One of Giovanni's other nephews, the one in the *Carabinieri*, arrived and shuttled John home.

"I want to thank you for doing all that," Patrick said when
Giovanni was done.

"Prego." Giovanni shrugged like it was no skin off his back.

"Still, *mille grazie*."

\*\*\*

"I'm sure we can arrange something," Patrick assured Mrs.
Boyle, but he wasn't so sure. John had been dispatched to a
nursing home and tended to by the most discreet nuns. They
were well used to casualties like him, especially at times like
these. But by all accounts, he'd settled down again and was free
to come and go—as long as he had someone with him.

"Well that's a great relief, Father, knowing that I can count on you."

On his way home, Patrick crossed the piazza and stopped to look at Bruno's statue. It was as it had been for over a hundred years. The night he thought he saw something different was nothing more than his mind playing tricks with him. He missed his uncle and, having only really gotten to know the man after he'd died, wished he could just sit down and talk with him.

Anything else was just the type of madness that lurked in the corners, waiting to take old priests to their resting homes. He had seen it with Dan Brennan, and now John. It would happen him too if he didn't watch himself.

*

"So?"

"So, yourself."

They were sitting at the island in the middle of Deirdre's recently remodeled and extended kitchen. It had needed updating and she had needed distraction. Life without Martin around was hard to get used to, but things were better with Grainne. Even though Deirdre was still furious with Billie for slapping her, it did seem to have smartened her up a bit. She was much easier to get along with, but that might have been because she didn't have to compete for her mother's attention.

"You've come a long way, baby." Miriam raised her glass in a toast. "How old are you now?"

"Don't ask. I'm forty-five and looking every year of it."

"Really?"

"You were supposed to say I didn't. That's what women do for each other."

"Lie to each other?"

"Well, I think I look good for my age." She was going to add that Eduardo did, too, but that would have been insensitive. Karl and Miriam had just separated.

"I'm fifty-nine, Deirdre, and I'm tired. I'm so tired of people. Nobody is what they say they are anymore."

"Nobody ever was, Miriam. The only thing that's changed is that you see that now. When you were a nun, people knew not to tell you what they were really thinking. Come to think of it"—Deirdre wanted to steer them back toward happier thoughts—"that part is still the same."

"How dare you." Miriam had taken the bait and was all ready to bluster her way forward. "I'm the most honest, open, empathic, kind . . . Did I mention honest?"

"Yes you did. You're repeating yourself."

"Well it bears repeating. And you could pass for thirty something."

"Something?"

"Six . . . five . . . four . . . three?"

"Fine, thirty-three. It's the perfect age for me."

"It didn't work out too well for Christ."

"Miriam, one of the many things I've learnt along the way is that you have to let go of your ex."

"Easy for you to say. Mine was the Son of God."

"Mine has an Irish mammie."

"Do you still hear from her?"

"She calls every few weeks and still sends money to the kids. She's okay. She never mentions Danny but I know she calls him too. And she's been back to Rome."

"And how is the eternal bastion of misogyny?"

"She saw Fr. Reilly."

Miriam softened at that. It had been so hard on her. She and Karl broke up when he took a contract in Iraq. He insisted that it was just a consultancy—that he was only going to advise on cultural sensitivities—but she didn't believe him. He was joining in on the gold rush.

"Do you really think," she had asked him, "that after you destroy their government, seize all their wealth, and throw the whole country into civil war that they will still want to buy whatever it is your paymasters are selling?"

"He didn't even answer," she had told Deirdre on the phone. "He just walked off and packed his bags and we haven't spoken since." He had left a note trying to explain that he was still a soldier at heart. And he was still an American, and he had to do what he could.

That was when Deirdre insisted that she come for a visit. She even made it sound as though Miriam would be doing her a favor—now that she had to deal with Grainne without a wingman.

"Woman," Miriam had corrected and showed up a few days later.

"I'm here to escape the toxicity of my adopted Christian nation's response," she announced after she had taken off her coat and scarf. "Preserving freedom and democracy has always been a bloody business and truth has always been the first casualty. My relationship with Karl was the second."

"Well," Deirdre considered as they hugged. "You're very welcome. Only, I'm afraid I just have French wine."

"Freedom wine? Make mine a big one."

*

"She says he's fine."

"Who?"

"Fr. Reilly. Jacinta had dinner with him in Rome."

"Oh, poor Patrick. I hope he survived it okay."

"Maybe you should go over and find out."

She had time on her hands. She'd lost her job teaching in a community college. She knew she would when she'd asked her students to write letters to the president. With her record she was lucky they didn't send her to "Gitmo."

"Oh, please. I'm the last thing the poor man needs to see these days. John is in and out of hospitals and I'm sure Patrick is busy enough with him."

"Maybe he could use some help? Unless, of course, you're one of those pseudo-liberal types that talks about things but never gets off their arses to actually do something."

"No, Deirdre. I can be accused of a great many things but that isn't one of them. It's only that . . . well he used to have the biggest crush on me."

"That's so cute."

"No, I mean when I was back in Dublin—after he'd become a priest."

"It's still cute. Besides, you're both much older now."

"Thanks, and by the way I lied. You look at least thirty-seven, at the very least."

"More Freedom wine?"

"I don't mind if I do."

"So, you'll think about it?"

"Yes, Deirdre, I will think about it. Now can I have some?"

*

Patrick still looked boyish and, even though his hair was thinning, it wisped out around his ears and his collar. He was still awkward, too, and when she put her cases down he didn't know what to do. Miriam did and hugged him tightly. "Oh, Patrick, it's so good to see you again. Are you well?" she asked as she let go and stood back to look at him.

"As well as can be expected. And how are you? How was your flight?"

"It wasn't bad, once we actually got on the plane."

"Did you have any trouble?"

"Not after they went through all of my bags; but I made it and it's wonderful to be back in dear old Rome."

"Well it's wonderful to see you again and I have a car waiting."

One of Giovanni's nephews owned a taxi and his uncle didn't hesitate to offer his services. "He's waiting just over there." Patrick picked up her cases and she followed to the shiny gray and silver car. He had arranged lodgings for her, too, in a convent that now functioned as a guesthouse. He hoped she didn't mind.

She didn't. She was there to pitch in and help save the body and mind of John Melchor, her second oldest friend in the world.

The plan was that Patrick would get John to Giovanni's and everyone would meet them there. Signore Pontecorvo and Miriam would be sitting at a table at the back discussing books and Giovanni would steer Patrick and John there as if it was all coincidence. Giovanni had left instructions with the waiters that the surrounding tables were to be reserved so they could have some privacy. They would lay it all out, rationally and reasonably. They would make it clear that they would always be there for him, but he had to accept that he couldn't go around preaching anymore, and that he should move into a retirement home.

But John threw a spanner in the works. He was fussy and, even though he'd agreed to go for dinner, he wasn't very hungry. He said the nuns, whose cooking lacked subtlety but not quantity, had stuffed him like a goose. He'd put on some weight and looked well. He wasn't so wild eyed anymore. Patrick had to think on his feet and convinced John to go for coffee instead.

John agreed but insisted on going to a place he liked on the Campo De' Fiori. He said he didn't like the water in Giovanni's and, even though Patrick usually avoided the place, he decided not to push it; but he did stop to make a call while John was busy offering tourists directions.

"Change of plan," he told Giovanni and gave him the details. They would meet there, but Patrick had to dawdle to give them a chance to get there first.

They were sitting in the patio shade, pretending to study their menus as the early tourists passed through, some stopping to read Bruno's plaque. They still hadn't worked out how they were going to handle it when John arrived—they were still a bit divided on what they were going to say.

"Dearly beloved, we are gathered here . . ." John greeted them all as if he was perfectly lucid.

When Patrick signed him out the nuns had warned him. John could be lucid for hours and then something would just come over him. The medication helped, but he didn't always take it. They asked Patrick to have a few words with him about that—it was for his own good.

"And Miriam? News of my madness has spread, I see."

"John." Miriam rose and hugged him, almost startling him. "Can an old friend not drop by to say hello?"

"Now I know how serious it is." He laughed and hugged her for a moment. "But is it serious enough to warrant an intervention?" John smiled at each of them but no one smiled back. Giovanni and Signore Pontecorvo looked as if they didn't understand and shrugged, while Patrick and Miriam exchanged sidelong glances.

"Not at all, John, it's just you haven't been yourself and we all wanted you to know that we're still here for you." Patrick joined in as they had planned. They were to play good cop, bad cop, like the two detectives long ago. They had no choice; someone had to tell him. The Society of Jesus had been patient but they were recommending a home in Tuscany, somewhere out of the way. Either that or a discreet clinic in Switzerland.

"So I am to believe that I have gone mad?"

"Well no, John. Nobody is saying that. It's just that you haven't been well, and we thought a nice trip would do wonders for you." Patrick added to the pile of little white lies he used to tell Dan Brennan.

"So even my Irish friends think I'm mad." John asked and turned to the two old Romans who had been nodding while Patrick was speaking. "And you two statues, what do you have to say for yourselves?"

"John," Miriam interrupted before they could answer. "There's no need to use the word madness. You know what has happened to you. You've been dealing with a lot of stress and you just need some time to come to terms with a few things. It'll be like going away on a retreat."

"Miriam, you have always been honest with me. Don't stop now."

She reached out and touched the back of his hand. "You're just tired, John; an old war horse in need of rest."

"It's not like that," he addressed them all, and looked from face to face before continuing, hesitantly. "My friends, if you really want to help me, then would you let me unburden something on you?"

Patrick and Miriam looked unsure but the Romans nodded encouragingly.

"I have been a priest for fifty years. And I have tried to be a good priest in the manner I was taught. But all the time I was just hiding from something." He looked around again as the afternoon's shadows began to edge across the piazza, and Bruno's face began to glow as if it was burnished. "I was hiding from the devil." He tried grinning but his tears were already trickling down. "And now he has come to claim what he is due since that night over Tokyo."

"There's no need to be upsetting yourself there, John." Patrick tried to intervene, but Giovanni and Signore Pontecorvo discouraged him and waited for John to continue—as if they had seen it all before. Miriam was silent, too, softly crying as she brushed the back of John's hand.

"He offered me a deal that night in El Salvador. He would let me live if I could prove that the god I was hiding behind was real. He said that if I could stop the terrible things we do for our gods, he would let me be."

They all blessed themselves, except Signore Pontecorvo.

"And after 9/11 he challenged me again. He said that he would have us at war again in months and that there was nothing I could do to stop him. And he told me that my god would not lift a finger to help."

He stopped and shook his head. "Maybe they're right. Maybe I am mad." He looked up at them all but they didn't speak.

"I suppose"—he tried to smile again but it was only a flicker—"there is nothing left but banishment to Helvetia?" He began to cry again and they all looked down, or away, except Signore Pontecorvo.

"Maybe you're not mad. Maybe you are just one of those people who have gotten too close to their god."

"Like a prophet," Giovanni agreed, trying to look wise. "This is Roma. These things happen here."

"Thank you, my friends, but perhaps it is time for me to face the truth." He rose and wiped the tears from his eyes. "I will do whatever it is you want me to do. And now, I will leave you to decide."

He walked out into the piazza, toward the statue.

"Maybe, I should go with him?" Miriam was already on her feet, one arm reaching out toward the old, frail Jesuit. "He shouldn't be alone."

"No, you're right," Patrick agreed. "Go on over to him."

As she caught up with John and linked her arm in his, Patrick thought again about Dan Brennan, crushed and broken by the cross he bore. And John's was so much heavier. "I suppose we have no choice, really."

"Patricio, we always have choices."

Patrick was in no mood for Giovanni's eternal optimism but tried to hide it. "I suppose you're right, but what can we do?"

"We could leave him alone. He is not doing anybody any harm."

"You don't think he's . . . not sound?"

"Patricio, you are in the business of gods and devils. Why is it so hard to believe that they still exist? No, Patricio, it is you that is not thinking sound."

"But we can't have him wandering around preaching like John the Baptist. They'll lock him up. Or worse," he added as he watched John stand and look up into the face of Bruno, who seemed to be smiling the way his uncle did. He shook his head, but he couldn't shake the feeling.

"Here, the past never goes away," Giovanni went on, with Signore Pontecorvo nodding along. "That's why all the people of the world come. They won't mind."

"Won't the police?"

"Them?" Giovanni shrugged again, this time disdainfully. "They only get involved if the merchants complain and they won't. I can talk to them. I will tell them about John and they will understand. He could come here, by Bruno, and talk to the people. No one will mind. It will bring more people into the piazza."

"I'm not sure I want my friend turned into a tourist attraction."

"And I do not want our friend sent away to one of those places. They will not help him there. They will give him things to make him stop—that's not the same thing."

"Giovanni is right." Signore Pontecorvo nodded as he watched John and smiled. "Besides, we need all the prophets we can find right now. They are the only ones who can guide us out of the darkness."

"That's all very well, but even if the Jesuits go for it, he's going to need someone to care for him."

"We are his friends. We will look after him."

"So," Miriam asked as she returned, leaving John in doleful meditation by the statue. "What has the council of the wise decided?"

"His friends will take care of him. We won't let them put him away."

"And how are you going to do that?" Miriam asked, and Patrick was curious too. Giovanni couldn't even get his own coffee anymore, preferring instead to get one of his grandnieces to do it. And Signore Pontecorvo was even worse. He was totally dependent on his granddaughter, who devoted her days to driving him around in her bright little red Fiat.

"Perhaps," she continued, when it was obvious that no one else was going to, "I should consider moving here to help out. I'm sure I could find a teaching position here."

"Of course," Giovanni enthused. "I have a nephew in the university. I will speak to him."

"Giovanni!" Signore Pontecorvo laughed. "He's like one of the old popes—he has nephews everywhere."

And while Miriam broke the good news to John, Patrick looked away. But he knew his uncle was smiling down at them.

# Chapter 8 – 2004

A H, DANNY, ARE YOU WELL?" the barman asked.

Danny wasn't. It had only been a year and half but already all of the old bitterness and resentments were surging back. And his drinking was getting out of hand again. No matter how much resolve he tried to muster—when he had a few drinks in him it all melted away. It didn't matter. He was on his own again.

He really missed Billie but he couldn't go back to her—not after what she did to his own flesh and blood. He still grew indignant when he thought about it but, a few drinks later, another realization waited for him. It wasn't really her fault—it was his. Everything in his life fell apart, sooner or later. He was a fool for ever getting his hopes up again. He could never have a relationship with anybody without screwing it up.

"I will be after I get a few pints into me." Danny smirked and settled on the stool just down from the corner of the bar, where he could join conversations on either side—and turn away from any he didn't want to be part of. He'd had a rough day. He'd been called into the HR department to discuss complaints about comments he was "alleged" to have made. "Comments," they told him, "that were no longer appropriate in a culturally diverse workplace." And he had to sit there and take it. He already had two strikes against him over his drinking and his absenteeism.

"And after I get to enjoy a few smokes before those feckin' social engineers take that away too."

"They say they're bad for you." The barman laughed as he placed the pint on the counter.

"Well feck 'em. It's my life and I'm getting sick and tired of everyone telling me how to live it."

The HR lady had told him that his comments on the recent tragedy in Mina were, "at the very least, insensitive and could be construed as offensive to more ethnic colleagues." All he'd said was that there were a few less Towel-heads for the Yanks to kill. He didn't mean anything by it. He was only trying to lighten things up a bit.

"First today," Danny lied and downed a large gulp.

The HR lady had made him feel as if he was back in the headmaster's office. Only she didn't have a cane—she didn't need it. She made it sound like she was concerned for him—him having been going through so many "personal issues lately." Only it was more like she was tearing off bandaids and assuring him it was for his own good. She also said he should seriously consider going to a cultural sensitivity workshop. It would look so much better for him when he faced the scheduled hearing.

He had wanted to point out that it was all fine and dandy for all the politicians, and all, to be going on about fighting to protect our way of life and slaughtering Muslims, but when he joked about it it suddenly became offensive. But he didn't and just nodded, until she forced him to say "yes," like she was making him "baa."

It was getting more and more like that every day. They were trying to get rid of guys like him—the old guard that used to just get the job done without worrying about everybody's feelings. Guys with a bit of character and not a bunch of feckin' cardboard cut outs.

The feckers that really ran the world wouldn't be happy until everybody was all the same. He'd just read that somebody in Korea was already learning how to make clones. He could save himself the bother. Everyone was already walking around like feckin' zombies, buying the same shite and believing in the same crap and never stopping to think about what was really going on.

That's how the feckers liked it—when everybody was plugged in and following subliminal commands. And now they were supposed to get all fired up and start fighting each other. Between everybody talking about weapons of mass destruction and terror alerts, a fella couldn't even think for himself anymore. It was like in that book 1984, only he hadn't actually read it. Deirdre had and told him all about it.

It was enough to drive a man to drink. Besides, when he was drinking, if he did say something they weren't allowed to think, let alone say, he could blame it on having drunk.

Sometimes, after he had a few, he thought he might be the only sane one left. Nobody could say shite anymore, even though they were all drowning in it. He finished his pint and ordered another in resignation. He had nowhere else to go anymore. McMurphy's was one of the few really Irish bars left in Toronto. Most of the others were all "come-all-yas" with young women running around in short little tartan skirts like naughty school girls.

"*Sláinte,*" the barman intruded softly, and placed the fresh drink in front of him.

In McMurphy's a fella could have a few quiet pints and contemplate his life. It was one of the habits they made him do in AA. He still did it, only a bit differently. Now, he'd try to shut out all the other stuff they had tried to teach him. But it kept coming back.

*Rarely have we seen a person fail who has thoroughly followed our path,* his reflection behind the bar reminded him.

"So, you're back on it?" McInerney sat down beside him and nodded when the barman looked over at him. He looked at Danny with curiosity rather than judgment. He was one of the last straight shooters and Danny liked him.

"I am, yeah, but I'm okay now. I learned how to handle it."

"How long were you off it?"

"A few years. I did a full drying out and now I'm grand," Danny said as affably as he could, while avoiding himself in the mirror. He was tired of talking about it.

"Wasn't for you, then?"

"It's not that, Sean. It's a great program and I learned a lot from it. Only I learned that I wasn't really . . . ya know? I'm more of a social drinker with other problems."

*One of those who do not recover?*

*Could not,* he corrected himself. He'd tried the program but what good had it done him? All it had done was make him too soft in a world that was getting harder and harder. And it made him guiltier. Not only was he a drunk, now he was one of those lost souls that even AA couldn't help.

*People who cannot or will not completely give themselves to this simple program, usually men and women who are constitutionally incapable of being honest with themselves.* His reflection smirked the way Anto used to. Sometimes, when he was plastered, Danny missed him.

"Well, as long as you're all right now," Sean agreed and devoted himself to his own pint. He'd just have one or two and go home. Not like Danny who had no choice anymore. He had to get as much in as he could hold. Only then, when everything had been blotted out, could he go home and lie down and get some peace. It wasn't his fault; he'd been born that way. *Naturally incapable of grasping and developing a manner of living which demands rigorous honesty.*

That's probably why it hadn't worked for him. He was finally being totally honest with himself and the rest of the world, only they couldn't handle shit like that.

Nobody ever could, and he was tired of trying to hide it. He had known what was going on from the start. It was all a load of bollocks. You got born, you put up with every piece of crap life threw at you and then you died. It was like what Deirdre used to say about living in the moment when she was all into yoga. He was living in the moment. He was having a few drinks and feck anyone who couldn't handle that. He was one of those whose chances had *always been less than average, one of those who suffered from grave emotional and mental disorders.* He just had to look back at how he grew up. He never had a chance to begin with. *Fecked from the start.*

"I'm off then," Sean interrupted him. "I'll see you later."

"Yeah," Danny agreed and ordered another, coming face-to-face with himself in the mirror. *But many of them do recover if they have the capacity to be honest,* the voice in the mirror quoted straight out of *The Big Book.*

He'd just have this one and get himself off home and, not for the first time, he wished someone would be there, waiting for him.

*

"Man, this place really rocks."

They had gone to the Windsor, and Doug was on his third beer. The bare-faced band was blasting away and the place was full of young Irish women. Martin hadn't wanted to come but Rachael insisted. They'd been home for over a month and had spent every evening together. She felt he needed a boys' night out, even if it was at the Windsor.

"Yeah, it's okay. My dad used to play here."

"Wow, man."

"It's no big deal."

"No man, it is. That's the first time you've mentioned him in years. And it's the first time I've ever heard you call him 'dad.'"

"Must be the beer."

"Seriously, man, what's the story between you two?"

"There's no story. I just don't get on with him."

"Martin, you don't just not get on with your father. Spill it."

"There's nothing to spill. He and I just never got along." They hadn't. His father had screwed his mother over and that wasn't something Martin could ever forgive.

"That's kinda cold, don't ya think?"

"Maybe. I just don't think of him as my father, that's all."

"How's it going with Eduardo?"

"It's okay. He's pretty cool. And he treats my mom really well."

"Cool." Doug let it go and leaned closer. "Hey, horny older woman alert, two tables over, on the left."

Martin was about to look over when Doug held his shoulder. "Cool it, stud. Let an expert show you how it's done."

Doug picked up his beer and ambled over to Billie's table and Martin just let him. Doug was a good guy, but he'd been riding Martin's ass about all the time he was spending with Rachael. "Sure," he agreed. "Go for it." He sat back to watch him crash and burn.

Billie was hot. Martin had never really noticed that before. She had to be in her mid forties but she still had it. Her skin was almost perfect and her bright red lipstick made her mouth seem warm. Her eyes were a deep sea-green, deepening as Doug came closer. She wore a long, gray dress that showed every curve and swell. She wore gray stockings and black, high-heel shoes. She blew out a long stream of smoke and looked Doug up and down. "Yes?"

"My friend and I," Doug nodded back toward Martin, "were just trying to remember which movie we saw you in."

Martin had followed him over and was about to bail him out, but Billie just winked at him and turned back to Doug. "Cute, and what do you do?" She managed, without even a flicker of a smile as they sat down on either side of her.

"Well, my friend"—Doug nodded toward Martin again— "and I are new in town."

"Is that right?"

"Yes, we just came in to sign all the paperwork."

"You don't look like lawyers."

"No. We're hockey players. We just signed for the Leafs."

Martin should have stopped him, but what the hell.

"Hockey players. Hmmm. Should I be impressed, Martin?"

"You two know each other?"

"Yup."

"And you didn't tell me?"

"You didn't ask."

"Man!"

Billie was okay with it all and even bought them a drink, after asking Doug if he was sure he was old enough. "How's your father?" she asked Martin when they were finally alone. Doug had left to get over his embarrassment and hit on someone else.

Martin had never really talked with her since that day on Queen St. He'd wanted to like her, but it felt like disloyalty to his mother. "I don't really keep in touch. Do you?"

"No." Her eyes looked sad when she said it.

It was the same look he'd often seen on his mother's face, and Martin wanted to try to make her smile. She'd been pretty cool about Doug. "Maybe you're better off." He meant it lightly but it didn't work. If anything it just made Billie sadder.

"You don't think much of him, do you?"

"I usually avoid thinking about him."

He didn't mean to but he felt himself growing stiff and cold. Any mention of his father still brought out that reaction. Rachael said it was something he had to deal with someday, but Martin wasn't ready. He said he could never forgive what his father had done, but it was more than that.

"I'm sorry," Billie answered as she watched his face. "I shouldn't have mentioned him. It's just that I knew a very different man."

"Well, I guess you were a lot luckier than me."

She lit another cigarette and blew her smoke up in the air. "It wasn't all his fault. He never should have become a father."

His eyes hardened as he checked to see if she was taking a shot at his mother.

"That didn't come out the way it should." She looked embarrassed and a little vulnerable, the way his mom used to. "I just meant he was never going to be much good at it."

"No arguments here." It was one of the things that always got to him. His father seemed to have the ability to really get into the heads of the women he had been involved with. It didn't make any sense.

Billie was looking directly into his eyes, trying to tell if he really meant it. "I get what you're saying, but you never knew the other sides of him. He could have been a great musician. He really was an artist."

*Piss-artist.* Martin smiled but didn't say anything. He could tell she was still very much in love with him.

"I'm sorry." She blinked back the little tears that were forming in the corner of her eye. "I shouldn't be talking about this with you. Tell me, how have you been?"

And he did. He told her all about school and all about Rachael. She seemed interested and even smiled a few times, except when he mentioned his sister.

"I'm so sorry about that. I don't know what came over me."

And when it was time for her to leave she kissed him on the cheek, leaving the bright red prints of her lips for Doug to see.

"Wow, that could have been your stepmother."

"Yeah. Cruel, isn't it?"

"You better wipe that off before Rachael sees it."

"Dude," Doug almost burped during the cab ride home. "We got to make this a regular thing. You and me, Martin. Boy's night out. Eh?"

*

As the summer ended, as Martin and Rachael prepared to be separated again, Deirdre decided to have a fiesta. It was the best way she could think of blowing all shadows from her mind. She could see how much they loved each other and she was happy for them, only she wished it hadn't happened before they had a chance to go out and see who they really were in the world.

*And not make the mistakes you made?* Miriam's voice echoed. She missed her visits. They were like reality checks. Still, it wasn't all bad. Jacinta had come over to spend a few weeks with them all and to meet Eduardo. And she kept Grainne busy, indulging her in every store they walked into. Deirdre didn't mind. Grainne had been so well behaved that Deirdre had to believe that, even though she would never admit it, Grainne missed her brother when he was away at school.

Eduardo and Jacinta were getting along too. She'd even started to use his name when she talked about him. And he referred to her as *Dona* and treated her like his own mother—and far better than her own son ever had.

"And I"—he had puffed himself up when she mentioned the fiesta—"will cook *tipo de peixe* for *Senhora* Boyle."

"Is that Mexican?"

"Dee-dree. *Sardinhas.*"

"Ah, I'll make sure we have the fire brigade on standby. You do know in this house fiesta night means Mexican?"

"Dee-dree, we're in Canada. Let's try to be more multicultural."

"Okay, but you're messing with tradition and I won't be held responsible."

"For what? For bringing those you love together?"

"Please don't mention love. We have a bit too much of that going on."

"You're still worrying over Martin and Rachael?"

"They're too young to know who they want to spend the rest of their lives with."

"They've already found each other. Why should they look for anything else?"

She had no answer, so she laughed and kissed him. "You're the last of the great romantics, you know that?" And so was Martin. He would love Rachael the way his father should have loved her. It made her proud, but it made her sad, too, and a little guilty. All that had happened between her and Danny had made Martin far too serious for someone his age. And he was in such a hurry—wasting time was abhorrent to him.

"And there's one other little thing. Martin's been bugging me to invite Rachael's parents over."

"Good. It will be good for us to meet them. We'll all be one big happy family one of these days."

"I'm not so sure about that. Martin tells me they don't get on very well."

"Good. Maybe our love can inspire them." He took her into his arms and nuzzled behind her ear while his hands traced down her spine and gently pressed her against him.

"I can't leave you two alone for a minute," Martin chided as he came through the patio door with Rachael in tow. "Sorry." He smiled over his shoulder. "They're at it again."

"What?" Eduardo puffed up his chest and stood between Martin and his mother. "I'm not afraid to show the whole world that I'm in love with the most beautiful woman I've ever seen." He raised Deirdre's hand and kissed it.

"Shucks," was all Deirdre could manage.

"Ew."

"Martin!" Rachael pushed him away, "You're beginning to sound like Grainne. Besides, I think it's cute. I wish my parents were more like yours."

Eduardo loved when they included him as family, but sometimes got carried away. "And, as the senior man in the house, may I extend an invitation to your parents to join us for a Portuguese-Irish fiesta."

"Fiesta?" Grainne bundled in with her shopping bags. "Are we having a fiesta? Oh, Granny, you're going to love it."

"I hope so." Jacinta fussed her way through them all and sat on a stool by the counter. "Only it sounds awfully foreign to me. No offense," she added in Eduardo's direction.

*

And afterwards, after everyone had gone home or gone to bed, Deirdre sat by her night stand brushing out her hair. Her skin was still dark from their trip to the Algarve. She wore her long satiny, pearl nightgown and waited for Eduardo to come up.

He had put the bones of the *sardinhas* in the recycling bin and the racoons had got to them. She had told him they would, so she didn't feel bad that he had to go back down. Besides, it gave her time to get ready. Watching him all night, being the man-of-the-house, made her realize how much she loved him. And when he came to bed she would show him how much.

Afterwards, as they lay entwined, she was still quivering in his arms. Despite a few awkward moments their multi-cultural fiesta had been a great success. Eduardo had been at his charming best and paid a lot of attention to Rachael's mother, topping up her wine glass and showing her the correct way to eat *sardinhas*, from head to tail. It was too much for Adina who, after a margarita and a few glasses of Portuguese wine, was almost flirting back. She seemed like a nice person, shy and reserved at first, but she warmed as the evening went on.

For the most part her husband, Joel, ignored her and attached himself to Jacinta, who was sitting by the trolley Eduardo had designated the portable bar. After telling her that she was far too young looking to be Martin's grandmother he went on to tell her how much he admired the Irish. "A race of noble poets and dreamers who set the world afire with their passion for justice and equality for all."

Jacinta had glanced at Deirdre to see if he was taking the piss before replying. "Ah, now, Mr. Brand, I wouldn't go that far."

"Please, call me Joel, and please let me get you another drink." He was hitting it a bit hard but Jacinta could keep up—no bother.

"I will then, but you must call me Jacinta."

"Jacinta. Isn't that a Spanish name?"

"I suppose it is, but my mother said she loved the sound of it. And I like your name. It's very . . . fancy."

"It's Jewish."

"Is that a fact? Wonderful people, the Jewish. We have Jewish neighbors back in Dublin. They're the nicest people you could hope to meet."

"Yes." Joel nodded like he had heard it far too often. "We can be when we're not making a cult out of all we have suffered."

"Sure the Irish are like that too."

"Maybe, but did the Irish condemn seven hundred thousand of their own people to death?"

And before Jacinta could answer, Adina scolded him for talking politics. "Can we not have one evening that is free from the past," she hissed at him while everyone pretended they didn't notice. Poor Rachael looked as if she wanted the ground to swallow her.

"I realize that people get offended by the things I say and I'm sorry about that," Joel explained to Jacinta. "But I can't look the other way and pretend I don't know what really happened."

"Ah sure, don't worry about it. We have the same thing back in Ireland. Deirdre's father ..."

Doug, of all people, saved the day by showing up uninvited and disturbing everything before settling between Grainne and Rachael. "So, dudes, what's happening?"

"I don't remember inviting you." Deirdre jumped at the chance to change the subject.

"Grainne did."

"Oh?"

"Beer?" Martin had asked, but Eduardo beat him to it and refreshed all their drinks.

"Well, all in all it was a success." Deirdre stroked Eduardo's skin as she lay with her head on his chest. "Though it was touch and go there for a while. Poor Rachael."

"What was it that *Dona* Jacinta was about to say about your father?"

"Never mind. You'll find out." They had agreed to visit Ireland at Christmas. Her parents were getting old and there might not be too many more chances.

"Do you think he'll like me?"

"Well, he used to hate Danny but then he got to like him."

"So he'll like me?"

*

"Ah, Danny, pet, they're just getting on with their own lives. You can't spite them for that."

"I don't, Ma. I just find it hard to believe they can forget about me so easily after all I did for them."

They had met for lunch at the Rose and Crown. Jacinta had been putting it off. She wasn't in the mood for him and all his darkness—not after spending such a great time with Deirdre and the kids. But she had to. "Ah, Danny, you don't really mean that. They're still your own flesh and blood."

"Yeah? Well maybe you should remind them of that the next time you all get together for a barbecue with him. My own feckin' family—behaving like he was their father."

"Well, son, I'm sorry that you feel that way but I'm happy for them and, if you want to point fingers, you might want to have a look at your own behavior."

"Yeah, like you were a saint."

"Ah, now son, I've made my fair share of mistakes. And your father, too, God love him, but you have to take a long hard look at yourself too. You're the one that did this to yourself and it's time you stopped trying to blame everybody else for it."

"Jazus. Now even my own mother is turning against me."

"No, Danny, I'm not. I'm still on your side, only you're not. You're the one who has turned against you."

"Ah, the cult of motherhood. You all stick together, even against your own."

"They're my family, too, Danny, and I hope one day you'll remember what that means."

That night, as she fell asleep in the beautiful bedroom that Deirdre had decorated so perfectly, Jacinta cried quietly so that nobody else could hear. She cried for her son, Daniel Bartholomew Boyle, who was slipping down into a hell of his own making while his children slept like angels. And when she was done crying she looked to the ceiling. She had done what she had promised and brought peace to Mrs. Flanagan. Was there still to be no peace for her own son?

*

It was a peaceful afternoon in Rome. The summer had passed and the cool fall was thinning out the crowds. Life went on, and it was Signore Pontecorvo's turn to look after John Melchor. Miriam had taken a teaching position so he and Giovanni, along with an assortment of nieces and nephews, kept the old Jesuit occupied. It wasn't hard. Davide Pontecorvo just let him loose in the back room of the store. It was where they stored the boxes of books that had come in and not yet been shelved.

His granddaughter drove John over and, when she wasn't busy, stayed to help. She said the old priest had sad eyes, just like her grandfather. She said the only time they brightened up was when he was reading. Tivia was an old soul that was still wandering in a changing world.

She made coffees for them, too, and served them with *biscotti*. "For the *studioso*." She always laughed as the old men looked up. Then she would sit between them and make them tell her what they had been reading. She reminded Davide of his sister who was stolen and, while that sometimes made him sad, it also made him smile.

"And what are you reading today, Padre?" she asked after she had settled the tray between them.

"I found a copy of Giordano Bruno's *De Magia*, the Toccu edition from 1891."

"Where did you find that?" she asked her grandfather.

"I have my sources but"—he winked and touched the side of his nose—"a Pontecorvo never tells."

"*Nonno*, you have so many mysteries."

"It was hard to find, and I got a copy of *Cabala del Cavallo Pegaseo*. They are a special order for a friend."

"Who still reads these things?"

"Patricio."

"Patricio Irlandese?"

"Yes, he has developed an interest in the old heretic."

"I wonder why?"

"Because of his uncle," John commented without looking up, not even when he sipped his coffee. "Patrick and Bruno are destined to become very close friends."

Tivia and Davide exchanged glances but didn't say anything, like they had seen it all before.

*

Christmas in Dublin was a total disaster. It hadn't stopped raining and Eduardo wanted to go sightseeing.

"Take one of the kids," Deirdre suggested distractedly. It had been non-stop since she got off the plane. She had forgotten her parents had become old and her children were being difficult, so she was trying to compensate. Martin was love sick and had to be by the phone all day, and Grainne only wanted to go shopping. They hadn't brought Rachael, and Deirdre was regretting it now. "Or ask my father. I'm sure he'd love to show you around. And it would give you guys some time together."

Her father had received him very well, calling him a "cut above." But couldn't get his name right and had taken to calling him "Eddie."

"He's forgetting everything."

Her mother had taken her aside when she first arrived, to kiss and hug her in private in case they didn't get another chance.

"Your father?"

"Sure. Dad!" Deirdre called into the living room. "Eduardo wants to go sightseeing and who knows Dublin better than you?"

"In this weather?"

"No, Mr. Fallon, I couldn't ask that of you."

"Do you not think I'm up for it? Us Irish are made of stern stuff. I will if we can stop in at the Yellow House on the way home. I want to introduce you to all the lads. We don't get many Port-a-geeses over here. You'll be the talk of the parish."

Eduardo looked like he was being arrested as her father put his arms around his shoulder and puffed himself up. "I'd be honored to show you the finest city in all Europe. You don't mind me sayin' that? Only it's true. I'm sure your place is fine, too, but wait until you see me 'Jewel and Darlin' Dublin.'"

"Sorry," Deirdre mouthed as he left, but she had no choice. Her mother couldn't get things ready on her own. Her father had taken her aside to ask her to keep an eye on her. "She's not herself these days. She's getting very forgetful."

Her mother was standing by the kitchen table as if she was trying to remember something.

"Are the kids enjoying their holidays?" she asked as soon as she noticed Deirdre. "I wouldn't know them anymore; they've both gotten so grown-up."

"They're fine, Mammie. Everyone is fine. We're just a little jet-lagged. We'll get over it in a day or two."

"And are you fine? Are you happy with him?"

"Yes, Mammie, I'm very happy with him. Where's the turkey?"

"I had your father put it out in the scullery to keep cool."

"Why didn't you put it in the fridge?"

"Because your father had to buy the biggest one he could find and half a pig. He wanted to show Eduardo that we have good food in this country too."

"Wow." Deirdre struggled back with the large, featherless turkey in her arms, its neck dangling along before her. "A real turkey? I'm used to the ones that come in bags." And even as she said it she realized how much life had changed her.

"And how is Danny? Is there any hope for him, at all?"

"It's over between us, Mammie. I'm with Eduardo now."

"I know that, dear. It's just that I wish he had somebody to help him get back on the right track."

"Well it certainly isn't going to be me."

"Ah don't say that. We won't know until it's all over. What about that nice uncle of his?"

"He's dead, Mammie."

"Lord bless us and save us. When did that happen?" She was so shocked she had to sit down.

*

Deirdre woke when her father tried to creep down the stairs in the early morning. It was Boxing Day and everybody else was sleeping late. Eduardo was snoring. He had overdone it on the whiskey the day before, trying to fend off a cold.

"About Mammie," she began when she got to the kitchen.

Her father finished filling the kettle and placed it on the stove. "It's Alzheimer's."

He turned away before she could see his face and turned on the TV.

They both stood in horrified silence and watched images of the Indian Ocean rise and surge over everything.

*Tsunami,* she thought. *What a pretty name for something so terrible.*

# Chapter 9 – 2005

DESPITE ALL THE TERRIBLE THINGS THAT STILL WASHED OVER THE WORLD, Patrick Reilly sipped his morning coffee with a certain degree of satisfaction. He'd come a long way from the shy young lad from Windgap. He was now forty years a priest. His mammie was probably smiling down on him as he sat by his open window and watched life dawdle by on the quiet little streets of Trastevere. Patrick smiled when he thought of her while the rest of Rome bustled off to work.

He remembered her hair most of all. His father used to say that when he was first walking out with her it was the color of butter, but Patrick only remembered it as a brown, sandy bun with the few strands that always got loose. She had told him from the start: there was no greater calling in life. His father would nod along, not wanting to upset the apple cart, but after him there was only Patrick. Who was he going to give the farm to?

"Sell it off and take the money and enjoy yourselves," Patrick had encouraged them every time he came home for holidays. "You've been working all your lives and now the good Lord has decided to let you have a bit of rest."

"He'll make a grand priest." They would smile at each other as if they had been in cahoots all along, but his father kept the land until after his mother died. Only then did he sell it off, piecemeal. And even though his father had died at peace with it, it still bothered Patrick from time to time. But what else could he have done? Since he was little, the priesthood was all he ever talked about. And even after all the other children started saying he was a bit "serious" and began to avoid him, he knew: he was going to try to follow in the footsteps of the Fisherman.

When it was time, his uncle found him a place as a boarder with the Holy Ghosts at Rockwell. He even drove him there in a big black car. "This place used to be called 'The Scot College' back when they made men ready for the call. These days, most of them will only hear the call of the bar, and not the legal kind." He tried to make Patrick laugh. "But they'll teach you all you need to know, and by the end of it you'll know whether you'll want to or not."

"But I know now," Patrick had insisted as they drove up the gravel drive and the strangeness of it all started getting to him.

"Maybe, but you'll know better after. 'Amidst things of necessity changing, constancy.'"

"I beg your pardon, Uncle." Patrick had been feeling less and less sure since he left his mother and father waving from the gate to what had been his world, growing smaller and smaller. Almost insignificant now as the college towered over them.

"It's the school motto. You'd better get to know it."

He did, for the next six years. As everything else about him changed, Patrick found constancy in his studies. When the other boys began whispering about girls, he closed himself off so that the Holy Ghost could flow through him and everything he did. And even in the seminary, when the other young men assumed the airs and graces that would come with the collar, Patrick remained pious and humble. The god that he was dedicating his life to was the god of the poor and those who suffered. But in the year before his ordination he came to a realization: he really wanted to do some frontline work in a parish rather than become a teacher.

"You want to learn something about life before you try to teach it?" The bishop had laughed and assured him that he would arrange everything. He was good to his word and installed Patrick with Fr. Brennan. But as it turned out, Patrick wasn't really cut out for that. The whole business with Danny Boyle had proved it—he wasn't really able for the way things were done in the world.

And then there was his acting like a love sick schoolboy over Miriam. It was a wonder she ever forgave him. "It's a lonely life, Patrick," his uncle had warned him when he'd asked for parish work. "Not being able to hear or see the god we're supposed to intercede with."

Patrick wasn't concerned. Everything he had been taught said that if he asked on behalf of some poor sinner that had lost his way, God would act. But the killing of Anthony Flanagan was hardly the action of a loving, forgiving god. It was more like the terrible god of the Old Testament.

That type of thinking wasn't encouraged in Ireland, where the Church was woven into the fabric of the country, but here in Rome, with old stone pagans on every street corner, such heresy lingered on the breeze. And when he first came over and read his uncle's papers, the threads of everything he had accepted without question began to unravel. That was why he tried to lose himself in teaching—that he might rid himself of doubts with the words of those who were far more certain.

Like François-Marie-Paul Libermann, who had come into the world as Jacob Samsonssohn, to a family that wandered Europe, running from pogroms and forced conversion. His father had been a rabbi and the poor man had to shun his own son, closing the gates of the ghetto on him when he had accepted the Messiah.

Patrick had read all about him in a book that Davide Pontecorvo had found for him, *The Life of the Venerable Francis Libermann*, and often found comfort in the passage that read,

> Then it was that, remembering the God of my fathers, I cast myself on my knees and implored Him to enlighten me regarding the True Religion.

He'd remembered it every time he felt like one of those that Joe had described long ago as "tearing the collar off and running, screaming into the world."

Joe had stuck it out, too, deep in the bowels of the archdiocese, working with legal teams to save what could be saved; but it was John Melchor that kept Patrick going. Him and Liebermann:

> I conjured him to make it known to me that the
> belief of Christians was true, if it was so; but if
> it was false, to remove me instantly far from it.

John seemed to know what he was going through. He missed nothing with his Jesuit eyes and had smiled when he reminded Patrick,

> The Lord, who is near to those who invoke
> him with their inmost soul, heard my prayer. I
> was at once enlightened; I saw the truth; faith
> penetrated my mind and heart. Setting myself
> to read Lhomond, I assented easily to all that it
> recounted of the life and death of Jesus Christ.

Patrick had never spoken of his doubts to Giovanni, but he and Signore Pontecorvo seemed to sense them too. They both had a depth that was almost disconcerting. Especially Signore Pontecorvo. It was as though he had absorbed all that was contained between the covers of the tattered books he'd spent his whole life with, absorbing all their joy and pain, and the wisdom that came from knowing both. "When the words of God become the law of man," he often reminded Patrick, "then even the most loving god becomes a stern judge."

He met them all for dinner at Giovanni's. Miriam brought John, who was calmer these days, and Tivia drove her grandfather and agreed to stay, after much coaxing. Patrick was happy that she did. She was so young, and everything around him was so terribly old. Even Miriam, who was turning into an old lady.

It was even beginning to happen to him. First it was his hands, and then the face that looked back at him from mirrors and shop windows.

"Congratulations," they all remarked, and raised their wine glasses several times during the meal and again when it was time for the older men to go home to bed.

Patrick wasn't tired and wandered for a while, thinking on all that the day brought back. And because it was the day it was, he walked to the Campo De' Fiori and stood to look up at Bruno. It was time he started facing up to things.

*

Danny never liked Eduardo, and seeing him again recon-firmed it. They were around the same age, but Eduardo was one of those guys that always looked as if he were going on a date or something. He was wearing jeans, but they were dark blue and fitted him right. Danny's were faded and stained, and sagged around the crotch as if he'd slept in them. He had. After Grainne had gone to bed he'd passed out on the couch while he was watching TV and having a few nightcaps.

Even though it was Sunday Eduardo was clean shaven, and Danny could smell his aftershave from a few feet away. And he had sharp-looking gray shoes. Danny was wearing his tat-ty runners and hadn't shaved since Thursday morning. He got away with it on casual Fridays, though they wouldn't let him wear his sweat pants. They'd even given him a written warning.

He didn't really give a shit anymore. He was hung over most mornings and his new supervisor was a real bitch, calling meetings first thing and expecting him to contribute. And she called spot meetings right after lunch. That wasn't so bad; he'd chew mints and say it was because he'd had something garlicky. She tried leaning closer to him a few times until he joked that he might have to file a complaint about her invading his per-sonal space.

"Hi Danny. Is Grainne ready?" He acted all friendly, look-ing him straight in the eye and all, but he was probably just taking a mental picture so he could describe it all later when he was back with Deirdre.

"Yeah." Danny smirked trying to be cool. "Grainne," he called back into his apartment.

He had finally persuaded her to come over again and she had spent the weekend. It was hard on them both. She wanted to be with her friends and he wanted to relax and have a few beers. They both tried, but things could never be the way they once were.

When she came out, Eduardo took her overnight bag and she kissed him on the cheek and turned to go.

"Don't forget to say goodbye to your father and thank him."

She turned and waved at Danny, but he was already turning to go inside.

"Piss on him, anyway," he repeated as he poured himself a beer and a stiff shot. "The greasy, slimy bastard. Who the hell does he think he is anyway, acting like he's her father?"

He fumed about it all evening as he finished the whiskey, and the beer was almost gone. He always kept one for the morning in case he woke up with the drys—something that was beginning to happen more and more. He was a bit wobbly as he pissed and avoided looking at himself as he splashed cold water on his face. He thought about brushing his teeth but he'd just have to do it again in the morning.

Besides, he was getting the spins and didn't want to risk leaning over the sink. He left the bathroom light on and turned off the light in the bedroom. He left his clothes in a pile on the floor and climbed into bed in his socks and underwear, bemoaning how life was treating him until he fell into a fitful sleep.

\*

"And how did he look to you?" Deirdre asked as she got ready for bed

"He looks like a man walking around without his heart."

"Perhaps he sold it to the devil?"

"Dee-dree, you don't mean that."

"No, I guess I don't, not really."

"You have won, Dee-dree. He is a broken man who knows that he has lost all that was really important in life."

"You could tell all that after just meeting him?"

Eduardo lay down beside her, took her hand in his and raised it to his lips. "It's how most men would feel. But all men are not willing or able to say it when it matters."

She kissed him goodnight and turned away. She'd been so busy calling Ireland every day that they still hadn't found the time to sit down and talk about it. He had gotten calls from his own children, who were old enough now to reach out on their own. He'd always wanted to see them but hadn't been allowed. He could have sued for access, but they both agreed that it would only make things more poisoned. Deirdre had said that he should just let some time pass and wait until they were ready. He accepted that and had suffered in relative quiet for a few years, not wanting to burden their relationship with it, but always probing for her opinion. She wanted him to see them and in time have them over, but she didn't say any of that, not until she was asked directly. She already had far too much to worry about.

*

"How was she?" Dermot Fallon asked as he shook the rain off his coat. Jacinta came over most afternoons to give him a break. Poor Anne couldn't be left alone anymore.

"Not a bother. We had a great time going through old photo albums. It's amazing what she remembers."

It was. Anne could remember the names of everyone in the old pictures, but she was unsure of those of her children and, from time to time, was surprised that she had children of her own.

"Yes," he agreed as he slumped into his chair. "Some days she's as sound as a bell."

He'd been down for a few pints and the smell of porter wafted toward Jacinta. She felt sorry for him. Of all the people she knew, he was the least capable of dealing with this type of thing. His daughters did all they could but they were away dealing with their own lives. They phoned almost every day, and Jacinta often got to talk with them. They preferred talking with her as their father was still reticent about what was happening.

"Dermot, what would you think of taking her to Rome?"

"Wouldn't Lourdes or Fatima not be better?"

He was still a pagan Catholic at heart but she ignored that. "Well, I know a priest in Rome that knows about things like this."

"Not the old bishop's nephew?"

"No, a friend of his. He's a Jesuit."

"A Jesuit, you say, but what could he do?"

"Well, I don't want you to be getting your hopes up but he has a way about him. He was a great help with Mrs. Flanagan."

"But Mrs. Flanagan was as mad as a hatter. Anne's not mad, you know. She's just getting lost."

"Mrs. Flanagan was lost too, in grief, and the Jesuit was able to help her. What harm could come from trying him?"

"Would you go with her?"

"I will indeed. Will you?"

"And what are you two planning?" Anne Fallon asked from the doorway.

"Ah, darling, you're up. I hope we didn't wake you. Mrs. Boyle and I were just talking about taking a trip to Rome. Would you like that?"

"Rome? I'd love to, only who will stay home and mind the children?"

*

Deirdre wasn't sure but kept her thoughts to herself. She knew there was no hope, but she couldn't say that to her father. He was grasping at anything, even as he blamed himself. He hadn't been a good enough husband to her mother.

She had tried to reassure him but he didn't want to hear. It was his Catholicism; everything that happened in his life was a result of his own behavior. His god didn't work in mysterious ways. His god rewarded the good and punished wickedness and, as Anne Fallon had never put a foot wrong, it was all down to him. She was paying for his pride and arrogance through the years. He'd even gone back to the church every morning he could and knelt down and repented.

"They should go," Eduardo agreed. "And you should go with them."

He had been seeing his children but still wasn't ready to really talk about it.

Deirdre wasn't worried for herself, but she knew his son was getting into trouble. He was seventeen, the same age as Grainne, and there were whispers that he was getting involved with drugs, something that his ex-wife didn't hesitate to blame on their broken marriage.

Perhaps she should go and give Eduardo the time and space to figure out what he was going to do. She didn't want to lose him, but he had to figure it out and he had to figure it out without her.

"Maybe I will."

Martin was taking an internship in Montreal for most of the summer and she could take Grainne with her. It would be nice for the two of them to spend some time together.

"Will you be okay here on your own?"

He took her in his arms but didn't answer, and that confirmed it. She would go, and when she got back they would sit down and have it out, for better or worse.

\*

The Hotel King on Via Sistina wasn't what Deirdre and Grainne were expecting, but Jacinta said it was close to everything and they could all be together. She also warned them to make sure they got rooms on the other side of the courtyard. The first two floors on the front had been converted into a theatre, and the

finales could echo right up into the bedrooms. "Arias for lulla-
bies and sweet cakes for breakfast, and just beside the Spanish
Steps. What more could you ask for?"

Internet connection would have been nice, but the tall
woman who checked them in said they didn't have it—as if it
was not important.

"But we need it," Deirdre and Grainne said, almost in
chorus.

"The café on the corner," the tall woman advised, patron-
izingly, and handed them their key, attached to a large brass
medallion. "You can get internet for free there. And pizza," she
added for Grainne's benefit.

Deirdre checked her room number before asking, "Are we
away from the front?"

"Si. Signora Boyle already spoke with us."

She smiled as she said it and her face grew a little warmer.
Her hair was dyed a dark red and almost matched her lipstick,
and her cheek bones were high, making her eyes seem deep and
dark.

"Grazie." Deirdre smiled and picked up her bags.

"Prego," the tall woman answered, and looked her up and
down as she walked away.

The room was basic but charming. Faded since the days of
*La Dolce Vita*, but so much nicer than the cookie-cutter same-
ness Deirdre had grown used to on her business trips. Shaded
and facing the east, it was cool even though the afternoon was
still hot.

"Can we go now?" Grainne asked again after she emptied
her bags and stuffed her things into drawers.

"What's the hurry?"

Deirdre was still carefully folding and hanging the selected
pieces she had brought. She hadn't brought a lot and hoped to
get some shopping in—as well as helping out with her mother, of course. The others had gone out for the afternoon but
had left a message that they would all meet up for dinner. Her

father had dragged them out on a tour of churches, Jacinta had added in her childlike handwriting.

"I want to have my first Roman pizza."

"And check your Myspace?"

"Maybe."

"Checking to see if anyone is missing you?"

"Mom! Besides, maybe I'm hoping to find a boyfriend here."

"Me, too, kiddo. Me too."

And even though they were separated from all they loved they were happy together as they walked down the hill toward the *Piazza Barberini*, pretending to ignore all the passing glances.

*

"The *Piazza Navona*?" Patrick asked after Miriam had explained the plan over the phone. "It'll be full of tourists this time of year."

"I know," Miriam agreed, "but Mrs. Boyle is the tour manager and you don't want to cross her, do you?"

"Certainly not. Is John going to be there too?"

"He better be—he's part of the tour. Deirdre said that Mrs. Boyle asked me to make sure he was coming. I'm just going to pick him up."

"Will he be all right?"

"He'll be fine. He's so much better these days." She didn't say it, but it was implied: Patrick hadn't been as available as he once was. He had become overly introspective lately. "See you then?"

"Of course, Miriam. I'm looking forward to it."

"It won't be as bad as you're expecting—Deirdre and her daughter will be there."

"No Danny, I suppose?"

"No, but I'm sure there'll be news of him."

"I'm sure there will."

*

As the evening began to cool and crowds eddied back in from the shade, Jacinta and the rest of them took their seats on a patio just across from another Bernini's tribute to the pagan river gods. The waiters, sensing windfall, converged from all sides, making a fuss and recommending only the best.

Pastas: *alla Carbonara* for Jacinta and *all'Amatricana* for Miriam; Gnocchi *alla Romana* for Anne, who couldn't decide for herself but had always liked potatoes. John chose the pasta *ai Cariocfi* while Patrick picked the *Fiori di Zucca* and Deirdre and Grainne opted for the *fettuccine Alfredo* as it sounded more familiar. Only Dermot remained and wanted something with meat.

"Carne." The waiter nodded and recommended the *saltimbocca alla Romana*.

"I hope I like it. Does anybody know what it is?"

"It's veal," Miriam reassured him, "with ham. I'm sure it will be very good."

"So, Mr. Fallon, are you enjoying Rome?" Patrick asked after the bruschetta arrived and they all dove in.

"I am indeed, Father, and I give thanks to God that I was spared long enough to have the chance to see it for myself."

Patrick had seen it all before. A few days in the basilicas could make even the most lapsed a believer again. His uncle used to laugh at that. "They only have to see and touch a bit of the spectacle of God's grandeur—then they'll be the best of believers again for a while."

"You can't help but be affected," Dermot added with a faraway look in his eyes.

"But do you not think that it might be better if they used all they had to make life better for the sick and the poor like they used to?" Jacinta sipped her wine and tried to appear earnest.

"Ah, now, Mrs. Boyle, don't you think the good Lord deserves a bit of honor in His holy name?"

"I don't think he'd care one way or the other. I think he'd be happier if we did what he asked us to do. Don't you, Father?"

"Well," Patrick hesitated and sought the middle ground. Miriam was deep in conversation with Deirdre but smiled over at him. "I suppose we all have different ways of showing our love."

*

"Either way," Deirdre said softly so only Miriam could hear, "we will do whatever is right, whether or not it is right for us."

"That's very noble of you."

"Not really. We both agreed that our children would always come first."

"Are you sure that ending your happiness will do anything for his son. You know what addicts can be like."

"I do, but I also know that I don't want our relationship to be blamed in any way."

"No reasonable person would ever think of doing that."

"And that's the problem, Miriam. His wife is not a reasonable person."

"A woman scorned?"

"Like a scalded cat."

*

"I am so happy," Anne Fallon confided in Grainne as they shared a large dish of gelato. "I always wanted to bring you and your sister here."

"You mean my brother." Grainne wasn't really listening. Her head was on a swivel, watching all that passed in the piazza.

"No, dear, I mean you and your sister—Deirdre. I've been after your father for years but the time was never right before." She raised another spoonful to her lips and shivered in anticipation. "But at least we're all here now."

When Grainne realized what her grandmother had said she looked around, but everybody else was busy in their own conversations; except John Melchor, who had been sitting silently, watching and listening to Anne Fallon.

*

"What we must arrange," Miriam decided as they all stood around waiting to take their leave, "is a shopping day."

"My two girls will love that," Anne agreed, causing a little ripple.

"But," Dermot asked before she could say anything else, "didn't you want to come to the Vatican with me?"

"Maybe," Jacinta jumped in, "she's seen enough churches for a while?"

"But we're in Rome."

"And we'll do as the Romans do," Miriam decided. "I'll call our friend Tivia and see if she has time to show us all the best places. You'd like that wouldn't you, Grainne?"

"I guess so." Grainne smiled. She looked doubtful about shopping with a bunch of old women but agreed.

"You and I can go to the Vatican," John offered when Dermot looked like he might sulk. "And we can bring Patrick too."

"Grand so," Jacinta announced. "It's all decided."

*

Tivia met them at Babington's, at the bottom of the Spanish Steps. Jacinta couldn't start her day without a proper cup and the tea at the hotel was "nothing but hot, colored water." Only she didn't complain too much as Deirdre, Grainne and Anne all enjoyed having breakfast there, sitting outside on the terrace, stuffing themselves with sticky pastries as if they'd never seen them before. Even Dermot, too, helping himself to the scrambled eggs as if there was going to be a shortage.

"We will begin on Via Condotti," Tivia began as she moved her dark glasses up like a hair band. "It is where we have the *haute couture*. But we will just look," she added when Deirdre looked a little worried. "And then we go along Via del Corso where all the young shops are. But there, we no shop either. For that we go to Porta Portese and Via Sannio. That's where the smart Romans shop—in the market for fleas?"

"Flea markets?"

"Si." She laughed at herself and headed toward the door. "Signora? We go windows shopping now?"

"Si," they all agreed and gaggled along behind her, Jacinta taking Anne by the arm as they went across the Piazza Di Spagna and into the warren of narrow streets beyond. "There won't be anything like Dunnes," she explained. "It's all very hoity-toity around here, but I'm sure we'll find something further down." Anne didn't seem to mind and just smiled to herself as the sun peeped down between the rooftops.

"Now that"—Deirdre paused in front of a boutique window—"is just made for me." It was a long, dark blue gown, strapped around the shoulders and gathered around the waist. It would be perfect for a night out with . . . anybody.

"It's fifteen thousand euros." Miriam had looked inside as Deirdre positioned her reflection so she could see what it might look like on. "That's like a gazillion dollars."

"Not to worry. I'm sure I can get a deal on it at the market for fleas."

They giggled like young girls until Tivia looked back at them.

"Soon we come to the young people's shops." She sympathized as Grainne lingered by another street corner while the others dawdled along.

"I don't mind."

"No," Tivia agreed and smiled. "Not when you have all the men in Rome watching you?"

"Really?"

"Prego. So do you have a boy back home?"

"Yes, only my mother doesn't know."

"She will not like him?"

"Oh, see knows him. She just doesn't know about us."

"How romantic. What is his name?"

"Doug, but don't tell anybody."

"Don't tell anybody what?" Deirdre caught up with them.

"She said we must look for a gown like that at the flea market." Tivia smiled sweetly and gave Grainne's hand a little squeeze.

*

While Dermot Fallon bowed at every craven image and blessed himself as though he was swatting flies, John Melchor walked serenely among the whisperings. The Society of Jesus had been gracious once more, but they had made it clear too: he was to see his days out quietly. Even Miriam and Patrick warned him that he couldn't be running around like a mad man. It made him smile, even as he watched the pilgrims file in and out. Madness had to be observed with silent reverence. That was the way of the world he had helped to shape, for good and bad.

"Father." Dermot Fallon approached, whispering penitently. "Will you say a prayer with me—for my Anne's sake?"

John hesitated. He hadn't been asked to act as a priest in so long. "I would be delighted."

They knelt together for a while until John rose and helped the other man to his feet. "We have prayed for your wife, my friend, and I have prayed for you. You don't need to worry about your wife anymore. She is not mad. Most of her mind is already with God."

Dermot Fallon kneeled before him again in a darker corner and kissed his hand. "Thank you, Father, and may God bless you."

John withdrew his hand slowly so as not to give offense and walked toward Patrick.

"Do you really think you should be telling him things like that?" Patrick whispered, while Dermot distributed his loose change evenly among the collection boxes strategically placed for the grateful.

"Patrick, there is no harm in giving some comfort."

"Even if it's false?"

"Hope is nothing without Faith."

\*

Those words stayed with him, right through another dinner with them all, and while he walked John home, Patrick knew he had to go back. It wasn't far and it was late enough that most of the tourists would be gone.

When he got there, he stood and looked up into Bruno's face. "And what do you think I should do?"

*What harm can it do?*

"That was Johann Tetzel's argument too."

*Oh, Patrick, you were always such a serious young man. Tetzel was just trading on futures. I hear that's all the rage these days. Even our own bank is up to it.*

"I suppose you're right."

*I usually am—when I'm not wrong.*

"You're getting very humorous in your . . ."

*Old age? I'm done with all that.*

"Why are you still here?" He'd been meaning to ask for so long.

*Well now, Patrick, there're two reasons. The first is that I'm getting to enjoy some well-deserved time with Benedetta. We're getting the chance to be together now. And, while I'm on the subject, spend more time with that friend of yours. You're both old enough now not to create too much scandal.*

"And what was the other reason?" Patrick asked after his uncle had been silent for a while.

*Actually there're two, Bart and Nora Boyle.*

"About Danny?"

*Yes, about Daniel Bartholomew Boyle. I can't face them until he is right. I promised them both I'd keep an eye on him.*

Patrick stood for a while and considered it all. That was a part of life too. It was a web of interconnectivity, no matter how hard he tried to avoid it. It was about lives that were woven together. Not all the time, but they were all part of each other's story.

Still, he was reticent and who could blame him. He had tried with Danny Boyle. He might even have done some good.

But problems like Danny's were beyond him. Other than offering the same old platitudes, what could he do? He knew so little about the demons that haunted Danny. Still, he was a priest and he was duty bound to help in whatever way he could.

"And what is it that you would have me do?"

# Chapter 10 – 2006

DANNY WASN'T TOO IMPRESSED WHEN THE NEWS OF THE TRIP FILTERED BACK TO HIM, but what really bothered him was when he vomited all over the new shirt Grainne had brought back and given him for Christmas.

It was more like something that Eduardo would wear, but he liked it. He had worn it every time he went out and for the last few months he hadn't felt so shabby. Only now he'd gone and puked all over it. He had stopped for a burger on the way back from McMurphy's and it hadn't sat well. He'd had a bit of a bug lately and couldn't keep things down—that and the seven pints he had knocked back while the lads, Ryan and McInerney, came and went about their lives.

It was another miserable February and he couldn't take much more of the cold and the mounds of dirty snow. But at least he didn't have to shovel it anymore. And, if fate would ever finish shittin' on him, he might even win the lottery one of these days and go south until Paddy's Day.

After he showered, and left his shirt soaking in the sink, he sat in bed with the TV on and watched a rerun of *Amadeus*. He saw a bit of himself in Mozart. Not the music part—the part that was all messed up. And he could drink as much as him. Or he used to be able. These days it was taking such a toll on him, but there was nothing he could do anymore.

McInerney and Ryan had been at him about it too. They said that he'd done a great job being off it for so long, and now he was in danger of sliding all the way back down. He didn't mind. He knew they were only trying to look out for him. They were good friends—the only ones he still had.

Frank had packed up and moved to Africa to teach kids carpentry with some churchy agency. He said he wanted to spend the rest of his life just giving back. That made Danny feel guilty—along with the shame of having gone back on the drink.

He had to admit it; he was getting as bad as ever. Some nights when dehydration woke him—not that he slept much anymore, tossing and turning while being tormented by the horrible things that lurked in the dark—he'd make resolutions. He'd go back to meetings one of these days. It mightn't have been the answer, but it was better than being like this.

He'd stop smoking, too, and he'd get himself in some kind of shape again. There hadn't been anybody since Billie. She still called him every once in a while, but he always acted cool as if he were still pissed at her over Grainne. Only that wasn't the reason. He was a mess and he didn't want her to see him like that. Although he did think about her on those nights when he wasn't so drunk and jerked off remembering all the things they used to do together.

Drinking, drinking, and masturbation. He often laughed sardonically as he enjoyed an "afters" smoke. His life never really changed that much no matter what he did. And if anybody tried to help him—they just got screwed over too. They all had: his uncle, Deirdre, Billie, his mother—he couldn't even think of her without getting teary eyed. And seeing the bit about *Don Giovanni* didn't help. His father had asked him to keep an eye on her the last time they spoke.

He would, he resolved as he wiped away his tears. He'd get organized and have his mother move over with him. She was getting far too old to be looking after herself, and she could get him to look after himself a bit better too.

He'd have to get Deirdre to give him his share of the house, but she wouldn't mind. Not if he stopped drinking again. Even his son would have to start cutting him a break now and then.

He saw him briefly at Christmas. They met for lunch, but Danny could tell he clearly didn't want to be there. His girlfriend did and was friendly, but it was all very stiff and painful. He got drunk after they left, but who could blame him? Drinking was the only way guys like him and Wolfgang could cope. The rest of the world just didn't understand them. And, as he lay in his bed watching Mozart dictate his requiem, Danny began to cry again.

Mozart was one of the lucky ones. He could put all his pain and suffering into something that would live forever. Danny's legacy wouldn't be so grand. He couldn't watch anymore and switched the channel, but it wasn't any better. He loved Bill Murray but *Groundhog Day* was far too close to the bone.

In the morning, when the alarm finally woke him, he knew what would happen. He'd reach into the fridge for a beer and forget about the resolutions he'd made the night before. He had no choice. He couldn't face the day without something to settle him down and calm the trembling in his hands. And tomorrow was going to be tough. He was up before HR again, and this time they were going to stick it to him. The union rep told him he'd be better off going on long-term disability for a while. At least until the heat was off. He had no choice really; they'd been out to get him for years. The man-haters were getting even and there was nothing he could do about it except fume and rant at the darkness.

"There are two days in every week about which we should not worry, two days which should be kept free from fear and apprehension," they used to say at meetings.

When he first heard it he always thought they were referring to Saturdays and Sundays.

"One of these days is Yesterday, with all its mistakes and cares, its faults and blunders, its aches and pains. Yesterday has passed forever beyond our control."

"That's all very well," he argued with the darkness. "But try telling that to all the people who have the knives out for me." But it was his own fault; he should've known better. That was another reason he needed a drink every morning. "Each new beginning is the start of the next failure," his father used to remind him when he was young. He missed him now and sometimes wished things could have been different between them.

*All the money in the world cannot bring back yesterday. We cannot undo a single act we performed; we cannot erase a single word we said. Yesterday is gone forever.*

"Feck it," he decided. He'd never get to sleep like this. He fetched a few beers and placed them on his nightstand. He'd be wrecked for the meeting and they'd all be delighted to see him like that—like he was proving their point for them.

*The other day we should not worry about is Tomorrow, with all its possible adversities, its burdens, its large promise and its poor performance; tomorrow is also beyond our immediate control.*

This time the voice was outside his head, something that hadn't happened since Anto.

*Tomorrow's sun will rise, either in splendor or behind a mask of clouds, but it will rise. Until it does, we have no stake in tomorrow, for it is yet to be born.*

"Look. I don't know who the hell you are, or what you want, but would you ever go and haunt some other poor fecker and leave me in peace. Haven't you heard—haunting doesn't work on me?"

*This leaves only one day, Danny. Today. Any person can fight the battle of just one day. It is when you and I add the burdens of those two awful eternities, Yesterday and Tomorrow, that we break down. It is not the experience of today that drives a person mad. It is the remorse or bitterness of something which happened yesterday and the dread of what tomorrow may bring.*

"Yeah, yeah, yeah. Let us, therefore, live but one day at a time. I know all that. Only it's one thing to be going on about it; it's another when everybody is out to get you."

*Nobody ever said it was going to be easy, Danny.*

His uncle's voice became clear and, for a moment, almost made him think about hope, but he deflected it. He wasn't getting back on that roller-coaster.

"I thought you'd given up on me."

*Never, Danny, never.*

"So why are you back then? Did ya miss me?"

*People are talking about you.*

"Don't ya think I know that?"

*Not the people you're thinking about.*

"Oh, great. Who else has it out for me?"

*Patrick Reilly.*

"Jazus, is he not dead?"

*Not yet, Danny, not yet.*

*There's no point getting all excited.* He calmed himself as the room went quiet again except for Bill Murray's alarm. He wasn't getting another chance. It was just his mind messing with him—getting his hopes up before it smashed him down again. He opened a beer and changed the channel. In the morning he'd take sick leave and feck the begrudgers. There was no point anymore—life was just one big shit heap. It always was and it always would be, and anybody who said otherwise was in denial.

*

When Patrick arrived, John was sitting outside the old bookstore in the early summer sunshine, flicking through the pages of an old copy of the Talmud. Miriam had dropped him off earlier and Patrick would pick him up and keep him occupied for the afternoon.

"I wouldn't go in," he advised as Tivia's voice reached them. She was always a bit excitable, but today she sounded really angry about something.

"What's going on?"

"Her brother is coming for a visit and Davide won't agree to see him."

"I didn't even know she had a brother. He never mentions him."

"He shunned him a few years ago."

"That's a shame. Did he join the Holy Ghosts?"

"Worse, he moved to a settlement in Palestine—occupied Palestine, according to his grandfather."

"Is he against all that?"

"He's a Torah Jew. He calls Israel the new 'Golden Idol.'"

John went back to his reading but Patrick knew he was waiting for his reaction. He never wanted to comment on what was going on in the Middle East. It was all too tribal and nobody could discuss it rationally.

"I don't suppose there's anything we can do? It's a shame to hear them like this."

"I'm trying." John raised the Talmud between them. "But everything in here seems to support the old man."

"I suppose you're right. Perhaps we should just sit back and let them sort it out themselves."

"That's pretty much what the world has decided too."

John might have calmed on the outside but Patrick could see the fire of passion still smoldering inside, smoldering old coals of heresy and truth. And whatever was happening inside the bookstore had come to a head, with Signore Pontecorvo using his most authoritative voice to issue what sounded like a stern command, while his granddaughter made the strangled sounds of total frustration.

"And you two," she snapped at them as she emerged in a tizzy. "I suppose you agree with him?" She put her hands on her hips and Patrick was afraid to look up. She had that fieriness that all the women of Rome had—an intensity they seemed to be able to call upon at will.

"Ah, Tivia, are you well?"

She looked like she was about to boil over but thought better of it and stormed off.

"Wait," John advised when Patrick rose to go inside. "Let our old friend regain his composure."

Patrick sat down beside the old Jesuit in the warm sun as the city rushed to get through the day. The World Cup was on and everyone had to have everything done in time to sit and watch the games undisturbed. The whole city was united in cheering for the *Azzurri*.

"Did you ever wonder," Patrick asked after Tivia had roared away in her angry red Fiat, "what it would be like to have a family of your own?"

"Hell no, life's hard enough. You and I only have ourselves to contend with and as we both know by now, that's more than enough."

"Oh to be an idle priest on a sunny day in Rome." Signore Pontecorvo greeted them as he came out. He had regained most of his composure and settled into the chair between them.

"And what would you have us do?" John asked. "Convert you?"

"It might yet come to that." The old bookseller tried to laugh but Patrick could see his heart wasn't in it.

*

Deirdre wanted to run upstairs and stop him from packing but she didn't. She just sat in her kitchen sipping a small glass of wine. She didn't really feel like drinking but she wanted something to hold in front her face in case her resolve wrinkled.

They had discussed it in a calm and considerate fashion and the only resolution they had been able to come up with was that he really had no choice but to move back to his family. He had cried, but she just held him against her and began the struggle back toward detachment.

He'd been spending more and more time with his children, and they were worried that their mother was going to kill herself—or at least that's what she kept telling them, wailing and moaning as she did.

She had also made it clear to anyone and everyone that the blame for their son's drug problems lay entirely on his infidelity—accusations that were echoing through the Portuguese part of town that was, even after fifty years, in many ways still a village unto itself.

Eduardo used to take her to College and Clinton for dinner on Saturday evenings, to "the Dip" or some new place he'd read about. There they would meet his friends—an eclectic bunch of Continentals and a few Brazilians to add spice. They were all darker than her and had flashing passions in their eyes. They were suave, educated and assured, and privileged enough to be able to speak about the world with a casual indifference while flaunting all things D&G.

She loved it. She loved sitting in her finest across from him so he could look at her all night. He would watch her lips while she was eating something exotic. And no matter who was talking, he only had eyes for her, even when his friends told her that the dish had once been the staple of slaves.

Or when they took turns trying get her name right. They were friendly enough, though it might have been the wine. They used to go through several bottles and various liqueurs, but that was with coffee after she and Eduardo had shared dessert.

"Do you really think they like me?" she sometimes asked in the cab back to Leaside.

"They love you."

"Are you sure? I don't think your cousin and his wife do."

"They're just jealous that we're happy. Miguel just spent their savings on a pool table and Maria wanted a new car."

"Really?"

"Yes, he grew up in a pool hall on St. Clair hustling Italians."

"No, I meant are they ever going to be okay with me being with you?"

"If they're my true friends, they will."

"I hope so. I can't go back to hanging out at Originals."

"What's wrong with Originals? I like it."

"You would. They're not your daughter's friends dressed like beer-slinging little sluts. Would you let your daughter do it?"

"No, but it's just young girls showing off their bodies."

"For tips?"

"Okay, we won't be going back to Originals."

His friends were true, and when everyone else stopped talking when he approached—and started again when he had passed—they said it straight to his face: he had to go back to his family.

Only not in so many words. More like in novellas that stretched out over weeks of lunches and hours of phone calls. "Everybody is telling me different things," he'd complained as he lay across her on the couch one night. "I don't know what to believe anymore."

She resented that and was about to say so, but what was the point? They would talk and talk, slowly drifting into argument, until he'd just shrug and ask her what she wanted him to do.

"Just look in your heart," she said as calmly and as bravely as she could, hoping against hope.

"But she's the mother of my children."

Deirdre couldn't compete with that. No matter where they went for dinner, or who they met, if his ex-wife actually did anything, she'd become the whore that had turned him away from his family.

She really wanted him to stand up to everybody and tell them all the things he'd told her; about how his heart wouldn't beat without her, how he couldn't bear a single day when he couldn't hear her voice. And about her kisses; how they were like manna to his very existence. But that wasn't fair; she knew he couldn't risk it.

Besides, she'd done the same thing when she let Danny back into her children's lives. No, she would have to be fair minded and noble about it all and let the scheming bitch have him back. If he really loved her he wouldn't . . .

That wasn't fair, either. He did love her. She was sure of that. But he loved his kids too. That was why she wouldn't make it any harder on him, or her.

When he came down the stairs he paused by the door, unsure if they'd said all that had to be said. He looked like such a lost little boy so she rose with her wine glass between them and walked closer to him. "Okay, then." She blinked as bravely as she could.

He couldn't face her and looked at his feet. "I wish," he mumbled, "there were some other way."

She wanted to take him in her arms and tell him that she didn't blame him, but she also wanted to kick out at him. Here, on the parting edge of everything they had been together, he was leaving her for someone he didn't even love anymore.

"Do you have everything?" She couldn't think of anything better to fill the awful silence.

"I think so." He tried to reach out to her but there was no point anymore.

"I'll drop by and pick up the rest later."

She just nodded. He would come by while she was at work and spare them any more goodbyes.

After she had leaned against the door and listened to him drive off she poured a larger glass, lit some candles, put on some Nora Jones and settled on the couch. And, sadly singing along with "What Am I To You?" she let herself cry for a while.

Later, when Grainne came home, she'd pick up the pieces again and get on with life. And after that, she'd get up each morning and go to the office where her dispassion and composure would be rewarded. But for now, in the privacy of her large, empty home, she would indulge her broken heart. And by the end of the song, when she had no more tears left, she would begin to glue the pieces back together again.

Love was such a transient thing anyway. It came and turned everything upside down and, just when you finally let down your guard and settled into it all, it left, leaving you alone and feeling broken. Only it had never broken her before. Not even Danny Boyle had managed that.

*

"Mom?"

"In here, sweetie."

"Is everything okay?" Grainne hesitated. The room was dark and the candles were spluttering.

"Come over here, sweetie," Deirdre made space for her on the couch. "I need one of your special hugs."

"Mom, I'm so sorry."

"Don't worry about me, sweetie."

She held her daughter against her, rocking slowly back and forth. "I'll be fine. I just needed to feel a little sorry for myself but I'm okay now." She drained the last of her wine, a dark, moody, Portuguese red, and roused the two of them. "We have corn chips."

"Fiesta." Grainne jumped up and changed the music. Ricky Martin could always get them dancing again.

"So?" Deirdre asked as they sipped from their salty glasses—their reward for doing all the chopping, dicing and grating, like best friends.

Grainne had been dealing with her own changes for a while but, between her mother's illness, and all the drama around Eduardo, Deirdre hadn't had a chance to have a real chat with her since Rome.

She'd seen a different side of her there, dashing around with her sunglasses on top of her head, just like Tivia. Even Miriam noticed. Grainne was becoming more confident and seemed far less concerned about what her friends thought.

Deirdre was happy about that. Life wasn't easy for young women, and all the changes she and Miriam had once endorsed hadn't proved to be too helpful. But sitting there over a platter of nachos, one half covered in ketchup, sipping margaritas, she couldn't help but feel that somehow everything was going to be all right, after the healing. She really wanted them to be able to talk like women but she wasn't ready for that. Not with her daughter.

"How's school?"

"Mom, I'm almost eighteen. Can't we talk about something else?"

"Yes, you're getting very grown up, but I'm still your mother and I want to make sure you are going to take advantage of all your potential."

"Mom, you don't have to worry about me anymore."

"Perhaps, but it is a very hard habit to break, so tell me."

"It's okay."

"Just okay?"

"Mom, it's just high school. You just show up and pretend you're interested."

"That's a bit cynical."

"Not really. Most of the other kids are on meds. Teachers are just happy if you seem like you're paying attention."

"It won't be like that when you go to university. Have you decided where you're going?"

Grainne wasn't sure but Deirdre was insistent. She had to get a degree. It didn't really matter which one.

"I'm thinking about OCA."

Deirdre would have preferred U of T. Grainne was smart enough to do anything she put her mind to. "Art?"

"Maybe."

"I see." It was a conversation they would have to have, but now wasn't the time. "Hey, how come I don't hear you talk about boys anymore?"

"Mom!"

"Well?" Deirdre knew she shouldn't but she couldn't help herself. It was so nice to be sitting chatting like friends.

"Okay, okay. I've gone out with Doug a few times."

"Our Doug? How long has this being going on?"

"Since Martin left for school."

"Does he know?"

"Who cares? It's nothing to do with him."

"He is your brother, sweetie, and Doug is his best friend. I don't think you should keep it from him."

"God! When are you going to stop interfering in my life?"

"Maybe after I'm dead, but I'm not making any promises."

Deirdre wasn't upset. She liked Doug and, right now, she liked being Grainne's mother. "I still think one of you has to tell him and"—she refilled their glasses—"I think it should be Doug."

"He's going to see him in a few weeks and can tell him then."

"Now, was that so hard? Sharing things with me is not as painful as you always make out. I used to be a young woman too." She managed to stop herself from saying: and then I met your father. But it wasn't really like that. She'd had a crush on Danny since the day they were Confirmed. And then, that day in the park, when they were stoned—it was like magic.

"Mom, do you ever miss being in love with Daddy?"

For a moment, Grainne looked like the little girl she once was. Where Martin had learned to be dismissive of his father, Grainne always seemed to be clinging to the hope that someday everything would be better and they could all be a family once again. They were the two sides of Deirdre's dichotomy. It might have brought her down despite the margaritas but she remembered all she'd learnt in her days in Al-Anon. "Yes, sweetie. I miss the times I was in love with your father. I still think of him."

"Really? Do you ever think about . . . you know . . . you guys . . . ever again?"

"Oh, Grainne, I'm afraid that ship has sailed. Let it go, sweetie." She sipped her drink and looked for the perfect thing to say. "I suppose one of the things that love has taught me is when to hold on and when to move on."

"Are you going to start seeing somebody new?"

"Young lady." Deirdre drew herself up and tried to look parental. "That's not really your business."

"But it was okay for you to ask me?" Grainne stuck out her lip as she did when she was a child. "I thought we were becoming friends."

"I'm your mother, sweetie, not your friend. And besides, I'm getting far too old for that type of thing.

"Mom, you're only forty-nine. That's like the new . . . thirty-nine.

*

"I don't know who you think you are but you're not my daughter. My Deirdre is only nine years of age."

Her mother looked at her the way she did when she was trying to tell if Deirdre was lying. It was breaking her heart. Her father had warned her on the phone, but it was still far worse than she'd wanted to believe. Her mother had been moved to a nursing home and he needed her to come home for a few days to help him deal with all the changes.

"Mammie, it's me. Please try to remember me." She said it the way she used to when she was a child, pleading to get her way. Her mother always softened to that. But that was before. Now Anne Fallon was reduced to sitting in a chair, staring out the window and waving at people who'd been dead for years. "It's like there's nothing left of her anymore," her father had warned.

"Of course I remember you, Mary, and I'm so glad to see you again."

Mary was her mother's sister who had emigrated to Australia and died a few years back. They hadn't seen each other in years. She was the one that everybody said Deirdre looked like.

"Come closer." Anne beckoned from her chair and Deirdre didn't hesitate. Her mother took her in her arms and whispered into her ear. "Promise me that you'll look after my Dermot and the girls when I'm gone. Promise me?"

Deirdre agreed as she lowered her head and cried into her mother's lap.

"There now, Mary, there now." Her mother stroked her hair as she used to.

\*

"I'm still not cool with it."

"Oh, Martin, you're such a cute big brother." Rachael linked his arm as they came out of The Pickle Barrel. The winds that swept the corners of Yonge and Eglinton in December could kill.

"Would you like it if it was your sister?"

"I would because it would mean having a sister. Oh, Martin, Doug's been your best friend since . . . forever. I hope you're not going to be like this when we have kids because I want a big family—all daughters too."

"Yeah, maybe you're right; but when we have daughters, I get to interview the guys in my office."

"We'll even get you one of those swinging lights that you can hit every now and then."

"I'll need a leather chair, too, so I can sit and crush nuts."

"Red or black leather?"

"I mean it. He just showed up one night and says, 'Hey, bro, let's go for beers. I got something I want to lay on you.' You don't lay that kind of thing on a guy in a bar."

"Was it a strip bar?"

"No. Why?"

"A strip bar would have been sleazy."

"It was a sports bar if that makes any difference—and I had to pay."

"Hey, when we're all married, Doug can be the brother-in-law that always borrows stuff."

"Great. And how many of your crazy relatives will we have to carry?"

"So, Doug is a relative now? And don't talk about my family; you know what things are like."

He did and he shouldn't have, because even having to deal with Doug, Martin was happy. They were home for the holidays and he always got excited for Christmas. Eduardo was gone and he wasn't too happy about that, but he could tell from the moment he got home that his mother was determined they would have a good time. Determined enough to make life difficult for anyone not willing to go along with family tradition.

She really made him laugh sometimes but he was always so proud of her. She'd given a talk to the graduating class last semester and blew everyone away. Especially the young women who flocked around her afterwards. Even guys did, but some of them said they were just hitting on her until he told them she was his mom.

"I'm sorry."

"Don't be. My father is perfectly happy being alone and miserable."

"But what about your mom?"

"She is happy making him miserable. She usually drags him out to see some horrible movie and makes him take her for coffee afterwards like they're dating."

"Wow, she must really hate him."

"So much that she can never leave him—for my sake."

"Are you sure we should get married and have kids? I mean, look at our families. It's a wonder we're both not strung out on crack."

"It's not funny, Martin. At least in your family people talk. In my house it's all silent gestures and knowing glances."

"You should write about it."

"Maybe I already am."

He kissed her by the CIBC, out of the wind. "You know, when we graduate I'm going to ask you to marry me."

"My father will have to interview you in his office."

"Red or black."

"Red of course."

"What's he crush his nuts with?"

"His head. Besides, he'll never accept you."

"Because I'm Irish? Don't worry. I inherited some of my father's charm. I'm sure I can come to some arrangement. Maybe we can do a deal with a few pigs and goats."

"You might do better with trucks and oil."

"Really?"

"Never mind. It's not going to be like that. I'm going to ask your mother if I can have your hand."

"She'll never go for it."

"She will if I can get you to lay off Doug over the holidays."

"So she got to you too?"

"And she asked if I wanted to invite my parents, but I said they were busy."

"Well I'm going to tell her they're not."

"Only if you invite your father. We can put them together."

Since she had met his father, Rachael seemed determined that Martin should reconnect with him. He didn't want to but he couldn't say no to her.

"You're father has suffered enough."

"So has yours."

"Is this what it's going to be like when we become Mister Boyle and Ms. Brand?"

"No. I'm changing my name."

"To Boyle?"

"Don't be silly. Fallon."

He smiled and kissed her again. He couldn't wait until she found her gift under the tree. A little silver Claddagh ring that Deirdre never wore anymore. It had been a gift from Danny, but she didn't mention that as Martin wrapped it in bright red paper.

# Chapter 11 – 2007

Two hours west of Clifden, Deirdre gave up and raised the blind a little. She'd never really been able to sleep on planes. Grainne and Martin had no such problems and slept against each other. In the low cabin light they looked like children again.

Outside there was nothing but miles and miles of pearly, fluffy clouds, growing brighter as they flew toward the dawn. It was like flying over heaven, and Deirdre couldn't help but look down in hopes of seeing her mother finally at rest on a soft, billowing seat.

She had died two days ago. She had slipped in the bath and drowned. Her father had just gone to fetch something and had left her alone. "I was only gone for a minute," he'd explained through his tears when he called.

Deirdre hadn't taken the time to cry yet. She'd been too busy rearranging life so she could fly over. And coordinating the kids, who'd dropped everything and hurried to join her in waiting at check-ins, security and gates. They talked but they were careful not to say anything too meaningful until they arrived. It was how they got through stuff. She wished they didn't have to be so drilled but it was the only way of really handling things. Her mother hadn't slipped. She had said her goodbyes—only not in so many words.

Deirdre didn't know how to feel about that. It was brave and, in strange way, the most selfless thing a mother could do.

She'd have to be careful around her father though. He'd never see it like that. He'd changed but he still couldn't handle thinking like that. The older he got, the more Catholic he became. But he was less critical of others. And a lot more apologetic. He'd probably be blaming himself.

There would be a break in the clouds near the coast and she'd see it soon: Ireland, that sorrowful old place that became more beautiful each time she came back. Soon they'd be able to see the little patchwork of life below.

When she could see it, she couldn't help it and nudged the kids, even as they were trying to rearrange themselves as their breakfast trays were cleared away. It was tradition; they had to look at all the things she and Danny used to point to. She made Eduardo do it, too, the year he came with them.

She'd wanted to call him when she heard but stopped herself in time. She phoned Danny instead. It took him a while to understand—it was six in the morning and he didn't have to go to work. He was on some long-term disability deal the union had worked out for him.

"Hold on, who's dead?"

"My mother."

"Your mother?"

"Yes, Danny, she died last night."

"Jazus, Deirdre. I'm so sorry to hear that."

"The kids and I will be going back for the funeral."

"Did you want me to go with you?"

That caught her. She hadn't even thought of it. "Well . . . I'm not sure. Do you want to?"

"I'd love to, only I'm not sure I'd be up for it right now. Unless you want me to go?"

"No. It's very kind of you but I was just calling to let you know where the kids were."

"Oh. Okay, then."

"Well I better go. I have so many things to sort."

"Yeah. Sure. I'd better let you get on with it.

"Deirdre," he had added before she hung up. "I'm really sorry about your mother. I always really liked her."

"She liked you too, Danny."

They both hung on that for a moment.

"Tell your dad I'm very sorry for his loss too."

"I will, Danny. Thank you. Good bye."

"That's Galway Bay," Deirdre mentioned as the clouds parted below.

"I know, Mom. Wake when me when we get to Dublin." Grainne closed her eyes again and rolled her head on to Deirdre's shoulder. "Love you, Mom."

"She can still do it?" Deirdre laughed and looked at Martin. "Eat breakfast and go straight back to sleep."

"I guess all those late nights were not a waste."

"Martin!"

"I heard that, too, Mr. Goodie-two-shoes."

"And that"—Deirdre turned back to the window so they couldn't see her smile—"is some bog of a place."

"You okay, Mom?"

"Yes, I'm fine."

"No she isn't," Grainne added from her shoulder like a second head.

"I'm fine."

"Really? Have you even had time to process it?"

She knew what Martin was really asking. "Sweetie, please, I'm fine."

"Mother," the second head joined in. "You don't have to be all brave in front of us."

"You sure?" Martin checked again the way he did when he wanted her to know that they would talk about it later. When they were alone.

"I'll be fine. My sister is coming and we'll manage everything between us." She had already made the funeral arrangements over the phone. The same ones that had looked after Danny's father—Jacinta had recommended them.

"Are they all coming?"

"No, just your aunt."

"What are you going to do about Granddad?"

"I don't know."

"We could bring him back with us?"

"Not long term."

"Why not?"

"Trust me, Martin, I know my father. *Bas in Eireann* and all that."

"Maybe we could get Dad to move back there and look after him."

"Two birds, eh?"

"You two are awful," the second head scolded; but they were happy together, even in their grief.

*

"And how are you, really?" Miriam asked with very real concern.

Deirdre sat across from her in one of the old booths they had often sat in when they were younger and funerals were for much older people. Bewley's hadn't changed but everything else had.

"I've told you, I'm fine."

"Your kids tell me you haven't even had time for a good cry yet."

She hadn't. Even when her father and sister dissolved by the graveside, Deirdre had stood like a stoic with her children beside her, greeting old neighbors and friends.

"Oh, trust me, I will."

And even as she said it, it began; a soft whimpering that she didn't even try to stop.

Miriam sipped her coffee and glared at any gawkers. She and Patrick had come over, and Dermot had prevailed on him to say the Mass. He seemed a bit reluctant. That was understandable. He hadn't been back since his father died. It must have been dredging up all kinds of feelings in him too. He managed to get through it with a soft informality and remembered Anne Fallon so kindly.

"Excuse me," Deirdre finally managed as she struggled to regain composure.

"Take all the time you need." Miriam smiled and stroked her hand. She was enjoying being back in Dublin—even if it was for a funeral. Death had long been a regular visitor in her life, as most of her family and friends were quietly dropping away. Soon it would just be her and Patrick and John, seeing out the rest of their days in the endlessness of Rome.

"I'm okay now." Deirdre wiped her eyes and put on her bravest face—just like when they first met all those years ago. Life had taken its toll on her but, if anything, she looked more beautiful because of it. She had a poise that could be confused with detachment, but when she smiled it was still so warm and engaging. Back when she was banished to Dublin, Miriam wouldn't have made it without Deirdre. Dear, open, honest, trusting Deirdre of the sorrows.

"You don't need to be brave for me."

"Why does everybody keep saying that to me?"

"Because you're doing it again. You're shouldering the whole problem and trying to protect everyone else from what they have to go through."

"I don't think so."

"Deirdre. You haven't stopped since you got back. You've been running around looking after everything and everybody. It's like you're avoiding yourself."

"Perhaps it's because I'm trying to come to terms with the fact that my mother killed herself."

She said it so matter-of-factly that Miriam was caught off guard. "And why do you think that?"

"Isn't it obvious?"

"It isn't. And even if it were, what difference would it make?"

"I suppose so, but I can't help but feel that I could have been a better daughter."

"Oh, Deirdre, you know better than that."

"Was there anything else I should have done?"

"I can't answer that, but I can say that I think your mother was very, very brave. Right to the end."

"I just wished she'd told me."

"What difference would that have made? Would you really have wanted to stop her?"

"No. No I wouldn't, but I would have liked to have been there . . . when it happened."

"What would you have done?"

"Held her hand."

"Ah, Deirdre, that's the sweetest thing I've ever heard."

"Sweet? I find it very bitter. I just wish I could have been there so she didn't have to die alone. I wish . . ." She never finished and began to cry again. This time from the pit of her sorrow.

After a while people began to look over, thinking Miriam was being a bit indifferent, but she didn't intervene. Deirdre just needed a little time and space to let it all out before she climbed back into the pressure suit she now wore every day of her life. It was all okay, Miriam understood. Life had changed them all.

*

Miriam asked him one more time as they passed over the Alps.

"What is it, Patrick? You haven't said a word since we got to the airport."

He hadn't. He was still preoccupied with Dermot's confession and was determined not to let any of it slip out.

"Bless me, Father," Dermot had blurted out when Patrick had dropped by the house, just as Dermot had asked.

"I'm after doing a terrible thing, Father."

Patrick wasn't sure if it was a confession or a normal conversation. "Ah now, Dermot. Don't be so hard on yourself. What could you have done?"

He'd hoped it was just the poor man pouring out all the regrets he'd been storing up over his lifetime, but Dermot shook his head and knelt on the floor before him. "You don't understand, Father. I'm confessing that I killed my Annie."

Patrick hadn't meant to look so shocked but couldn't help himself. Dermot, however, wasn't deterred. "Do you have your stole with you, Father? Only, I want to make a proper confession."

He didn't, but he assured Dermot that it was optional and sat while he listened.

"I did it for her, you know? She'd been begging me. And then, the other day, she sat down on the couch in front of me and, as clear as a bell, asked me again. She said she knew what was happening to her and she couldn't take any more of it."

He seemed to expect Patrick to say something, but what could he say?

"You don't think it was wrong, do you, Father?"

But before Patrick could answer, Dermot started to cry. "Forgive me, Father, I shouldn't have said that. Of course it's wrong. I knew it as I held her head under the water. She didn't even struggle. She just looked up at me like a child.

"Only now, that's all I see. I wake up in the night and see her looking at me. I killed her, Father, and now I'm heartily sorry. Is there any way that God could forgive me that."

*Well?* The memory of the bishop intruded when Patrick took too long to answer. It had always been the voice he listened to when he was in doubt. *You're not going to deny the poor man the peace his wife sacrificed herself for?*

"No."

"Oh no, Father, don't say that."

"No, no, I meant there is nothing to forgive. God understands these things and is always merciful."

"So you'll be able to give me absolution, then?"

Patrick nodded and muttered the dusty old words: Dominus noster Jesus Christus te absolvat; et ego auctoritate ipsius te absolvo ab omni vinculo excommunicationis et interdicti in

quantum possum et tu indiges. Deinde, ego te absolvo a pecca-
tis tuis in nomine Patris, et Filii, et Spiritus Sancti. Amen. And
halfway through, his uncle's voice joined in.

"Okay, don't talk to me."

"I'm sorry, Miriam, I'm getting very distracted in my old
age." He was torn—and not because of any legal ramification.
He was a priest and was bound to secrecy. But he was also a
human being and just wished he could tell someone.

"Don't worry. A few days with the *Magi* will have you feeling young again."

"Do you think they were able to manage without us?" He
was glad of the distraction. Miriam had always known when
he needed drawing out. He wished he could tell her, but he
couldn't. Besides, why burden her with this?

"Oh, I'm sure they did. John had my number and I haven't
heard a peep from him."

"Is that a good or a bad sign?" Maybe, if he could catch
John on one of his lucid days . . .

"We'll find out soon enough when we land. You know"—
she laughed and nudged him—"I feel like we're parents coming
home to our children."

\*

While Miriam and Patrick were flying over the Alps, the three
old friends sat on the patio like gargoyles, overlooked by most
of those who passed. They didn't care; their time together had
become far too precious, even if at times they still argued.

"I don't want to talk about all that, Padre John." Giovanni's passion was aging and he didn't use his hands so much
when he spoke, preferring instead to shrug at almost everything. "Yes, there are terrible things happening in the world,
but today I want to sit in the sun with my friends. Have I not
earned that yet?"

"Ah, the sins of omission. The greatest crime of all." John
had been brooding since Miriam and Patrick left, sulking like
a child, even at his age.

"Signore Pontecorvo," Giovanni implored. "Can you try to talk sense to this impulsive young man?" John was the youngest of the three by just a few years.

"What would you have me say?" Davide Pontecorvo nodded like a sage. His old head seemed too heavy for his scrawny neck to support. "There is nothing to be said to the young and the rash."

"What is the matter with you, today?" John asked the old bookseller.

"I'm old and my heart is heavy."

"We all get to feel like that from time to time."

"It is Tivia. She is still angry with me." He had refused to see his grandson when he visited, even when the poor young man came by the café. Even when Giovanni tried to intervene.

"Didn't she drive you here?"

"Yes, but we didn't speak. We haven't spoken in months. We just go on with life as if there is nothing between us."

"But she did drive you here?"

"She is doing her duty, but she has no love for me anymore."

John couldn't comment on such a familial matter so it was down to Giovanni, who looked genuinely concerned. "Signore, sometimes we get angry with the people we love, but we don't stop loving them."

"She says I am a pig-headed old fool."

"And sometimes we say things that are not ... so nice."

"So you agree with her?"

"Well." Giovanni shrugged again. "It's not for me to say."

One of his nieces had explained it all and Giovanni had shared it with John. Tivia and her brother wanted the old man to retire and move to Israel. They wanted him to see out his days in some ease and comfort—and Tivia was planning on starting a family with a man her grandfather knew nothing about. He wasn't Jewish and they weren't planning on getting married. Giovanni said he wasn't surprised. Nobody was getting married in churches anymore.

"Do you think I should?" Davide turned to John who would have preferred to stay out of it.

"Well, you know my thoughts on Israel, but yes, I think that you should go and spend some time with your family."

"And you?" Davide looked back to Giovanni.

"Yes, for family. You have great-grandchildren. It would do you some good to be with them. They might remind you how to smile."

"I cannot go there. That land was given to us by God and then taken from us until the true Messiah returns. Some of us have given up waiting and broken our covenant. I cannot be a part of such godlessness. I am a wandering Jew and I will stay that way until the Messiah."

"Our lot say you've missed that boat." John tried to lift the mood but he felt no different. His own country had broken its covenant and had become what it claimed to defend against.

"Here." Giovanni raised his hands, imploring the two of them. "We have seen all these things before. This is not what the people really are. This is what happens when they are frightened and herded. We have seen it here many, many times."

His words stayed on the warm air as the evening slipped in around the piazza, gathering in drifts around the walls of the temple to all gods, still standing when others had fallen, or had been pulled down, still offering hope to any who were looking for it.

*

Dressed in gowns and tasseled mortar boards, the Class of 2007 stood in tiers. Smiling and waving discreetly as the speeches promised the whole world that this would be the group that would change everything. Bright, energetic and full of promise, they were about to make their way in the world.

*You must be very proud,* a soft warm voice whispered in Jacinta's ear.

"I am, Martin. Look at him. My own grandson up there getting his degree."

*Yes, he's a good lad.*

"He reminds me a lot of you. He's very caring, you know. Not so much with his father—but that's understandable—but he never stops thinking of his mother. Sometimes, I pretend not to be paying attention and I watch the way they are together. He's always been the man of the house, only he's like the way a man should be, you know; kind and attentive. He must get that from his grandfather."

*Not that one,* the voice joked as Dermot took her photo.

"No, not that one, God love him. He insisted on coming over for it. I didn't mind. He's afraid to be on his own right now."

They were all family now and family marked the big occasions. Even Danny came. He looked more like his father with each passing year, only now he looked like Jerry when he had his heart attack—scared and a bit guilty. She hadn't had a chance to chat with him yet but she would. She hadn't given up on him yet.

*He doesn't look too good.*

"No, Martin, but between you, me, and the wall, I'm not done with him yet."

*Get him to Rome.*

"I've mentioned it to him, but he has no interest in going anywhere. Couldn't you have a word with him? It would mean more coming from you."

*Sure, Jass. Are you crying?*

"Oh don't mind me, I'm just being silly. I was just thinking how nice it would be if you could be in all the pictures with us. Dermot is in charge of them and has it all planned out."

*I'll be in them.*

"How?"

He had no chance to answer as the Class of 2007 threw their hats into the air and rushed out to hug and kiss their families. Proud, but not so proud to forget everything that had been done for them. Jacinta liked that. People didn't take enough time to say a bit of thanks every now and then.

Martin kissed his mother, his girlfriend, and his sister, then came straight over to Jacinta to kiss and hug her in front of everyone. "I only wish Granddad Jerry could have been here. I was thinking about him when I was up there."

"Ah now, pet." Jacinta tried not to snivel. It wouldn't have killed him to show his face, but she wasn't surprised. Fr. Reilly said it might be because he had already gone to the better place. Jacinta wasn't too sure. Knowing Jerry he would have stopped for a few pints on the way. "I'm sure he's smiling down on you. He's probably boasting to all his old friends about you as we speak. And your uncle Martin, he's so proud of you too."

Before Martin responded, Danny came through the crowd. He looked the way he did when he was little and unsure of everything around him. He was clean and well-dressed, and he was wearing his fancy shirt, even if it was a bit wrinkled. She was just glad he had the decency to show up. She knew what a struggle it would be for him.

"Congratulations, son." He held a shaky hand toward his son and waited.

Jacinta watched her grandson from the corner of her eye. She could count on him to do the right thing when it came to everything else, but he was still very hard toward his father. It was understandable, but regrettable too. It was one of the things that stuck inside of Danny and, sooner or later, became an excuse for getting drunk again. She'd seen the same thing between Jerry and his father—only that was the other way around. She really wished things could be different between them. But she needn't have worried. Martin took his father's hand and shook it. "Thanks, Dad. And thanks for coming."

"I wouldn't have missed it, son. Not for the world."

They both lingered, trying to find something else to say. Jacinta understood and her heart ached for them. They were still father and son, despite all that had happened. She was about to intervene when Dermot interrupted them all.

"C'mon now. Let's all get together for a few photographs while the light is still so good."

"Jazus," Jacinta filled in the gaping pause that still lingered, "when did he become such an expert? He probably doesn't even have the right film in the feckin' thing." She linked arms with her son and his son and brought them a little closer. "Let's go then; otherwise he'll be at us all day."

Deirdre joined them and stood next to Martin and Rachael, with Grainne next to Danny. And after giving numerous instructions to a kind-hearted passerby who was roped in to take the picture, Dermot joined them and stood by his daughter.

"Cheese."

"Cheese," they all replied, and repeated for a few more shots before Dermot took back the camera and started taking less formal shots as they mingled. "They'll be more natural that way."

"Did you really have to bring him?" Deirdre laughed as she and Jacinta posed informally.

"Ah now, dear, you don't really mean that."

"Just one more, ladies, only try to look like you don't notice the camera."

"We might," Jacinta snapped like an impatient wife, "if you'd stop bothering us."

"He must be driving you mad."

"Oh, he's not the worst of them. He's good company for me."

"And you don't think he should be in a home?"

"He has his own home, pet. Let him enjoy it a while yet."

"Is he still capable of looking after himself?"

"He can manage, and I drop in and do a bit of washing for him now and then. Sure it's only over the road for me."

"Jacinta, are you and my father . . . you know?"

"At our age, pet, it's more about having a bit of company."

"And one with the proud mother and the happy young couple." Dermot ushered Deirdre over to where Martin and Rachael were posing informally.

"Hard to believe?" Danny sidled up beside Jacinta and watched the family he had lost.

"It is. They grow up so fast, but it's all part of life."

He looked a little teary eyed as he watched, but Jacinta was in two minds. It was sad, but there was no point in trying to soften it. He needed to see the harm he'd done so that he might be able to see that there was still so much to change for.

"Your uncle would have been so proud of him."

"Yeah, I wish he could see this."

"I'm sure he can."

Danny looked directly at her and was about to say something when Dermot called her away. She had to stand with Grainne and Martin and Rachael, as if they were just chatting.

"Jazus, how much bloody film does he have in that camera?"

The kids all laughed and Dermot made them do it again.

"Ah c'mon now, Dermot. Maybe you've taken enough."

"But we want to have a record of the day."

"Granddad." Grainne waved her phone at him and smiled.

"But they're not real photos. Wait 'til you see. When I get these developed you'll all be thanking me."

"Thank you," they all mouthed during the next one, so Dermot made them do it again.

"And try to look happier; only don't make it look like you're trying."

\*

"I can't believe it," Dermot fumed when Deirdre got the pictures back from Blacks. "Half of them didn't come out right. They all have this white blotch in them. Are you sure those people knew what they were doing?"

"They said it was a problem with the camera."

"There's nothing wrong with my camera."

"Here." Jacinta leaned across him and took the photos, smiling as she looked at each one. Bright and full of color, her own flesh and blood in one of the happier days of their lives. "Sure they're grand. What are you going on about now?"

"Look at these. It's like there's a ghost standing behind Martin. Look. This one too."

"Oh." Grainne came in to the kitchen, gleefully. "Did the pictures not come out? Don't worry, Granddad. I'll share mine."

"Grainne," Deirdre chided.

"Oh, let her alone. She's probably right." Dermot sighed like he was leaking.

"C'mon," Grainne offered magnanimously, "we can look at them on the computer."

"Poor Dad," Deirdre muttered as she leaned forward and looked at the pictures again. "Well I must say, some of the shots of Martin are beautiful. I've never seen him looking so handsome."

"He does," Jacinta agreed. "They both do."

*

Danny sipped his pint and smirked to himself. Life was still one screw up after another, but some things were working out okay. He might be a total disaster, but his son was doing all right for himself. That was the whole point of being an immigrant—you sacrificed yourself for the next generation.

Martin's girlfriend had been really nice to him, too, and had insisted that they take a photo with him. And when Martin was talking to someone else, she squeezed Danny's hand and said she hoped she would see a lot more of him.

It made him feel a bit better but, being there, watching them all together, just made him sad in the end. Of all the things that had gone wrong in his life—that was the one that got to him the most. Sometimes he wished he could go back and . . . But what was the point? He'd only fuck it up all over again.

Still, he was doing a lot better than Saddam Hussein. It was on the TV behind the bar.

He'd just been sentenced to hang. His whole trial was a load of bollocks. It was just for show. They had wanted him out of the way, and it wasn't because of what he did to the Kurds—or the WMDs that weren't. They weren't too concerned about shite like that when they put him in power.

Gaddafi would be next or the Iranian. They'd get them all one way or the other, sooner or later. The world was run by cruel bastards, and Danny just had to make the best of it, just like everybody else.

He was trying. He'd just finished his grocery shopping and that was something to feel good about.

He hadn't bought a lot of food—there was no point. He just ended up throwing most of it out. He did buy lots of soup though. He could still manage that. And sugar, tea, and milk. And toilet paper. He'd forgotten the last few times and had to wipe his arse with junk mail. And he was having a few stomach problems.

He was probably getting an ulcer or something, only the doctor kept on at him about his drinking—as if that was the reason for everything. He'd done his laundry, too, and was rewarding himself with a few quiet pints like a normal person would.

That was the real problem all along. Life was so fucked up that they all had to overdo it on something just to get through. Like food, or money, or sex. They all had something they abused—even each other.

At least he wasn't murdering anybody and saying it was just to defend his fuckin' way of life. Yes, the world was a fine big fuck up, and as long as people were making money out of it nothing would ever change. If he didn't have a drink once in a while, he'd go mad altogether.

*If only it was once in a while.*

"Ah, Martin, don't be getting on my case again," he whispered to his reflection.

*I'm not going to give up on you.*

"Well, maybe you should." Danny raised his glass between him and the mirror behind the bar. "Because I'm done fighting it all. I'm just floating now like everybody else. Life is not worth it, you know. Everything that is supposed to be good and nice about it is just fairy tales.

"Tell me something." He lowered his glass and stared straight into his own eyes. "Are we all really being judged or are we already in hell?"

# Chapter 12 – 2008

WHEN THE SPANISH COURTS REOPENED THE CASE OF THE MURDERED SCHOLARS OF UNIVERSIDAD CENTROAMERICANA, they also let loose a flood of emotions that John Melchor had penned up for years. In a way he didn't mind. He'd been walking around in a pharmaceutical haze for far too long.

He needed to feel something again, even if it was painful. And he needed to be able to clearly hear the voices of the dead again. They had become so vague and muddled with everything that was happening around him. But he was also reluctant. At heart he was still from the old school, where men quietly suffered their burdens without complaint, even if it meant they were crushed under them, or lashed out at something in frustration. He saw it all around him. Old men who had given up all that life offered to devote themselves to a god who cared so little for any of them in the end. Bitter now and imposing their restrictions on everyone else.

Sometimes he envied women. They could share their feelings and their empathies even if they were often just enabling each other. Tivia had been to the café to plead with them all, and Miriam quickly became her advocate. Tivia's child was on the way and she still hadn't found a way to tell her grandfather, as they still weren't talking. Miriam suggested that Giovanni should do it, but he didn't feel it would be right coming from him. He was afraid her grandfather might think he was judging him. He thought Patrick should do it as he still saw Signore

Pontecorvo regularly at the bookstore, and it would seem less of an issue if Patrick brought it up casually.

Patrick looked horrified at the prospect and turned to Miriam, but she avoided his eyes.

"Please?" Tivia turned from one to the other, her pretty brown eyes growing softer and softer.

That always fascinated John, how easily women could cry sacred tears from the depths of bruised hearts. Or were they just little girls getting their way? He could never decide. He usually depended on Miriam, but with Tivia she had become. . . almost maternal.

"Very well," he announced when the silence became unbearable. "I will go and talk with him."

"Are you sure?" Miriam asked. She looked at him until he responded, trying to understand what was going on inside him.

"Yes, I am. He and I are old enough and wise enough to be able to sit down and share this wonderful news."

"Yes," Giovanni agreed and rearranged himself as if the matter was settled. "It would be best for Padre John to talk to him. Signore Pontecorvo would appreciate it more coming from him."

"Grazie, grazie, grazie." Tivia fluttered from one to the other, kissed Miriam and Giovanni on both cheeks, lowered her dark glasses and turned to leave. "Ciao. Grazie mille.

"Ciao," she called again over her shoulder, and walked off across the piazza without once getting her heels caught in the cobblestones. She waved again before sliding into her shiny, new Smart Car and, nosing her way through the crowd, waved again and was gone.

"That poor young woman," Miriam commented to no one in particular.

"The poor old man," John muttered into his raised coffee cup. It was the last thing the old bookseller needed. The whole business with his grandson had torn at his heart, and even though he still went about his day as he had for decades, John knew better. The old man had become distant. He'd still find time to talk with his friends but he always seemed distracted. "I will go and see him right now."

He pushed his chair back and rose like Jesus from the supper. He might have argued but there was no point. He couldn't leave it to his friends; they were stretched enough looking after him. He knew they all took their shifts keeping his devils away. He had gone along with it because he was lost, but now that all that had happened that night in San Salvador was to be re-examined, his life was coming back into focus. He was still a member of the Society of Jesus and he would bring what comfort he could to the poor old Jew whose granddaughter was about to leave the tribe.

"I will come with you," Miriam decided and drained her cup.

"There's no need," John assured her, half-heartedly. "I'm sure I can manage very well alone."

She insisted, and soon they were walking toward the river, slowly so he could keep up. When they first met, he was the one who led her. He was okay with that. He trusted her now.

"We all need a little bit of help with our crosses." She smiled when he looked over at her.

*

Signore Pontecorvo still kept an apartment over the bookstore. It was far too big for him now, so he allowed clutter to gather in the corners. The place wasn't dirty. His nieces took turns coming over to cook and clean for him, always ensuring that he had fresh clothes laid out for the week, laid out by day and spread on the large bed he hadn't slept in for years.

He rarely spoke to them and gruffly when he did, as though it was expected of him. His nieces were good, kind women, but he couldn't remember who was who so he didn't risk getting into conversations. His nieces didn't force the issue either, in case he started another of his tirades about Israel and how Zionism was the rejection of their covenant with God; about how they had turned the Promised Land into hell; about how they were becoming all that once terrorized them.

Even John was reluctant to get him started on the subject, given how he felt about his own beloved country, distracted again by the contorted voices of righteousness citing the twisted passages of the Old Testament to rationalize support for hate and intolerance, while those who had died in the towers cried out to him in shame. The dead were unanimous in that; they never wanted vengeance.

Old Pontecorvo often said the same thing. His people had been trapped by inherited fear. Cultivated around the mantra of "never again," they used their dead as human shields against all that might dare to question them, careening hand-in-hand with those who wore Jesus as the mark, closer and closer toward Armageddon. And all the words of love offered so little solace. If the meek did inherit the world, it would be a barren, war-scarred wasteland.

"How are we going to raise the subject?" Miriam intruded as they turned the last corner and strolled toward the book store.

"In deference to his age, I think it should be a short, sharp shock."

"Are you not concerned about giving him a heart attack?"

"No." John laughed. "Old Davide will bury us all."

He looked up from his desk as they entered. "Ah, a visit from the Catholic clergy. This type of thing has never ended well for Jews."

His nephew, a short bespectacled man who Davide always accused of being underfoot, looked out from the back room. "Coffee?" Efraim asked and smiled in the hope that they might accept.

"We do not need coffee," Davide chided and waved him back into the storeroom. "Go back and unpack those boxes while my friends and I talk."

"Thanks anyway," Miriam offered as the poor nephew looked crestfallen.

"You are well?" John asked, and sat directly in front of the old man, meeting his eyes.

"As well as can be expected, but I doubt you have come all this way to discuss my health."

"No." John smiled a little but held the old man's gaze. "We are here with news from your granddaughter."

"News? Should I presume that she sent you because it is bad?"

"That will depend on you. She is with child."

"And the father is not . . ."

"No he isn't, but by all accounts he is still a good man."

The old man lowered his head and stared at the floor for so long that they were beginning to wonder if he hadn't nodded off.

"Signore?" Miriam checked after a while.

"And Tivia had to send you here to tell me all of this?" The old man raised his head and his eyes were dewy.

"She did. She wants you to know but she is afraid that you might reject her."

The old man lowered his old gray head again, into his long bony hands that wrinkled around it.

"Is that what she thinks of me?"

"No, Signore." But Miriam wasn't convincing, and the old man stared some more.

"She is still your granddaughter and she is still a good woman. Please try to remember that, Signore." Miriam reached toward the old man's shoulder but John shook her off. The old man would need his time and space.

He started to shudder and they were both convinced he was crying. But when he looked up, he was smiling. "Please tell Tivia that I am very happy for her and, if she is willing to forgive such a stubborn old fool, I would like to give her my blessing for what it's worth."

Miriam rose with her phone in hand. "I will call her right now."

She went outside to fill in the details in private.

"So," John asked unsurely. "You are happy about this?"

"You do not have children, or grandchildren, do you Padre?"

"You know I don't."

"Well then you do not understand the joy this brings to me. So, for now, my great-grandchild is to be Goyim but I'm sure that can be negotiated."

"And what if it isn't?"

"Then one of the Pontecorvos might finally meet this Messiah you speak of."

*

"So how can you be sure? It's not like we're surrounded by people living happily ever after."

Martin and Rachael had just had dinner in one of the fancy little places on Mount Pleasant and had shared two bottles of wine, but they were walking some of that off. He never liked to let the world get out of focus. When you did that in hockey, there was always someone waiting to blindside you.

"My mom's doing okay."

"That's my point, Martin. The only happy, successful person we know is divorced."

"Then let's get married, have two children, and you can divorce me."

He had started on his dream job, straight out of school, and just had his first promotion. It had seemed like the perfect time to pop the question.

"See!" Rachael spun around without letting go of his hand, raising their arms like a bridge and gliding beneath it. "I knew you weren't serious about it." She was just teasing him, pouting a little while her eyes sparkled. "So how can you be so sure that we'd get to stay . . . happy?"

"Because I will never let anything make you unhappy."

He tried to hold her close to kiss her soft lips, but she rolled out along his arm like a ballerina or as if they were about to tango. He hadn't told her yet; he'd gone to see her father to ask if he could propose to her. It was the right thing to do. He felt bad about not telling her but it was still the right thing to do.

"Oh, Martin, don't say things like that. What if I go crazy and start knitting for my twenty cats?"

"Only twenty?"

"Yes, but I'll have a parrot too. And you'd have to make sure the cats didn't get it—so I'm not unhappy."

"I'll get a big dog."

"What if I dress it up in a chicken-lady costume and cover it with catnip?"

"I'll hire a live-in shrink. Listen, you know if you don't want to . . ." He held his arms open and exposed his heart. "Just tell me now, and I won't ask again . . ." he sang as she tried not to giggle.

"No, I'll let you marry me, but I want you to know from the beginning, I'm only marrying you for your money."

"Shit. Really? I thought you had money. It's off then."

"See, you're starting to make me unhappy already and you're not doing anything about it." She stepped closer so she could bat her eyelids directly at him, gently coming to rest against him.

He had to tell her. It was starting to bother him. He put his arms around her and drew her closer, almost lips to lips. "I went to see your father."

She stood away abruptly and blinked. "Why? We already talked about that."

"I know." He rubbed his chin before lowering his arms and turning his palms forward. "But I had to."

"Why?"

"It's a man thing—and no I'm not saying that you're chattel."

"Martin, listen to me. I'm not angry. In fact I'm very touched, it's only . . ."

"It's only nothing," he interrupted. "It's the way it should be. For good or bad. He's still your father and I respect that."

"That's all very well, Martin, but I wasn't ready to talk with him about it. Not yet."

"Oh, shit."

"Yes, Mr. Goodie-two-shoes. Shit. But, as a matter of interest—not that it matters to me—what did he say?"

"Thank Christ or Hallelujah. I can't remember. He was so happy."

"'Christ?' Really Martin, 'Christ?'"

"He says he's converting—for the sake of the children."

"They're going to be Jewish."

"All of them?"

"No." She grew serious for a moment and then smiled again. "Let's have one for every religion in the world—except Rasta. We can't have the kids smoking ganga. They'd have to go to Northern."

"But we agreed: only two. And I'm sure Grainne can be relied on to produce the Rastas, especially if she sticks with Doug." He was really down on Doug these days. He hadn't got over not making it in the draft and had retreated back into his mother's basement, only coming out to see Grainne and to eat at their house.

"Okay, we'll just have two, but we'll teach them all the religions."

"Or no religion at all?"

"Or no religion at all."

"So really," she asked as they passed the cemetery and were almost at the corner of Moore and enough of the wine haze had floated away, "what did my father say? How did he react? Tell me! Tell me!"

"He got down on his knees and thanked me for making an honest woman of you again."

"It's the least you could do. After all, you are the only person I was ever . . . never mind. What did he say about inviting relatives?"

"I can't remember, but he did say that he'd be proud to call me son."

"Did he really? Did you have to sneak some Irish whiskey into his coffee?"

"Please, no racial profiling—you'll set a bad example for the kids."

He had thought about it though. Joel was hard to read. He had sat behind his desk and said that he would welcome Martin and he would be happy to see Rachael as his wife, but he would not have his wife's family there. He did invite Martin to sit though, as if the matter were negotiable. "There are matters between me and those who drove us out of Montreal."

"Sir . . ." Martin had approached it carefully. He was getting good at that—convincing hesitant clients to place their trust in him. "I understand there are issues, but I would ask you to consider the happiness of a woman we both love dearly." It was subtle. Charming on the surface, but also a very soft declaration that he was going to be the man in Rachael's life from now on, with all due respect.

"Do you know what the issues are?"

"No, sir." Martin lowered his eyes.

"My wife's family was in Montreal during the war, espousing Zionism while my family was sacrificed for their precious Promised Land. And now, when you try to confront them with the truth, they shun you, saying you have taken sides with the enemies of Israel. Zionists. They were once hand in glove with the Nazis and betrayed us all."

Martin was in way over his head but that wasn't going to stop him. "Sir," he began, but Mr. Brand stopped him.

"Please, do not call me 'Sir.' It's far too militaristic. Call me Joel or Papa."

"Joel," Martin began again, more determined. "I'm Irish, and we're no strangers to wars and suffering and dark family secrets, but Rachael and I have a chance at a whole new beginning."

"True."

"But we would like to have the blessings of our families when we start out. It would mean everything to your daughter."

"I can't. They drove me out, you know. Every time I mentioned my uncle they said he was nothing but a drunk and I was a self-hating Jew. Me, who lost everything."

"Mr. Brand." Martin was trying to think on his feet and needed something to sway the balance. "My father is a drunk and I will be inviting him."

"Why?"

"Because your daughter asked me to."

She had. She'd insisted on it and got his mother to agree too.

"And what did he really say about my relatives?" Rachael persisted.

"He said he'd think about it."

"Thank you, Martin." She leaned in and kissed his cheek but was careful to brush her breast against his arm. "I know I should have dealt with it myself but thank you. I owe you."

"Yes, you do." He pulled her closer and ran his hand down her back. Joel had agreed to consider it for his daughter's sake but it had taken some convincing. "And you can start repaying me by being the one to invite my father."

"So. You have finally agreed to that."

"I had to; it was part of the deal with your father."

It was. When he said it, her father had sat back as though he had been slapped. "You're a good man, Martin Boyle." He finally looked over and smiled. "And I will be proud to call you son."

"You made a deal with a Jew?" Rachael smiled and nudged him with her hip. "You'll lose your shirt."

"That's a little bit anti-Semitic, don't you think."

"You can't be anti-Semitic when you're Jewish."

"What's with that, anyway? Like you're 'ish,' but not really?"

"I was put on probation when they found out I ate pork with your family."

They both laughed at that and drew a little closer to each other.

"Are you sure we can pull this off?"

"Yes, Martin. We can be as happy as anybody else; raise two perfectly normal, well-adjusted, non-judgmental, uninhibited children and be fabulous together, until you make enough money to make divorcing you worthwhile."

"You've been talking to my mother, haven't you?"

"Every step of the way."

"Every step?"

"Well, not every step."

He kissed her again at her father's front door and was about to turn away.

"Come in," she whispered as she fumbled with the lock. "Only be quiet. My father sleeps with his Uzi."

*

Fortunately, he didn't bring it to the reception, as he got a little drunk and began to argue with his in-laws. Most of the guests didn't notice but Jacinta did. She never really relaxed at weddings anymore—not since Gina's, when they took Danny to the mountains to shoot him.

Not that he seemed too concerned with that anymore as he danced with Grainne and looked rather well, all things considered. He had put on weight and was a bit pasty and flabby. He said he wasn't drinking that much anymore but Jacinta knew better. He did, however, stay away from the bar where Mr. Brand was getting heated.

Jacinta saw Rachael and Mrs. Brand exchange glances and decided to step in before Martin noticed. It had been a perfect day so far and she wasn't going to allow anything ruin it.

Joel looked cornered and was ready to lash out at those around him. He was also getting a bit fat and pasty. Jacinta had said hello to him, of course, when they first arrived. She had been to enough weddings to know that establishing entente between in-laws was the best gift a young couple could get. And she promised him one dance—as long as it wasn't one of those modern things the kids were all doing, like they were all wearing itchy underwear.

"Excuse me, gentlemen." She edged in between him and his in-laws, who seemed relieved. Deirdre had told her that most of those invited had declined, most of them politely.

Deirdre had also said that Rachael had cried her eyes out about it but didn't want Martin to know. She came to Deirdre about it, too, instead of her own mother. She was far too busy coordinating travel plans and checking for reasonably priced accommodation that wouldn't be too far away. Jacinta just listened without saying a word. It wasn't her place to comment.

"We'll need to keep an eye on the father," Deirdre had confided as they stood for more photographs in the hot hazy sun, right outside City Hall, with the big spaceship thing behind them, but at least it wasn't Dermot taking them.

He hadn't been able to make the trip. He'd just had a hip put in and wasn't allowed to travel, but he'd be over as soon as he could, and maybe they could organize something with a bit of church in it. Martin and Rachael had decided on a civic service. It didn't bother Jacinta. She'd seen enough young couples in her life to know: her grandson was madly in love with a beautiful young woman who was just as much in love with him. It mightn't last forever, but it did the whole world a bit of good to see it now and then.

"Which father?" she had asked as the photographer herded them all together: Martin and Rachael in the center, with Joel and Adina on either side. Jacinta stood with Deirdre on their left while Danny and Grainne stood on the other side.

"We don't have to worry about Danny. He won't let Martin down—he's just so happy to be invited."

"Did Martin invite him?"

"Yes, with Rachael. They took him out for dinner and they shared a bottle of wine."

"Just the one?"

"I didn't ask. Martin seemed okay with it all—must be Rachael's influence."

"She means a lot to you too?"

"Like the daughter I never had."

"Oh, don't say that. You don't really mean it."

"No, I don't. Grainne has been a doll with all this going on."

"What does she want now?"

"Now, now, Granny. That sounds like cynicism."

"Well, it's better than sarcasm."

"Mr. Brand, you promised the grandmother of the groom a dance," she interrupted.

His in-laws took the opportunity to introduce themselves, complimented her on Martin and, one by one, slipped away, leaving a flustered Joel seething on his own, swaying slightly.

"Mr. Brand, am I going to have to stand here much longer? My shoes are starting to get to me."

"I'm so sorry, Mrs. Boyle. Please forgive me. I have let myself get a little upset. My in-laws . . ." He shook his head, took her by the arm and led her closer to the band.

"Sure we all have those." She waited while he found a tempo she could move to. "It's all a part of being family."

"You don't know what it's like, Mrs. Boyle."

"Maybe not, Mr. Brand." Jacinta talked as calmly as she could. The dancing seemed to be relaxing him a bit. "But even in Ireland we have to put things aside for the sake of the day that's in it."

"I can't do that. I have tried but just seeing their smug, self-righteous faces . . ."

"Sure we all have relatives like that. You should have seen my mother-in-law. She turned out to be a good old soul in the end, but at my wedding—even the priest had to watch what he said. My poor father was afraid to even have a drink."

"You do not know these people like I do. They hide behind the Holocaust while our own people are over there burning olive trees and acting like the SS."

He was getting flustered again and Jacinta smiled as sweetly as she could. "You know, Mr. Brand, you'll drive yourself insane thinking about things like that, and I know. I was in an asylum."

"Mrs. Boyle, I'm a Jew that has been cast out by my own tribe. I carry my asylum around with me."

"And that's what I'm trying to tell you. No good ever comes from dwelling on the past. We used to be like that in Ireland. Everybody was always up for having a go at the English, you know, because of all the things they did."

"I am no fan of the English, either. They went along with it all."

"Well, after all the fighting was done and we had our own place in the world, all we had done was to teach our children that it was all right to go around shooting each other. My own poor Danny nearly got murdered in it all."

"My people do not like to learn from the mistakes of others, Mrs. Boyle. We have been raised to believe that we and we alone were chosen by God. We won't admit that we are raising a generation of soulless young people who will go out and kill all before them without thought. And when we have killed all the Arabs we will turn on ourselves and kill all who disagree. We are becoming the fourth Reich."

"You know, Mr. Brand," Jacinta said softly as the song came to an end, "the world has to go through all its twists and turns and we can't let ourselves get caught up in it all. What we can do is to make sure that my grandson and your daughter are given every chance to have their bit of joy without all the shadows of the past."

She waited while he absorbed what she was trying to tell him. She felt for him. He had seen through the veil of lies that the world told itself. He'd never find peace again. In a way, he reminded her of Danny. "Besides, you're part of a new family now."

"You're a very wise woman, Mrs. Boyle."

"I'm not really. I've just learned what is really important. And now, if you want my opinion, you should go over and dance with your beautiful daughter."

She left him and walked toward Danny, who was inching his way toward the bar.

"C'mon now and dance with your mother," she coaxed until he smiled. "C'mon quick, while they're still playing something I can dance to."

Danny obliged and swept her off, almost waltzing while everyone else did some type of jitterbug.

"You must be very proud of your son."

"I am, Ma. I just wish I'd been a better father to him."

"It's never too late, son."

"It might be for me, Ma."

"Not a bit of it. All you need is a bit of a holiday. Why don't you come to Rome with me? I want to go over and see Fr. Reilly again."

"I'll think about it."

"Promise?"

*

After the bride and groom had danced one last time, and taken the time to talk with each of their guests in turn, and the band had played a few slow songs as the catering staff cleaned up, Jacinta and Deirdre finally got home and sat at the kitchen island.

"Well that went well," Jacinta decided as she took off her shoes and settled over the cup of tea before her.

"It did," Deirdre agreed. "And didn't they both look beautiful?"

"They're a real credit to you." Jacinta nodded as she raised her cup. Canadians had all kinds of fancy ways of living but they still couldn't make a proper cup of tea. "Both of them."

Grainne joined them after she had said her goodnights to Doug. They had seemed a little deflated throughout, and when he made his best man's speech he'd seemed distracted.

"I want to say a special thanks, sweetie. You've been a real angel through all this."

Deirdre reached out to touch her daughter's face but she pulled away.

"Mom. I need to tell you something."

"Oh," Jacinta joined in. "Are you getting a touch of wedding fever too?"

Grainne seemed a bit unsure so Deirdre coaxed her. "What is it?"

"I'm pregnant."

They froze for a moment, teacups half raised.

"Are you sure?"

"Yes, Mom. I've known for a few weeks, but I didn't want to tell you before."

Deirdre took a few breaths and touched the back of her daughter's hand before she spoke again. "Sweetie, have you decided what you're going to do?"

"What do you mean 'do?'" Jacinta blurted. "You're not thinking of murdering it?"

"Of course not," Deirdre assured her, but Grainne didn't look so sure.

# Chapter 13 - 2009

As the winter dragged on and on, Danny spent his evenings at the corner of the bar in McMurphy's, the only warm, happy place he could find along the frozen desolation that was Eglinton Avenue East. He'd walk over in the cold, brittle sunshine of the afternoon and stay for three or four hours. Then he'd get a cab home and have a few more in privacy. He didn't want people knowing how bad things were again.

Even he had to admit that he was hitting it hard, but who could blame him? The whole world was going to shite around him and nobody knew what the fuck was going to happen next. Everyone on the TV was saying the same thing—the sky was falling—and this time they were right.

The Great Recession threatened to engulf the whole world. He'd even started watching the business channel and couldn't help but feel totally vindicated. He'd been saying all along that it was going to happen—only nobody ever listened to him. It was the obvious conclusion to the fuck-everything-for-profit shite they'd all bought into. And they were properly fucked now. Especially when all those lying, cheating bastards who had preached against socialism in all its forms were now more than happy to dump their gambling debts on the backs of tax-payers; and everyone went along with it like they had their heads up their arses.

He didn't really blame them though. If people really stopped and thought about it there would be a revolution in the morning; and who had time for that anymore? That was the type of thing their grandfathers had done and nobody was like that anymore. They were more like frightened sheep who kept their heads down and hoped that any shit that fell would land on someone else. It was enough to drive a thinking man to drink.

"Gimmie another while I go out for a smoke." He smiled at the young woman behind the bar. Her name was Siobhan and she was great in that really Irish way—hard when she had to be but soft when sympathy was needed. She always knew when he wanted to talk and when he didn't.

He shivered and coughed a few times as he tried to finish his cigarette as quickly as he could. It was too cold to be outside. "I hope the fuckin' social engineers are happy." He flicked his half-smoked cigarette out onto Eglinton Avenue where buses and cars crawled along, their exhaust fumes like ghosts in the frozen air.

"Tá sé fuar go leor inniu," he announced when he settled back on his bar stool.

"Why don't you quit, then? They say they're bad for you."

He was about to tell her why, but he couldn't. She had a touch of innocence about her and he didn't want to be the one that shattered it. She'd stand like an angel, even when the TV behind the bar was spewing out all kinds of lies in sound-bites and talking-points, like none of it got to her.

It got to him, though. He could see what was really going on no matter what all the spin-merchants tried to sell them. It was a mad race to see who could destroy the world first: the banks, the oil companies, and the righteous whackos, Christian, Islamist or Zionist. All emboldened by their distorted interpretations of what their gods wanted, and all so hell-bent on making Armageddon a reality. It wouldn't matter in the end. Whoever survived was only going to get to sit around gnawing on bones, up to their necks in pollution and garbage.

Nobody had the balls to admit that they were all fucked, and no amount of social engineering was ever going to change that. None of them, not even that bitch Miriam—the mother superior of the hand-wringing, shocked and appalled liberals who picked their causes by gender, color, or creed, but stuck their heads in the sand when it suited them.

No, the human race was totally fucked now, and they had the nerve to say he was the one with a problem.

If he did die from drink, then at least there'd be some point to it. Only something else was probably going to get to him first—like getting stabbed by some crack-head terrorist with the swine flu. The four fuckin' horsemen were on the loose and everybody was going around like it was no big deal. They were all scared shitless about losing their jobs, or their houses, or their savings. That almost made him laugh. The warning signs had been there for years and nobody paid them a damn bit of attention.

*It's like they're all alcoholics.* The face in the mirror smirked back at him.

Danny was beginning to dread his uncle's visits. He always came by when Danny was really down—as if he was rubbing it in. Only Martin wasn't like that—or at least, he wasn't when he was alive.

"What's the point in even trying to get well anymore?" Danny mouthed at his reflection. "The end isn't far off now. And the meek? They're going to be fucked over more than anybody."

"Gimmie another." He nodded at Siobhan. There was no point getting bitter about it. What was done was done, and now it was just a matter of sitting back and letting the chips fall where they may. "We reap what we sow," he added, much more fatally than he had intended.

Siobhan just smiled as she placed the fresh pint in front of him and turned to add another tick on the pad she kept behind the bar. She called it his score card as she totaled it up when he was leaving.

He was carefully raising the full glass to his lips when Doug came in and sat beside him. "Mr. Boyle." He nodded and ordered himself a drink like he was a regular. He wasn't. Danny had never seen him in there before.

"Doug, what brings you in here? Put that on mine," he added to Siobhan.

"Thanks. I was just passing and I felt like having a pint." He tried to sound casual but Danny didn't buy it.

"Well, you're in the right place."

"Yeah."

They'd never been alone before. Danny had been out with him and Grainne a few times, but other than when she went to the washroom they never really had to talk to each other. "How's the hockey going?"

"I didn't make it." Doug looked surprised that Danny had asked. Grainne had said something about that, only Danny had probably forgotten or just wasn't really listening. It was hard to keep track of everything these days.

"Ah, shite. I'm sorry to hear that."

"Yeah. Bummer, eh?"

"Well like I always say: When life gives you lemons, cut them up and put them in gin."

"Yeah." Doug nodded but didn't really laugh. Something else was bothering him.

"So, what are you going to do with yourself now?"

"Become a working stiff."

"Good luck with that. Haven't you heard? The fuckers have taken the economy away too."

"I already got a job. Martin got me in where he works."

"He did? Well good for him. At least he hasn't become one of those heartless bastards yet."

"There's something else, Mr. Boyle. Grainne and I are going to have a kid."

"When?"

"In a few months."

"But that can't be. I just saw her . . ."

He hadn't. She'd spent Christmas with her mother and then afterwards got the flu or something, and they hadn't gotten together. At the time he didn't mind. He was having a rough Christmas and had been on a bit of a spree. He didn't want her to see him like that.

"Well that's . . . great." He looked up at his reflection. It was still smirking, but with the hint of a smile. "Siobhan, give us two Black Bush—large ones."

"Cheers, me old son," he toasted when they arrived and looked over as Doug gingerly raised his to his mouth. "Get it down ya."

Danny downed his in one, just as he used to. Only it didn't go down well and almost made his stomach churn. He probably shouldn't have had it. He rose to let his stomach settle and reached his hand out, trying to stop it from shaking. "Put it there, me old son. And congratulations." He slapped Doug on the shoulder with his other hand and sat back down as the room teetered a little. "And tell my Grainne that I'm so happy for her."

"I will." Doug sounded relieved, downed his whiskey too, and rose to leave.

"You'll have another?"

"No. I gotta get back. Grainne said I had to come straight back and tell her what you said."

"She has you whipped already—that's my little girl."

After Doug had left and Siobhan had let him hug her a little, Danny sat back and stared at his own reflection. He wanted to feel good about the news but he couldn't help but think that the poor child was coming into hell on earth.

"You must be thrilled to bits," Siobhan suggested as she took the empty whiskey glasses away.

He looked at her and smiled but didn't answer.

"I always think that new babies make everybody feel hopeful again," she added as she turned away. "It's like what Obama is always going on about—we all need a bit of hope, now and then, especially now."

Danny stared at his reflection and decided she was right. They might all be fucked right now but they'd find a way out of it, just as they always did before. The guys on the business channel said it might take years, but they would. Someone had to start sowing a few seeds of hope for future generations. It cost so little and could do no harm. They had to. They'd all become grandparents one day.

All the doom and gloom they had been listening to for years was getting them all down—that and all the warmongering and hating each other. That was why everyone was going around being hard with each other all the time. There was nowhere else to go from there but to start killing each other.

He knew what he was talking about—he'd been a bit like that himself once. But getting married—and having kids—had made him look at things differently.

Only, he argued as he took another swig of his beer, it had made him soft and he'd been beaten down until he just gave up and went along with it all. But he never bought back in, he comforted himself. He knew what happened to the guy in 1984—he'd finally read it. That was when they put the bullet in your brain.

Some mornings, when he was retching his guts out over the toilet bowl, he might have welcomed it, but now with a few drinks under his belt, the world was a bit more manageable. The trick was to believe in nothing and expect the worst. Anything else was just delusion—or denial.

He finished his beer, settled his tab and called a cab. When he got home he'd phone his mother with the news. Only he'd wait a few hours so it wouldn't be too early over there. She was getting on and all the economic shite was hitting Ireland really hard. Not that he didn't feel a little smug about that. He hadn't really begrudged them during the good years, only what was the point of emigrating if things were going to get so good at home?

He'd have a few more drinks while he was waiting. He had to—to wet the baby's head. Besides, she'd be on at him about going to Rome. But now he had an excuse. He'd have to be around for when the baby was born.

*

"But we all feel like that," Jacinta reassured Dermot as he laid his latest sorry tale of woe before her. She dropped in every afternoon to check up on him and to share whatever bit of gossip was going around. Lately, however, he was preoccupied with all that was wrong with him. His hip still wasn't right and the other one was starting to go too. It was getting to the point where he could barely look after himself. There was talk of moving him into a nursing home, but he was adamant that he could still manage on his own.

"C'mon now, Dermot. We both know you can't make it up or down the stairs."

"I'll buy a flat. They're getting much cheaper—they're practically giving them away."

"Do you have money for that?"

"I will when I sell this place. I'll have enough for a nice small place and still have enough to leave for the girls."

"You'll get nothing for it right now—if you get anything at all. You'd be better off going where there are people to look after you all day. That way you can hold onto the house for a bit. At least until things start picking up again. There'll be more for the girls that way."

She tried to sound reassuring but no one was really sure about anything anymore. All the bravado of the Tiger years had evaporated and was being replaced by a dull, sickening feeling. They'd been enjoying the fat cows for years and now the lean, scrawny reality was coming home to roost. And most of them had been spending like drunken sailors, even those who should've known better.

She hadn't done too badly though. Her solicitor, Old Davies' son, knew people that knew people, and based on the whispers and nods that were the language of those in the know, had divested what was left of Bart's investments from the crumbling banks into something far more solid just before the bubble burst.

She had actually done very well out of the whole thing. She didn't feel too guilty about that, as she'd never really thought of it as hers. Danny had signed it all over to her years ago, and she would use what she needed and leave whatever was left to Deirdre. If she left it to Danny, he'd probably drink it all and kill himself into the bargain. Deirdre would see that the right thing was done. Only she couldn't say a word of that to Dermot. Between his hip and his house and all the news about the Church, the poor man looked like all the wind had been let out of him.

"Besides . . ." She tried to cheer him up and poured more tea. "Don't you still have your pension?"

"They'll try and take that away too."

Jacinta sipped her tea and thought about her answer. There was talk about scaling back pensions, but on the other hand Dermot probably wouldn't live that much longer. There was really no way she knew of saying any of that, so she decided to offer him a little bit of nagging instead. "Don't be fretting over things like that. It's not good for your health."

As if to defy her attempt at optimism, Dermot coughed a deep, phlegmy cough. He still smoked more than a pack a day and it was all starting to catch up with him. "Health be damned. Why would any decent, honest, hard-working man want to live through times like these? They've all betrayed us. Our own people too."

She wasn't sure if he was talking about the clerics or the bankers so she let it pass without comment. The whole country was acting like they were shocked, but she felt they'd known all along. The people had always been in denial. First with the Church, despite rumors that had been going around for decades; and then with the bankers—and their cronies in the government. And now the people were getting angry—like they were surprised. She wasn't. She'd known the jig was up when Gina and Donal sold up everything they had and moved to Spain.

"How will we ever survive it all?" Dermot pleaded with her as if she'd have an answer, the same way Mrs. Flanagan used to.

"Well now, Dermot. We've been putting up with worse for centuries. We'll get through this too."

"You might, but I'm getting far too old for all of this."

"Ah there's a bit of life left in you yet."

There wasn't really but she had to say it. Dermot hadn't been the same since Anne died. And he had to be a least five years older than Jacinta and she was turning seventy this year.

She wanted to do something nice to celebrate it and was hoping to make it back over to Rome while she still could. She was still after Danny to come with her, but with Grainne having the baby and all, nothing had been decided. She could have gotten Deirdre to organize it for him but that didn't seem fair. She had enough on her hands right now.

"Well, Dermot, I better be getting on with my day and let you get back to reading your paper. Is there anything you need down at the shops?"

He wanted the usual, a pack of cigarettes, the evening newspaper—in case anything had happened since the morning—and if she could manage it, some more whiskey. He just liked to have it around—to add to his tea he'd explain every time he asked for some.

She didn't mind. He had little left in life and it wouldn't do him much harm at this stage.

*

Grainne and Doug had a very quiet wedding in late December when everyone was still occupied with Christmas. Grainne didn't want to make a big deal of it. City Hall, dinner with both families, his father getting a bit tipsy and telling her that Doug would have married her anyway, and her mother putting on her bravest face throughout. Grainne knew she was disappointed.

She had wanted her to finish her degree and go on to do something great and fulfilling with her life.

Grainne assured her that once the baby was old enough she would go back and finish, and her mother seemed to accept that. Almost. But she just couldn't hide her disappointment from Grainne—they knew each other far too well for that. They'd discussed her options, obliquely, and Grainne wasn't sure if her final decision was what her mother would have wanted. She said it was Grainne's decision to make, but she was always saying stuff like that. She did go along with the outcome with seemingly good grace and just a hint of reservation that only Grainne could detect.

Martin had been much more accepting once Doug had told him that he was totally committed to raising the child together. He even arranged for Doug to get an interview where he worked. It was an entry-level position, but after spending so much of his life on hockey, Doug wasn't really qualified to do much else. Martin had even taken to mentoring him privately and was sure that Doug would be promoted within months. They'd need that. Having a baby was far more expensive than either of them had realized. They were living with Deirdre until they had time to sort everything out, but still.

At first, Grainne had assumed that she could keep up with her studies while the baby slept. Her mother had told her that it mightn't be possible and to give herself the time to get used to all the changes babies brought. After a year or so, she could think about the rest of her life.

Her mother was right. Douglas Jr. was more than a handful and was only really content when he was latched onto her breast. The rest of the time he fussed and squirmed until her mother took him and calmed him. She said Grainne had been the same, but Grainne didn't believe her. Douglas was almost impossible.

And Doug was of little help. He worked late, and when he was home he always had homework. He said he had so much to learn, so she didn't complain. She knew he was doing it for them, and because Martin had gone out on a limb for him. But it was starting to get to her.

She didn't even bother getting dressed anymore and went from morning to night in one of Doug's old hockey sweaters and her tartan pajamas under her old, tattered robe. She kept her hair tied back because she hadn't had time to wash it, and she avoided her reflection in the mirror. Douglas Jr. had really taken a toll on her and she didn't want to be reminded. She couldn't seem to shed the thirty pounds of padding. She was about to cry about it again when she heard her mother's key in the lock.

"Oh, Mom, you're home earlier." She hadn't even got around to tidying up the kitchen and had hoped to have dinner started.

"No earlier than usual," her mother answered without looking directly at her. Grainne knew why. She must look a total mess.

"How was your day?" her mother continued, as if there was no issue. "Did you get out for a walk?"

Grainne hadn't. She had promised she would, but when the time came she couldn't; and it wasn't just the way she looked. She was exhausted all the time.

"Well, why don't you run upstairs and take a shower and I'll take DJ out into the garden?"

"No, Mom. I couldn't ask you to do that. You just got in from work."

"You weren't asking, sweetie, I was. Now get up stairs before Rachael gets here. You don't want her to see you like that. It might put her off having children and you know your brother. He and Doug are probably planning on rearing their own hockey team."

She smiled that smile she used when she was being the good cop, and that made Grainne feel even worse. Her mother had managed two children—practically on her own.

"Sweetie? Go now." Her mother nodded as Grainne blinked back her tears. And when she still didn't move, her mother turned her and, with one hand around her arm, just above the elbow, steered her upstairs. Grainne couldn't help it and began to sob a little.

"Have a long shower, sweetie, and we'll have a chance to talk later. Rachael will sit with DJ while you and I go out for a coffee or something."

"Look at me, Mom. I think we should go to McDonald's instead."

"Don't be silly, sweetie. You're nowhere near as big as I was after having you."

"Really?"

"Yes. I looked like a beached blimp and back then there was no consideration for the plus-sized woman. I had to cut a hole in a sheet and wore a pillow case over my head."

"Did you ever get . . . you know . . . a bit resentful?"

"All the time, sweetie, but you were worth it. Now get in the shower. Please?"

"How long did it take?" Grainne asked as she slipped behind the shower curtain before disrobing.

"Physically, not long. Emotionally . . .? Well, kids do permanent brain damage."

"You don't really mean that, do you, Mom?"

"It's true." Her mother took her discarded clothes and put them in the laundry hamper. "But don't worry, grandchildren are the cure." Her voice trailed away as she went and picked up the baby, who had woken and was beginning to fuss.

Grainne just stood and let the water run over her while her mother and her baby laughed as though they were happy to see each other. Her mother made all the little things they did together seem like fun. Everything. "We can't have your mother coming home and changing diapers," Doug had protested indignantly when he first found out. Only he was never available to do it. He was always working.

By the time Grainne had showered, and washed and conditioned her hair, her mother had changed the baby and taken him outside. Grainne could see them from the bathroom window. Douglas gurgling and mewling in his swing chair while Deirdre rocked him slowly with her outstretched leg as she sipped a glass of wine. She'd told Grainne, many times, that it was the happiest part of her day.

After she rummaged through her clothes a few times and tried on things that would never fit again, Grainne settled on her maternity pants and her extra-large, bright jazzy top. They were too big for her but she hoped they would make her look smaller. She put some shadow around her eyes to cover the dark circles and a little lipstick. Her hair was clean but still lank, and her bra was far too tight.

"You look wonderful," Rachael assured her as she came down the stairs.

"Considering?"

"Considering nothing. You're getting your own face back again."

Rachael probably meant well—Martin said she just got a little flustered and had been since Grainne was pregnant—but Grainne couldn't help feel there was more going on. Rachael probably found the whole thing repulsive. The bloating, the lactating, the dirty diapers and all the stuff that people didn't discuss.

"It's the makeup." Grainne blushed a little.

"Well, I hope I look as good as you when I get pregnant."

"Trust me." Grainne smiled at her tall, slim, perfect sister-in-law. "You'll look perfect, even while . . ." She stopped when Rachael's eyes grew too big.

"Well." Her mother stepped between them and handed the baby over to Rachael. "We will go and have a coffee and be back before his next feeding."

"You have my number?" Grainne checked with Rachael as Deirdre steered her toward the door.

"Yes, silly. You know I do."

"And you'll call, no matter what?"

*

Deirdre couldn't help feeling that she was kidnapping her own daughter, but something had to be done. She and Martin had been talking about it for a while: Grainne needed help and they couldn't put it off any longer. So they arranged for Rachael to come over while he took Doug for something to eat after work so they could have a little chat in private. And so that Deirdre could get Grainne out of the house for a while.

Martin had tried to sound nonchalant about it all but Deirdre knew he was concerned. Deirdre had told him not to be, that it wasn't that unusual; but she knew he would never accept that. He could be such a man-of-the-house sometimes.

Still, there was no denying it; Grainne was a mess. She hadn't shed any of her pregnancy weight yet and that was only an issue because it was clearly bothering her. And when she complained about it, Deirdre had gently suggested a little more exercise and a little less gorging, but she didn't make an issue of it. She knew what it was like and remembered how grateful she was when Jacinta and her mother kept their opinions to themselves and just helped out. Still, she agreed with Martin. It was time.

"Please stop checking your phone and enjoy a moment for yourself. You deserve it."

Grainne nodded and tried to smile but it was so strained. Deirdre remembered what that felt like; smiling because you didn't want anyone to know how totally drained you really were.

It was another one of the really stupid things women had done to themselves. These days you were expected to give birth one day, hit the gym the next, and be back to looking fabulous in weeks. Celeb-mums had thrown down the gauntlet and too many women were foolish enough to pick it up. They could blame men all they liked but women really were their own worst enemies.

"Grainne?"

She looked up from her phone and tried to put it away. "I'm sorry, Mom, it's just so weird to be away from him."

"Then try being in the moment and enjoy it."

"Is that even a thing anymore?"

"I would have thought that by now you would have developed a greater appreciation for the more important things in life—like actually getting a full night's sleep again," she added, so she wouldn't sound like such a mother.

"People still do that?" Grainne almost took the bait and for a moment looked like a brash teenager again, but she checked herself. "He wakes every two hours still. And Doug is talking about sleeping on the couch. He's beat before he even gets to the office. But"—she seemed to correct herself—"he's such an angel. I just want to hold him all the time."

"Of course you do, sweetie," Deirdre encouraged and Grainne grew more animated and proceeded to repeat the litany of all of Douglas Jr.'s recent milestones, almost becoming frenetic as she swelled a little more with pride.

Deirdre remembered what it was like. Once her babies had been her entire universe. Danny's, too, for a while. And even as she remembered that, she remembered what it was like the first time Jerry and Jacinta visited. At the time she had resented everything about them, intruding and smoking everywhere; but then she remembered what she was like.

Baby blues was such an old-wives' way of describing something that was one of the lowest points in her life, even rivaling some of the things Danny had done. It had all been so straightforward with Martin, but when Grainne came along everything she thought she knew about motherhood went out the window. With Martin, every little first was pure validation. That and the fact that he looked so adorable from the moment he emerged.

Grainne had fussed and resisted her every step of the way, and every regression was a ringing condemnation. She had felt like a total failure and probably would never have gotten out of it if she hadn't gone back to work. Miriam had been the catalyst. "It's all very well basking in the aura of motherhood for a while," she'd said, "but it's not really something to hang your hat on. Birds do it, bees do it. Even educated fleas do it."

Grainne was still talking and still talking about the baby. Deirdre loved the little tyke. It was easy; it was just an emotional investment without all the work. But her first loyalty was to her daughter. That would probably change, but right now her daughter needed her.

"Grainne, we need to talk about you for a while. It's been almost six months and I think it's time you started to get back into life."

Grainne reacted as if she had been slapped and, for a moment, looked as though she might cry.

"You think I'm being obsessive. Don't you?"

"It's not that. It's just time to start doing things for yourself again. It won't be long before DJ will be off doing his own thing."

"Mom! He can't even stand up by himself. He needs me for everything." And even as she said it, her eyes grew wider. "He's just a baby still—my baby."

Deirdre didn't answer. She didn't want to force the issue.

"Besides"—Grainne sat back and pouted a little—"I'm not ready."

"I know, but you must start getting back into the swing of things."

"Really, Mom, what else am I supposed to be doing?"

Deirdre reached out and touched the back of her hand. "I'm not criticizing you. I'm just trying to help."

"And you think I need help?"

"We all need help from time to time."

Grainne checked her phone again and sipped her decaf latte. She looked the way she did when she was young and frightened. "You don't think I can do this?"

"Of course you can, sweetie. You will be a perfect mother."

"As long as?"

"There's no 'as long as.'"

"Mom, there's always an 'as long as' with you."

"Now, Grainne, let's not start criticizing my maternal skills." Deirdre raised one eyebrow to let her daughter know she was joking. "You can only do the best with what you're given. Now, let's finish and get you back before Rachael's good deed turns bad on her."

"Thanks, Mom." Grainne finally smiled as Deirdre unlocked the car. "You were right, I really needed that."

"We all do, sweetie, from time to time."

*

By Christmas, Grainne was almost back to her old self. She had slimmed down enough and had weaned Douglas Jr., but she still fussed over him. Doug and Martin had teased her about that until Rachael announced that she was expecting. Deirdre had known, but hadn't told them and just sat back while they dug themselves in too deeply. She enjoyed watching Martin skillfully extract himself while Doug blundered on as the two girls turned on him.

Deirdre sat back and smiled. She would wait until they had blown it all off; all the little niggling things that were better casually discarded before they grew into the types of things that could tear them apart. She loved them all, even Doug. He was doing his best and that was all that anybody could ask.

They all were, even as the rest of the world was shrouded in doom and gloom. Except Canada, floating along in a bubble. Serenaded by songs of self-promotion crafted by spin masters and paid for by tax dollars. The Canadian banks were, for the most part, unaffected—something the smug took credit for despite the fact that the real credit was due to a man that voters had soundly rejected. But for Deirdre, things were solid. She had paid off the mortgage and house prices in Toronto were still rising. She would sell the house and find a nice condo closer to Yonge and have plenty left over to help her children set up their own homes. She would have to make an allowance for Danny, too, but it might be better to dole it out rather than risk him with a lump sum. That would be tempting fate. She still cared about what happened to him—that would never change—even if everything they once shared had turned on them. But they had created a family too. His mother was still after Deirdre to get Danny to go to Rome and she had talked with him about it.

"And why on earth would I want any part of all of that?" he had asked and smirked. They had gone for coffee after she helped him pick out a few gifts for his new grandson. She didn't mind doing it. She had moved past all her harder feelings and was comfortable just seeing him, as long as it was about their family. "Next she'll want me to go back to Confession—and start going for Communion again. I wouldn't mind, only she doesn't even believe in any of that stuff."

"Maybe she just wants to have a vacation together," Deirdre lied. Jacinta had told her all about Fr. Reilly and the Jesuit, and all that they had done for Mrs. Flanagan. She was convinced that they would be able to help Danny.

Deirdre had talked with Miriam about it, too. She'd told her that poor old John Melchor was struggling to cling to whatever was left of his sanity. But she also said that she didn't think there would be any harm in Danny visiting. She thought Fr. Reilly might appreciate it. She said that, even though he never mentioned it to her, she always had the feeling that Danny Boyle was a piece of unresolved business for Patrick.

As far as Deirdre was concerned, Danny had enough unresolved issues around Catholicism and the way he had been brought up. "Besides"—she smiled at him and kept her thoughts to herself—"it might do you some good to take a trip somewhere. Grainne and I really enjoyed ourselves when we were there."

"Yeah. I'd love to go on a trip like that with her, only that's not going to happen anymore."

Deirdre was tempted to say something reassuring but she knew better. She didn't want to become involved any more than she had to. "Well I think you should consider it. It would mean the world to your mother."

She drained her coffee as he thought about that. She'd done as Jacinta had asked but she was getting uncomfortable. It was all very well meeting him, but she didn't want any more involvement in his life. There was no point. It had always been a downward spiral and she would have more than enough to do helping Grainne, and Martin, with their unresolved issues when it finally came to its sad and sorry end.

"Thanks," he said and tried to smile as she rose to leave. Only his smile was tired and forced. "Thanks for coming out and doing this with me."

The kids were now bickering over music. They were all tired of Ricky Martin and Grainne wanted to listen to Michael Jackson. Since his death it was all she listened to, but Rachael and Doug wanted something more traditional, so Martin dug out the Bing Crosby CDs and soon they all sang along to "White Christmas." And as she sat there, surrounded by family, Deirdre couldn't help but feel a little sorry for Danny Boyle. He'd cut himself off from everything he loved to wallow in his pools of self-pity.

Yes, life was full of ups and downs, but together, as a family, they would muddle through. They would deal with everything life threw at them and get up and go on to the good times that always followed. That was the biggest difference between them—Danny just sat in his misery decrying the world around him.

It wouldn't have mattered but for one thing; even in absentia, Danny was still a part of their family. They all were.

# Chapter 14 – 2010

"Sure you'd hardly recognize the country anymore," Jacinta told them all as she placed fresh flowers on their graves. Bart, Nora and Jerry, all lying peacefully on the hillside across from Glenasmole on a fine spring afternoon. The sun was warm but there was still a chilly breeze running through the long grasses.

She hadn't been to see them since last autumn. It was getting harder and harder for her to manage the trek and she couldn't ask Dermot. He was so bad it wasn't safe for him to drive anymore. Deirdre had her hide the car keys from him. He still insisted that she help him look for them every time she called in, but he was getting so forgetful that he was easily deflected by a cup of tea. By the second cup he would have forgotten all about them and begun another rant about the sorry state of the country.

"It's all a bit down now," she told the dead. "The poor old Celtic Tiger has been and gone but it's still a great difference from the way things used to be. Only the young are leaving again—not that they aren't well up for it. They all have university degrees these days and they've been going on holidays to places like Thailand and all, so they'll be well used to it. Jaze, isn't it well for them all the same. In our day the Isle of Man was far enough—if you could even get that far. Most of us had to make do with Butlins.

"Not that I haven't done my own bit of traveling too." She pulled at the new crop of weeds that were poking up around the graying, lichen-stained stone. Her own parents, and Anne Fallon, all had nice, clean, polished granite stones, but Bart's was an old stone. They had put Nora beside him when her turn came. And Jerry too. He'd asked her to.

"They're better off getting out of here and going somewhere they might have a chance at having a life for themselves. This country is nothing but a bloody disgrace. We raised them up to expect the world and then when the Germans wagged their finger, packed them all off into exile. We should be ashamed of ourselves."

They should. They had let themselves be led back to the way things used to be under the old landlords. "Fiscal Connaught," Dermot used to growl every time she brought him the newspapers. And this time it was their own that did it—no matter how much everybody went on about Mrs. Merkel. It was their own flesh and blood that had sold them out this time.

"Nobody is going to church anymore and who could blame them? Every day there's news of another bishop who didn't do the right thing. I suppose they think they were just protecting the good name of the Church when what they should have been thinking about was the poor little innocents who had been brought up to trust them.

"I suppose," she conceded as she lowered her head, as her own share of their collective guilt rose up inside her, "we're all to blame really. We all knew, only we wouldn't let on and now we're all wandering around like we're lost in the fog. And," she added with a nod to Bart's name on the stone, "there's nobody left to give us a good kick in the arse and drag us out of it. We've gotten awful lazy, and even the idea of rising up and changing things has us worn out. We've had a taste of the good life and we'll never be happy going back to the way things used to be."

She paused for a few moments but none of them answered her. They didn't have to; she knew what they would have said. Bart would have fumed and snorted like a bull. Nora would have clucked and sniffed as if she wasn't surprised. And Jerry? He would have had a good laugh about it all. "What did the people expect?" he'd ask. "Sure didn't Karl Marx warn them years ago that this would happen?"

That would've set them all at each other's throats again—or at least it would have when they'd been alive. None of them had ever been shy about their views. Still, Jacinta missed them more and more with each passing year as she grew older and more alone.

"I suppose Danny and Deirdre were better off getting away when they did," she said to lighten the mood again. "But I'm afraid it's a bit of a mixed bag over there too. He's getting worse every time I see him. It's like he's just waiting around for the end now.

"It's such a pity, too," she added as she struggled with her composure. "His children are a credit to us all. And they're hardly children anymore and are off starting families of their own. That must make you all proud? Being a part of something that goes on long after you."

She took solace from her own words as she pulled a tissue from her purse and cleaned the dust and dirt that was gathering in the grooves of the inscriptions. "And you'd all be so proud of young Martin. And Grainne, too, but Martin is a bit like you, Bart. He's not afraid of doing what has to be done. And he's a real gentleman too.

"He's shrewd too. Sometimes, when I see him thinking, he reminds me of you, Nora. But when he laughs it still sounds the same way it did when you made him laugh, Jerry. He still remembers you and often tells me that he misses you."

She knew that would make them all happy, but even as a cold breeze rustled past her, her news of Danny lingered over the place.

"I'm still trying to get him to come to Rome with me this year—if we ever get to fly again after all the ash. It would do him the world of good to see Fr. Reilly again.

"And he could meet the Jesuit. You'd like him, Nora. He's nobody's fool and you can tell, just by looking, that he knows what's really going on. Fr. Reilly tries, God bless him, but it always feels like he is just telling you something that he's read in a book.

"Not that he isn't the heart and soul of good, but the Jesuit has the eyes of a man who can see what nobody else can.

"I'm sure that sounds like I'm going a bit daft again but that's how he made me feel. He was able to get the soul of Mrs. Flanagan's brat out of purgatory. I'm sure he'll be able to do something for our Danny yet.

"Please God he'll come with me this year."

She got ready to rise as the new curate approached. He'd been off saying his few prayers at some of the newer graves. He was a decent enough young fella—taking time out to drive her and all—but God he was so young. "How is one so young and innocent ever going to survive," she'd confided in Nora before he got too close. "But still, he's a huge improvement on Fr. Dolan—or Bishop Dolan as his eminence now likes to be called. He'd drive me all right but he'd have kept the meter running."

"It's so nice to see you smiling, Mrs. Boyle," the young curate whispered after he had made the sign of the cross and kissed the rosary beads that trickled from his fingers. He was very old school like that—a bit like old Fr. Brennan, God love him.

"You'd be smiling, too, if you knew them." Jacinta laughed for his sake as she took his outstretched hand and hauled herself up. "They were the best of characters. We'll never see the likes of them again.

"Bart, my father-in-law, fought for Ireland back in the Troubles. And my mother-in-law, Nora, she'd have put the skids under them all, from the bishops all the way to the Vatican, if she'd known what was going on. And she'd have put those bankers in their place, too."

But it was Bart and Nora's fault too. They'd known and had known for years. The Republic that Bart had fought for was nothing more than what Jerry always said: "A rotten little fief-dom of liars and thieves and buggerers."

"And what made you take the collar?" she asked the young curate.

"Well, Mrs. Boyle, with all that happened I thought some-one should be reminding the people of what Jesus really stood for."

"And do you think you know that?" It was unfair of her to say that, and the poor curate looked like a rabbit that was trying to decide which way to run.

"Never mind me," she soothed him as she linked her arm in his for steadying. "Tell me, did you ever hear tell of Fr. Patrick Reilly. He was the curate here years ago, only he's off in Rome now. I'll give you his address—if you're ever going over. He was like the Sacred Heart, he was."

She wondered what Patrick was making of it all—and the German pope. Jacinta didn't really care for him. He had a face like a man who had squeezed all joy out of his own life and was more than happy to squeeze it out of the people too. Every time she heard him speak she couldn't help but remember what Jerry used to say, back when he was Cardinal Ratzinger—the Pol-ish pope's Rottweiler: "Ve must follow orders." And, he'd been a bit of a Nazi too. Only he was just a young fellow then and everyone did foolish things when they were young.

"That's very kind of you, Mrs. Boyle. I've been dying to see it and I might get the chance next year. It'll be nice having somebody to go and see—someone from around here, that is."

They drove for a while in silence but the curate was the chatty type. "I hear that the Saville Inquiry will finally say that they were all wrongfully killed."

Jacinta turned and stared at him in silence.

"The poor people from Bloody Sunday," he added for clarification.

"Since when did we need the British to tell us that," she asked, far colder than she meant to. Her mind was wandering and she'd been thinking about how nice it would be after the

Jesuit had cured Danny. "Sure didn't we all see it on the TV?" But he wouldn't have—he would've barely been alive then.

"Please excuse me, Mrs. Boyle. I didn't mean to be bringing up all the pain and sorrow, only I thought it would be good for the country to finally have a bit of closure. It helps with the forgiveness."

"Are you even Irish?"

"I am, indeed." The curate relaxed when he realized she was joking. "Only I'd like to think of myself as the new breed."

"Well, I hope you're right."

How was one so young and innocent ever going to survive?

*

Martin's head was still spinning as their shots were placed on the bar in front of them. Doug had insisted that they drink Irish whiskey and Martin just went along with him. Deep down he remembered that he didn't like whiskey—not the taste and not the smell—but everything else had changed. Maybe he'd like it now. He'd just become the father of a beautiful boy—a new addition to the long line of Boyles, glorious and otherwise. He thought he was ready as he and Rachael had spent the last few months preparing, but nothing could have prepared him for the flood of emotions that surged up and loosened the tight grip he kept on himself. Joy, pride, hope and forgiveness. They all surged around inside him, unchecked.

"You know . . ." Rachael had laughed and leaned toward him, as much as her enormous belly allowed. It was just days before she was due and they were going through the check-lists one more time. "We're going to have to involve your father."

"Why?"

"For ballast. Being around my father will turn our children into Goths."

"I could live with that."

She reached out, took his hand and placed it on their baby. "Martin, please?"

She hadn't swollen up the way Grainne had and was again. Rachael was still so pretty and thin but for the enormous bump that kept growing. And, as it grew bigger, she had to push it along in front of her, having to lean back and waddle the more it grew.

She never once complained—not really—but he could see what it was taking out of her. She worked right up to the end, too, even though he disagreed. He'd kept bringing it up, more and more as the time got closer, but she was adamant. She had to see out her project. He admired that and, as a compromise, they agreed she would take at least a year off after that. His mother had almost snorted at the idea of it being a "year off," but agreed with him. She'd told Rachael that she sometimes wished she had spent more time at home with her babies.

"Okay. I'll let him know when the time comes." He withdrew his hand from Rachael's belly but kept his smile. He would, but he'd phone him so he wouldn't have to struggle to contain his disdain face-to-face.

"Martin, call around and see him tomorrow."

"I'm so happy for you, son." Danny had lit up when Martin shared the news with him. "And Rachael too. I'm so proud of both of you." He tried to get up from his barstool but was too unsteady. Martin stood over him and tried not to look disgusted.

"You'll sit down and have a drink with your old man, won't you?"

"I can't. I was late at the office and I have to get back to take Rachael somewhere." It sounded plausible. He didn't want to be rude but he didn't want them to get any closer than they had to. He was doing this for Rachael—not for his father.

"I understand, son, but you'll tell that lovely little wife of yours that I can't wait to see her and the little one. When you're all settled in again," he added, realizing that he might be imposing.

"Don't worry. Rachael's going to have everybody over to celebrate."

"Is he going to be Jewish?"

Martin could tell he was joking and went along with it. They could share a quick laugh before he left. "Half. Half Jewish and half Irish. The poor kid doesn't stand a chance."

"He'll be fine. He or she, it won't matter. With you for a father, he's going to be a winner."

Danny looked as though he was hoping to have a father-son moment, but Martin wasn't ready for anything like that. Instead, he checked his watch and began to turn away.

"I want you to know something." His father reached toward him, as much as his balance would allow. "It'll always be my greatest regret. One that I will carry to the grave. I'll always wish that I could've been a better father to you."

He should have stayed with him and had a drink. Martin knew that now. Watching his own son come into the world had changed the way he looked at everything. His father would have looked at him the same way. Martin was sure of it. And now . . . He almost shuddered as he tried to imagine his own son acting the way he had.

"Cheers." Doug raised his glass and waited for Martin to respond. "Welcome to the club."

They drained their glasses, both shivering and grimacing until the barmaid returned with beer.

"Well?" Doug tried again after Martin had stared off into the distance for too long.

His mind was wandering, and he had been replaying the faces Rachael had worn during the birthing. First it was frustration and impatience, giving way to irritability, beading with sweat as her hair began to cling to her face. Then she had been angry and reddened as she pushed between every breath. He was supposed to coach her but he would have been better off going somewhere and boiling water. And then, when he was feeling totally helpless and useless, she began to smile as their child emerged, smiling as he had never seen her do before.

"I told you. It changes everything. Doesn't it?"

"Yeah," Martin agreed and struggled to get his head straight. "Can it get any better than this?"

"Wait until you have to deal with your first shitty diaper."

"I'm serious, Doug." He didn't want the day-to-day reality to rush back in just yet.

"So am I, Bud. So am I."

"You're killing my buzz."

"Chill, Bud. I'm just a few steps ahead of you. Another shot?"

"What the hell, but let's try tequila this time. Whiskey is an old man's drink."

"Tequila? Are we having a fiesta?" Doug was ready for a night out. Between the baby and his pregnant wife, and taking work home with him every night, they hadn't had a boys' night in months.

"Not me. I'm just going to get a good buzz on and then I'm going home to get some sleep."

Martin needed to unwind. They'd made it this far, keeping all the balls in the air. He'd been bringing work home, too, and dealing with it after Rachael nodded off on the couch every evening. He let her sleep even though she was always embarrassed when she awoke. Her hair was always tousled and she'd have the marks of the cushion across one side of her face, and a silver string of spit dangling from her lower lip. He never let on and kissed her anyway, but sometimes he wondered if she would ever look normal again.

"I hope you haven't said any of that aloud?" his mother had asked when he mentioned it to her. "It's the last thing a woman needs to hear."

He had tried to look offended that his discretion was questioned but knew his mother could see straight through that.

"I wouldn't worry, sweetie." She came closer and he could almost feel her heart beat. "Rachael will be back to her beautiful self before you notice. Besides, after a few months of midnight feedings neither of you will be too concerned about things like that."

"Thanks, Mom. That makes me feel a whole lot better."

He could talk to her about stuff like that—or that's what he told himself when he was really asking her what he should do. All the other stuff—hockey, school, work—was easy to figure. Family—that was hard and he was determined to get it right.

"Martin, you and Rachael will be fine. You'll pay the price all parents do. You'll have your lives hijacked for fifteen to fifty years. Things will be very different, but you and Rachael will make it a very beautiful thing." She stood in front of him, a tall slender woman who had taken the proverbial basket of lemons and made a very good life for herself, and Grainne and him too.

"Thanks, Mom, but I bet you said the same thing to Grainne."

"You know," she said and hugged him, "you guys are becoming so competitive since you started having children. It's cute. Disturbing, but cute."

He held her longer than normal and drew from her calm strength. "So what did you say to her?"

"Grainne and I talk about other things."

Martin had let it go at that. Grainne was bloated again and they all trod carefully around her.

"So what did you guys decide to call him?" Doug asked.

"Martin. Martin Joel Boyle." He and Rachael had discussed names and had thought about going hyphenated. She thought Brand-Boyle had a certain ring to it, but he suggested Fallon-Brand. But they couldn't. It sounded like something from a marketing pitch.

"We're calling the next one Daniel."

"If it's a boy."

"We know already. There's more than enough to be uncertain about. At least this way we can plan some things."

"Do you ever get worried?" Martin asked as he sipped his beer and ordered two more shots. "You know—about bringing a kid into this world?"

"Me, no. Just think about how fucked up my world would be if I didn't let your sister have what she wanted."

"Good point."

"Besides, we'll teach them how to skate and they can figure the rest out for themselves. My old man always said that. He wasn't such a bad guy. He used to make a backyard rink every year—before he fucked off with his secretary. I used to be mad at him about that."

"And you're not anymore?"

"Not so much. I'm still pissed at what he did to my mother but I get it now. Being a father is much harder than they said."

"Really?" Martin sat back and smiled.

"Yeah, newbie. But don't worry; you can come to me for advice."

"Right. Maybe you could do me a PowerPoint or something."

"I'm serious, dude. You have no idea how much bullshit you have to go through trying to make everything perfect so you can sneak off for a few hours to watch a game every now and then."

"You still get to watch games? Grainne must be getting soft."

"Yeah. You gotta keep that part of you alive, bro, otherwise you go crazy worrying about money and all the other shit."

When Deirdre sold the house she gave them each enough for down-payments. Rachael's father had matched it, and Martin and Rachael had a really nice place near Mt. Pleasant and Lawrence. Not to be outdone, Grainne had insisted on buying a place on Cameron Crescent. A place she and Doug couldn't really afford.

"Hey, that reminds me. I got some news that might interest you." When Martin had found out that Rachael was expecting, he'd gotten another promotion. They liked that he was becoming a family man and wanted him to know he had a future there. "I'm putting a new team together and I might be able to get you in."

"More work?"

"Of course, but the money will be better."

"Thanks, Martin. You're a life saver."

"I didn't say it was for sure. I said I might be able to get you in. You're not the best candidate."

"Yeah, but you could teach me all the stuff I need to know."

"Yeah, while Rachael and I are dealing with a new baby?"

"Welcome to my world, bro."

*

"We'll all be arrested for this," Patrick Reilly protested meekly, but Miriam ignored him and pushed John Melchor's wheelchair closer to the concrete prow of the Isola Tiberina. All around them the river rushed by as if it had caught the scent of the sea and could no longer be restrained.

"It was his last request." John looked back over his hunched shoulder and smiled as if to encourage him. Only now poor John was so old that his smiles looked more like grimaces.

"Most of the *Carabinieri* are probably related to him one way or another," Miriam joined in, nodding in agreement as she pushed John far too close to the edge. She had often joked about doing it but stopped and looked back at Patrick. "Besides, I'm sure we can plea bargain with them."

"Then why didn't he get one of them to do it."

"Because it's illegal, and Romans have always been very particular about which laws they break."

Patrick was getting nervous—he'd never done anything illegal in his life.

"Oh, Patrick, don't be such a worrier. If anything happens you and I can make a run for it and leave John to face the music. You won't mind, will you John? It would be such a grand gesture—another felony for humanity."

"No," the old Jesuit agreed. "But I have my price. I will want a statue. Me, sitting high in my chair, right beside my old friend Bruno."

"Okay, then," Patrick agreed as both Miriam and John laughed, something they almost did as one—like the hardened felons they were. "Throw them in quick and let's get back up before someone sees us." He scanned the banks above but no one was watching them. The World Cup was on and everybody was busy following it, the older crowd in front of their televisions while the young checked their devices as they dashed around from place to place.

"Our dear friend Giovanni has honored us with his last request. We will see it out with all the dignity that he deserves." John fondled the urn as he spoke, as if deciding if he still had any time for Patrick. He was close to the end, too, and had grown very impatient with the world and everyone in it. Except Miriam, but he was totally dependent on her.

The night before Giovanni had died in his own bed, in his own house filled with grieving relatives, cooking and eating to deflect their grief, he had asked to see them all. Patrick had brought his stole but that wasn't what the old Roman wanted. He told them he was going to be cremated, despite the operatic chorus of objections from his family, and he wanted his ashes poured on the river. And, as there was no one else he could trust, he needed them to promise him that they would do it. He would have asked Davide Pontecorvo but he was far too old and rarely came out of the backroom of the bookstore anymore. "Like an old spider." Giovanni laughed, his shuddering almost shaking the last of life from him. "They'll find him there when his time comes, leaning over a book behind a curtain of spider webs." They had laughed along with him but they knew: here at the end of his days the dying man missed his oldest and dearest friend.

"There are no better words to remember our old friend than those of Bruno," John decided after some contemplation: "That I shall sink in death, I know must be; but with that death of mine what life will die?

"Fear not the lofty fall," he continued, holding the urn like a chalice,

> Rend with might the clouds, and be content to
> die, if God such a glorious death for us intend.

Patrick lowered his head so his face couldn't be seen. Poor old John had finally lost his grip on reality and now lived among the whispering shadows that seemed to hover around him everywhere he went. He had discussed it with Miriam but she didn't seem too concerned. "He's just passing between the worlds," she had answered, strangely intent on her own words. "Soon he will pass on from us. Let him have his eccentricities until then."

"The Divine Light is always in man," John emphasized in Patrick's direction, as if to assuage his doubt,

> Presenting itself to the senses and to the comprehension, but man rejects it.
> From whom being, life, and movement are suspended,
> And which extends itself in length, breadth, and depth,
> To whatever is in Heaven, on Earth, and Hell.

Patrick kept his head down in case anything he did might encourage more, while John fumbled with the lid of the urn.

"Here, let me help," Miriam fussed, but John was determined.

"I can manage this." His old gray face grew red as he struggled and his long white fingers grew whiter until Miriam had had enough and reached forward and grabbed the urn as John's fingers tugged at the lid. It opened in the struggle and covered him with a fine white dust.

"The fools of the world have been those who have established religions, ceremonies, laws, faith, rule of life," he continued as Patrick carried his chair back up the stairs. Miriam had taken John by the arm and was coaxing him from step to step. They had gotten most of the ash off but some had settled into the pores of his skin and made his face seem stone-like.

The greatest asses of the world are those who,
Lacking all understanding and instruction,
And void of all civil life and custom, rot in
perpetual pedantry;
Those who by the grace of heaven would reform
obscure and corrupted faith,
Salve the cruelties of perverted religion and
remove abuse of superstitions,
Mending the rents in their vesture.

"Not far now, John. Perhaps you should save your breath until we get to the top." Miriam was losing her patience.

"It is not they who indulge impious curiosity," John continued regardless, slowing their progress as he stopped again to speak,

Or who are ever seeking the secrets of nature,
And reckoning the courses of the stars.
Observe whether they have been busy with the
secret causes of things,
Or if they have condoned the destruction of
kingdoms,
The dispersion of peoples, fires, blood, ruin or
extermination;
Whether they seek the destruction of the whole
world that it may belong to them:
In order that the poor soul may be saved, that
an edifice may be raised in heaven,
That treasure may be laid up in that blessed
land,
Caring naught for fame, profit or glory in this
frail and uncertain life,
But only for that other most certain and eternal
life.

Patrick reached the top and unfolded the chair, gasping as he did. Miriam and John were halfway up and he was conflicted between going back down to help or just waiting to catch his breath.

John, however, was determined to continue, pausing again after taking just two steps.

> Pray, O pray to God, dear friends, if you are not
> already asses
> That he will cause you to become asses...
> There is none who praiseth not the golden age
> when men were asses:
> They knew not how to work the land.
> One knew not how to dominate another,
> One understood no more than another;
> Caves and caverns were their refuge;
> They were not so well covered nor so jealous nor
> were they confections of lust and of greed.
> Everything was held in common.

"That's enough now, John," Miriam chided as she tucked him into his chair and draped the rug across his knees. "This beast of burden needs a bit of peace and quiet."

"Let me push for a while," Patrick offered, but Miriam was stubborn. She was still teaching part-time but most of her days were taken up with John. She picked him up most mornings and pushed him around until the day grew too hot. Then she would return him to his home where he could nap the afternoon away. Patrick often joined her in the evenings as they took the old Jesuit somewhere for dinner—not that he ate much anymore, but was content to be spoon-fed some soup.

"Oh holy asininity! Holy ignorance," John went on regardless, blessing those who walked by.

> Holy foolishness and pious devotion!
> You who alone do more to advance and make
> souls good
> Than human ingenuity and study...

\*

It was almost winter and it was a cold, numbing type of day, with a regular sprinkling of rain. Rome didn't suit the rain. It brought out all that was old and mildewing and the faint smell of rot.

"I heard from Deirdre the other day," Miriam mentioned after they had taken John for his afternoon outing. He'd been brooding and muttering dark portents and, after they had dropped him off, they had walked in silence for a while. "She's just had her third grandchild. It's hard to believe she's old enough."

"How old is she now?" Patrick asked, but Miriam could tell he wasn't that interested. He was becoming more and more reticent about people as time went on. John had said that it was avoidance and Miriam was concerned.

"She's fifty-two."

He nodded but didn't answer.

"I don't suppose you want to go for a coffee or something?" Miriam wanted to reach out to him. She couldn't bear to see him like this.

"Not tonight, Miriam, it has been too long a day."

"Patrick, what's bothering you?"

"Oh, it's nothing, Miriam. I'm just feeling a bit down in the dumps."

"Anything in particular?" She should have let it go but she suspected there was something in John's ramblings. He had, amid his other pronouncements, insisted that until Patrick dealt with the Danny Boyle issue, he would never have peace. He said that was why Patrick was retreating further and further into himself. "He feels he has failed Danny as a priest. Help him with that."

"It's nothing for you to be concerned about," Patrick finally answered with a hint of resignation. "It's just something that old priests have to go through."

"Everyone has to look back and evaluate their lives, Patrick, not just priests."

"That's true, but other people have families and accomplishments. Priests have so little to show for it all."

"Only if they ignore all the good they have done."

"But have we, Miriam? Have we done anything other than offer platitudes?"

She might have argued but it wasn't going to change his mood. She knew him far too well for that. Instead, she just stood as the rain misted and the whispering shadows of the past closed in around them. There would be better days ahead. Days when the sun shone and everything around them came back to life. That was when she would sit down and talk it out with him—on a fine sunny day. That was the best time to talk about things like that.

Besides, what had she to offer? While Deirdre had filled her life with her career, her children, and now her grandchildren, Miriam was almost alone. She had tried with Karl, but now all she had to show was her friendship with John and Patrick. She wanted to be content with that but, as their days dwindled . . .

\*

Patrick felt bad about not being able to respond more honestly and wandered aimlessly for a while. It was another of those evenings when the emptiness of his life billowed around him. Being with Miriam and John was having that effect on him lately. They had all given their lives in the service of a god that had nothing to give back.

*I tried to warn you,* his uncle's voiced whispered as he crossed the Campo.

"You did indeed, Uncle, only it sounded like you were contradicting yourself."

*How so?*

"Because you always said one thing and behaved completely differently. And you always had such confidence and assurance. You seemed like everything I wanted to become."

*And do you regret it now?*

"Tonight I do, but it's probably just the weather. I'm sure I'll feel better about everything when the spring comes."

# Chapter 15 – 2011

H ER EYES, THEY SHONE LIKE THE DIAMONDS," Danny sang in a phlegmy, hoarse rattle. He had difficulty reaching the lower notes and had to be careful not to start coughing.

> Ya'd think she was queen of the land.
> With her hair thrown over her shoulder,
> Tied up with a black velvet band.

He tried to finish with a flourish but his chords were blurred and his strumming was erratic—not surprising, given that he hadn't picked up a guitar in a few years. He was just happy that he even remembered how. He'd been promising himself he'd get back into it one of these days but his hands were far too shaky. Or at least they were until he got a few drinks into him. Only then, when he finally managed to keep them down, he'd be back on the merry-go-round and wouldn't feel like it anymore.

He drank alone in his apartment these days, right through the gloom of the afternoon until the night closed back in around him, hiding all that was defective or broken. He'd even stopped lighting candles because he kept seeing the ghosts of his past in the flicker of the flame. He'd tried to ignore them, but they'd just grow and sneer at him from the shadows on the wall. They'd stopped talking to him, too. Even his uncle Martin just stood there along with everyone else he'd ever let down.

Billie was there, too, and now just looked at him with haughty disdain.

He still tried talking to them. He'd start out with his polished rationales and hope that at least one of them still had some sympathy for him, but they didn't.

It wasn't all his fault—and they knew that. Yes, he had fucked up so many things on his own, but he was an alcoholic and everyone knew it was a disease. And, as he had learned in AA, he had been from the beginning, long before he'd even started to drink.

That was the thing nobody could understand. He had a disorder that made the things that normal people dealt with impossible. He'd obsess over every little slight—real or imagined—until they grew like cancers inside him and blocked out everything else. He'd heard it a thousand times at meetings: alcoholics suffered from a spiritual, physical and mental disorder. He was just as much the victim as any of them. Probably more, given that he had all that guilt and shame to deal with too.

Every time he thought about the way his life had gone, all the old feelings of worthlessness would rise within him as thick as fog, and the only way to dispel them was to have another drink and wait for the warming comfort that only alcohol brought.

Only even that didn't work the way it once did. Now any comfort just shriveled up in moments and he constantly needed to boost it. He mostly drank wine—cheap red wine in bottles, bags and boxes. The taste didn't matter anymore. He just wanted the old reassurance it used to give him, and that was getting harder and harder to get back to.

He still drank whiskey and beer when he was out and had to show them all he was just an ordinary man out having a few—that he'd finally got the monkey off his back. But home alone, with no one to impress, he could drink as much as he wanted. He wasn't doing anyone else any harm. He'd just get himself to the point where he could pass out and not have to think about anything for a while. Only before he slipped back into the darkness inside himself, his last few thoughts were always about the morning and having to deal with it all again. Sometimes he'd almost pray to be taken out of his misery while he slept. Nothing painful or messy—just something quick and painless. Then they'd all see: he might have been a fuck-up but at least he had the decency to go in a quiet, dignified manner at the end. People remembered stuff like that.

Some nights he even showered and changed his underwear in case it happened, but most nights he just collapsed on his bed in all his sweaty stench. If it did happen, he'd tell himself, somebody would clean him up before everybody got to see.

Probably Grainne. She hadn't given up on him. She still believed in him and encouraged him every time he promised to try to get his shit together. He could still convince himself that he really meant it. But every morning when he was trying to cure himself, he'd miss the tipping point and just get drunk again.

Even then she wouldn't cut him off, and right up to just before the new baby was born, still got together with him; but only for coffee in The Second Cup or Timothy's.

He didn't mind. He always brought a mickey of vodka and could swig from it in the washroom if he had to. Most of the time he didn't. She was always rushing off right after and couldn't stay long.

She always brought something for him; mostly socks and underwear, or jeans, or a fresh new shirt. She'd wanted to take him to buy shoes but now, with the new baby and all, she hadn't been able to find the time.

He didn't mind. She always slipped him a few bucks, too, before she left. She was the only one who knew what he was really going through. He was in hell, only it wasn't the way they'd all told him. His hell was inside him and instead of burning fires there were steaming piles of shit stinking up everything while the devils of his conscience poked and prodded him.

"Fair play to ya, Boyle," the crowd along the bar cheered him anyway. "Ya never lost it."

They were the hard core who had been drinking since noon. Refuges from all the other Irish bars in town, now over-run by hordes of wanna-bes who wore green and thronged to anything that was remotely connected to St. Patrick's Day.

Packed in crowds, the more brazen sipping Guinness while others settled for O'Keefe's or Bailey's, with a touch of green food coloring, they talked in what they thought was blarney and acted out every garish Irish caricature they could think of.

No such foolishness was tolerated in McMurphy's. There, the true sons and daughters of Eireann just carried on as if it were any other day, but with more than a hint of manic determination.

"Give us another one, Danny Boy," someone called.

"Yeah, do something by the Pogues."

"Feck the Pogues—bunch of feckin' punks. Do something by Luke Kelly."

Danny fingered the fret board. His fingers were begin-ning to throb. He'd just come in to get a few beers into him but someone had the guitar behind the bar and, as long as he played, he was getting his drinks for free.

He needed the break. He was almost broke again but he couldn't ask Deirdre for help—not for drinking money. He'd seen her when Grainne invited him to her house to meet her new child, before Martin got there.

Danny had a few before he went—to settle his nerves—but he didn't drink when he was there; not even when Doug and Grainne tried to tempt him into having a few beers. He knew Deirdre would be watching him so he said he didn't feel like drinking when he was around the babies.

It was a struggle, but he had to make the right impres-sion. He wanted to have some part in his grandchildren's lives. Grainne and Doug seemed happy with that and promised to invite him over at least once a month. He told them he'd be delighted, promising himself that when he went he'd be as clean and sober as he could manage.

Martin arrived as he was leaving and, as far as Danny could tell, still wanted nothing to do with him, barely acknowledging him, even though Danny could sense that Rachael was working on him. She'd always been very nice and made a point of bringing her father over to talk with him. Danny didn't care too much for him but went along with it. He liked Rachael and knew that she was his best hope of ever having any kind of relationship with his son.

"I then put my head," he sang on. "Peggy Gordon" was always one of his favorite songs.

> To a cask of brandy.
> It was my fancy, I do declare.
> For it's when I'm drinking, I'm always thinking...

The crowd at the bar pressed in all around, making him feel like a star. And when he finished and handed the guitar back, he saw Joel Brand standing near the door. He'd bugged Danny about getting together to celebrate the day. Danny had told him where he'd be but had never expected him to show up.

Joel edged his way toward him as though he was afraid that any misstep might upset someone around him. Danny could have called out to put him at ease but he didn't and just sat there and watched.

The crowd was rambunctious but still in a good mood— though they were getting drunk and a little unpredictable. He could mooch a few more drinks from Joel but he would have to be careful and not mention the Holocaust. Grainne had said that Joel always reacted to that—and not the way normal Jews did. She said he went around calling people pro-Semitic and was always trying to explain why that was a bad thing.

Personally, Danny didn't give a fuck one way or the other. As far as he was concerned Israel was just like everywhere else. The whole world was following right-wing extremists down the same path that Hitler had dragged his people, and now it was the Palestinians turn to pay for someone else's crimes.

But he knew it was better to keep his opinions to himself. If you spoke out you were going to be labeled anti-Semitic or a terrorist. Nobody really discussed things anymore. Instead they just snapped and snarled at each other and recited sound bites and spin. Nobody gave a fuck about anybody else's point of view—and they said he was the one with the problem.

"Happy Saint Patrick's Day, Danny."

"Ah, good man, Joel. Are you well? Sit down beside me and have a drink."

\*

By nine in the evening, Danny was far too drunk to continue.

He was beginning to slobber and stagger and he didn't want people seeing him like that. Joel had been trying to coax him to leave, but even though he should Danny resented that and could feel himself becoming belligerent.

He couldn't let Joel see that, so he joined in with the crowd at the bar, undulating like an ocean, arm-in-arm in heartfelt camaraderie, unified by drink against all the terrible things the world had done to their race. They'd been cast out from their own little place, painted as half-simian and called terrorists when they rose up against imperial savagery.

"A Nation once again," they all sang; discordantly, but it didn't matter.

A Nation once again.
Ireland long a province be a Na-tion once again.

"C'mon." Joel tugged on Danny's arm when the song was over. "Let's go for something to eat."

"But why?" Danny asked more petulantly than he intended. "We're just starting to enjoy ourselves."

"Because you're getting drunk and Rachael would be upset if she found out I didn't take care of you."

Just the mention of Rachael had a sobering effect on Danny. "I suppose you're right." He couldn't afford any stories getting back to Rachael and Martin.

He finished his drink and looked longingly around. Paddy's Day was the only day he still fit in anymore. It was when everybody around him drank the way he did. It was the one day he didn't have to hide what he'd really become; but he was getting a bit sick and tired of it all, too. And he was dreading what the morning would bring—another day of shivering and shaking until he could get the cure into him. He'd stashed a few cans of cider around his apartment in all the strategic places, but it was still going to be hell.

"C'mon then." He nudged Joel and followed him toward the door as everyone along the way stopped him to ask why he was leaving so early, their cross-eyed concern obvious through their clouds of boozy breath. "Jazus, Boyle, you're not leaving? The *craic* is only getting started."

"You're a lucky man, Danny," Joel commented when they got outside and waited for a cab.

"Tell me about it. I shit horseshoes every morning."

"Why would you say something like that? I just think you're lucky because you have so many friends."

"I suppose you're right," Danny agreed as he decided to go along with it all. He knew about Joel and, even though he could be such a morbid fecker, Rachael was the only connection he had left to his son and he wouldn't mess that up.

He would go along with him and get something to eat. It would soak up some of the alcohol so he'd be less likely to fuck it up. And he could still get himself back in the mood when he got home. But he hadn't eaten all day and wasn't sure if he was able. Solid food was getting so hard to keep down. Still, he could have soup. "C'mon then, let's go to The Pickle Barrel." He hailed a passing cab and they tumbled in.

"So what's happening over in Ireland," Joel asked after they'd ordered food and settled down over two more beers. Danny assumed he was just trying to take the piss and was about to tell him to feck-off, but decided that maybe Joel was just trying to be friendly. He had sad eyes and long shaggy eyebrows. His skin was sallow and his mouth was tight. He was the type that drink had the worst effect on—one of those that opened up and tried to share their feelings. Danny hated guys like that, but he couldn't help feeling a little sorry for him too. They were both outcasts, and while Danny could always convince himself that he could handle it, Joel seemed so helpless.

"They had to go and beg money from the Germans." He paused to see how Joel was going to react. Jewish guys usually did whenever anything German was mentioned—not that it stopped them from driving Audis and BMWs, though.

"What happened?" Joel ignored it. "Everything seemed to be going so great for them."

"Ya know when George Bush said that Wall Street got drunk? Well, the Irish banks went on a total fuckin' bender and wiped the whole country out—them and their buddies in the government. And now the whole country is going to have austerity rammed up their arses. It's all a fuckin' scam, ya know? They're just rolling back all that the people gained over the last hundred years. My old man was always going on about stuff like that and everybody said the old fecker never knew what he was talking about. Even me."

"Yeah," Joel agreed. He seemed in awe and Danny liked that. No one else took him seriously anymore. "Hey, you don't think we could have problems like that over here?"

"No." Danny leaned back and laughed. "Haven't you heard? We've the best banking system in the world, or at least that's what those lying bastards in Ottawa would have us believe. It was Paul Martin, you know?" Danny waved his fork at Joel who sat transfixed. "He was the one who saved the banks from themselves—back in the nineties. And the first chance we got— we gave him a good kick in the nuts.

"Personally, I think it would be a good thing if we all went down in it. That way we might get up off our knees. Even the

Arabs are rising up but over here—we're far more concerned with our jobs and our house values."

"You don't really mean that," Joel argued softly. "It would be so hard on our kids and their kids."

"Yeah," Danny agreed as the waitress placed his soup in front of him. "I suppose there is that."

They talked about what they both agreed was wrong with the world while they ate, Joel munching away on his burger while Danny struggled with his soup, leaning over his bowl so his hand didn't have so far to wobble. And they agreed on a lot. Joel was a lot like Danny—except for the drinking. He was just as twisted by life and Danny was beginning to enjoy being with him.

"You know," Joel enthused when their coffees arrived—he'd insisted they finish the evening with a few and Danny went along with it. He still had a bottle of Bailey's waiting for him in the fridge and could get another buzz going when he was alone. "It's so good to sit down and talk with someone who's not afraid of telling it the way it really is." He had become a little more relaxed as the evening had worn on, and Danny couldn't help but smile at that.

"It's the curse of the Irish. We're burdened with the need to speak out—except when it is our own who are fuckin' us. Then we pretend there's nothing goin' on and that the whole world is just pickin' on us again. And being Catholic makes it even worse. We bow and scrape to the biggest mafia in the world, even while they're buggering our children. And do you know why?"

He paused long enough for Joel to look up again.

"Because they sold us shame. The moment we were born they slapped us with Original Sin."

He was still feeling a bit drunk but the soup had gone down so well he was almost enjoying himself. "And if you dare stand up to them, they send all these bleeding-heart do-gooders around to work on your guilt."

His mother was still bothering him about going to Rome with her, and while the idea of having to see Fr. Reilly again didn't sound too bad, the thought of Miriam put a shiver through him. She was probably still going around bitching about the way everybody else was trying to live their lives. It was easy for people like her who had no idea what it was like in the real world where people had to do real work to get by.

"I suppose," he finished as Joel just sat smiling at him, "that you know a thing or two about guilt, too."

"Yes." Joel nodded and kept smiling. "We've made a culture out of inflicting it on ourselves and everyone else. In our tribe no one can speak about the truth anymore and we have lost all sense of right and wrong."

"Not my crowd," Danny enthused as Joel signaled for the check. The bottle of Bailey's was getting closer. "We know what's right; it's just far more fun to do what's wrong—even when it's not fun anymore."

*

"What harm was there?" Rachael asked as off-handedly as she could.

She always got up to have breakfast with Martin before he rushed off to the office. It was one of the few times they could have some time to talk and she didn't want to upset him. She sensed that since the baby, he was softening toward his father, but there was still some way to go before they could ever be cordial again. "They just had a few drinks to celebrate."

Her father had told her all about his evening with Danny and how much he had enjoyed himself, having never done anything like that before in his entire life. He had called her the following morning and kept her on the phone as she pushed the stroller along through the park. She didn't mind. It was a warm, bright morning and the world was coming back to life.

Martin, however, seemed less impressed. He looked up for a moment as he sipped his coffee. "I'm not sure we should be encouraging them," he commented before going back to his phone.

She didn't want him to shut her out so soon and laughed at that. "They're our parents, Martin, not our children."

"And if my father ever starts acting like an adult, I will treat him as one."

He tried to look stern but Rachael could see past that. Whatever change he was feeling toward his father, it would take some time before he could admit it. Rachael let it go at that. He already had too much on his mind.

Things were tight at the office and he was spending every free moment dealing with calls and texts. She might have complained, but they both knew it was going to be hard and that sacrifices had to be made. Sometimes, she felt they should lower their expectations and have a simpler life, but he would never go for that. Martin was out to conquer his corner of the world. He'd always been like that. It was one of the things she loved about him.

"Grainne and Doug want us to go over on Saturday night."

"Can we get out of it?"

"I don't think so. We've been putting them off since the baby." She understood that he needed a break from Grainne— parenthood was bringing out their old sibling rivalries—but he'd always been able to relax and enjoy himself with Doug. "And I've already agreed."

"Great, there goes the weekend."

"It won't be that bad. Besides, your mother will be there."

"How did she get roped in?"

"She said that Grainne needs this right now. She called right after to make sure we would be there."

"Great. Why don't we invite our fathers ,too, and really wallow in our collective miseries."

"Oh, Martin, can we?"

He did smile at her before draining his coffee. "I got to go."

"Here." She pointed to her cheek and waited for him to kiss her. "And come home at a reasonable time. Your son is beginning to feel fatherless."

"He should be so lucky."

She knew he was joking, but there was something hanging over him—something he wasn't ready to tell her about. Maybe she could get Deirdre to help extract it. She went upstairs and carried their infant to the window where they could both wave as Martin backed out the driveway. Sometimes it felt as though he hardly lived with them anymore.

*

"*Fianna Fáil* were well and truly paid for their sins," Jacinta said with more than a flutter of anger in her voice. "And nothing more than they deserved. Wasn't it the biggest crime the country has ever seen? It's a good thing that Bart and Nora weren't around to see it."

She and Danny were having lunch in Scruffy Murphy's. She'd come over to see her great-grandchildren but took time out for her son. She was shocked by the change in him. He looked older than a man of fifty-three and had a terrible shake in his hands. They'd ordered fish and chips but he hardly touched his, sipping on his pint instead, spilling some of it at first.

"And Gerry Adams got elected too. I'm not sure about him but at least he might stop Enda from ruining what's left."

Danny nodded but she could tell he wasn't really interested. Deirdre had warned her that he was getting worse, but Jacinta was still shocked and saddened. But at least he was spending a bit of time with Grainne again. They had him over to meet his new grandson and Grainne could get a bit of dinner into him. "And you know the Queen came for a visit?"

"I heard that. I wonder what Bart and Nora would've made of that."

"I think they would've been delighted. We all have to learn how to apologize, and forgive, again."

"Do you really think that's what she was doing?"

"Danny, she made a point of going to the Garden of Remembrance. Even if she just stood there and took pictures—it meant everything."

"It might to you, but I don't forgive so easy."

"And that, son, might be why you're all twisted and bitter. Hate is the greatest poison in the world and it will be the death of us all."

"At this stage, Ma, death wouldn't be the worst thing that could happen."

"Oh, don't be talking like that, son. You still have so much to do and see."

"Like what?"

"Well," Jacinta seized the moment. "You could come to Rome with me. You know what they say about all roads . . ."

"When are you going?"

"Next summer, if I'm spared 'til then. Will you come with me? Will you, son?"

*

As May gave way to June, Rome grew warm again and filled with tourists who made getting around a little harder. But the warmer evenings were nicer for wheeling John around and Miriam didn't have to swaddle him in his blanket. Since Davide Pontecorvo had passed away, quietly in the bosom of his much-extended family, reconciled with all that life had put him through, John had become more taciturn, speaking to fewer and fewer people. And being a bit more terse whenever he did speak.

The staff at the home put it down to the grief of having lost two good friends in a short time, but Miriam knew him better than that. Here, at the end of a life spent spreading hope, John had grown very tired. And a bit cynical, often snapping at Patrick when the poor man tried to cheer him up with some heartfelt platitude or other. "Do not waste what time I have left with your nonsensical idiom," John would say in his iciest voice, almost bringing Patrick to tears. Miriam told him to pay it no mind—that John was just preoccupied with what was going on in the Spanish Court.

After three years of deliberation and hearing the evidence of an anonymous eye witness, they had finally issued a verdict on what had happened that night so long ago in San Salvador. She had printed out everything she could find on it before she came out and was waiting for the right moment to bring it up.

John was still reciting the litany of Imperial crime—from Rome, Pagan and Christian, right through to America—working himself up as he did. Miriam used to try to deflect him until she realized it was how he kept conviction pumping from his scarred and battered heart.

"And now we have slain the Bogeyman," he had included since the death of Osama bin Laden, "who made the fatal mistake of forgetting whose creature he was."

Miriam waited to see if there was any more. Each month there was a new addition or two, and when he had been silent for a while she stopped and locked his chair by the parapet that overlooked the Piazza del Popolo. She, too, had grown tired of the ways of the world and now found her happiness bringing comfort to her oldest friend in his last days.

She still saw Patrick, too, whenever he could be coaxed out, having become very reclusive himself. He'd never admit it but she knew: he was second guessing his own life choices. Not becoming a priest; she hoped he was content with that. What was probably getting to him was the type of priest he'd become—a hermit scholar, retired now but still sought out for his deep and compassionate insights into the written warnings from the past.

"They have sold us a new brand of fear." John nodded toward the open space where convicts were once publically executed, killed by hammers to the head. "To keep us in line so that the truly evil can do what they will.

"When I was younger we were taught to hate communists. Back then they told us they were the greatest threat to all that was white and decent in the world. Television had so much to do with it. After we all came home from the war, we sat down each evening and learnt how we were supposed to think, act, and live. It was a black and white world back then and always in the shadow of the mushroom clouds we had just learned to create.

"But we got to see Vietnam in color. We saw the angry orange of our napalm and the red, red blood of our dying young men. I thought back then that we had seen enough to change the world but, as Nietzsche teaches, 'Battle not with monsters, lest you become a monster, and if you gaze into the abyss, the abyss gazes also into you.'

"I was so full of pride back then, and while I resisted the urge to become the all-American Second Coming, I would have settled for nothing less than being one of his more favored apostles.

"Not a Peter, and certainly not a Judas. But look at me now, Miriam. What type of disciple have I become?"

"If I had to pick one," Miriam decided when she was sure he wanted an answer, "I would say that you are somewhere between a John and a Thomas."

She pushed the printed articles back into her bag; the news of overdue justice could wait. For a little while they would enjoy the warm breeze that drove the shadows of clouds across the streets below. And, when the street lights began to glow, all that was old and time-worn would become beautiful again for a while.

\*

Deirdre lay on her back and stared at the ceiling. She couldn't put it off any longer; she had to change the color. It was time to redecorate the whole place anyway—and maybe change some of the furnishings. It was a bit indulgent, given that the whole world was still shivering in fear of contagion.

At work, everybody rushed to reassure themselves. "The Canadian banks," they all repeated, "are the envy of the whole world." But as the European debt crisis spiraled down and down, and the Americans opened the vault and greased symbolic gears with imaginary dollars, even that seemed insignificant as a financial tsunami surged across the world.

She decided there was little point in worrying about it though. The foundations of everything they had might be damaged but they would be repaired. It would take time and probably a few false starts, but ultimate disaster would be averted. And, hopefully, long before it reached anywhere near her.

*Only after all those on the lower rungs are washed away.* Miriam would have chided her for feeling a little smug.

She was right, but Deirdre's first responsibility had always been to her immediate family. She didn't have to worry about Martin, though. He was well able to thrive in times like these. And he'd look out for Doug too. And, if anything did go wrong, Deirdre could help out for a while.

"Besides," she decided aloud for Miriam's sake. "We have responsibilities to the economy. We need to show our consumer confidence."

"Oh, for God's sake." She laughed as she stretched from her warm wide bed and stepped into her satin slippers—another indulgence. "Why am I explaining myself to an ex-nun?"

She enjoyed mentally bantering with her old friend. It helped her get ready to face another day, and today was going to be a difficult one. Grainne was hosting Thanksgiving and, if past experience was anything to go by, a day of family dramas beckoned.

\*

When she got home she poured herself a larger glass of wine. She had earned it. She had spent the day indulging Grainne as she directed the preparations in her recently remodeled kitchen. She could hardly be expected to do it with a baby on her lap.

Deirdre had bitten her lip and accepted assignments and instructions without complaint or comment, except for some mock grumbling with Rachael when Grainne was distracted by the pestering of her toddler.

When she did redecorate, Deirdre would try something more Zen. Something clean and uncluttered to allow for more organic flow through her private space away from it all.

She sipped her wine and kicked her shoes under the coffee table. She loved her family but her life had changed, and now she had to wait for them to catch up to that. Martin and Grainne still wanted to involve her in everything that happened between them—looking for her approval and using it as an endorsement when she gave it.

Grainne wanted to stage an intervention for her father, something she announced after everyone had taken their turn giving thanks. In the silence that followed, Deirdre avoided looking at Martin but she could sense him. And she could sense Rachael watching him.

"Perhaps," Deirdre had suggested after no one else spoke, "we should discuss it another time."

"I would be more than happy to help, anyway I can," Joel Brand offered obliviously, before Adina could nudge him.

"Well thank you, Mister Brand." Grainne smiled at him before turning to her mother and brother. "It's nice to see that not everyone has become cold and heartless."

Joel seemed happy with that but everybody else kept their heads down, except for Doug who was gnawing on a drum stick.

"I don't see why it has to be such a taboo," Grainne complained as she supervised Deirdre and Rachael as they tidied away. "We all know it's the right thing to do."

"Not all of us," Deirdre corrected as mildly as she could.

"Martin just needs to get over it. Don't you agree, Rachael?"

Rachael looked to Deirdre before answering. "I agree, but now is not the time to try to force the issue. Things at work are very tense and . . ."

"Things are always tense where Martin is concerned."

Deirdre thought about intervening. Martin had told her what was bothering him: Doug was struggling at work and there was talk of letting him go. But what was the point? Grainne would have her say regardless and Rachael was more than capable of fighting her own corner.

She had to when Martin drove them home. He was still simmering about it all. "It's well meant, Martin. She's just trying to do what she thinks is right."

"Well it's not. It would be different if he was trying to make things right."

He checked his mother's face in the rearview mirror but Deirdre didn't look up. She was determined to keep her thoughts to herself. As they were leaving, Grainne had suggested that they should have Danny join them for Christmas and that she would be delighted to host it.

"Martin," Rachael tried to reason with him, "that sounds so hard-hearted. Perhaps this could be the catalyst he needs."

"Perhaps, but his drinking is as bad as ever. I just don't want him showing up drunk and ruining another Christmas on us."

"So what do you want us to do, stay home?"

It was the first time Deirdre had ever seen them disagree about something—Grainne always said that it was so unnatural but Deirdre understood. It was just a pity they should be arguing about Danny.

"No, I'm not saying that. I just don't see why Grainne always has to indulge him."

"What if we host it instead? You know he will be on his best behavior at our house."

"Grainne will never go for that."

"We could keep it to ourselves and present it as a *fait accompli* when the time is right."

"And when will that be? You know what she's going to be like."

"Not if we involve Doug."

Deirdre smiled as she reached toward her wine glass. She would have to help sell the idea, but Grainne was so busy with the kids she might appreciate the break. And if Danny did come to Martin's house he'd be more likely to behave himself.

Though, if she were to be honest, it might be better if he just stayed away.

She felt bad thinking like that but she would make up for it by taking him for lunch one day. They usually met up in late November. She'd give him another piece of his shrinking share of the house to see him through the holidays. He'd always go through the pretense of insisting that she had already given him more than enough, but she knew; there was still about twenty-five thousand left.

After that, she'd figure something else out. She still kept a glimmer of hope that he could get his act together for the sake of his grandchildren. She knew he would want to and he deserved that chance—regardless.

# Advent 2011

Rejoice in the Lord always. I will say it again: Rejoice!
Philippians 4:4

# Chapter 16 – Advent 2011

A T 3 A.M. DANNY CAME TO WITH A REALLY BAD CASE OF THE DRYS but he didn't dare get up to do anything about it. Even rolling onto his back had caused a bout of retching and heaving. He hadn't really slept; he'd just passed out in his underwear again. So he lay in a tangle of sweaty sheets and tried to keep his mind from wandering into darkness inside him. That was where his guilt and shame simmered and bubbled and everything stank like shite.

At meetings, the old-timers who'd gone all the way down used to talk about this stage. They made it sound like something out of *Dante's Inferno,* but one of them described it as having a never-ending court case in his head. When it started happening to him, Danny tried arguing his case, but even his ghosts had stopped listening to him.

*Denial,* he reminded himself in total resignation, *works both ways.*

By 4 a.m. he was wandering through his resentments. The old-timers used to say that they polished theirs and kept them sharp for the day that they would get even—even though they kept stabbing themselves while they were waiting. He knew what they meant. He'd met with Deirdre a few days earlier. She'd given him some money and brought him up to speed about all that was going on with their family.

She also told him they were making plans for Christmas and Grainne was thinking of inviting him. She didn't say it, but he knew what she was implying: if he wanted to be part of it, he'd better get his act together.

Later, after he'd stopped and spent some of the money on a fresh supply and a cab home, he'd sat up drinking and stewing about it. As the booze surged through him and rekindled his bravado, his outrage grew. She was always doing shit like that to him—like his own children were something she could dangle in front of him. She was always going on about not letting emotion get in the way when it came to dealing with the kids but he could tell; she loved seeing him grovel.

But now, in the cold pre-dawn, after a few days on the spree, and with his indignation spent and shriveled up, he was shivering and quaking. He knew what she was really trying to tell him. He was a mess and he couldn't let his kids, or his grandkids, see him like that.

By 5 a.m., the sweats and the drys were really getting to him, and he still wasn't able to move without almost passing out, lucidity began to dawn and everything that had been hidden in the dark began to look so shabby. He'd become one of the guys who was finally hitting the bottom. He'd had enough. He had to quit if he was going to be in any shape to spend Christmas with his family. He'd begin today. He'd get himself back to the meetings, right after he got himself settled.

At 6 a.m. he finally managed to sit up on the edge of his bed. He had to steady himself as the room began to spin. His stomach was churning and his head was burning and there was a very sharp pain between his eyes. He didn't dare stand up. He leaned forward slowly and picked up the can from the side table.

He'd learned that, even if it was tepid, it was better than trying to get up to reach the fridge. He'd also opened it to avoid having to pick at the tab. His hands shook uncontrollably these mornings and he'd have to get a few drinks into him before he could use them again. The cider was flat but he preferred it that way. If it was still gassy it might cause all kinds of expulsions.

"The first today," he announced aloud to reassure himself. "I'll just get myself settled and then I'll do it. I'll get my arse back to meetings. I promise."

He tried to steady his hands but spilled some of it. The can rattled against his teeth as he tried to swallow. The cider burned like acid as it went down, and when it reached his stomach the revolt began. Heaving and choking, he couldn't contain it and spewed it back up and across the room. He wiped his mouth with the back of his hand and tried again. He had to get some inside him or his suffering would never end.

"Steady now," he encouraged himself.

It still burned and churned until his stomach gave in. His body was finally crapping out on him—not that he could blame it. He hadn't treated it very well. He sweated and shivered and waited for the cider to take effect.

When he was sure it wasn't coming back up, he risked the next sip. It was a gradual process, not unlike spoon feeding. He'd done all of that, too, and he hadn't done such a bad job, given that he'd no idea what he was doing. But Deirdre did.

From the beginning she'd always been such a natural. He'd done his best, playing in the park and going for McDonald's afterwards. And then taking them home and tucking them into bed where he could fill their eyes with wondrous stories of *Finn MacCool* and the *Fianna*, or *Oisin* and his trip to *Tir Na N'Og*.

Then, when they started to grow up and he and Deirdre started having a few problems, it all got away from him. Part of it was he'd been so busy working and doing gigs; he wasn't around as much as he should have been.

Part of it was his drinking, too. He couldn't deny how much it had cost him. He'd left them all to end up sitting in a cruddy little bachelor flat. But he was going to change all that now. He was going to show them all that there was still something for them to believe in, especially Rachael and Martin.

He managed to raise the can again without spilling any and got another mouthful into him. It still burned on the way down but it was beginning to work. A few more and he'd be grand. He thought about reaching for his cigarettes but it was too soon. He couldn't risk a coughing fit just yet. That could upset the delicate balance.

He was going to have to tough it out and cold turkey his way through—there was no other way. There was no point going to doctors. He'd seen enough of them to know—changing to a new one every time they threatened to withhold his prescriptions.

He'd been on Diazepam and stuff like that to lift the darkness, even if they just made everything gray. The doctors kept trying to get him back on anti-booze, too, but he couldn't. It just made him sicker when he drank. He had to go back to meetings.

"I'm done with this fuckin' merry-go-round," he announced as his body slowly started to come back to life; and by the time he'd drained the last of the can he felt well enough to try to get up. He really needed to fart but couldn't risk it, sitting on the bed. His stomach was unpredictable and he couldn't risk shitting on his sheets; they were the only ones he had left.

He'd left the light on in the washroom. He couldn't bear the total darkness anymore—too many faces in the shadows. Lately it was just Deirdre and the kids, but their faces were distorted as if the very thought of him filled them with revulsion. Other times it was his father and his mother. His father looked at him with resignation but his mother always cried and blamed herself.

He couldn't stand the brightness either. He turned on the light in his bedroom as he left, turned off the light in the washroom and settled himself on the toilet. These days it took forever to piss so he lit up and coughed a few times, hacking up tacky blobs of yellowish-brown phlegm and bitter spittle. But he'd be all right in a little while. He'd left another can in the cool water of the cistern but he couldn't reach around to fish it out just yet.

He had to admit it: the last few mornings were worse than usual. He was shivering and sweating more than normal, and even when he wrapped himself in his old robe he couldn't get warm. His hands shook like crazy and his skin was the color of dead fish—only a bit more blue. It would be his luck, he tried to joke with himself, to die on his way back to meetings.

His heart was pounding, and even thinking about what might be wrong made his stomach clench with fear. He raised his cigarette but couldn't take another pull—the smell was sickening and his lungs were aching.

*Sacred Heart of Jesus,* he prayed as he relaxed a bit and began to piss. He didn't really believe in any of that but he'd take help from anywhere. *I'm sorry. Get me through this one and I'll never drink again. I mean it. I'll really try this time, ya know? Just get me through this one and I'll never touch another drop. So help me, Sweet Jesus. Hail Mary, full of grace . . .*

There was no harm in appealing to maternal instincts too. He needed all the influence he could muster.

In time he felt a little better and rose and turned on the shower. Flushing his half-finished cigarette away in a dark swirl of piss, he lurched forward and fished out the cool can. He'd just have one more to settle himself and get him right to meet the day. Then he'd begin his reformation.

That was the danger in trying to go cold turkey—a fella could get brain damage that way. No, he'd have to ease his way off it. He'd have this last one and then get to a midday meeting. *Moderation,* he reminded himself, *moderation in all things.* It was how he was going to rebuild his life.

He clung to that hope in the shower. His legs were shaky so he leaned against the wall and let the hot water beat on his back like punishment. It almost felt like some of his sins were being leeched from his skin and were swirling away down the drainpipe.

He retched a few more times and coughed up more phlegm, and each time his head spun and he had to steady himself. Crouched over as he was, each cough forced an expulsion from his other end—a watery, yellowish brown that stank like death before it mixed with his sins and his snot and slithered away.

*Jaysus.* He tried to laugh. *I don't remember eating anything like that!*

He took another swig, almost defiantly, and wiped his hand across his mouth. He couldn't remember the last time he had eaten. That was probably why the last few mornings were so bad.

He had to eat something, but the very thought of food made him retch again and this time some of the bilious bile in his stomach bubbled up; acidic and greenish yellow, mingling with the watery yellowish brown that dripped from his ass, mingling with his sins and his withering resolve and slithering off down the drain.

He avoided looking at himself when he finally toweled off. His skin hurt; even the lightest touch felt like a rasp and the effort was proving too much. He had to sit on the side of the bathtub because the room was spinning again. He drank some more cider and started to breathe slowly and deliberately—the way he'd learned the few times he'd tried to get into yoga.

It was another one of Deirdre's efforts to help him before she gave up on him. But yoga wasn't for him. He couldn't meditate to save his life. The breathing worked a little though. The room stopped spinning and his heart's pounding began to ease, as if it had realized it couldn't break out through his ribs and settled for grumbling protest against all that he'd done to it.

*I'm the real victim here,* he reassured himself like so many times before. *If I had cancer, or even AIDS, then everyone would feel really sorry for me, but I've alcoholism and nobody gives a shit about that.* But he shouldn't have said that. *Admitting you have a problem is the first step,* a chorus of memories reminded him.

He had spent the previous evening prowling the pubs around Yonge and Eglinton; the *Duke*, *Scruffy's* and *McMurphy's*, anywhere where he might find someone who would still sit and have a drink with him. He just wanted one last fling before he quit.

He'd done all right, too. Everyone was getting into the Christmas spirit. He'd ended up with Ryan and McInerney, who always had time for him even as they teased him. "Oh Danny boy," they'd sing when he approached, "your pipes are blocked and croaking!" He didn't mind, as they always made sure he got home okay, calling him a cab when he began to dissolve into a slobbering mess, and making sure he had the fare.

He'd spent most of the money Deirdre had given him but he wasn't destitute, not yet. He still had his disability pension. That wasn't bad, but after he shelled out for rent and stocked up on essentials like wine and cider and cans of soup, there wasn't much left. His check arrived at the end of the month and he'd be tight again within a few weeks. But he couldn't complain. He just needed to catch a break.

Maybe if he could get his hands to steady up he might start playing the bars again. His voice was shot but it was like riding a bike . . .

After all, he hadn't come all the way to Canada to end up like this. Deirdre might be finished with him, and Martin was hesitant about having anything more to do with him—not that he could blame him—but he wouldn't give up on himself. He'd show them he could beat this yet. Right after he finished this can he'd do the only thing left to him. He'd pick himself up, dust himself off, and start all over again!

He started to cough. He should have known better than trying to sing at this hour of the morning. "Today," he announced when he'd calmed down, "is going to be the first day of the rest of my life."

When he got to the kitchen he opened another can and sat down at his table. He pushed aside the bowl of congealed soup and began a mental list. He'd phone Grainne; she always made time for him. He'd tell her that he wanted to know if there was anything he could bring—like a pudding or something. He wouldn't mention alcohol and maybe, if he played it right, Grainne would tell the others that he was really trying this time. But the bending over to reach into the fridge caused him to break out in a sweat and his heart was thumping again.

He'd be fine, he told himself, once he got a few more into him. "And I'm still going to the meeting," he reminded himself. And afterwards, before he met up with Grainne, he'd go for a haircut, and maybe a shave. He wanted everyone to see that he was serious this time.

It was almost nine and it was starting to get bright—well, a brighter gray. It was going to snow; he could feel it in his bones. He didn't have a good coat anymore. He'd lost the last one—left in a bar somewhere. Maybe when he met with Grainne, she'd help him pick out a new one.

Christ! He was sweating badly. A cold, clinging sweat, and his heart was off beat. He had to remind himself to breathe before he drained the can. That was the end of it. There was no point in kidding himself anymore. He'd die if he didn't stop.

*

Deirdre wasn't that surprised when the call came—a call from a total stranger who had tried so hard to sound sincere and comforting. She always knew it would happen—sooner or later—but why did it have to be now, just before the holidays?

She rose from her desk and closed the door of her office; a sign to her staff that she was not to be disturbed. She didn't want anyone barging in while she took a few moments to sort her feelings out. She'd always been so careful to keep them private, even through the worst years.

She walked toward the window, taking her phone with her. *Was there really a good time for bad news?* her mother's voice asked from just beyond the veil that divided the living from the dead.

A part of her was a little surprised that she considered it bad news. Sometimes, when life with Danny had become impossible, she'd almost hoped for it, but now that it was happening . . .

Her reflection reproached her, looking ghostly against the gray clouds outside, so she smiled. She just needed a moment to compose herself.

Men were not the center of her life anymore. Both Danny and Eduardo had been replaced by her professional life. She had earned the respect of the old boys' club and had been promoted all the way to the glass ceiling and, as far as they were concerned, she was completely un-besmirched by any hint of failure—professional or personal.

Not that she considered her life with Danny a total failure. They had their fair share of good times once, and they had a family together. She was detached enough to see all of that. But he was still the father of her children and this was something the whole family had to deal with.

She straightened her skirt and tugged gently at the flaps of her jacket—pulling herself together. She was ready to manage this just like every other crisis life threw at her. Her years with Danny had taught her many transferable skills. She would break it down and deal with it piece by piece, and she would delegate. She folded one arm across her waist, flicked her phone open and called.

"Martin."

"Oh hi, Mom. I've been meaning to call. What's up?"

"I just had a call from St. Michael's." Deirdre paused. She knew it was going to be difficult; his initial reaction was always the same. "Your father is in a coma and it doesn't look good."

She waited for him to speak as the snow fluttered down outside, slow and lazy. It was mid December and the winter had just begun. It would take and hold Toronto for months. The salters had been out—they were always so eager at the beginning of the season—even though the fresh white flakes quickly dissolved into mush. She stood above it all, aloof and alone.

"I'm sorry to hear that."

He almost sounded as he did when he was a child and tried to act as though he was unaffected by all the turmoil that was life with his father—even when his voice quavered and his little face reddened.

"Yes, Martin, and no matter what else we may feel, he's still your father and he is seriously ill."

"I am sorry, Mom. I didn't mean to sound so indifferent. It's just that I'm swamped at the moment."

"And that's it?"

"What else would you like me to say, Mom? Of course I feel bad for him, but what can any of us do? We all knew this would happen."

"Well I think, given the season and the fact that we will all be getting together, we all need to try being a little more compassionate and you could offer to be of some help." She returned to her chair in case she had to negotiate with him. She rearranged the greeting cards on her desk—insipid wishes for a Happy Holiday Season to every race and creed.

"Okay, Mum. What can I do to help?"

"I'm going to the hospital and I would like you to come with me."

"Mom, it's a bad time right now. Work has been so crazy lately and I promised Rachael I'd be home for dinner this evening."

"How are Rachael and MJ?" Deirdre rearranged the cards from naive to insidious as she waited for his response.

"They're fine, Mom. Getting excited for Christmas—and looking forward to seeing you," he added like an afterthought.

"That's nice, Martin. Family is what Christmas is really about."

She knew she was being mean, but she didn't have time to be more diplomatic. Sometimes it was better just to reach into him as she did when he was young and didn't have the right words to express himself. And now she would wait patiently for a moment or two.

"Martin?"

"Okay, okay. Let me just check and see if I can get out of a few things and I'll get right back to you."

"I can't wait, Martin. I am going over right now and I could use your support."

She swiveled toward the window and watched snow drift down on the solid, old brick town of "Old Fort York," one of the few parts of the city that still had some of the old character from before Toronto began to fret about its place in the world. She preferred that part of town. It was not as sterile and restrictive as the bland, polished glass towers. "This place is soulless," Danny often reasoned when he came home drunk, when they first started living together, and she thought it was a phase he would outgrow. "You can't expect someone like me to be able to survive here without blowing off a little steam every once in a while." That used to frustrate her, but now it just made her smile.

"What about Grainne?"

"She's didn't pick up and I need to go right now."

She hadn't actually called her yet but he didn't need to know that. She knew her family and she knew how to get them to do what had to be done. She just had to seem impassive all the time so she could seem impartial when she had to dictate. "This is not about him, Martin. This is about you. How do you think you will feel if he dies?"

"Relieved?"

"Martin!" She ignored his attempt at black humor—something he had inherited from his father. "You've always had a tendency to be a little judgmental when it comes to your father. It's probably time you grew out of it."

That was a little harsh but she was growing impatient with him. This was life; sometimes you had to deal with things you didn't want to.

"That's not fair, Mom."

"Please, no part of life with your father has been fair."

She knew her tone would register with him, tinged as it was with more than a hint of righteousness wronged—the voice of the real victim in it all. She hated guilting him but it was the fastest way. She was doing it for his own good. If she didn't force him to deal with it, it would just become another lingering issue. She wanted to protect them all from any more

of those. What mother wouldn't? But she couldn't help feeling
that she was using him as a foil.

"Okay, Mom. Give me ten minutes and I'll be waiting
outside."

She called Grainne while she waited for the cab but she
didn't pick up—probably fussing over her Christmas shopping. Deirdre wanted her to know as soon as possible to avoid
touching off simmering sibling rivalries that might mar an
already delicate Christmas. And she wanted to tell her in person. It wasn't the type of thing that she would leave in a message: "Grainne, dear. It's Mom. Just called to let you know that
your drunken father has landed himself in the hospital. He
might even be dying." Instead she just said, "It's Mum, hun.
Call me as soon as you can." She called Martin, too, to let him
know she was on her way as she slid into the back seat of the
teal and orange cab. "Bay and Queen, then St. Michaels."

"Very good, Madam. Would you like me to take Richmond?"

The driver seemed eager to talk so Deirdre just nodded
and pretended to be busy with her phone as they inched along.
The snow fluttered down and most of the passing pedestrians
shivered as they waited to cross at the lights, across ridges of
shoe-destroying slush. It took two lights to cross Yonge, where
someone always got stuck in the intersection.

"These people don't know how to drive in the snow," the
driver complained in a thick accent.

His name was Abdullah and his license photo made him
look like one of the faces she had seen when she Googled the
Taliban, right after Canadian soldiers started dying in Afghan-
istan. "And it's the same thing every year!" He looked back
through his mirror. He had very deep, sad eyes.

She wondered if there was a Mrs. Abdullah and if she was
the reason his eyes were so sad.

Perhaps she had become westernized and had renounced
all that had once been their way of life. Deirdre had seen it often
enough at work and, as a woman, she automatically agreed
with them and went out of her way to help those she could,

making sure they knew about promotions and other opportunities. She had never stopped to think about the impact all that would have on a couple trying to stay together in a strange new land.

Perhaps it was because she was on her way to see Danny, but she couldn't help but feel a little sorry for Abdullah and stole a quick glance at the rear-view mirror. He had fine cheek bones and bright white teeth, and for a moment she tried to imagine what he would look like on the back of a stallion, riding across a Persian landscape.

She shuddered a little when she realized where her mind had gone. It was beginning to do that. It was starting to rebel against the regime she had followed for years. It had worried her at first but now she just smiled to herself and tidied it away as she watched the storefronts pass by. It was almost Christmas and had been since Halloween, but the snow added credibility to the glittering in honor of the ancient festival of excess, jangling with jingles about peace and love, all gift wrapped at no extra cost.

"Pull over here." She nodded toward Abdullah who was still stealing glances at her through the mirror. It was a no-stopping zone and traffic was tense, so she smiled at his frustration and brushed her hair behind her ear. Men were so easy to deal with.

*Except the ones you really care about,* she reminded herself as Martin dashed toward them and climbed inside. He was beginning to look more like his father, except while Danny had always been languid, Martin did things so frenetically. She kissed him on the cheek as Abdullah turned away and reasserted his place in traffic. They crawled along Queen, behind a lumbering streetcar with fogged up windows, and waited to turn into the hospital. Deirdre wasn't in a hurry. She was carefully rearranging her emotions.

"Would you like me to wait for you?" Abdullah offered as he tried to touch her fingers when he reached for the twenty.

"No thank you, but you can keep the change."

"Thank you, lady. Thank you very much and have a merry Christmas."

"You too, Abdullah!"

Martin held the door as she stepped from the cab. "Mom!"

"What?"

"You're going to visit your dying husband!"

He hadn't been comfortable with the idea of her seeing anybody since Eduardo so she usually kept that part of her life to herself. She'd even tried to be on her own for a few years, but it just became too lonely. While Martin and Grainne grew up and had lives of their own she had waited, and now it was time to move on.

"Ex-husband," she corrected and walked towards the door. She'd wanted to tell him but now wasn't the time. There was someone.

She hadn't gone looking for him. They met at the supermarket and got talking when he stopped and asked for her advice. Deirdre had hardly noticed him until then. He was trying to buy feminine hygiene products and was quick to explain they were for his daughter. He was divorced but had the kids every other weekend.

That made them both smile and she couldn't help but notice his eyes and his teeth. He was probably about seven or eight years younger than she but he didn't seem to notice. His daughter had cut her last visit short because it was "her time" and she didn't have "her things" with her. Deirdre could see that he was embarrassed and nodded to spare him. "It must be hard sometimes?" she had asked to encourage him as they pulled their trolleys over to make room.

"Sometimes? Try all the time."

She turned and picked a few items from the shelves, explaining each one as she handed it to him and moved farther down the aisle. He followed, pulling both carts effortlessly. He was smiling but she knew he was still embarrassed.

When they reached the end, they both lingered. "Well, I am here around this time most Saturdays—if you ever need help again." She couldn't believe she had said it but he seemed happy that she did.

"My name is Ritchie and if you tell me your name I could have you paged—in case we don't bump into each other?"

"Deirdre."

"Deer-dra?" He repeated as though he was committing it to memory. She liked the way he said it, as if he were savoring it.

They met a few more times before she decided to let him ask her out for coffee. He had seemed delighted when she agreed, but was a little more hesitant when they did meet, fidgeting with his spoon and looking over each shoulder.

"You are divorced?" she had asked as flippantly as she could. She could see he was uncomfortable—like he was afraid of bumping into someone he knew—and she was beginning to regret it all. He seemed to pick up on all that and turned to look at her directly, as though he'd just been caught in a lie. "I'm sorry. I guess I'm just not ready to do this."

He waited for her reaction but she took her time. He might be one of those that got their kicks trolling while doing the family grocery shopping. Most of them were younger and none of them ever hit on her in the feminine hygiene section. But he didn't seem like that. He had that look that all divorced people had—a wariness that never really went away.

"Ready for what, exactly?"

"Dating again." But even as he said it, he began to smile. "What did you think I meant?"

They had laughed at that and, after a second coffee, agreed to see each other again. They had begun spending Saturday afternoons together, walking around Yorkville or through the cemetery as fall gave way to winter.

They'd started to sleep together, too, and he was anxious to meet her children. She had been deciding the best way to do it, but now . . .

*Damn you to hell, Danny Boyle.* She almost chuckled and prepared to return to the past. The hospital was just around the corner from the Windsor. She hadn't been there in years. Not since the kids. But they'd had a few great years, too, when they were warm together sharing the good and the bad. Danny, in his old-fashioned way, had once won her heart and softened her hard edges.

However, the little glow that memory rekindled was quickly doused when the nurse explained: Danny was suffering from severe alcohol poisoning. He had collapsed on the Queen Street platform and the paramedics had got there just in time. "He is stable now but he's in critical condition. I'll have a doctor drop by to talk with you. Try not to be alarmed. His skin looks blue."

"Your poor father," Deirdre whispered as she tightened her grip on Martin's arm and entered the ICU. "He's going to die looking like a Smurf."

\*

"Oh Mom, I came as quickly as I could."

Grainne crossed the sterile room with her arms extended like someone in a trance, her face contorting as she grew near. "But I'm here now so we can get through this together. Oh Mom!" She closed her arms around her mother and squeezed a little. "I'm here for you."

She finally loosened her grip and turned toward her father. "And how is Daddy? Is he going to be okay?"

"We just have to wait and see, dear."

"Can't they do anything? Have you checked with the doctors? You know when we came in here with Doug's father— they weren't very good. They didn't find anything wrong with him."

"That must have been very disappointing for you."

"Oh! Hi, Martin. I'm surprised you could tear yourself away long enough to visit your father."

"I'm here for Mother's sake so let's not make this into an emotional sideshow."

"Martin, Grainne, please!"

This was what Deirdre had been dreading. For all her efforts to normalize their life together, anything their father did could always turn it upside down.

"Well at least I'm not afraid to show my emotions."

"Grainne!"

"No, Mother, he needs to hear this. Otherwise he'll sit there like a constipated fool and if Daddy dies, he'll be riddled with guilt. I'm only thinking of you, Martin. I just want you to be happy, that's all."

"I was until you came in."

"Of course you were. You just love seeing him like this."

Deirdre just gave up and walked away, looking for somewhere quiet to sit, somewhere she could think in peace. Somewhere she could talk with the doctor alone.

"If he does pull through," the doctor said, "he'll probably need constant care for the rest of his life. We have to expect brain damage, especially if his coma is prolonged."

Deirdre turned away from him. She didn't want him to see her struggle. *You mean more brain damage?* But she couldn't say that aloud. Danny would have seen the funny side to it, though.

"Rest assured, Mrs. Boyle, we will do everything we can for your husband."

"Ex-husband," Deirdre corrected, reflexively.

"Sorry." The doctor seemed a little flustered and Deirdre wondered if he was really old enough to understand. He couldn't have been more than thirty, but he managed to compose himself and continued. "We will keep him in the ICU and monitor him as the alcohol leaves his body. After that . . ." He seemed unsure how he might phrase it. "We'll just have to wait and see."

When Deirdre returned to the room they were still bickering. Grainne now sat in the seat closest to her father and rested an arm on the bed beside him, staking her claim. And Martin was staking his claim too. "Mom called me to come down with her. I guess she didn't want to have to deal with . . ." His voiced trailed away as his mother approached.

"Oh yeah! Well, I'm sure Daddy is much happier now that I'm here," Grainne hissed unaware, as her mother stood behind her. They really hadn't changed all that much. They had grown up and filled their lives with children of their own, but when it came to their father they were still as they had always been. Deirdre used to resent Danny for that but now it was theirs to deal with. It was just anger, the first manifestation of grief.

"I think"—she reasserted herself between them—"he might be aware of us so please, let's put everything else aside for now."

Grainne rose to let her mother sit but perched on the arm-rest between her and her brother.

"You're right, Mom. That's what Daddy would want."

*

As the afternoon darkened, they had to leave. Martin first, when the office called, and in time Grainne had to pick up the kids. A neighbor had been kind enough but she didn't want to impose. But she hoped her mother would be all right alone. How long did she intend to stay? Did she want to come over and have dinner with Doug and the kids? No? Maybe another night?

"As you can see, Danny"—Deirdre leaned forward and absently began to stroke the back of her ex-husband's hand—"we're still pretty much as we were when you left us."

It almost sounded bitter, and a little judgmental, so she searched for something lighter. "And we still haven't figured out what to make of you. I was just thinking that it could be fun to put a big question mark on your gravestone. Not that I want you to die or anything. In fact . . ."

She paused as she searched for her most honest feelings— it was the least he deserved on his death bed. "I suppose I just want to see what fate has in store for you next."

He didn't respond, of course, and just lay there. The only signs he was still alive were the gentle beeps and the pulsing lines on the monitor beside his bed.

"I don't know what else to say, Danny, and I must warn you: I have no more tears. You've kind of used up your store." She did stop to sniffle a little and laugh. "I suppose I still have a little love for you and, God love you, Danny, you always needed all you could get."

She relaxed as they shared a silence broken only by the beeps and the noises from outside, where nurses and doctors passed in quiet deference. It was peaceful, but Deirdre couldn't stay much longer. She left her numbers with the desk. They would call if there was any change and she'd be right over. And if nothing had changed she'd be back in the morning.

"Have a good night, Danny," she whispered into his ear before she rose and left.

# Chapter 17 – Christmas 2011

THE FIRST THING GRAINNE THOUGHT ABOUT WHEN SHE OPENED HER EYES WAS HER FATHER. She rose quietly and checked her phone. There were no missed messages and that was something to be positive about. But as she wrapped herself in her warm robe she began to feel guilty. Her daddy was still in a coma. Who knew what kind of suffering he was going through?

She left the bedroom and ghosted downstairs, not wanting to wake anyone. She was considerate—something she never got enough credit for. She knew they all thought she was such a drama queen. She had to be; she was the central nervous system for two families, and every now and then she just had to vent. And she wouldn't have to if only they would stop and listen to her once in a while.

It was always down to her to try to make everybody happy. She'd done it with her parents and her brother, then Doug when his hockey dream died, and now her own children. Sometimes she'd tried not getting involved but that only made things worse. Things would fall apart, and then she'd have to try to put them all back together again. If only they listened to her once in a while and not go on making the same mistakes over and over.

Her mother would have chided her for giving in to self-pity, but she needed to indulge herself a little. Doug had been working late again—and had been for weeks. And when he did come home he hardly had time to speak to her. She couldn't help wonder about that, even though it was like poking an icicle into her heart. She told herself not to—not now when everyone was so upset about her father. Besides, she might be wrong. He might really be busy. Or maybe he was just out drinking with his friends? He and Martin still had their boys' night, though they hadn't in a few months.

*But what if he met someone when they were out and Martin liked her too?* He always joked that Doug would be better off with someone else, and she sometimes wondered if he really meant it. Deep down, she knew he really loved her. Very deep, and Doug too. So what if they went out and drank and flirted for a while? It was just a phase men went through.

She and Rachael used to have a girls' night out, too, until they both realized they were just far too tired and took turns visiting each other's houses for girls' movie night instead. But even that became an effort and just died out. Doug still encouraged her to start it up again. He said that Rachael told him she really liked spending time with her.

Grainne was never sure about that. Rachael always acted very nice with her but sometimes she seemed condescending. And she never complained about things and always looked bemused when Grainne did. Martin had probably told her all kinds of terrible things about when they were kids.

Sometimes it got to her. Doug always told her that she was more beautiful even though he did admit that he thought Rachael was beautiful too. And no, he never once wished that Grainne could be more like her—something she always asked after the four of them had been out together.

She had to. Whenever they were out at a restaurant it felt as though Rachael and Doug were the happily married couple. They just seemed to fit better together, always supporting each other with knowing glances when their respective spouses jokingly complained. Even her mother had noticed but just laughed. She said that Doug and Rachael had probably formed a survival pact. Grainne had laughed along with her, but later it began to gnaw at her and now it was becoming obvious; something was going on.

She moved mechanically around her kitchen but it followed along behind. She had checked his shirts and his underwear but could find nothing. She called his office often but always got to speak to him directly. But she knew; she had women's intuition. She always knew things were going to happen before anybody else. Everything that could happen to a family like them happened, and each time only she saw it coming.

That was one of the reasons she never cut her father out. She always knew a time would come when only she could make it better. Her mother and her brother were in denial. They were always like that—bottling everything up and turning their frustration on her. "Just because you've got feelings," they'd chide her, "doesn't mean you have to impose them on the rest of us."

Grainne knew they really loved her, even Martin. He'd always been there when things started to turn bad. He'd come into her room when their parents were arguing. He'd start clowning around with her, rearranging her dolls or trying to read whatever she was reading. That always drew her out of herself and they'd pretend to fight to drown out the noise below. Only somewhere along the way, it started to get serious. It was around the same time her father left. That was when Martin started to become impatient with her and rolled his eyes whenever she spoke. Her mother said it was because he was becoming a teenager but Grainne knew; it was because her father wasn't there to stick up for her.

*Oh my God.* She was a typical little sister and she knew it back then. She knew what she was doing when she got their father involved. She couldn't help it, even though he always became really angry at Martin. Then her mother would get mad at her father and, no matter how hard she tried, Grainne could never put all the pieces back together.

She paused for a moment to check. The table was set— pulp-free orange juice, whatever cereal was on sale, coffee in a pot—and the diet pop tarts were in the toaster oven. She would take one more deep breath and call up to them. Doug had got them out of bed but had rowdied them up.

"Doug the pug! Doug the pug! Doug the pug!"

"Mom?"

"Doug the pug! Doug the . . ."

"Listen to me, Daniel." She bent so she could make eye content.

"But he . . ." His little face grew redder in ignominy. She always tried him first. Douglas was more stubborn and couldn't be reasoned with. "Mommy is asking you to please stop teasing your brother. For Granddad's sake?"

"Oh no!" their father announced from the doorway. He was clean shaven, freshly showered and dressed in his good suit. Recently he'd been dressing up more for work. It was a sure sign; men only did that when they were in love with someone new.

"Did I hear any naughty kids in here?" He put his hands on both of their heads at the very same time. He seemed to know how to turn them up and down at will—like the surround sound. She always pressed the wrong buttons. "I just got a text from you-know-who and he was just checking that his lists were up to date."

The boys forgot about their rift and gazed at him in shock and awe. He could always do that. He just had to walk into the room to settle things. Where she would fumble and try to out-negotiate them, he'd just pull out something like Santa Clause and they'd stop. When she tried it, they just looked at her as if she was crazy. Their father always bought them the latest, bright shiny gadgets while she tried to find fun underwear and hats, gloves and scarves, which they lost by the end of January. She was just there for all the everyday stuff. Still, she appreciated when he did it. If only he would do the same for the two of them.

"The Big Guy was asking about you, too, you know?" He stood so close to her as he poured his coffee and reached across her toward the toaster. She could feel his breath on her cheek but she couldn't look up into his eyes. She mightn't be who she saw in the reflection.

"You were very late again." She moved past him so she could watch her children—with her back to him. She didn't want him to see she was furious at him. He was out betraying her and the boys, but for their sake she would ignore it for now. At least until after the holidays—and the crisis with her father had passed. After that she would confront him and, after he'd made a full confession, see if she could give him another chance. But only if he promised to stop seeing her. And admitted that it really meant nothing—that he just got a little drunk and made a mistake.

He'd have to get down on his knees and beg her to forgive him. She would, but she wasn't sure if she could ever forget it. She'd try—for the kids' sake—but she couldn't promise. And they would have to go to counseling. This would never have happened if they took time to work on their relationship. But who had time for things like that?

They would have to make the time and, in time, when they'd talked everything out, she might be able to forgive him. But only after he'd come to realize how much he'd hurt her and the kids. In time, she would admit that a little bit of it might have been her fault too. She was always pushing him to be better. He'd told her he needed that when they first got together. He asked her to help him become a better man—just like in the movie—but somewhere along the way he stopped wanting that.

After that, all he seemed to want from her was that she dress up at night and be somebody totally different. And they hadn't even done that in months. She still wanted to, but she wanted him to be somebody different too. She wanted him to be more smoldering and mysterious. Someone who was walking along a boulevard and saw her and couldn't take another step without her. And it had to be him so she would be able to look into his eyes and see herself sparkle the way she did before. She couldn't think of being with anyone else.

"Sorry, Gra, but I had to work late. You know how it gets?"

"You work too much. It's Christmas." He only called her "Gra" on special occasions, like when he was trying to reassure her about something.

"Yeah. But I'm trying to get something finished. I'm right up against another deadline."

"I hope it's worthwhile—spending all that time away from me and the kids."

That got his full attention and he put down his coffee and took her in his arms. "What's the matter?"

"Nothing." She couldn't look at him; she was wondering if he held someone else that way too.

"I'm sorry. I know I promised but it can't be helped. It's end of the year stuff and I'm swamped." He tried to lift her chin with his fingers but she wouldn't let him and turned her head toward the kids who were watching them in stunned silence. She had to step past it, for now.

"I know, dear, and we all appreciate it. Don't we?" she encouraged the boys and nodded her head. She didn't want anybody to see the corners of her eyes where little tears were welling up.

He noticed and took her into his arms again. "I promise. I'll be home on time tonight. I promise."

She stole a glance at his eyes. Damn, he was good. There wasn't a trace of lies to be seen. Instead he was looking at her a little quizzically, as if he was wondering if it was all getting to her.

"Any news on your dad? I didn't ask already because I thought you might need a break from it."

"So why are you asking now?"

"Because you seem upset."

He stood waiting for her answer until his phone rang and, as he raised it to his face, she read the caller ID.

"I gotta take this," he explained, looking as though he'd been caught in his lie as he walked from the room. She smiled at her children and turned back toward the stove before she betrayed herself. Nothing would ever be the same again.

*

They hadn't been to The Windsor in a while. Doug was surprised that Martin even suggested it but it was just around the corner from the hospital. When they first started having boys' night, they hung out there under the watchful eye of Jimmy McVeigh who looked after them, even sending his bouncers to bail them out the night they'd tried to pick up two girls who were with a couple of guys who would have kicked the shit out of them. But the bouncers were bigger, and far meaner, and the matter was settled subtly enough.

That was back when he and Martin could afford to be young and foolish—the way young men were supposed to be. That was when they bonded forever. That was when Martin started to let down his shields and open up to him. They'd been the best of friends since they made the same team, closer in some ways than to their wives. And when they got together, away from the wives and kids, and all the bullshit of the week, they always got around to talking about it.

The "Windsor Years" Doug called them, some of the best times of their lives.

Until Danny found out and started showing up. Even Doug could see that he was begging for another chance, but Martin didn't want to know and they stopped going. Martin found them a new place but it was never the same. Nothing ever came close, but Doug didn't complain. He knew things would never be right between Martin and his father.

He also knew Martin's mother still saw Danny. Grainne told him, but she closed like a steel gate when he asked how she knew. Doug didn't have to pry; he knew she was seeing him too. He could tell from the credit card bills. Lunch at places like Swiss Chalet, purchases at the LCBO and, recently, a new winter coat. Her father went through a lot of coats—and visits to the LCBO. Doug never said anything; he still liked her father.

Danny always knew how to enjoy himself. But Doug kept his views to himself. Grainne was very prickly on that subject and Martin was even worse.

The Windsor was a very different place during the day. Efficient, with just a touch of quirky humor. The lunchtime crowd was mostly men grabbing a beer and a sandwich, rebelling briefly from their cubicles, but with their phones on the table in front of them where they could see them. No one could really disconnect anymore.

Doug ordered a beer and sat at the bar. He didn't feel like eating. His stomach was knotted enough. The beer would help loosen it so he could breathe again. He had to hang in there. Martin was his last hope.

On cue he walked in and looked around the whole room before seeing him. When he sat, he carefully tugged his shirt sleeves so his golden cufflinks could be seen, and the gold strap of his watch. Doug had never seen him act so ostentatiously before but he could understand. It was the thing that drove him—never wanting to be compared to his father. It was what had driven him so far up the ladder—something Grainne was always reminding him of.

"Thanks."

"I haven't agreed to anything yet." Martin slapped him playfully across the shoulder to mask what he really meant. They both knew why they were there and they both knew they both knew.

"You agreed to lunch. My treat." Doug had enough for lunch, at least for now.

\*

"I'm here now." Martin finally answered his phone. Grainne had been calling for over an hour. "I'm just getting off the elevator."

She had called while he was talking with Doug but they both agreed that he should ignore it. He was tempted. He wanted to tell his nosy little sister that he was having lunch with her husband who was about to lose his job and would have to try to make ends meet by delivering pizzas over in North York where no one would know him. Doug hadn't told her, and as far as she was concerned everything was fine.

Martin had agreed to see what he could do. He wasn't making any promises but he'd try to call in a few favors, and Doug seemed happy enough with that. He wasn't really cut out for the job but Martin would sort something out.

"It's about time you got here."

"Oh, can it. I work for a living, you know?"

"Well maybe you should consider investing in some time with your father. Or are you concerned about your ROI or something?"

Christ did he want to tell her, but he couldn't. Behind all that drama, self-serving and manipulative as it was, was his little sister. He often forgot that until later—after he had said something stupid; but she really knew how to piss him off.

She'd been doing it since they were kids, before running off to tattle to their father. But she was on her own now and he wanted to take her in his arms. He hadn't felt like that in a few years. They had grown so far apart. It all started when their father moved out. Martin had tried to make her realize that it was for the better but she wouldn't listen. She probably still believed that someday they would all get back together and be one big happy family.

"How is he?"

"No change, but they say that is good." She looked at him, expecting him to say something derogatory, as he usually did.

"Are you okay?"

"Fine. Why?"

"No reason," he lied. "I just know that these things are harder for you."

"Martin . . ." She hesitated as if she was deciding if she could trust him.

"What is it now?" He'd meant it to sound funny but it didn't and she seemed to change her mind.

"Never mind."

"I'm sorry. What were you going to ask?"

"Nothing, I have to go. I have to pick up the kids. You'll stay until Mother gets back? She said she would be here after six."

At Grainne's insistence they all had to take turns being there—in case Danny woke up.

Martin just nodded but he did stand up and take her in his arms. She melted against him for a moment but quickly stiffened and grew cold again, and very brittle.

After she'd gone, and after he'd checked his phone, he sat by his father and watched him breathe, his chest rising and falling gently. His father was still bluish and was covered in pieces of tape, holding drips and sensors in place. Martin reached forward slowly as if to touch his arm, but he didn't. He wasn't ready; but as he sat and watched his father, he felt himself softening.

Much of it was Rachael's influence. She'd made him see that none of it had been personal. And the times they got together with his father she made a point of treating him with respect and civility, and chiding Martin for not doing the same. He'd gone along with it for her sake but now, as his father clung onto his miserable life, Martin felt a surge of compassion. He'd never accept the drunken oaf his father had been, but if he ever got his act together . . .

\*

"Has there been any change?" Deirdre took off her coat and settled in the chair on the other side of her ex-husband, never taking her eyes from her son's face which, in the low light, looked exactly like his father's when he was that age.

"Nothing has changed. We're still in a holding pattern until his Lordship deigns to leave."

"The King is dead, long live the King?'

"What does that even mean?"

"I don't know. It was something your father used to say when he heard that someone died."

"Figures."

"Martin, do you think we should still go ahead with Christmas?"

"Well, Rachael is a secular, anti-Zionist Jew and has just spent every waking moment of the last few weeks plotting and organizing. What do you think?"

"I was thinking more about your father."

"He's in a coma. It's Rachael I'd be more concerned with."

"I hope you weren't talking to him like that." She didn't mean to but she put her hand on her ex-husband's arm as she spoke. It was like something Grainne would do. Martin seemed to think so, too, and shrugged as he rose and reached for his coat.

"How late are you staying?"

"Why?"

"Because." He fussed with the buttons on his coat, just like he did as a kid. "I was wondering if you'd like to go for something to eat after."

"Are you not going home?"

"Rachael is going to her mother's. It's the first night of Hanukkah."

"I didn't think they . . ."

"Normally they don't. And they haven't told her father yet."

"Is that wise?"

"She's taking MJ. Joel gets so busy spoiling him that he mightn't notice."

"You're such a considerate husband."

"Mother, don't be so mocking."

"That wasn't mockery; that was jealousy."

"Mother!"

"Okay, okay. Give me a hug and go back to your office and call me when you're leaving."

She watched him walk to the elevators before she turned back to Danny. "You must be so proud of him, Danny. He turned out to be the you you couldn't be.

"I'm sorry. That was a little bitter."

Her ex-husband didn't move but he looked a little less blue. Now he just looked fish belly white—like a normal corpse. She didn't chide herself for thinking that. Danny liked his humor dark. It was how he'd gotten through all the terrible things in life. That, and getting drunk.

*

Being almost dead wasn't the worst thing that had happened to him.

In fact, in many ways it was far better than the way Danny had been feeling lately. His body was calm, with no heaving and churning, and his mind was clearer than it had been in years. He couldn't lift a finger but he didn't really want to. It was like he was outside of himself, looking in. And from there he could see himself for what he'd really become—his own worst enemy, poking and provoking himself with his own indignation and outrage. Prodding himself until he gave in and picked up the next drink, even though his body and soul were screaming at him.

He had no other option. It was the only way he knew to drown out all the condemnations and accusations that surged up from deep inside. He'd been a total and utter failure as a human being, and part of him had been hoping that the drink would kill him and be done with it. But it hadn't. It almost did, but he was still there.

Another part of him wasn't surprised and laughed sardonically—he wasn't going to get off that easily—while another part of him was relieved. He was like someone who'd survived a tornado and, even though everything was smashed to pieces around him, he was still alive. There was still some hope.

He sensed Deirdre as she leaned over him. She seemed to glow like candle flame and talked in delicate whispers, but he couldn't make out the words. It sounded like Latin, or Gaelic, or some language he'd forgotten. He tried to remember her eyes when she looked at him like that, deep and dark and peering all the way inside of him, looking for some reason to believe in him again. They hadn't always been like that. There was a time when she looked to him for hope. But when it was obvious that he could never deliver any, she began to look at him with growing derision.

It was so Catholic of him, lying on his deathbed recanting. He'd always despised that but now, at the end, he was no different. He was almost resigned to it all. At the very least, when all was said and done, he'd finally be at peace. Poor Daniel Bartholomew Boyle, who'd never known a contented day, and still full of regrets and remorse, was to finally be released from this hell on earth.

"It doesn't have to end like this." His uncle's voice was clear as a bell and tinged with the same concern Danny remembered from all those years ago—when his uncle Martin used to take him for burgers and chips.

*Look at me, Martin. I've become everything they said I'd be.*

"This doesn't have to be the end."

*I can't do it anymore. I just want to lie here and die.*

"But, do you really want to die like this?"

*I don't, but what can I do about it now?*

"People haven't given up on you yet, so you shouldn't either."

*What people?*

"Deirdre and the kids have been taking turns sitting over you; and there are others."

*Tell them to stop wasting their time. I'm not worth it. Even when I promise to get my act together, I can't.*

"It's not the end yet, Danny. There is still hope."

\*

*I hear that young Boyle might finally be ready?* Bruno's statue called out as Patrick tried to cross the Campo De' Fiori unnoticed. He hadn't meant to come that way but he had his head down and was deep in thought. But he wasn't that surprised.

Miriam had told him that Danny Boyle had been in a coma for more than a week. Jacinta had phoned, too, to ask if Patrick would remember him in his prayers and, if wasn't too much bother, maybe say a Mass for him. She said she was at her wit's end with worry and even though she didn't really believe in all that anymore, it couldn't do much harm—especially if the holy Jesuit would say a few too.

"Ah, Uncle. Are you well?"

*Well enough for one of the faithful departed, but enough about me. Boyle's uncle came to see me and he says it's time. Don't you think we should get him over here so we can try to straighten him out once and for all?*

"But he's in a coma, Uncle."

He could hear the reluctance in his own voice. He'd been praying a lot for some guidance, and for some reassurance, because his world had become a very cold and sterile place where old people gathered to linger until their ends. Only he had been hoping for something a bit more theoretical.

Saving Danny Boyle would be more than a challenge—and one he had handled so poorly before. But if not him then who? John had clearly crossed the line—just like Dan Brennan. And Miriam went along with it all—she probably just didn't want to upset him. And the bishop was dead and just a voice in his head.

*Patrick.* The bishop sounded as he did back in his palace in Dublin—when he used to call Patrick in for a little chat. *I'm talking to you from the other side. Do you think a coma is going to stop us? We must strike now, while the iron is hot.*

"But what can I do?" He stopped himself from adding, "Your Grace." It just didn't seem relevant anymore. "It seems that poor Danny is bound and determined to drink himself into an early grave."

*And that's precisely what we're not going to let happen. I'd never be able to look Bart and Nora in the face again.*

"But what can I do, Uncle?"

*You can be ready for him when he comes over. He'll be here by the summer and you'll get your chance. I know you think Boyle was your own personal failure but he wasn't—you were just trying to do your part as you had been told how. It's the likes of me that owe people like Danny Boyle, you know?*

*Me and the rest of crozier crowd. We were so busy blocking the devil from getting through the door that we never noticed him climb in the window. He was there among us all the time, Patrick, whispering in our ears about all the good we were doing and stroking our pride until we got so full of ourselves that we became everything we were supposed to be against. And I was as bad as the rest of them.*

"Ah now, Uncle," Patrick argued reflexively—something he wouldn't have done back in the palace. "Don't be so hard on yourself. You were only doing what you thought was right."

The bishop snorted the way he had done so often before. *But that's the point, Patrick. We weren't. We were telling the people about the love and forgiveness of the Sacred Heart while threatening them with the eternal fires of hell. It's no wonder so many ended up like young Boyle.*

*You were right back then, you know? It was the young priests like you that should've been running the whole thing all along. Young fellows who could still remember what it was all about*

His uncle seemed to smile down on him before raising his eyes and staring at the Vatican—as Bruno had done when they burnt him to death. *You know, when all the cardinals and the likes were inside, the good people of Rome should've locked the door and not let them out. They should've let them sit there and rot and, when their stench was gone, the place could've been turned into a museum.*

Patrick couldn't help but smile, too. It was like something Giovanni might have said. "C'mon now, Uncle. They weren't all that bad."

*Patrick, the day Gelasius turned his back on the monastery and took the keys of this city, all that we stood for was lost. And, like most of us, he started out with the best of intentions; but you can't build a stairway to heaven with the bricks and mortar of this world.*

*We soon forgot about all that the good Christ had left us and it was no time at all before we were building the Holy Roman Empire. And we were better at it than all the old pagans. We had half the world bowing and scraping whenever we walked by. They were lined up from Iceland to* the tip of South America, on their knees, kissing our rings and giving us anything they had of value. We became the greatest racket this world has ever seen.

"Is that you talking, Uncle, or have you been spending too much time in Bruno's head?" Patrick could hear the anguish in his uncle's voice and wanted to lighten things up a bit. It was the same thing he often tried to do with John—only he wasn't very receptive anymore.

*You always had a touch of sass about you. I'm glad that wasn't beaten out of you.*

So was Patrick. He had done what he had never been able to do before. He had moved them on from talking about Danny without having committed, one way or the other. He knew it was the right thing to do, only he wasn't ready to face that yet and would need a bit of time. Not that he wasn't up for doing his priestly duties—he just wasn't very good at them. "I suppose," he added to distract himself, "that you'll get to move on after this."

*I suppose I will, unless, of course, you might need something else from me.*

"Are you not looking forward to it, Uncle? You're always complaining that you feel like you're stuck in limbo."

*You should know by now not to put much stock in anything I say.*

"Go on with yourself. Won't it be nice to go to whatever is in store for you? Will Benedetta be going with you?"

*Who knows, Patrick? She has about a dozen relatives praying to her every day as if she was a saint. There's always someone who needs a little miracle every now and then. She's busier than the pope.*

Patrick smiled at that and thought about it for a while. They'd been selling saints to the people for so long that they were now making their own. Then again, they always had and that was why the Church went along with it.

"Is any of what we've been telling them true, Uncle?"

He had always wanted to ask but it had never felt right before.

*I can't be telling you things like that, Patrick. You have to find out for yourself; otherwise there'd be no point in faith. Besides, it's different for everybody. Some people just get to drift off and become something new. Some of us wait around to attend to anything we left undone and others . . . well, they get what's coming to them.*

"Like in heaven and hell?"

*I can't tell you, Patrick, except to say both of them are inside us all the time. We just have to decide which one we want to live in.*

Patrick let it go at that. He could understand his uncle's reticence. He felt just as guilty about the part he'd played in it all; telling everybody they were supposed to believe that things would be better and that all the trials the world threw at them were part of a plan.

And even when trials turned to torments, and the love of God had become stern and strict, all they could tell them was to try to emulate the example of Jesus.

Still, that was what he'd devoted his life to, hoping that the little bit of good would offset the bad. It was clear what he had to do about Danny Boyle.

"Thank you, Uncle." He nodded as he turned toward the river. "You always had the knack of bringing me the comfort of a bit of sense when I needed it most."

*

"Will he be all right?" Benedetta asked as she stood with the bishop, casting only the faintest ripple of a shadow on the darkening piazza below.

"He'll be fine," the bishop assured her but she could tell he wasn't convinced. She knew Patrick and she knew he was far too kind and decent for the world he lived in.

"Well, you know better than to worry."

"I do, but it's a hard habit to break."

She slipped her hand into his, and when he turned to look at her she smiled with all the love in her heart. They didn't have much time left but she would enjoy it. "Let's go over to the Pantheon. Giovanni will be there by now."

"Has he not moved on yet?"

"Why would he go anywhere else? This"—she waved her arm across the Roman skyline—"has always been heaven to him."

*

On Christmas Eve Deirdre sipped her wine by the twinkling lights of her little white tree. She wasn't looking forward to what the next day would bring.

Rachael and Doug had arranged everything without Grainne knowing. As far as she was concerned Christmas was going to be postponed until there was some development with her father—one way or another. Doug would find some way of coaxing her over to Martin's, telling her they were just going to have a quick gift exchange for the kids' sake.

Deirdre wasn't against the idea; she just knew how Grainne would react. Lately she had a bee in her bonnet over Rachael—probably over some imaginary slight—and had become very critical, passing comments and knowing glances. Deirdre could see it for what it really was—insecurity; but she knew enough to keep her opinions to herself.

Martin was on a short fuse too. He'd been going to bat for Doug's job and it wasn't going well. Doug wasn't really cut out for that type of work and Martin's loyalty was sure to cost him some credibility. Deirdre had seen it so many times before, but he hadn't yet asked for her advice so she kept it to herself.

Perhaps if the right opportunity presented itself tomorrow she would, as subtly and diplomatically as she could. The last thing she needed was his getting upset too.

She might just mention it to Rachael; she always knew how to get Martin to listen.

Ritchie was a bit miffed too. He really wanted them to spend Christmas together but she couldn't, not with all that was going on. She had offered to have him over on Boxing Day—just the two of them. She would cook for him and they could spend the evening together. He tried to look happy with that but she could tell; he was beginning to wonder if she was ever going to tell them about him. He said it made him wonder if she was serious about him.

She almost laughed at that. It was a ridiculous thing for a grown man to think but she understood. His wife had left him. After almost ten years and two children she discovered that she could not be fulfilled in their relationship. He was still scarred by that and, even though Deirdre really liked him, she had hoped for something far less complicated. She wanted them to have the chance to be together without any ghosts of the past whispering in the shadows. She hoped they could work it out but she wasn't prepared to settle.

Her phone rang as she poured another glass—the one she took to bed as she watched some silly Christmas romance movie. She thought it might be Ritchie or one of the kids. She never expected it to be from the hospital. For some reason she had expected all of that to wait until after Christmas.

IT WAS A MIRACLE, FATHER. A Christmas miracle."

"Well, I'm very happy to hear that, Mrs. Boyle."

Patrick was happy, but he was worried too. He didn't want this to be like the night in the Church of the Dead. He had decided he would reach out to Danny, but he'd do it his way. There'd be no miracles or magic. He'd just sit him down and talk, man to man, and if God had anything to say to Danny, he could say it through Patrick.

"It's funny," Jacinta replied in a voice that almost sounded like when she was young. "Just when you think there's no hope left in the world a miracle happens, like they used to do in the Bible."

Patrick smiled to himself. Jacinta, like most people, knew the Bible more through hearsay than through actually reading it. And most of those who had read it were convinced by every word, even though each page contradicted the last. That was probably why the Church had discouraged people from trying to read it on their own. But the Reformation changed all that. The Bible had been given to the people so justification could be found every time the old order had to be changed.

Patrick knew what he was talking about; he had given a course on it for years. At first he found the going very dry until it dawned on him to shift his stance and became the *Advocatus Diaboli*, picking and poking at it all. That forced his jaded students to engage, but it raised a few eyebrows too. It might even have drawn a bit of censure, but there were far worse things going on further up.

He had read all the bishop's writings again as he had weighed Danny's problem in his mind, and had finally digested them. They were not the ravings of heresy he had once taken them for. They were the simple words of a man trying to make peace with all that he had harmed in trying to make the world a better place. His uncle had not renounced his faith; he had just torn away all that was wrong with how they had gone about things.

> From the story of Adam and Eve on, we sold
> them shame and unworthiness in the hope that
> they would turn back to God. We told them
> they should not give in to the ways of the world
> when all along we were a part of everything that
> was wrong with it.

Patrick had read them like scriptures and his understandings had changed as life had changed him.

> We, even those of us who were not yet corrupt-
> ed, went along with it all because we wanted to
> believe that, in the final balance, all the good we
> did would outweigh the bad. We spent hours
> telling ourselves that and hounding out any
> and all who would try to speak against that.
> May all the gods forgive us for we have sinned
> against everything we held as holy.

Since he had retired Patrick was happy to become a forgotten old monk in the library. They had made him a Monsignor a few years back but he never got used to it. He wanted to remain unaffected by the pomp and glamour of Rome and a call from Dublin, even if it was from Mrs. Boyle, always made him feel like that. He was just a simple priest, and all he had to offer was a bit of kindness. "Well I'm so happy for you. It must be a great relief to you all."

"Well it is and it isn't, Father. We're still not sure how right he'll be after. He'd become awful dark and brooding the last few years. Not that I'm not happy that he has been given the chance, only what if he has to live in an iron lung for the rest of his life? Or a wheelchair? There'll be no living with the moods he'll get himself into. I'm just afraid he'll go back on the drink as soon as he's well enough again."

"Well, maybe the Good Lord is finally showing Danny a bit of mercy."

He wanted to sound comforting and he didn't want to sound impartial. He agreed with the bishop; they did owe the Danny Boyles of the world—and all belonging to them.

"And I'm sure we have you and the holy Jesuit to thank for that."

"And how are Deirdre and the children?" Patrick switched the topic as subtly as he could. He had never actually gotten around to telling John about Danny's coma. He knew he didn't have to. John and the bishop had probably been in cahoots for years.

"They're over the moon, especially Grainne, even though it spoiled Christmas for her little ones. I told her I would make it up to them all. When Danny is well enough, they're all going to come over and visit Rome with me. It'll do Danny a world of good to see yourself again and your friend."

Patrick wasn't so sure about that. Lately all John talked about was the Mayan calendar. "It's not the end," he'd say every time he mentioned it. "It is a warning from the past that the time for complacency is over. The meek must rise up before everything is taken and destroyed."

"Now that is something to be looking forward to. And will Deirdre's father be with you?"

"I doubt it, Father. He's gotten very bad. He gets lost on his way to the toilet. And then he forgets why he was going and wets himself. We can't have the children see him like that."

"No, Mrs. Boyle, we couldn't have that."

"Deirdre says she might try and spend a few days in Ireland if she can manage it but she'll have her hands full enough."

"Will it not be awkward for her—being here with Danny?"

"We'll manage. After all, we're still family."

"Of course, Mrs. Boyle. And please tell them all that I can't wait to see them."

*

"Have you gone mad? It will be worse than a Griswold movie."

"Rome survived the Barbarians; it will survive us." Deirdre couldn't look him in the eye; she wasn't crazy about the idea either. It was something Jacinta and Grainne had cooked up between them and left it to her to break the news to Martin.

"I don't think I'll be able to get away this year. We've got so much going on at work."

"You might not have a choice," Deirdre said softly. She had noticed the change in him where his father was concerned. Before, he would just have refused flatly. Now he was just coming up with excuses. "Grainne is already working on Rachael."

"She never said anything."

"What could she say? But she did ask me to talk with you."

He thought about that for a while. He really didn't have an option, so she sat patiently while he digested it. He'd probably vent a little more but he'd do the right thing. He always did.

"Isn't it too soon? He won't be well enough to travel."

"I hope that's concern for his wellbeing. Besides, if it proves too much for him we can just drop him off in the Catacombs."

"You're taking this very well. Have you even thought it all through?"

"As a matter of fact I have. That's why I will be bringing someone with me."

"Who, an exorcist?"

"In a way. His name is Ritchie and we have been together for a few months. We feel that it's time he met all of you." That, and she didn't want anyone to think that she and Danny might ever . . .

"In the lion's den?"

"Don't be silly. I've told him how well adjusted you and your sister are."

"I see. You get me to go along with it so Grainne doesn't get upset. Mother, you can be very Machiavellian."

"Not at all. You and I are allies. And we have backup. I suggested to Rachael that she invite her parents."

"Don't you think they've suffered enough?"

"Joel and your father have become friends. Joel goes to see him every day and wheels him outside so he can smoke."

"He's still not able to walk?"

"He can, a little, but the doctors want him to ease back into things and you know your father: why walk if someone is willing to push you around?"

"And there is nothing I can say to get out of it?"

"I doubt it. Your grandmother and your sister have formed a pact. We must do the same. Help me with this and I will see to it that you spend as little time as possible with him. That way you and Rachael can have a reasonably romantic vacation."

"With deranged family in tow."

"When in Rome, Martin. When in Rome."

He'd be fine. For all his grumbling, he would be the perfect gentleman to Rachael and Grainne and her and Ritchie. He'd be cordial with his father and that was the best that could be hoped for.

※

"You want to bring your new boyfriend along?"

Deirdre moved the phone to her other hand and rose and closed her office door. This was going to take a while. "Yes, Grainne, I'm bringing Ritchie."

"Have you even considered how Daddy might feel?"

"Grainne, he just came out of a coma. I think he'll feel so grateful he won't care."

"Mother. Why don't you just throw him to the lions when we get there?"

"Sweetie, listen to me. Your father and I are okay with all that has happened. We accepted it and have both moved on. It's time you did too."

"I can't believe you're saying this—after all he has just been through."

"Grainne, the only reason I agreed to this trip was because of what we've all been through. And we all have to deal with it in our own way. Now stop trying to impose yourself on the situation. Give everyone the space to deal with it as they want."

"Sometimes, I can't believe you're my mother."

"I know. It's still a bit strange for me, too, but don't worry. We'll all behave ourselves and we'll have a wonderful time. And your father will just be delighted to be included."

"Until he sees who you're with."

"I could keep Ritchie locked in my bedroom only I'd probably never come out either."

"Mother!"

"Oh, relax. I'm just trying to lighten the mood. Besides, your father will be so busy with Joel Brand, he won't even notice."

"And that's another thing. Why are they coming?"

"Because your father has finally found a friend who doesn't spend his whole life drinking. It might be the positive influence he's going to need."

"But they're not even family."

"They are to your brother and you know your grandmother is hoping that this might be the chance for your father and him to get closer. It could be nice."

"That's if Rachael doesn't drag him off all the time."

"Sweetie, what's the issue between you and Rachael?"

"There's no issue. Why would you say that?"

"Because you haven't said a kind word about her lately."

"That's not true. How could you even say such a thing?"

"Well, forgive me if I'm wrong. It just seems that you had a falling out with her. Is there anything the matter?"

"No, only she thinks she is so much better than the rest of us."

"I don't think she'd ever have a thought like that."

Grainne didn't answer, and in the pause that followed Deirdre laid out all the pieces in her mind like a jigsaw. She would take the time to put them all together but not now. "I should say goodbye for now. I have a few things waiting. But I'm going to visit your father later. If you're not too busy, we could go for coffee after?"

"I can't. Doug's working late again."

Martin had pulled it off. He'd managed to save Doug's job for now. It had cost him a few favors and he'd made it very clear to Doug: it was his last chance. Doug would be grateful and, when they were in Rome, gambol about like a dog. But it would keep Grainne occupied. All in all, it might not be such a bad trip when everything was said and done.

\*

"I'm just not up for it, Joel. Look at me." Danny still looked like death but it was understandable; he'd been almost dead for weeks. "I'm payin' for my sins now, I can tell ya. Do they really think that a trip to Rome is going to cure me?"

Joel was wheeling him across Bond Street and into the park. They'd told the nurses that they just went around the block for some air but nobody bought that. The doctor had been very critical of his smoking, but other than that Danny was being a model patient—charming but with a touch of contrition—so nobody said too much. They were never gone more than twenty minutes and he wasn't drinking. That was the big concern. Other than that, as long as he was warm enough, everybody just looked the other way—and it was good for Danny to have the company of a friend. Everybody knew the value of that.

It was very cold and brittle outside but the sun was bright and, out of the wind, warming. There were still piles of old snow everywhere, crusting at the blackened edges.

"You gotta love the spring in this country," Danny tried to joke when the cold reached in between his new coat and the robe he wore over his pajamas. "It's no wonder the whole country is going mad. We're not designed for living like this."

"It will be nice and warm in Rome," Joel finally answered. He was still red faced from the exertions he had to go through to dress Danny, who was still getting dizzy spells. Joel had brought him the coat, an extra blanket to cover his legs, and had wrapped Danny like a toddler. And he had brought him a fresh pack of cigarettes.

He wasn't the worst of them, Danny decided, as he looked up at him. He'd offered to wheel Danny over to St. Michael's Cathedral, nestled in behind the United Church, but Danny just wanted to get a few drags into him and get back inside. He didn't like smoking near the entrance where the other patients gathered. They looked so pathetic with their coats on over their gowns and wearing slippers. And some had to bring their drip things too. He didn't want to be seen with them.

"It's all my mother's doing, isn't it?"

"Well, Danny, you can't blame her for wanting to have her family around her again."

"I thought you didn't care much for family."

"Just my wife's. Yours, I like."

"Yeah, but she's probably still hoping I'll be saved or something."

"She's your mother; of course she'd want that."

"How come you never talk about your mother?"

"What can I say? She was a sad woman. Nobody in our house ever smiled. As a child, I always had to hear about all the terrible things life would do to us. I know she had every reason to be the way she was—she was only eleven when they took most of her family away. I just wish she didn't have to pass it all on!"

He looked guiltier than usual and Danny couldn't help but try to reach out to him. Only people who went through things like that could really understand, but Danny had a bit of an idea what it was like. He'd spent enough time in his own hell. He wanted to nudge Joel or something, just to let him know, but he was wrapped too tight. "Tell me about it. Only in our house, my parents used to get drunk and sing about our sorrows."

"I think I would have preferred that."

Danny looked up at him and realized he was right. It could have been worse—and it should've been after all the shit he'd pulled. And despite everything, he was still being given another chance. Only, that scared him. He'd screwed up every other chance he ever got.

He really wanted to believe that it'd be different this time. When he was in his coma he could hear their voices: his uncle and his parents, and the old priests. They were all telling him there was still time to set things right. He knew he really had to this time—only he couldn't say that to anybody. He'd been promising to get his act together so often that he'd sound like the boy with the wolf; but being almost dead had shown him how precious life really was. He just had to remember to look at it that way. He had to learn to become grateful and not always be harping on. "I used to be happy back when it was just me and my granny."

"And what happened?"

He wanted to be positive but even just thinking about it brought up the old shit that was still surging around inside him. "She died and I found out about all the lies she'd told me.

"I suppose it wasn't all her fault," he added for Joel's sake. If he'd been given another chance, he'd use it to try to make the world a little better for those around him, and he'd start with Joel. "After my grandfather was gone, she had to deal with everything on her own. Not that she wasn't more than a match for the world, I can tell ya, but she always worried about what people might be saying.

"Everybody was like that back then. All kinds of shite could be happening but as long as the neighbors didn't know . . . only they always did. Everybody used to make it their business to know what everyone else was up to. And nobody was good enough for anybody else."

"There are times when I hate my uncle," Joel answered, thinking out loud. "Because of his principles . . ."

He didn't say any more so Danny threw his butt into a snow bank. "C'mon then, let's get me back before my balls bang together and shatter."

"You should have let me put your pants on."

"Ah now, Joel. You're a good friend and all but I'm not sure I want you in my pants."

Joel looked horrified as he stepped out of view and began to push the chair back toward the hospital.

"Are you a bit homophobic there, Joel? I used to be too. Until I found out that my uncle was gay. Then he died and it took me a while to sort all that out. But now I'm proud to say—even though I'm a total fuck-up—I'm not the slightest bit against any of that. Live and let live, eh?"

Joel grunted something but it might have been because they were sloshing through the slush as they crossed Bond Street again.

"The Nazis were against them too." Danny decided to change the mood; they were getting a bit morbid. "Even though they were all closet-cases themselves."

Joel still didn't answer, but that might have been because he was pushing Danny up the ramp, gasping a bit as he did.

"Are you all right there, Joel? You know there're going to be lots of hills in Rome, don't ya?"

"We'll get a moped with a side car."

"Now that would be something for the kids to put on You-Tube, or something. We could become the Hell's Angels of Rome."

"Danny." Joel stepped back in front of him as they waited for an elevator. "Rachael wanted you to know that Deirdre will have someone with her."

Danny kept smiling even though a tiny little flame inside of him went out. It had sputtered back to life when he'd come out of the coma and the first familiar face he saw was hers. But he'd no right to expect anything. It was just nice to feel a little foolish about her again.

"Well you tell Rachael that there's nothing to worry about. I'm very happy that Deirdre has someone new in her life; she deserves it. And besides, I'm just delighted that we can all be together again, even if everything is different. Everything is anyway, so why should that spoil anything anymore?"

He knew Joel would repeat every word he said and Rachael would repeat them to Martin. "It took being in a coma for me see to see a bit of sense. And I do now. I can see that I was the luckiest sod around—when I got out of my own way. I've a family who's still willing to be seen with me even after all I've done."

He meant it too—most of it, anyway. When he'd been out of it, he'd got to watch his whole life right from the beginning. And it wasn't like when he'd actually lived it. It was more like a movie and he got to see things differently. And even though he could see all the shit that happened, he could see there were other ways he could have handled things.

"Joel." He almost smiled when he was tucked back into his warm bed. "Thanks for everything."

"What, for taking you out into the freezing weather so you can smoke yourself to death?"

"Yeah, and for all the other stuff too. And for Rachael. Martin really lucked out there."

"They're good for each other and we can both take some pride in that."

They nodded in agreement at that.

"Can I ask you something? How the fuck did you put up with me before."

"Because you're the only person I know that doesn't treat me like an outcast."

"Ya know"—Danny smirked—"when they get you to Rome—my mother's probably going to have a few Jesuits on standby to try and convert you."

"Perhaps we could get a deal—like a two-for-one."

"That's very Jewish of you there, Joel."

"I would have thought that being in a coma might have helped you see the ugliness of racial profiling, you Irish drunk."

Danny pretended to glare at him but he couldn't keep it up. "Thanks, Joel. I really mean it."

\*

"I just wonder if bringing her new boyfriend is wise."

Miriam was pushing John across the Ponte Sant' Angelo, the narrow pedestrian bridge that led to the Castel where popes often hid from the people of the city—and others who came to challenge their temporal power. John liked the bridge and always waved up at the stone angels along the parapets.

"Maybe she needs him as a foil." He didn't usually comment on her news of Deirdre but he seemed interested in Danny Boyle.

"Really?"

"Yes, she will want to support him but not give him any false hope."

"You have remarkable insight into people you've never met."

"Not really. What would you do in her place?"

"I don't know. I'd like to think that I could be like her but I'm not sure. Deirdre has learned how to be loving and detached and that's still beyond me. She's doing this for the sake of her family. It is Jacinta Boyle's grand scheme to save her son, and Deirdre is willing to go along with everything and play out her part as she must."

"And you don't think you could do that?"

"The role of motherhood was always beyond me. That's why I chose the veil."

"Do you have regrets?" John asked without looking back at her. Instead, he was staring down at the river.

"Yes and no. When I became a nun it was a revered vocation."

She locked his wheels and joined him in looking at the river. "And often the only way a woman like me could get an education and have some independence in the world."

"What set you apart?"

She knew exactly what he meant. They had both spent most of their days separate and apart from the rest of the world.

"When I was a child, my mother was an avid reader and would sit by the fire every night reading. My father could never understand and would get impatient with her. He wasn't such a bad person but he had little education. He was taken out of school to run the farm.

"When we were very young she read to us, but when we were more grown up, she gave us books to read on our own. But we had to wait until all our chores were done—so as not to aggravate my father.

"So for an hour every evening I got to sit and read, and it was the happiest part of my day. I knew then that I wanted to be a teacher. I wanted to share the joy I had found with others. I suppose I was vain, too, and wanted to be the one that turned on the switch inside them. But instead, I have just become an anachronism."

The river flowed slowly past them, sparkling in the sunshine. Books had changed everything for her. They had opened her mind to a world beyond the fields her family had farmed for years. Books helped her see beyond the hills that rimmed their world. They had made her different, even from her sisters who finished school and went out into the world looking for husbands.

They found them, too, and settled down to raise families of their own. When Miriam was in America they wrote often but it was more a sense of obligation to fading familial bonds. And, when she was defrocked and had gone back to Dublin in disgrace, they were cordial enough, but she knew her past was not something they wanted their friends to know about. They lived in places like Killiney and Howth and could never find the right time to have her visit. Those that were still alive wrote emails, at Christmas mostly, with vague promises about meeting up the next time they were in Rome.

"We're both relics." John smiled and his faded blue eyes seemed so sad. "But at least we're in the right place for that."

"Yes, there is that. And I must admit that I'm looking forward to seeing Deirdre's children again. They always make me feel that I belong to something."

She was determined to play her part too. She'd be as nice and as supportive as she could with Danny. She'd never really disliked him—she was just hurt by the things he'd done to Deirdre. But it was time to put all that aside. It might even be a nice visit for everybody, but she would have to make sure John was taking his medications properly. Sometimes he played around with them and could get very dark.

"Do you?"

"Do I what?"

"Have regrets?"

"A great many."

"I mean about choosing the priesthood?"

"No, not about that. Even though I had read that we should wear the world as a loose garment—I had to play my part. I could not stand by and let terrible things go unchallenged. I had to become a part of the good in this life.

"But, as it turns out, the saddest part of living is learning that so much that we held as good had been corrupted. Yes, great new ideals spring up, but it is only a matter of time before they are turned for profit. Even this." John waved his hands across the Roman skyline. "All the ideals of the Republic became nothing more than the rationalization of a pyramid built on the backs of slaves.

"And when it was the turn of the Christians, the simplicity of Christ was lost in the clamors that are matters of State and Politic. The voice of Love became the voice of censure and condemnation. This is our nature and this will be our fate. Blessed are the weak of mind for they can go along with it all, assured by the comforting lies of the world."

"That is the most un-Jesuit thing I have ever heard."

"Yes, I have become a heretic."

He was smiling again and she reached forward and gently stroked the back of his hand, old and white and wrinkled.

"What would you have done differently?"

"Very little."

"Even the war?"

"Even the war. That was what shaped me and made me for the paths I was given."

"Don't you think you might have been shaped and chosen before then?"

"No. Many men go to war and do not become Jesuits. This was my doing. At the end of the day, and despite all that happens to us, we make our own choices."

"I'm not so sure about that."

John turned his hand and took hers in his. He held it for a moment but she could feel all that was still kind and tender in him. "We can see it so easily in those around us. Look at Deirdre's husband."

"Ex-husband."

"Regardless. Was he made by the world or has he chosen poorly?"

"John." Miriam interrupted his musings as they approached the Via Giulia. She would let him pray with the dead for a while before she wheeled him home for the night. "We need to talk about Patrick."

"What about him?"

"You haven't been very nice to him recently."

"Haven't I?"

"You know you haven't. You've been very impatient and dismissive with him. He doesn't deserve that and especially not from you.

"John?" she asked again when he didn't answer.

"Very well then. I am jealous of him because he still has a purpose in the world and is reluctant to embrace it."

"I see, but isn't that his choice? Patrick was never one to go rushing off tilting at windmills. He was always the more patient sort who trusted that he'd be given his part when the time came."

John snorted and hunched his shoulders to urge them along.

"Not everyone is like you, you know? Not everyone is always up to fight the good fight," Miriam chided gently and let his chair come to halt. She stepped in front of him so she could see his face and he could see hers. "Patrick has a different approach. You have to allow for that."

"It's not just about what I want. Patrick's uncle wants to move on but he cannot until he fulfills some old promise he made."

"To Danny Boyle's grandmother?"

"Yes, and to Patrick himself."

*

"I have tried talking to him," Miriam told him when she called, but Patrick wasn't convinced.

He'd found it better to avoid John altogether and soothed any guilt for deserting the old man by convincing himself that it was better not to upset him.

"And do you think you got through to him?"

"Who knows, Patrick? But I do know that he does not mean the things he says. He's really very fond of you and admires all that you've stood for. He says that you're like the last of the Desert Fathers."

Patrick almost smiled at that. Lately he'd been finding solace in the writings of the *Apophthegmata Patrum*, something John had picked up on the last time they met. "Say something to your bishop," he had paraphrased, "that he might be edified."

"If he is not edified by my silence," Patrick had responded, almost with a smirk, "he will not be edified by my speech."

It was a bit petulant of him and he'd regretted it immediately, but he resented John harping on at him about his uncle.

"Well it was kind of you talk with him but, if you don't mind—I don't think this is something we need bother John with anymore."

"No," Miriam agreed and paused for a moment. "I suppose you're right."

After she had hung up, Patrick took the letter from his pocket. He'd found it at the bottom of the bishop's box of papers. Old and yellowed and addressed to him in his uncle's bold hand, and dated the evening of Patrick's ordination. He'd read it so often that he could recall it verbatim.

> It might be that my greatest sin was that I got you into it all. I could have tried to turn you away from this life even though you seemed bound and determined. Perhaps I could have done more but now I will pray that you can prove stronger than most and always be a true priest and not just another functionary in God's bureaucracy. I pray that the spirit you have shown since you were a boy is never diminished.

He put the letter back into his pocket and recited the rest as he walked out into the night.

"Are you well, Uncle," he called up to Bruno when he reached the piazza as the night closed in around them.

*No complaints, me boy. And are you well?*

"I am. You know Danny Boyle is on his way?"

*I do indeed.*

"And would you happen to know what it is I'm supposed to say to him?"

His uncle just smiled and didn't answer. He didn't have to. Patrick knew. All he had to do was to clear his heart and mind and let God work through him, for better or worse.

This was the moment his life had led up to. He was being given another chance to play his part in the great plan that would help save Danny Boyle from himself.

# Chapter 19 – Summer 2012

IT WAS, PATRICK HAD TO ADMIT, GOING TO BE A LOT MORE DIF-
FICULT THAN HE HAD ANTICIPATED. The invasion of Boyles
was far too much for him. It was nothing they did. He just
wasn't used to dealing with so many people at one time and
that made him sad. He'd become a shepherd who couldn't be
around his flock.

Not that they seemed to notice. Jacinta invited him over
to their hotel for lunch the day after they arrived and greeted
him as if he was a cardinal. Danny was very cordial, too, but a
bit more hesitant—at times contrite and at times embarrassed,
particularly when his mother spoke for him.

She didn't seem aware or concerned, sitting like a dowager,
the way old Nora Boyle used to.

Martin and Grainne had left their kids at home with their
mothers-in-law and sat at the next table over with their spouses and Deirdre. Patrick had met them all in the foyer and liked
them immediately. Grainne looked more like Anne Fallon and
Martin was the image of his father—except a lot more polished
and proud. He liked Doug, too, and Rachael, but he wasn't sure
what to make of her father. "Brand," he had introduced himself.
"Joel Brand," he went on as if Patrick should have known him
or something. But he seemed nice enough and Miriam had told
him that he never left Danny's side. Danny was walking with
a cane and Joel was never far away. He looked over a few times,
making sure that Danny was okay.

As far as Patrick could see he was, but he looked awful and Patrick didn't normally dwell on such things. He looked like a man who had been dragged through the fires of hell by wild horses. There was hardly anything left of him. Patrick had always remembered him from that day in Rathfarnham Castle—the day they walked around and talked about the trouble Danny was in. That was the day when he felt most Christ-like in all the years he'd been a priest. Nothing else came close. Funerals, weddings, baptisms—they were pretty run of the mill. Of course he had to act the part, being happy if it was a wedding or a baptism and sad when the other situations called for it. He did, however, like visiting the old people, even though he realized most of them were so lonely they would have looked forward to his visits even if he was selling insurance.

At the end of the day that was all he was doing, and that was the problem. Not even the pope could stop bad things from happening, no matter how much he asked them all to pray. That's what his uncle's letters said: the best they could hope for was to try to be able to clean up afterwards.

"And how was your journey over?" he asked Danny, as kindly and welcoming as he could. He wanted him to know that he was really happy to see him. From what he had read about alcoholics, they all suffered terribly from shame—at least until they were sober for a while. But Danny wasn't really listening; he was gazing over at the other table where his family sat.

Deirdre had come alone. Jacinta had phoned the night before to let Patrick know they'd arrived safely and mentioned it, almost casually. Jacinta had also confided in her that things weren't rosy on that front, but it was probably for the better.

They all needed to know the lay of the land, but it still felt like gossip. Old Fr. Brennan used to call it one of the delicacies of life but Patrick never felt proper about it. Still, as Miriam had rationalized aloud, they all had their part to play in Jacinta's plan.

"And what are you hoping to see in Rome?" Patrick tried again when Jacinta had finally fallen silent, having answered his previous question and talked all through the meal that she had just picked at. She said flying always did that to her; her stomach took a few days to land—not that it was great at the best of times, but she still had her health other than that, and there were many who'd be more than happy to change places with her.

"I'd like to see all of it but I'm really just hoping to spend a bit of time with my kids again." He tried to look happy but Patrick could see; for a moment he looked as though he might cry.

"And that will be very nice for you," Patrick agreed and tried not to look at him. There was too much of a question in the way Danny said it. He could feel Jacinta watching him too. "And you, Mrs. Boyle. What will you see this time? Now that you're practically an expert on the place."

"Well, today I'm going to have a lie-down until my tummy is better. After that, I'll just go wherever the rest are going. I want to see their faces when they see it all; and I'd like to see Fr. Melchor again. Is he still around?"

"He is. He's in a wheelchair now so he isn't as mobile. And he's a right old age, but he did say he'd like to see you again. Him and Miriam."

"Ah that's nice." She smiled back at him. "And make sure you tell him that I can't wait. It'll be so nice to sit down and have a chat about things. And he can meet my Danny."

"Is that the old Jesuit you told me about?" Danny asked with more than a hint of resignation. He wasn't the little boy who used to cling to his grandmother's skirts anymore, but he looked just as plaintive. And all the world had done to him just made it worse.

"Well he and Miriam are very excited about seeing you all again." Patrick gushed a little. Deirdre had told Miriam what the old woman had in store for her son. She was going to march him from one holy site to the next until every saint in Rome took up his cause. Poor Danny. He looked the way he did when Patrick used to give him his penance.

"Well, I want to see the Coliseum first. And the Temple of Venus is just across from it," Grainne announced for all to hear and waved the map on her phone around in case further proof was required. "And the Garden of the Vestal Virgins is right there." She turned her phone back and changed the zoom. "We have to take pictures of me there" She nudged Doug. "Only they'd be nicer in the moonlight."

"Well, Rachael and I are going to see the Sistine Chapel first and the Basilica." Martin flicked a crumb from his lap. "And we will probably have dinner in Trastevere."

"Why don't we all do that?" Doug asked hopefully.

"Because, silly, you and I are going to have the most romantic holiday of our lives." Grainne closed her hand on his and gave it a little squeeze.

"That sounds wonderful," Deirdre agreed as ambiguously as she dared, careful not to upset the apple cart. "I'm hoping to see Miriam today and who knows what we might get up too."

"And what about Daddy?"

"I'll take your father for a walk," Joel offered before Deirdre could answer. Martin and Rachael had told her that he was unhappy about Adina taking Martin Jr. to Montreal, but caved in when the consensus was clearly against him. "He'll probably get tired quickly and I won't mind bringing him back so he can rest."

"We could take your dad too. If you want?" Doug offered awkwardly, and checked Deirdre's reaction even before checking Grainne's.

Poor Doug. There was a storm brewing around him and there was nothing he could do but wait for it to break. Grainne had been difficult with them all for days before they got on the plane, but she did hug Deirdre tightly when she showed up at the airport alone. Deirdre knew she would read something into it. There wasn't. She had just taken the time to think things through and decided she was coming alone. Ritchie said he understood, but she could tell he was having a terrible time with trust. She didn't want to feed that fire but she wasn't ready for him to step on this stage just yet. It was a part of her past and she didn't want any of that between them.

"No, let's all do our own things today; but I will ask you to commit to dinner on Thursday. Your grandmother and Auntie Miriam want to get everybody together."

"Are we having the last supper?" Martin muttered as he rose and extended his hand to Rachael, to help her rise and go out and see the Eternal City with him. She smiled back and rose so elegantly. Rome, the sun and her bright blue summer dress making her look a part of it all.

"Of course we will be there." She wove her arm around Martin's. "Even if I have to frogmarch him there myself."

"I suppose he's getting used to that by now," Grainne muttered with her head down as she rose.

"Now, sweetie," Deirdre reached out as if to help her up. "Let's not trip and fall and ruin everything."

Grainne stood almost face to face with her mother and smiled. Deirdre knew that smile. Her little girl was in pain, and just like her father, would not be able to talk about it until it erupted. Hopefully it could be postponed for a while. Maybe Miriam could help; she always had a positive effect on her kids.

*

"Well I think it's terribly unfair. You're the one who still looks like a queen while I look more like a grandmother each year." Miriam wasn't kidding; she looked so old.

"I didn't think ex-nuns gave much thought to things like that." Deirdre tried to keep from smiling but she couldn't. Being with Miriam again made her feel as she had when she was young and Miriam offered her guidance. Life hadn't turned out the way either of them had expected. It was better and worse.

"Even beneath the veil still lurks the heart of a woman, as full of love and foolishness as any other."

"Is that the faint hint of bitterness or self-pity?"

"Neither. It's jealousy."

"That's so nice of you to say, Miriam, but we both know you don't do jealousy. Thanks for playing though." Deirdre raised her glass of red and paused for a moment. "This is the first time I've had a drink since I left Toronto. Somehow, it doesn't feel right to be drinking around Danny. And Grainne asked us all not to."

"She's still calling the shots?"

"Always, but there is something else going on. She's spoiling for a fight and her poor husband has no idea what to do with her."

"What did he do?"

"I'm not sure. He's not the brightest, but this strikes me as a bigger problem. I think Martin and Rachael are in the firing line this time."

"Mr. and Ms. Perfect. What could they have done?"

"Made a better life for themselves? Who knows? Grainne is so like her father minus the drinking. Every little thing gets stuck inside and . . . well, you know the rest."

"Will the peace last until we all have dinner? Jacinta has put so much effort into arranging everything."

"Tell me about it. She checks that I'm still available every time she sees me."

"Well, you have become a bit of a social butterfly lately." Miriam leaned forward the way she used to back in Bewley's when she was letting Deirdre in on some secret about life. "Can I ask you something? Are you happy?"

"Of course I'm happy. I stopped letting the world steal that from me a long time ago. I've worked hard and done my best and now I choose to be happy. I know it might be a disappointment to you, but I don't have much of a social conscience left. I recycle, though, and I support my causes. But beyond that I simply don't have time for all the terrible things in the world. I have done enough crying and worrying to last me a lifetime.

"Besides, Danny once told me about something that he heard at an AA meeting. Someone said it was better to light up your own corner of the world rather than sit crying in the dark. I don't think he remembers that, but it stayed with me. I guess you could say it became a mantra for me."

"Oh, Deirdre. You're the total opposite of disappointment. You're the only person I know who's truly happy." And in that moment everything was changed between them. Just as with her father and Jacinta Boyle, Deirdre was now the adult to everyone she knew.

"Miriam, you know better. I'm a mother. We only get to be truly happy when our kids are or until they act up again. Come on, we've come this far and we're sitting in the middle of Rome on a beautiful day. We have so many wonderful and happy things to talk about."

"Yes, you're right, and here's something wonderful and happy that I can only share with you. I was pushing John along by the river a few days ago when it struck me. I've always . . . well, carried a bit of torch for John. I never let myself think about it before but the other day it hit me. When I first met him I had silly little dreams of the two of us growing old together, and now I guess I have as much reason as any to be happy."

"And that"—Deirdre raised her glass, a beautiful red sparkle in the sunshine—"is the secret to contentment: how to make lemonade."

*

They gathered in a patio on the shady side of the Piazza Farnese. Martin and Rachael stylishly dressed from their shopping; Grainne and Doug, who wore his Maple Leaf shirt; Deirdre in a dark dress and gold earrings; Jacinta in her smartest linen suit; and Danny and Joel both clad in jeans and polo shirts, almost looking like mismatched twins. Patrick had called to say that he and Miriam were running late as John was being difficult, so Deirdre decided they should sit and wait. She was wearing higher heels and needed to get off her feet. The walk over would have been so enjoyable but there was something going on. Jacinta didn't seem to notice and just chatted away as they walked arm-in-arm through cobblestone lanes, but Deirdre did. Every time Rachael and Martin stopped to look in a window, Grainne would groan. It wasn't as if they were slowing them down—at Jacinta's pace they would have had time to stop in every store. Even Danny was able to keep up, and he and Joel wandered slowly ahead, joking and laughing. They shared a very dry sense of humor. Deirdre was happy for them—two black sheep who had finally found each other. It would have been so pleasant if her daughter wasn't in one of her moods.

"I didn't realize we were going formal tonight," Grainne commented as she sat and took a sidelong glance at Rachael.

"In Rome, no woman goes out in less than her best," Deirdre explained and smiled at her daughter. Grainne still carried some of her baby weight and dressed to cover it with shapeless things that she found in Winners. "But you look wonderful, too."

"I think Martin and Rachael look very Italian—very stylish," Jacinta chimed in as she checked each of the little streets that led into the piazza. "And you look wonderful, dear. You look very Canadian."

"Thanks, Granny. Doug and I like to enjoy our vacations and not feel we have to impress anybody."

"That's nice, dear," Jacinta soothed. "And are you enjoying yourself?" she asked Doug.

"It's great," he agreed quickly, "but it's different than I thought it would be."

"Really?" Deirdre joined in to distract Grainne from her brother, who looked like he was about to say something. "And why is that?"

"The Italians here are a lot nicer than the ones we have at home."

The waiter intruded before anyone had to answer and asked if they would like drinks while they waited. "Yes,"

Martin answered immediately and began to read the wine menu. "Rachael and I would like some wine."

"And why wouldn't you," Jacinta encouraged and turned to Danny. "You won't mind, will you?"

"Not at all," Danny enthused. "Please go ahead. It's not going to bother me."

"Are you sure?" Joel asked, and waited for Danny to nod before picking up his menu.

"It would bother me more if you weren't. I'll have a bottle of water, the gassy one."

"Aqua." The waiter smiled. "You don't like wine?"

"Not today." Danny smiled at them all. "And hopefully not tomorrow, either."

"And I'll have water too." Grainne announced and looked to Doug.

"I'd love a beer, if that's all right?"

"Really, Doug. Beer?"

"Oh let him have it," Rachael offered like an olive branch. "He's on holidays."

"Yes he is, with me."

"And what's that supposed to mean?" Martin asked as he leaned forward between his sister and his wife.

"Ask her," Grainne said as off-handedly as she could.

"Grainne?" Rachael looked confused.

"Oh, don't play the innocent with me."

"Grainne?" Jacinta joined in. "What's the matter?"

"Oh nothing, Granny. It's just that some people seem to forget who they're married to."

"Grainne." Doug tried to put his arm around her.

"Don't." Grainne stiffened.

The waiter returned and everyone sat back and waited while he served their drinks with a flourish. "And are you ready to order?"

"Not yet." Deirdre smiled up at him but it was a heartless smile. It was all beginning to make sense to her now. She didn't know for sure; it was more a case of her maternal instincts. "We are still waiting on our friends. And before they get here, please excuse me while I use the washroom. Grainne, will you come with me?"

\*

"You're after missing all the excitement," Jacinta explained when Patrick arrived and found her sitting with Joel and Danny. He had come alone as Miriam had been unable to get John to come out. "He needs to do this on his own," he kept repeating, and Miriam wasn't able to find out who "he" was.

"It's like we had an outbreak of the plague," Jacinta continued after Patrick had made their apologies. "They all suddenly got sick."

Grainne and Doug had left because she was feeling unwell. Then Martin and his wife had to leave, too, after a lot of running back and forth to the washrooms where Deirdre was trying to manage a crisis or something.

"I hope it's nothing serious," Patrick offered with real concern when Deirdre remerged looking as serene as she could.

"It's just an outbreak of family-itis." Jacinta laughed and patted the back of her daughter-in-law's hand. She could see she was upset and embarrassed. "They never really outgrow it. You think they're all grown up but as soon as they get together, it's like they're three-year-olds again."

They all laughed at that but Jacinta could see; there was no point in trying to keep her plan. "Maybe we should try and get everybody together some other evening?"

"Yes, I think that would be for the best." Patrick nodded back and waited for Deirdre. She took another moment to compose herself and smiled at them all. "Yes, I agree. Let's go back to the hotel and get a good night's sleep and see where we are in the morning."

"Where's Danny?" Joel asked as they gathered their things and got ready to leave.

"He was here a minute ago," Jacinta said but wasn't sure. With all the fuss that was happening, no one had noticed him leave. Joel checked the washrooms while Patrick looked around the piazza, but there was no sign of him.

"You don't think he's going to get himself into any trouble?" Jacinta asked; but Joel and Deirdre had no answer.

"Perhaps," Patrick suggested as soothingly as he could, "you ladies should go back to the hotel with Joel and I'll look for him."

Joel was reluctant but Patrick assured them. He knew the city better and he had friends to call on if the need arose. He didn't think it would—he had a hunch where Danny might be—but he didn't tell them that.

*

Deirdre lay on her hotel bed and wished she were at home. The whole misunderstanding between Grainne and Rachael had been smoothed over for now, but these things always took much longer to really resolve. Doug had sat in muted shock as his wife accused him of having an affair with his best friend's wife. That type of thing didn't just blow over; there would be fallout for months, maybe even years. Rachael seemed ready to forgive and forget but Martin had yet to have his say.

It was well past midnight but she couldn't get to sleep. She kept replaying the details in her mind. She might have been able to avert it but she hadn't been giving it her full attention. She had known something was going on since before Christmas. That was the misunderstanding: Rachael and Doug's effort to plan festivities in secret had been misinterpreted.

*No good deed goes unpunished,* Deirdre reminded herself and fluffed her pillows again. She needed to sleep so she could continue the smoothing-over process in the morning. They still had four more days to go and she was determined to make the best of it.

Shortly after one, just as she was finally beginning to drift off, Joel phoned her room. He apologized for disturbing her but he was worried; Danny had not come back yet.

*

After wandering the narrow streets of Rione Parione, Danny Boyle stood at the foot of Giordano Bruno's statue like the lost pilgrim he was. The scene at the restaurant had really gotten to him. Watching it all unfold, he knew he shouldn't have come. He wasn't sure what Grainne and Martin were upset about but it probably had something to do with him. They'd all been acting so carefully around him—as if he might shatter and break if one of them looked crooked at him. He should have stayed at home.

This was the part of getting sober that he dreaded—facing up to what he'd become and what he'd done. How could he explain to his own son and daughter—and his ex-wife—that he had chosen the life of a drunken bum over them? He couldn't even explain it to himself, other than finally admitting that he really was an alcoholic. And that meant accepting all that entailed.

At meetings they said that part of being alcoholic was that they were wired for denial—and rationalization. They told themselves they drank to try to take the edge off, when really it was the only way they could get comfortable around other people. And over time, as the few drinks became many, that created a whole new mess of problems—such as lying about how much they really drank or what they'd done when they were drunk.

Everybody did crazy things when they were drinking but other people could choose to avoid it—even if they chose not to. Alcoholics couldn't. As well as having a psychological dependency, they also developed a physical addiction that in time became an allergy. Then, to try to hide that, they had to learn to lie so convincingly that even the people who didn't believe them weren't sure.

It was a vicious cycle that made little sense to anyone around them, and even when they were trying to lie low and keep out of trouble, the shame of all of that would set them off again—that and the unmanageable compulsion. They'd start nitpicking about things at first, to release all the tension that was building inside them. Then, as it grew, they'd have bouts of bitching and complaining, chafing against restraints while sounding like spoiled brats.

Until they crossed that line. After that, it all became the thrashings of another soul in pain.

That was Danny to a tee, and even though he'd heard all of that a thousand times, he'd still gone back out, over and over, and that's what really scared him. After his coma, he couldn't risk it again.

He just couldn't see how he was going to manage. He still had all those terrible feelings deep down inside. He'd tried all the stuff in the steps about resentments and making amends, but no matter how hard he tried to believe he really meant it, he knew he was just kidding himself. His stuff was branded right into him.

A lot of it was from when he was a kid. He'd never felt good about himself. Especially with his granny. It wasn't her fault. That's the way people were back then. Once you started to screw up, you were done for. For all everybody went on about Jesus and the lepers and all, nobody really did stuff like that.

The kids at school were always picking on him, too, because his father was gone and his mother was in the loony bin. Even their parents spoke about him as if he was a bit soft in the head or something. His granny told him to ignore them—that they were nothing but gossips—but it got inside him and stayed with him all his life, gnawing away at him. And he'd never found a way to make it stop.

By the time he'd gotten involved with Anto he'd already given up. He was never going to be a part of all that was supposed to be right and proper in the world. How could he? They were never going to accept him.

He'd really tried again with Deirdre, but in the end all it brought was pain and sorrow—for her, the kids, and himself. He wished he could have done it differently but he was a lost cause and always had been. And now that he'd been well and truly beaten down, his only option was to do whatever it took to crawl out from under it all.

The old-timers—the ones who'd been all the way to the bottom—talked about the day they knelt down and really asked for help. They all said that was the day everything changed for them; and it wasn't about God and all—it was about admitting to themselves that they were powerless.

He shook his head and smirked as he stared up at heaven. He wasn't sure if it even existed, but he was certain about hell. He knelt down, resisting the urge to bless himself—but he couldn't help it, being in Rome and all.

"Dear God, if you're there I need help. And I'm not just asking for myself. I'm asking for my family. They've suffered enough."

They'd also said that the real power in prayer came when they put others first.

\*

"You know you're praying to a heretic?" Patrick Reilly offered as casually as he could. He'd been watching Danny from the shadows and his heart was almost breaking. In the low light he could almost see Danny as he had been long ago.

"Well." Danny smirked as if he'd been caught doing something he shouldn't. "I've tried everyone else."

"Can I be of any help?"

For a moment Danny looked like he was about to say yes, but then his face clouded over again. "I doubt it, Father. I think it's a bit too late for me."

"Ah now, Danny, don't be thinking like that. Where there's life there's always hope." It was a platitude but it was from the heart, and Patrick could see what Danny needed most was for someone to believe in him again.

"There is, but you know me, Father. It's only a matter of time before something flips a switch inside of me and I'll pick up another drink. And the next time . . ."

Patrick could see beyond his fatalism. Danny was frightened. "Not if you were to avoid the things that get to you."

"But it's everything." Danny sighed. "The whole world is lying and cheating and everybody else goes along with it—except when I do it."

Danny looked pained so Patrick tried to smile. Maybe John was right. Maybe it would have been easier to pretend there was some magic in the world that could help. But the bishop would have reminded him that, at the end of the day, they had abused that—and a lot of it was nothing more than superstition to begin with.

He'd do it his own way. He'd show Danny some of the love and kindness he'd been taught. Danny had always been too sensitive for his own good. He was never really cut out for the way things were. Not unlike Patrick, himself.

"Danny, did you ever consider that your granny might have been right about you? Maybe you were a born saint only you haven't come to realize that yet."

That seemed to make him stop and think, but only for a moment. "Well, I'm not like any saint I ever heard of."

Patrick smiled to himself. He could almost hear his uncle wanting to weigh in and have his say.

"Well, I think the difference between devils and saints is that no matter how bad a saint is behaving, they always keep their conscience. The devils throw theirs away the first time they become inconvenient. And some of those saints were right devils in their day—and I've read enough about them to know. Paul and Augustine, to name a couple. But they found a way to go on and become something better."

"I've tried, you know?" Danny answered after staring at the moon for a while, perched as it was just above Bruno's shoulder. "Probably harder than most people—and a lot harder than anyone gives me credit for—but I can't. Keep coming back, they kept telling me. It will get better. But it didn't, and the longer I went to meetings, and did all the things you're supposed to do, the worse I felt."

He was wringing his hands and his knuckles were white. "You know," he continued, looking Patrick in the eye, "in the program they make us do a moral inventory? Well, the only good I could find was that I'd die and it would all be over—only I can't even do that properly."

Patrick took a moment and thought about what his uncle might say. He'd said it often enough in his writings. Patrick just had to put it all in a way that Danny might understand. And he didn't want to be condescending either. He'd read up on alcoholics and everyone said they could be a bit prickly. No, if he was going to be of any help, he'd have to try offering a bit of humanity.

"Danny, sometimes the world can seem very dark."

"It's all lies and bullshit, isn't it?"

Danny wasn't being defiant—he was just at the end of his rope. "Well, there is that, Danny, but you have to understand: most people are just afraid and cling to whatever they need to get by."

"Then why doesn't everybody just come out and admit it?"

Patrick smiled at that—it was a bit rich coming from someone who'd spent so much of his life denying the obvious, but it wasn't for Patrick to judge. It was for him to bring a bit of comfort to those who were suffering and Danny was as much a victim of his environment as a product of his own choices. The bishop had been adamant about things like that.

"Do you remember my uncle, the bishop? He once said that we create the truths we need—and we go on doing that until we're so lost that the middle becomes the edge. He used to say it was one of our fundamental flaws—an original sin if you like. He also said that even after we're exposed to the truth, we go scurrying back to the like-minded and huddle in congregations to celebrate the great emptiness inside of us."

"You're not asking me to believe in all that stuff again?"

"No, I'm not, Danny. All I'm saying is that we've made this beautiful life into a hell on earth and instead of becoming the mindless followers of cults and creeds, we're supposed to be trying to be a bit nicer to each other."

"Then I'm fucked on that score too."

"In a way." Patrick nodded and ignored the profanity. "And in another way you've done most harm to yourself."

"I don't think my family would agree with you."

"They're still here for you, Danny, even after everything. How are you going to reward that? That's all that really matters now."

"Do you not think it's too late?"

"Danny, I'm sure you've often heard it said that there's more joy in heaven over one lost sinner who repents." Patrick was getting a bit religious so he switched tack—that was the last thing someone like Danny needed to hear.

"Have you ever heard the words of Yehuda Berg? He was the one who said 'hurt people hurt people.' He was asking us to stop making more pain in the world. We can stop causing pain, Danny, to ourselves and others. We may not find forgiveness in this world but we can know that we stopped causing pain, and sometimes that's the best we can hope for."

Danny seemed to be considering that and sat at the foot of the statue. He still looked scared, as though there were demons waiting for him in the little streets around the piazza.

"Do you know who Giordano was?" Patrick asked as if he hadn't noticed and sat down beside him. "He was burned to death on this spot for his heresy, but I don't think he was a heretic. I think he was more like a playwright or a novelist. He said things that frightened people, and those who ruled saw him as a threat. If Bruno could speak his mind then others would follow and the whole system of rule would come tumbling down.

"And the reason I mention it, Danny, is that you've survived the fires of hell, so to speak, and I think you could still go out and do a bit of good in the world."

"Like what?"

"You already know. You could start by bringing a bit of happiness to those that love you."

"Until I fuck-up again?"

"Don't be talking like that, Danny. You've been given another chance and I don't believe it's for you to fail again. I really don't. I think it might be Fate finally balancing out—or God's mercy. It really doesn't matter. What does matter is what you're going to do with it."

Danny hesitated, trying to decide. "I'd like to believe you. I really would, but how?"

Patrick wasn't sure what to say to that. He'd never been through what Danny had suffered. He'd read about people who had but, while that gave him empathy, he had little insight except to offer a bit of hope.

*For the love of God, Patrick,* the bishop's voice boomed down from above. *Tell him that I've been dead for decades and I'm still here trying to talk sense into you. That should tell him all he needs to know.*

"Danny," Patrick continued as he tried to shut out his uncle's interruption, "you know there are people who never gave up on you?"

"Like who?"

"Well, there's your mother. And I'm sure that Deirdre and the children haven't either—deep down inside.

"And I always like to think that those who've gone before are still there when we need them. We all have a few dead relatives that we like to keep in our thoughts and our prayers. We like to think of them up in heaven, advocating on our behalf. What decent human being could ignore that?"

"My father and my granny didn't seem to have any problem moving on."

"Your granny was just doing what she thought was best, and your father walked many of the same paths you did, Danny. Would you begrudge them a little peace and quiet now or would you want them suffering along beside you?"

"I suppose not."

"Of course you wouldn't. And if they were all here with you, I'm sure they'd tell you to put all the other stuff behind you and enjoy a bit of life before it's too late."

"But what if I drink again? After the coma . . . it'll kill me."

"Then you'll just have to choose not to."

"You know me and choices."

"I do, Danny, and I'm sure that this time you'll only make the right ones."

"I wish I could be so sure."

"Would it help if I told you that you might have been right all along? Life is one lie stacked on top another. It begins at the mother's breast because what woman could look into her baby's eyes and tell them the truth? Only you're not supposed to say that. What would happen if all our priests and politicians were to tell us the real truth?"

"So how am I supposed to tell what's true and what isn't?"

"There was something my uncle said: that if they're trying to get you to believe it, it's probably a lie. And if they try to keep you from knowing about it, it's probably true. He also said that in this age of lies, only the sinner is truly honest."

# Chapter 20 – Christmas 2013

H I, MY NAME IS DANNY . . ." He paused and looked around the room, trying to make eye contact with as many people as possible. "And I'm definitely an alcoholic."

"Hi, Danny," they all called back with a touch of festive cheer in their voices. It was Christmas Eve and, right after the meeting, he was going over to Martin and Rachael's to watch his grandkids open their presents.

"And I'm here tonight to tell you about how, after years of drinking and bouncing in and out of this program, I have finally found a bit of contented sobriety." Since he got back from Rome a new hope had grown inside him, and it had been two years since he picked up a drink. And, even more important, he hadn't wanted to either.

"I was one of those guys that had to keep going back out until I reached the bottom and then some. I once stayed sober for a few years and still went back out." This time it was different. He could have tried to explain it but who would believe him? It wasn't so much what Patrick Reilly had said to him—it was the effect it had on him. It was almost like Patrick was speaking directly to his soul.

"Keep coming back," someone shouted from the back row where Joel sat. He was waiting to drive Danny and he liked sitting in on meetings. He said he liked the positivity—and the black humor.

"You said a mouthful there, my friend. Keep coming back because it does get better—but only after it gets worse. A lot worse. And let me tell you something else. I was one of those guys that had to have proof, so I did a bit more research than most of you."

Most of them laughed at that, particularly those who had been in and out a few times; and especially those that were done with all that. He could see it in their faces and they could see it in his.

"I can see now that each time I went back out it was because deep down I never really accepted that I can't manage my own life—even when I'm not drinking. I used to think it was pride—that I could beat this on my own—but it was just stupidity.

"Now, I know that it means I can't trust myself. In trying to cover up all the totally insane things I did when I was drinking I had to lie and cheat and do all kinds of things that I wish I hadn't. And then, when I sobered up, I used to be ashamed, and that would get me drunk, over and over.

"Now, I know that if don't pick up the next drink, and I follow this program, and try to practice the steps, and admit when I'm wrong now and then, I just might have the chance of becoming a normal human being again. It sounds like a lot, but when you look at the way the rest of the world behaves—the standard isn't very high."

The whole meeting laughed at that and Joel beamed at him like a proud papa.

"But I have to have a bit of hope, too, and faith in something better—like being a part of this program and being around you people." He paused to look around and smiled. They were all damaged but were quietly rebuilding their lives.

"When I was a little kid, my granny used to tell me that there would always be guardian angels in my life. She was right. You people have been like guardian angels to me, and now I'm beginning to believe in a higher power.

"Please keep an open mind because my higher power might be different to yours." He wouldn't say it aloud, but Danny still wasn't ready to accept the god that so many at meetings evangelized for with their reformed zeal. It was the same god that the rest of the world fought over—or used as a rubber stamp for their inhumanities. It was one of the things that still bothered him, but he wasn't going to let it drive him out again. The old-timers always said that it was a spiritual program and to think of a higher power as anything that might inspire him to be a better person. "The rest of it," they had said about churches and the Bible, "are outside issues and we have no opinions on them."

"Mine is very simple. I just want to be a better human being. It's tough but the more I work on it—the easier it gets. I'm still not sure about what other people mean by god because throughout my life everyone who talked about stuff like that was usually trying to screw somebody out of something. That was one of the things that kept driving me back—that, and I could never get rid of the compulsion to drink." But since that night in Rome, whenever he thought about picking up a drink his next thought was about the following morning, when he'd be back to sweating and shivering. It might not be the next morning but it would happen sooner or later.

"And even when my drinking got to the point where I knew it was killing me, I couldn't stop. Part of it was addiction—my body couldn't function without it—and part of it was denial.

"I know that it seems like the whole world is drowning in denial, and that used to be my favorite reason for drinking. What was the point in trying to get better when the whole world was going to hell?"

The old Jesuit had talked to him about that when they all finally got to sit down for his mother's last supper. "Be a light in the darkness," he'd said. At first, Danny wasn't sure if he was talking to him or just muttering aloud. But then the old Jesuit had turned to him and beckoned him closer. "From the greatest sinners spring the truest saints." No one else seemed to notice, except his mother who smiled over at them as though her last care had been taken away.

"I don't worry about all that stuff anymore. I know that sounds like I don't care. I do. I care but, being the way I am, I have to practice a bit of tolerance and acceptance or I won't make it. I have to learn to stop looking for what is wrong with the world. Now, I try to look for what is going right and there's far more of that going on than they tell us on the news.

"I was brought up to believe that we were getting more and more civilized and that all the terrible stuff that happened in history was behind us. So, every time I realized that we were still a bunch of savages that could be riled up to tear at each other's throats, I'd get good and drunk to try to block it all out. Now I've come to realize that's just the way of the world that you and I have to try and get sober in.

"Keep an open mind," he added in deference to those that might not agree with him. "I'm just sharing what I think and feel. If it offends anybody—I'm sorry. And don't let anything I say become a reason to go back out. Go to another meeting and listen to somebody else."

He paused for a sip of water and to focus on his own message.

"When you listen to the news and stuff, it seems like everybody hates everybody else, and if you try to say anything against all that you get accused of something. If you're against war and killing, then you're with the terrorists or something like that. I used to get drunk back then because it was the only way I had to drown it out.

"I know many people feel like this and they don't get drunk but they do other stuff. Drinking was the way I tried to medicate myself against all the madness.

"Now, a normal person would cop-on after a while, but alcoholics don't think like that. It's like the way we go on using oil even though we're drowning in pollution and destroying the only world we have. Alcoholics are the experts in that, even if everybody else is catching up fast."

Everyone laughed at that but they laughed nervously. Danny had stepped out of the ordinary and no one could guess where he was taking them all.

"That's one of the things that really got to me about trying to sober up. Why did I have to smarten up while the rest of the world was racing to Armageddon?

"Anyway, after I came out of the coma, my mother took me to Rome. I think she was hoping it might cure me or something, even though she'd stopped believing in stuff like that. I went along with it all because there's nothing like a few weeks of being almost dead to make you realize that living is not so bad after all.

"I came to realize a great many things on that trip. My ex-wife and my kids came along and I assumed it was more for their grandmother's sake. They had no reason to be there for me and yet they were.

"Now I'd done a lot of damage to my kids when they were younger—collateral damage. My son despised me for the way I was with them, particularly with their mother. My daughter always tried to stick up for me even though I let her down every time. They had a bit of a blowout when we were there and, for the first time in my life, I could see how much of it was down to the way I'd been with them.

"When I was drinking I used to try and tell myself that I wasn't harming anybody else, but that wasn't true. Everything we do spills over into other people's lives—the good and the bad.

"What made this even harder to deal with was that I didn't have the best childhood. My own parents had lots of issues that spilled over into my life. Someone once said that 'hurt people hurt people' and I totally get that. Back when my son was born, I'd promised someone that I'd never let the stuff that happened to me spill over onto him. I failed—and not because I wanted to. I failed because when I drank, nothing else mattered and I became worse than anything I had to deal with growing up.

"That always bothered me and made me feel worthless. I despised myself and that, along with all the other baggage I had, led me to my next drink.

"I'm changing that now. Now, instead of feeling sorry for myself, I get off my arse and try to find some small way of making things better.

"Yes, I was a very poor father, but now I get to make up for some of that. By being sober and facing up to my problems, I can regain some of their trust. It's beginning to pay off and my kids now let me be a part of their kids' lives and I'm very grateful for that.

"Now I don't stay sober for their sake—it doesn't work that way. I stay sober for my sake, so that I can be a better person and a good grandfather. My kids might be able to forgive me but they'll never forget all the terrible things I've done and I wouldn't want that. I can't hide from what I was and I don't try anymore.

"Instead, I'm just happy that my grandkids will never have to know the drunk that I was. I've been given the chance to start fresh with them, and after all I've been through that's enough to be getting on with.

"You see, I've been given another chance and it'll only work if I can learn to love and forgive myself, and that's a tricky thing for an alcoholic to do. We're experts at self-justification and can find excuses for all the insane things we do.

"You hear a lot about rigorous honesty in this program and that's the thing that makes the difference. I have to learn to be totally honest—with myself and with others—or I won't survive.

"Before, I used to confuse it with all the stuff I'd heard as a kid—about the Church and Confession and all. It might have been well-intentioned but it just made me feel totally worthless—like without all that I'd always be an unworthy sinner. That's a big part of why I became a drunk and why I couldn't get sober—when you have people saying things like that to you, you start to believe them. I just don't listen to stuff like that anymore. Instead, I listen to what you people say. Here I'm told that I might be very damaged but if I can avoid picking up that first drink, and go to meetings, and practice the twelve steps, and be honest and promptly admit when I'm wrong, that there's hope for me.

"I know it sounds like a very tall order. It is, but what choice do I have? What choice do any of us have?

"You see, even after I came out of the coma, I still wasn't sure if I would be able to try again. I wanted to, but I knew myself. I knew it was only a matter of time before something would come along and derail me again. But when I was in Rome I met some people from when I was a kid back in Dublin and they told me a few things in a way that I could understand.

"They told me to forgive—myself and others. That was hard for me. I suppose it's hard for everybody. Everywhere you go you hear nothing but accusations and condemnations. It's a sickness that is plaguing all of us, and before that used to get to me.

"Now, I go to a meeting and look for someone who is doing worse than me and try to help them. Sometimes it means just sitting and listening, but that works too. At least it does for me. Being kind makes me kinder and that can only be a good thing. I used to be one of those guys that sat in the dark complaining about the darkness. Not anymore. From now on I'm going to try to be the kindness I want to see in the world."

Fr. Reilly had reminded him of that. Even though Danny had heard it lots of times, there was something in the way the priest said it—something very kind and loving. It got to him, right in the middle of Rome, and he'd cried like a baby.

"And now I'm going to sit down and shut up. But before I finish I want to share one last thing with anyone who is new or is coming back. I want you to know that if someone like me can make it then so can you, if you're just willing to try. Life will not be perfect, but you can learn to live in it without drinking. It's hard but it can be done."

*

Christmas Eve in Rome was a busy time. Pilgrims from all over the world flocked to hear the midnight Mass. Patrick stayed away from all that and sat on the patio, across from the Pantheon, waiting for Miriam. They hadn't gotten together since John had died.

At the closing of his days, John Melchor, who had spent his whole life fighting the good fight, had very little proof that any of it was worth it. It was the way of life for those priests who stayed true to their calling. It was the same for everyone, but it was more acute for old men who died alone and forgotten by the world.

**

"I know what's really bothering you," Miriam had said to John as she tried to coax him out one last time. He had looked up at her and tried to smile, or sneer, it really didn't matter anymore. Most of what he'd been was gone, leaving only a shadow.

"You're worried about your legacy. You want to be remembered. Perhaps, after you've gone, I will see about erecting your statue, just like you asked."

"At the foot of Bruno's?"

"Why not? And when there's no one around, the two of you can compare notes until the end."

He laughed at that, an almost strangled gurgle, but she knew it made him happy.

"Thank you, my dearest, dearest friend, for this and for everything. I have become a bitter old man and for that I apologize."

"You're not getting off that easy. We're still going to go and have dinner with Patrick, just like we agreed."

"But I am not hungry."

"You can have soup then and be happy with it." Miriam unlocked his wheels and began to push him forward. Despite everything, she was truly happy. She wasn't serious about the statue; he already had one in her heart.

He died in his sleep that night, peacefully, despite all the storms that had raged throughout his life. He died with a smile on his face, as if he were going off with an old friend. Or it could have been a grimace. Patrick had said the Mass. He kept it as simple as he could but Miriam thought he had rushed it a bit.

He had. He'd never felt comfortable in the Church of the Dead.

*\*\*\**

When she came through the crowd she was smiling. She looked so old—they both did—but when they were together they saw each other as they once had been: young, energetic and full of hope. The years had worn all of that down, but they still believed in each other and all that they'd stood for.

"You're such a creature of habit." She laughed as she sat.

"Now that's rich coming from a nun."

They ordered tea as it was far too late for coffee. Giovanni's nephew, who had taken over the café, stocked Barry's tea especially for them.

"Any news?" he asked.

"I just got off the phone with Deirdre. They're well and are getting ready for a big family Christmas. Jacinta went over—though how she manages at her age is beyond me."

"And why didn't you go over?"

"And leave you here on your own?"

"Now, Miriam, you know we're never really alone here."

She smiled at him as she sipped her tea. "Ah, the souls of the faithful departed."

"And the unfaithful, too. But tell me—how's Danny doing?"

"He's still off the drink. Deirdre thinks he might make it this time. I hope she's not getting her hopes up again."

"We must all have hope. The world would be far too bleak without it. And I hope he does make it this time. We need a few 'good news' stories to keep us going."

"Speaking of news—though I'm not sure if it's good or bad—I got a letter from Karl."

"Did you, indeed? And how is he?"

"Actually he's dead. He died in the spring and the letter was forwarded by his attorney."

"I'm sorry to hear that."

"There's more. He wrote to me to explain a few things. It seems that when he was helping to get John out of El Salvador, he had to make deals with a few devils."

"He never."

"He did. That was the price. They helped him and he owed them, and when they went into Iraq they called in their favors."

"Oh, Miriam, I'm so sorry to hear that."

"I'm not. It all makes sense now."

"Yes, it certainly does."

*

"So?" Danny asked Joel as they pulled out of the car park. "How was your trip to Montreal?"

Rachael had already told him about it. They'd gone to celebrate the Festival of Lights with her mother's family and it had passed without major incident. She'd said it was a bit stilted but it was a good beginning on the road to reconciliation.

"Don't ask. These people can't even say 'good morning' without schmearing it with hasbara."

"C'mon now, Joel. Don't be getting all dark and broody on me."

"But you don't know, Danny. You don't know what these people are like."

"Maybe not, but I know what you're like."

"You know . . ." Joel tried to sound serious but he was beginning to smile. "I think I preferred you when you were a drunk."

"And why is that?"

"Because, as long as you were like that, I wasn't the most pathetic person I knew."

"You know what your problem is, Joel? You're just like everybody else. We're all born into the wrong lives. Everyone's an expert on what everybody else should be doing."

"It's a Jewish thing."

"That's another problem right there—you know that? You guys think you wrote the book on everything."

"Didn't we?"

"Well . . . not everything."

"Do you know the difference between the Irish and the Jews?" Joel was clearly enjoying himself so Danny played along.

"Tell me."

"When the Irish do wrong, they say the devil made them do it. But when the Jews do wrong, they say it's because of their covenant with God."

"I hope you're not going to be saying stuff like that when we get there." It was the first time Danny had been invited to Martin and Rachael's and he was determined that nothing should spoil it.

"No, Danny. This is a private conversation—for heretic's ears only. And don't worry; everybody is delighted you're coming."

"Everybody?"

"Yes, even Martin. Rachael told me."

*

Rachael checked everything one last time. She wanted it to be perfect and it was. She and Grainne had combined their decorations, including those that Deirdre had passed on when she downsized into her condo. Jacinta had brought a few pieces, too, and some had belonged to Danny's grandmother. Rachael liked the sound of old Nora Boyle. She reminded her of the stories of her own grandmother who had smuggled her younger brother and sister out of Hungary and halfway across Europe when she was only eleven.

Since Rome, and the inevitable showdown between Martin and Grainne, all was calm. Martin, with some encouragement, was able to accept his sister's apology. He said he took it for the sake of peace but, since then, things had changed. He began to see his sister differently and they began to spend time together, alone or with the kids. So much of what lay between them was nothing more than the residue of childhood squabbles and most of that evaporated when Grainne miscarried.

She had taken it as a condemnation of herself as a woman and poor Doug was no help at all—constantly seeking assurance that there was nothing he could have done. Martin had stepped up and coaxed his sister out of the funk that followed, even getting her to join a gym. In time they became jogging partners and were learning to indulge their rivalries in much healthier ways.

Life with the Boyles was never dull but Rachael wouldn't have it any other way. And, as the shadows of Danny's past began to dissipate and blow away, a brighter future beckoned. Martin had been skeptical, but she knew how to get around that. She didn't force the issue but she did share her own father's growing admiration for Danny's daily reform. Joel almost made it sound as though he and Danny were taking the journey together.

Her mother's family was still an issue—they were having difficulty accepting Martin and the secular life he and Rachael had chosen, particularly as it pertained to their child. She had explained it all to them and it was their choice. If they wanted to reject her for that—she'd reluctantly accept it. Her mother understood and had begun to advocate on Martin's behalf. It was easy. He was doing so well at work and could provide for his family, and that was all that really mattered. Rachael and her mother were united in that, though they were careful to keep much of the matter from her father.

She was also concealing the fact that she was pregnant again. In deference to Grainne, they would keep the news until after the holidays. Deirdre knew; Martin shared everything with her to the point that sometimes Rachael felt that his mother was as much a part of their relationship as their own children. She didn't mind. She liked and admired Deirdre and understood that Martin would always feel protective toward her. He was the same with her mother and treated her with such respect and consideration that Adina had no difficulty seeing him as the son she never had—even to the point of siding with him whenever he and Rachael disagreed. Rachael didn't mind; Deirdre always sided with her.

She checked again as the doorbell rang. Everything was perfect.

Martin opened the door and Dougie and Daniel burst past him like loosed hounds hot on the trail. "Wait," Grainne called after them. "Take your shoes off first."

"But we gotta go see the presents," they both argued.

"Now!" Grainne commanded and they both froze. She had begun to be more assertive with them. She had told Rachael that she had to or they would turn out just like her. The kids tugged at their shoes and tossed them aside and were gone. Doug took Grainne's coat like a gentleman and hung it. He shook hands with Martin, but he was in a hurry, too, and followed his kids inside.

"He's worse than the other two." Grainne laughed as she brushed cheeks with her brother. "And you"—she smiled as Rachael came from the kitchen—"look radiant."

Rachael blushed a little and leaned forward to kiss her sister-in-law. "You're the one who looks beautiful." Grainne did. She had finally cut her hair, short at the back and sides with a long fringe. She had lost her weight and looked better than she had in years.

"Please!" She laughed again and hugged Rachael. "And thanks. I hope we're not too early. The kids have been pestering me since lunchtime."

"You should have come earlier then." Martin stood back and smiled at her.

"I would, but you know Doug. Too much excitement and he'd need a nap. Are mother and Granny here yet?"

"They're on their way. Granny had to do some last minute shopping."

"She should have called me and not bothered Mom."

"Mom offered."

"Hmm. Sounds like they're up to something. And when are your parents getting here?" She turned to follow Rachael into the kitchen.

"My dad is picking up your father and they'll collect my mother on the way. They should be here after nine."

Rachael poured Grainne a glass of red wine and raised her glass of grape juice. She had used a wine glass so no one would notice. "Happy Christmas, Grainne."

"Happy Holidays, Rachael, and congratulations."

"How did you know?"

"Don't you think I know what being pregnant looks like?"

"Well . . . we're not ready to tell everybody just yet, so if you could keep it quiet . . ."

"Mum's the word."

"Mum's the word."

Deirdre and Jacinta arrived and set the kids off again. Even Martin Jr. forgot himself and joined in with his rowdier cousins. Deirdre didn't mind, but it all became too much for Jacinta who had to be rescued and brought to the kitchen and fortified with a glass of sherry.

She said she didn't mind as Christmas was really for the children, and she was effusive in her praise for how well the house was decorated. "It looks like a real Christmas," she decreed and everyone let that one slide.

"I think it just might be the best Christmas ever," Jacinta added and winked at Grainne. "Your mother and I were just chatting," she added with another wink.

**

"I know it would be asking a lot of you." Jacinta had paused for effect.

They had stopped for coffee after a few hours of combing through what was left in the stores. Jacinta seemed determined to rid herself of the last of her money before going back—buying a few last minute things for the kids, and their kids. "But I was just wondering if there's any way you might consider giving Danny another chance?"

Deirdre didn't react. She knew the question was coming when Jacinta asked if they could spend some time alone. Instead, she looked across at the face of an old woman who just wanted to see her corner of the world right before she left. Deirdre's father had looked the same as he struggled with his last few breaths. He'd wanted Deirdre to know how sorry he was about her mother and all. He still insisted it was all his fault and Deirdre didn't try to argue the fact. There was no point; not at the end of his days.

Nor was there much point with Jacinta. She was nearly done and, even though she tried to hide it, Deirdre could see how much this trip was taking out of her. She was right to spend what she had left with those she loved—and those who loved her.

"I'm not going to rush into anything."

She and Ritchie had parted ways. It was inevitable when she returned from Rome. She knew he had felt excluded and nothing she could say could penetrate the distrust that was growing inside him. She'd tried for a while but she wasn't prepared to commit to someone who was fatally wounded. His wife had taken him for everything she could and he'd never recover from that.

She wondered if it wasn't a bit callous of her, but Martin and Rachael disagreed. Grainne was concerned she might be becoming unfeeling for a while, but seemed to have changed her view.

"But you won't rule it out?"

Deirdre avoided lying for the most part but what else could she do?

"I won't."

"Well, that gives me something to look forward to and, at this stage of my life, most of it is behind me. I just want everyone to be happy. Is that too much for an old woman to ask?"

"No, it isn't. And we are happy—for the most part. We've been through the worst of it and life goes on."

"You must be very proud."

"I am, and you should be too. You had as much to do with it as I did."

"That's awful nice of you to say and, if I was helpful—I'm glad. Only you promise that you'll consider it?"

"I promise."

\*\*\*

"What are you two plotting?" Martin asked as he poured the sherry.

"Can't I even have a moment with my own granddaughter?" Jacinta pretended to scold him. "You're not jealous, are you?"

Martin might have taken the bait but the doorbell rang and Danny, Joel and Adina arrived and set the kids into another tizzy. It was time to open the presents and Papa Joel had been selected to play Santa this year. He even wore a hat and beard that Rachael had bought for him. He wasn't plump but made up for it with loud ho ho ho-ing, until they all gathered around the tree in the large, warm front room with the dancing flicker of a log fire.

And when at last every gift had been opened, and the mounds of discarded wrap had been put away, and the children had fallen asleep where they played, the adults sat around and talked and laughed as a family should. Joel, still wearing the Santa hat, sat back and put his arm around Adina. Grainne and Doug, squeezed into a single chair, giggled and kissed as if they were alone. Rachael took time from attending to them all and stood with Martin and Danny. They were still a bit stiff and formal together but it was a start.

In time, Jacinta rose from her place of honor by the fire and quietly asked Deirdre to help her to the kitchen. She returned alone and whispered in Danny's ear before sitting back by the fire.

"Let's sing a few Christmas songs," she announced to them all as Danny sidled out.

Deirdre was sitting in the breakfast room. She had aged but she had done it with grace and poise. She smiled up at him when he entered and motioned for him to sit opposite her. "Your mother said that you wanted to talk with me."

"She told me you wanted to talk with me."

Deirdre laughed at that. "Well we better talk then. She has asked me to consider . . . you know."

"I know, and I want you to know that it wasn't my idea."

"Well I have considered it." She looked him in the eye and slowly shook her head. "And it is not something I can see myself doing." She paused to gauge his reaction but he was impassive. That was what was different this time. Since Rome, Danny seemed to be finding peace and it showed in his face. "I'm happy for you, Danny, and I hope with all my heart that you make it this time. But I cannot go back to what we once were. Do you understand?"

"I do, and I wish my mother hadn't tried to do this."

"It was well meant."

"The road to hell is paved with good intentions."

"Yes, it certainly is, but we've been there and now we're back."

"Yes we have, and now I just want us to be friends, Deirdre, and to share our family as that. I want our grandchildren to see us together—not as a couple—just as two people who'll be there for them for as long as we get."

"That, I can do."

"Then that's enough to be getting on with for now."

"And what about your mother?"

"We're going to have to lie and pretend that we're working things out. For a while, anyway. She can't live forever."

"Are you not afraid she might come back and haunt us?"

"She might, but I wouldn't worry about stuff like that. The dead understand life far better than the living. And I should know—they've been haunting me all my life."

Deirdre smiled a little. Drunk or sober, Danny would always have a touch of melodrama about him. He used to say it was because he was poetic. Deirdre used to like that about him, but then they had to grow up. That was life, regardless of whatever his ghosts had been telling him. "Oh Danny boy, you might just become a wise old man yet."

"I doubt it, but I'm going to do everything I can to die a sober one."

They smiled at each other and Deirdre rose to go back to their family.

"I'm not interrupting?" Martin asked from the doorway, hesitantly.

"No. No you weren't. I was just heading back inside." Deirdre walked towards him and extended her hand.

"Actually . . ." Martin almost stammered, "I wanted to have a word with Dad."

Deirdre smiled at both of them and left before her eyes welled up. She always knew that Martin would do the right thing in the end.

"I have something for you," Martin said, and looked his father in the eye. "It's not actually from me. An old friend of yours asked me to give it to you." He walked past his father and retrieved a battered old guitar case from a closet. "Billie found this in a pawn shop and thought you might want it back."

It was Danny's old Guild. He had pawned it years ago and lost the ticket.

"And if you can still remember how to play it, Rachael and I would like you to play for the kids. It would make their Christmases." And before Danny could answer, Martin reached out and hugged him. It was quick—and jock-like with backslapping—but it was the best he could manage.

After he left, Danny sat with his old guitar on his lap, wiping his eyes with his sleeve. He had been a lousy grandson and son—and he'd been a worse husband and father—but he was going to be the best grandfather ever. He strummed his way through a few chords and it wasn't bad. A bit muffled by his soft fingertips but he could still get the changes. He'd do "Jingle Bells." That would get everybody going. After that he'd just play it by ear.

And that would just be the beginning. He'd spend every moment he could telling his grandchildren the stories of *Finn MacCool* and the *Fianna*, or *Oisin* and his trip to *Tir Na N'Og*. His life up to now might have been a total disaster but he'd end on a high note, and his grandchildren would only remember a man who loved them for what they were—and not what the world said they should be. He'd use everything he'd learned along the way to guide them as best he could. It was the least he owed them all, and all who had gone before them: Nora and Bart, and his father.

Later, as he stood in the living room, surrounded by family, he couldn't help feeling that they were all smiling down on him. His uncle Martin, too.

Even Anto was there. "Fair play to you, Boyle," he seemed to say. "You did all right in the end." And even though the world was still spinning out of control, the Boyles and the Brands were at peace with each other.

# Acknowledgments

Throughout the book I have cited the mantras and slogans commonly used in Alcoholics Anonymous in recognition for the enormous impact they have had on so many lives.

Likewise I have "borrowed" from various writers—the saints and sinners of antiquity—and have credited them in the text. Their words still have resonance whether we agree with them or not.

I am, again, deeply indebted to my editor, Lou Aronica, and all the good people at The Story Plant, for allowing me to weave the tale of Danny Boyle and the times he struggled through. Without their encouragement and support Danny's story would not have been told.

Likewise, I owe a huge debt to the great many people who I have met in my own life and times who taught me to look into the shadows and how to listen to the voices of the dead. My late mother, who taught me to love reading; Padraig J. Daly, who leaves a trail of beautiful words in his poetry; Jim G., who plucked me from the fires of my own hell many years ago; and my brothers, Sean, Barry, Richard, Paul, and Ciaran.

My children, Damien and Aidan, who taught me so much about life as they grew into fine young men.

And of course to my wife, Eduarda, who not only loved and cared for me during the three years I was writing this trilogy but has joined me on my next great adventure.

And to all of you who have taken the time to read the books.

May we all find peace and serenity before the end.

Peter
Lisbon, April 19th 2015

# About the Author

Raised in Dublin, the city of songs and stories, Peter Murphy grew up on books and music. As a young man he spent time trekking around Europe before moving to Canada where, after a few years battling some personal demons, he fell in love and raised a family.

When his children reached adulthood and, having written four novels, Murphy packed up his life and moved back to Europe with his loving wife and faithful dog.

He now lives in Lisbon where he plans to study the lugubriousness of love.